SHE WOULD BE HIS MISTRESS ...

Althea Wintergreen leads a quiet life with her child, Effie, in the beautiful Lake District—far removed from London Society and gossip. Shrouded in scandal, she has no illusions about the amorous intentions of the wholly disreputable and devastatingly handsome Lucius Keene, the Duke of Traherne. Tempted by the sweet promise of passion in Lucius's kiss and her own secret desire to know love, Althea aids him wholeheartedly in her own seduction!

... BUT NOT HIS WIFE!

Though Lucius Keene is a confirmed rake and dedicated bachelor, he is above all a gentleman. Determined to set matters right, he proposes marriage to the unconventional, delightful Althea, never anticipating the *ton*'s most eligible duke would be turned down flat! But when Effie is almost abducted twice, Lucius knows that the little girl and Althea belong with him. Now, that his own heart is becoming dangerously involved in the matter, he vows to convince noble Althea that her "scandalous" past is no reason to deny them both a future of bliss in each other's arms. . . .

BOOK YOUR PLACE ON OUR WEBSITE AND MAKE THE READING CONNECTION!

We've created a customized website just for our very special readers, where you can get the inside scoop on everything that's going on with Zebra, Pinnacle and Kensington books.

When you come online, you'll have the exciting opportunity to:

- View covers of upcoming books
- Read sample chapters
- Learn about our future publishing schedule (listed by publication month *and author*)
- Find out when your favorite authors will be visiting a city near you
- Search for and order backlist books from our online catalog
- Check out author bios and background information
- Send e-mail to your favorite authors
- Meet the Kensington staff online
- Join us in weekly chats with authors, readers and other guests
- Get writing guidelines
- AND MUCH MORE!

**Visit our website at
http://www.zebrabooks.com**

HIS
SCANDALOUS
DUCHESS

Sara Blayne

ZEBRA BOOKS
Kensington Publishing Corp.

http://www.zebrabooks.com

ZEBRA BOOKS are published by

Kensington Publishing Corp.
850 Third Avenue
New York, NY 10022

First Printing: October, 2000
10 9 8 7 6 5 4 3 2 1

Printed in the United States of America

*In loving memory of Steve's dad,
Elbert Howl, better known as "Eb."
We miss him dearly.*

Books by Sara Blayne

PASSION'S LADY
DUEL OF THE HEART
A NOBLEMAN'S BRIDE
AN ELUSIVE GUARDIAN
AN EASTER COURTSHIP
THEODORA
ENTICED
A NOBLE PURSUIT
A NOBLE RESOLVE
A NOBLE HEART
HIS SCANDALOUS DUCHESS

Published by Zebra Books

Prologue

The arrival of a hired post chaise in the middle of a mid-September night at the Old Mill House, just up from Glenridding on Ullswater in the Lake District, must surely have been thought curious—had there been anyone to witness the event. Certainly the figures of two women alighting from the closed carriage—one seemingly ill and leaning on the other as they made their way slowly up the weedy flagstone walk to the door—would have caused no little comment. In fact, had there been anyone to glimpse the faces beneath the deep hoods of the cloaks, both fair and lovely and as near alike as made no difference, there would have been a buzz of talk all through the dale. As it was, there was no one but the coachman and the elderly caretaker and his wife to know that Miss Althea Wintergreen and her sister, Gloriana, had come home at long last—though not to Briersly. That fine, old house that had seen generations of Wintergreens come and go had been sold some years since. Some said to pay the colonel's debts. Others said it was too haunted with painful memories for the colonel, after the death of his beloved wife, Judith, ever to contemplate returning there. Still, he had kept the Old Mill House and a small acreage surrounding it, no doubt for purely sentimental reasons. And it was in this relic of Elizabethan days that his daughters took their refuge unremarked.

It was, in fact, a matter of almost a fortnight before Thaddeus Elright, the butcher, commented to Miss Louisa Thedford, the rector's spinster sister, that old Elias Treadwell up at the Old Mill House must be under the weather. In a single week, Mattie Treadwell had twice purchased soup bones. Then this, the very next week she had already bought lamb cutlets, a fine standing roast, a loin of pork, and six plump capons—and here it was only Thursday. It was clear the old man must have been poorly and in need of a good sustaining broth, but then he had obviously recovered. And now old Mattie was bent on feeding him to build up his strength.

"Fiddle-faddle," retorted Miss Thedford, clearly skeptical. "Mattie Treadwell's never indulged in lamb cutlets, a standing roast, and a loin of pork all in a single week in her life. Never mind the capons, which she'd never have put out good brass for at all. And *six* of them to boot. Why, it sounds like she's setting a table fit for the quality."

It was inevitable that such extravagance on the part of one normally accounted a more than frugal housewife must elicit a deal of speculation among the local inhabitants of Glenridding. Although it was generally known Mattie had on occasion helped out at the big house, it was common knowledge Briersly did not look to receive its lord and master anytime in the near or distant future, as he was reportedly abroad seeing to his foreign holdings. Since there was no other likely member of the quality for whom the Treadwells might be expected to be providing sustenance on the order of Mattie's recent purchases, it was variously theorized that either Mattie or Elias had come into an inheritance of some sort. Perhaps their only son, Jonas Treadwell, had fallen into a small fortune while serving in India as Colonel Wintergreen's batman, or perhaps living for so long by themselves in the relative isolation of the Old Mill House had finally addled their wits to such a degree as to lead them to fling every farthing away on the consumption of all the things they had for so long denied themselves.

Miss Thedford, more astute than the others, however, placed little credence in any of those far-fetched notions. Furthermore, never one to pussyfoot around when there was fodder for her highly developed palate for anything that smacked of the queer or curious, the rector's sister wasted little time in paying a morning call on Mattie and Elias Treadwell.

She was not to be disappointed. Indeed, she had no sooner been ushered into the small downstairs parlor and the door hastily closed "to keep in the warmth of the fire," as Mattie was quick to explain, than Miss Thedford detected the distinct creak of footsteps on the stair. "It's only Peg, the girl we took on to help with the cooking and the cleaning," offered Mattie, correctly interpreting her visitor's sharp-eyed glance, which she was later to liken to that of a ferret on the scent of a pheasant's nest.

An hour later, having been unable to pry anything definitive out of her hostess beyond Mattie's prized recipe for gooseberry cream and the admission that there was already a distinct nip in the air for the twenty-fifth of September, Miss Thedford noted that the biscuit dish was empty and that her hostess demonstrated little inclination to offer to refill it.

"I suppose I should really be getting home," said the spinster, reluctantly discarding the notion of a fourth cup of tea in the absence of biscuits and unable to come up with a plausible excuse for prolonging her visit. She was rewarded with the faintest of impressions that Mattie could not be more relieved to be rid of her guest, which only added fuel to Miss Thedford's already flaming curiosity. Still, there would seem to be nothing for it, save to gather up her reticule and gloves in preparation of taking her leave.

"It was kind of you to drop by to inquire into Mr. Treadwell's health, I'm sure," murmured Mattie, deftly guiding the rector's sister out the parlor door. "Fortunately, you may tell everybody he's fit as a trivet," she added, as she helped Miss Thedford into her pelisse. "I daresay we've never been better."

"Yes, well, I'm sure I could not be more pleased to hear it. No doubt we shall see you in church on Sunday then," Miss Thedford replied in the way of a last, hopeful effort to worm something of interest out of Mattie Treadwell.

Without missing a single heartbeat, Mattie smiled for all the world as if she had been anticipating that final thrust. "I'm afraid I couldn't promise you or the rector something I can't be certain of. As it happens, Mr. Treadwell and I've been thinking of taking a drive over to Hartsop to my sister Harriet's. It's been some little time since we saw Harriet and the family. Perhaps we'll stay a couple of nights and come back on Monday. Make it a proper holiday, y'see."

Unfortunately, perhaps, Miss Thedford did see. In fact, glancing up at the second story, she saw, framed in one of the windows, the figure of a woman standing with her elbows back, her hands pressed against the small of her back in the manner of a female exceedingly close to the time of her lying-in. Nor was Miss Thedford slow to realize the identity of the young mother-to-be. There was no mistaking the strikingly beautiful profile, the thick mane of hair shining a rich red-gold in the afternoon sunlight. She was the very likeness of Judith Wintergreen, who had died giving birth to a stillborn son twelve years before.

Mattie Treadwell, taking in Miss Thedford's triumphant glance, smiled grimly to herself. *So she thinks she has what she came to find out, does she?* Mattie thought, as she watched the spinster drive off in her pony cart. Miss Althea Wintergreen's come home, and now the whole town was about to know. A pity there'd be none to know the real truth of the matter.

Mattie sighed, her gaze going to the face peering down at her from the bedroom window. Well, it was the way *she* wanted it, and now would begin the reckoning.

Chapter One

Lucius Carroll Elbert Keene, the Duke of Traherne, came suddenly to the awareness that he had been regarding his private secretary in stony silence for what must have been several seconds. Wryly, he noted poor Phips appeared to be wilting beneath the protracted stare of his employer.

"She is in London, then," Traherne said, taking pity on his highly efficient personal agent. "You are quite certain."

"There is no mistake, Your Grace," replied Edward Phips, resisting the urge to mop his forehead with his linen handkerchief. "The woman staying at the Chesney under the name of Mrs. Praetorius is most definitely the Duchess of Traherne."

"And *Mr.* Praetorius?" The duke looked deliberately at Phips, who forced himself to meet that rapier glance unflinchingly. "Is he here with her?"

"*Yes,* he is here with her," snapped Lord Hilary Keene, a tall, elegant aristocrat in his middle fifties who, despite his fair hair in sharp contrast to the striking blue-black sheen of Traherne's raven locks, bore a marked resemblance to his nephew, the duke. "He is considerably altered by the passage of the years, Lucius, but it *is* Mr. Xavier Praetorius, as he styles himself. I have not forgotten him or his demmed silver-tongued oratory. He could talk the bloody bristles off a boar."

"Damme," drawled Traherne, mildly sardonic, his strong chiseled features betraying little of his innermost thoughts. "It would seem there is a deal more to Mr. Praetorius than one might have imagined. Twenty-six years, and they are still together."

"Curious, that," Lord Hilary agreed, his gaze, wary, on the duke. "But then, all those years ago I should never have expected Olivia Traherne to fling all away for a traveling thespian. She was never a flighty gel. You may be sure Lady Stanton reared her daughter to know where her duty lay."

"And where was that, Uncle?" queried Traherne, absently swinging his quizzing glass back and forth on its black riband. "Certainly not at Meresgate. In all these years my dearest mama has never so much as bothered to write, and now, suddenly, she is back. One is moved to speculate why."

Phips circumspectly cleared his throat.

Traherne favored his secretary with an elevated eyebrow. "You have some theory to offer, my dear Edward?" he queried.

"Indeed, sir. The duchess has expressed a desire to see Your Grace," he offered carefully.

"Really, Phips, you never cease to amaze me. And to what purpose, one must ask, would be such an interview? Personally, I cannot think of a thing we might have to say to one another."

Phips, who had served the duke for several years, evinced no surprise at what might seem a striking lack of curiosity on the part of one who had not had occasion to lay eyes on his mama for better than a quarter of a century. But then, Lucius Keene had been only nine when the duchess abandoned her husband and only child to elope with an itinerant actor. There had been no lack of news in the interim regarding the duchess and her paramour on the Continent, or in the East Indies, or finally, in Africa and the Mediterranean, for that matter. Her Grace, far from seeking to remain inconspicuous, had not hesitated to thrust herself into the center of Society in whatever foreign city she happened to make an appearance. She had, in fact, despite the scandal attached to her name, apparently enjoyed a more than modest success in the circles in which she moved. She was, by all accounts, a diamond of the first water, a woman of great wit and charm; she was, in fact, the delightfully Scandalous Duchess of Traherne. All of which the previous duke must have found more than a trifle galling.

It was generally held that the dread of adding to the scandal had prevented the duke from seeking the formality of a divorce. Lucius, however, considered it far more likely his father's hand was stayed by a harsh and vengeful nature. The previous duke had refused categorically to grant his errant wife her freedom. After all, in such an event, there would have been nothing to prevent her from wedding the man she presumably loved to the exclusion of all else.

Wealth, position, title, reputation—not to mention a husband and a son—she had gladly sacrificed for an all-consuming passion. But then, no doubt the last had counted less to her even than all the rest, cynically reflected Lucius, who had long since relegated his esteemed mama to oblivion. Indeed, he could think of only one reason the duchess should have returned and but a single motive for her to wish to see him.

"No need to answer that, my dearest Edward," he said with a cynical curl of the lip. "You will inform the duchess I am called away from Town for an indeterminate period of time." Ignoring Hilary Keene's sudden start at that announcement, the duke continued in his dispassionate, well-modulated tones, "You may further apprise her that I have commissioned you to set up a sizable allowance for Her

Grace on the condition that she is to make no further attempt
to communicate with me, save through you. You will be
quite clear on that point, Edward.''

"I understand, Your Grace," murmured Phips.

"Well, I do not," declared Hilary Keene, eyeing the
duke's tall, elegant presence with a fulminating eye. "Have
you forgotten you are invited to Dunstan's house party,
which is to be graced by five of the most eligible young
beauties who are to make their curtsies in Society in the
spring? And then there is Lady Crenshawe's gala in celebration of her daughters' birthday—twins, by heaven. And from
everything I've heard, as lovely as they are impossible to
distinguish one from the other.''

"Bookends, egad," drawled Traherne with a singular lack
of enthusiasm, which did little to smooth his uncle's ruffled
feathers.

"Hell and the devil confound it, Lucius. Need I remind
you of the matter we discussed a short time ago? You gave
your word you would at least look over the new bevy of
females making their appearance. You are five and thirty,
my boy. It is past time you were setting up your nursery.
We agreed on that.''

"Then no doubt you may be certain I shall give the matter
my due consideration, Uncle," replied the duke, favoring
his kinsman with his gently mocking smile, which little
reflected the immovable will that lay behind it.

Hilary Keene, however, had had the rearing of his brother's son from the time of the previous duke's untimely
demise in a duel when the boy was twelve. He knew full
well how fruitless any further remonstrance with His Grace
would prove. Keene gave vent to a sigh. Traherne would
keep to his word to think over the matter of finding himself
a wife, but he would not be pushed into committing himself
to more than that. It was little enough, but Hilary would
have to be satisfied with that—and with the knowledge that
the duke had a deeply ingrained sense of where his duty

lay. No doubt Traherne would marry to ensure the title when it suited him. He would have to have done. After all, save for Hilary, whose dearest wife, Ophelia, had borne him five children, all daughters, Lucius was the last male of the line.

Cursing the whim that had brought Olivia Traherne back to London just when his nephew had been persuaded to set aside his aversion to green girls barely out of the schoolroom in order to find himself a duchess, Hilary suppressed a sigh of resignation.

''Where, then, are you off to this time?'' he asked, though he hardly needed to have done. Nor was he surprised when he received in reply that Traherne would be leaving for the Lake District for a few weeks of shooting.

Since his salad days, whenever he wished to pull one of his vanishing acts, Lucius had ever retreated to Briersly, his hunting lodge near Glenridding on Ullswater. It was something Hilary had never fully understood: How a man of Traherne's polish and stature could actually *choose* to bury himself in the barren fastness of the Lake District for weeks at a time! But then, Lucius had always been something of an enigma. As a boy, he had demonstrated a dreamy disposition, which had manifested itself in a liking for poetry and music, pursuits fostered, undoubtedly, by his mama in the frequent long absences of her husband, the duke. At least it had not been too late to nip such feckless tendencies in the bud, reflected Hilary with grim satisfaction. As the young duke's guardian, Hilary had made sure Lucius's time was occupied with more manly pursuits, with the result that there was not his match with pistols or swords and few who would willingly choose to engage him in fisticuffs. He was, furthermore, a top-of-the-trees sawyer, a bruising rider, a Meltonian at the top of his class, and a Corinthian. That he was also an astute man of business who had tripled his already considerable income, while many another noble fortune had been tossed down the River Tick, his uncle accounted as a mere eccentricity, albeit a lucrative one.

It was, in fact, an eccentricity that was particularly well suited to what was generally viewed in Traherne as a singular coldness of nature. The duke, it was agreed, was totally lacking in any of the softer human emotions. Furthermore, he was known to be utterly ruthless in the pursuit of his various business enterprises, which included—aside from his several prosperous estates—numerous textile mills and mining operations, both at home and in India. No doubt those who acquitted him of possessing any of the finer sensibilities would have been considerably surprised to learn that he was highly regarded by those in his employ, from those who served him most intimately to those in the lowliest degrees. Everything the duke undertook was certain to prosper, but not at the expense of those whose labor profited him. At considerable cost to himself, Traherne had improved and modernized the machinery in his mills and his mines, and instituted policies ensuring the welfare of those who toiled in his employ, including the exclusion of children under the age of fourteen in the workforce and the limiting of shifts to a more humane ten hours. He had also personally supervised the renovation of the workers' tenement buildings to eliminate the health problems occasioned by overcrowding, poor drainage, and inadequate sewerage. With the result that production was maintained at a highly profitable level and his holdings had remained untouched by the strikes and riots that had recently plagued the textile industry in Manchester and Bolton, not to mention the shipyards in Liverpool.

His Grace of Traherne no doubt would have been no little startled to discover he commanded from those in his employ something approaching affection, not to mention a fierce sense of loyalty. Having applied his considerable intellect to the matter of how to maintain his investments at the greatest efficiency possible, he had simply taken those steps he had deemed necessary to achieve his ends. A reasonably happy, healthy workforce at his command had not been a motivating factor or even an accidental by-product of his policies. It had been one of the several building blocks determined by logic for laying a sound foundation for a thriving business enterprise. Nor had it been any different with the upkeep of his various estates, which boasted prosperous tenants and a healthy inflow of revenue, which in turn went to promote the latest in farming techniques, as well as the renewal and maintenance of the land upon which everything else depended. It was all a matter of cold, hard reason, he would have said, had anyone thought to ask him why he had instituted his various policies.

The business of getting himself a duchess in order to provide Meresgate an heir should have been no different, Traherne reflected humorlessly some little time later as he gave Greaves, his gentleman's gentleman, instructions to pack for a lengthy stay in the country. He was far too astute, however, not to acknowledge that taking a wife entailed the potential for just the sort of complications he would far rather have done without, had there been any other choice in the matter.

His uncle had been right to remind him of the various functions to which he had promised himself in order to expedite the business of finding himself a wife. Good God, did he wait for the Season to begin the hunt, he would be forced to court and woo numerous simpering females with little more experience of the world than chicks in the nest. This process of elimination must prove as tedious as it was promising of ennui. Worse, he would have to perform this onerous endeavor in a milieu of sycophantic mamas eager to promote their single darlings. That he had a particular aversion to attending the assemblies at Almack's, detested the commonality of dancing at Vauxhall Gardens, and abhorred the prospect of an endless round of balls, dinners, and soirees—not to mention all the impromptu musicales designed to display the dubious euphonic talents of middling young virtuosas—did little to sweeten his anticipation of a Season spent hunting a successor to the scandalous duchess who had so dramatically demonstrated she was not up to the position.

And there was the crux of the matter, he admitted humorlessly to himself. Having had the example of his own mother and father as an extreme by which to gauge marital bliss, in addition to having been made the object of numerous lures to ensnare his title and his fortune, he had long since come to intrinsically mistrust the institution of marriage. Indeed, he much preferred the sort of arrangement to be had with a mistress, who understood from the beginning there would be no possibility of anything of a long-lasting nature. It was not only a far more practical and, therefore, reasonable arrangement than one predicated on the idea of willingly leg shackling oneself for life to a single partner; but it was a deal more suited to human nature, which he cynically viewed as basically fickle. Nor could he console himself with his uncle's bromide that, once married, he might find that, in time, love would come to cement the union, as it had come to Hilary and his dearest Ophelia. In spite of the example of his aunt and uncle whom he considered the exception that proved the rule, Traherne, as a man of logic, must inevitably question the romantic notion of love. Premised as it was on an ideal of constancy, this quixotic concept, when applied to something as mutable as human emotions, could only be as difficult to realize as it was absurd to live in hopes of stumbling across one day.

Love, he judged in short, was at best a creation of fiction, a fantasy for the less logically minded, and at worst an illusion that vanished in the revealing light of reality. After all, as a man experienced in the art of the physical aspects of love, he had found that interest rarely endured much beyond the act of conquest. More than that, however, he looked with distaste upon the accepted practice of married partners who, disillusioned with connubial bliss, sought solace in the arms of illicit lovers. Love affairs, by their very nature, were most damned untidy and invited complications that must inevitably prove fatiguing. More than that, however, he detested the notion of opening himself up to the humiliation of a wife who, once she had obliged him with an heir, took her pleasures elsewhere. Had there not been the succession to consider and his duty to the name he bore, he doubted not he would forgo the dubious pleasure of saddling himself with a duchess.

Still, he found little to comfort himself in the fact that he had seized upon his mother's arrival in London as an excuse to put off the inevitable. He acknowledged sardonically to himself that, while he had never before in his life run from an obligation or from what promised fair to be an unpleasant confrontation, he was doing both in retreating to Briersly at such a moment. Marry, he must, and the sooner the better. He was demmed, however, if he must feel any obligation to humor his long-lost parent in an interview that could serve little purpose other than to dredge up memories long buried and better left forgotten. Nevertheless, he had the uneasy suspicion that he had slipped a cog in his own estimation, a notion he summarily dismissed as predicated on some lingering feeling of childhood guilt and, therefore, an utterly wasted emotion.

He was still vaguely displeased with himself when, little more than an hour later, he climbed into his traveling coach and, settling back against the squabs, gave the coachman the signal to drive on. No doubt he would be able to put everything in its proper perspective once he was settled at Briersly, he told himself. He was immediately aware of a familiar tingle of anticipation at the prospect of trodding once more the wild environs of Ullswater and the Lake District, which he had not done for various reasons for better than five years.

Of all his many houses, Briersly was the one that must be accounted singularly his own. He had purchased it on a whim while on a walking tour in the District with his tutor, Wendell Haverland. Even as a youth of eighteen, he had seen it as a welcome retreat from Meresgate, his castle on the coast, which his distant ancestor had caused to be built in 1475 in defense of England from the raiding Scots. Where the great pile that was his ancestral home reverberated with history, both ancient and more immediate, the picturesque sprawling country manor that he had purchased from a Colonel Wintergreen, presently with the King's army in Egypt from all accounts, was thankfully free of any personal ties and, especially, any memories that related to himself. Despite his very real pride in Meresgate, Briersly offered the sort of solitude he had long since discovered he required from time to time and was nigh unto impossible to achieve anywhere else.

It was undoubtedly the one thing he could attribute most certainly to his mother's early influence, this need to be alone to think and dream. It was where his ideas came from, his strength of purpose, the same driving force that had made him one of the most powerful men in England at a time when England needed men who could provide prosperity and stability to at least a segment of the population plagued by war.

He had thought it all out while at Briersly—how he could best support his country in the fight against French tyranny. His holdings provided meat, wool, and grain to help sustain a country fighting for its very survival against seemingly impossible odds, even as his mills supplied textiles and his mines coal and iron ore for the war effort. If they could be made to produce more efficiently despite the reality of shortages of manpower, dwindling natural resources, and the drain on the public coffers—not to mention a growing unrest fueled by low wages, paltry working conditions, and the work of insurgents—he could contribute far more to his country's war efforts than he could have done either in the diplomatic sector or as a soldier. More than that, he could provide a stabilizing influence of no little significance on the local economies as well as on the populace to whom he provided lucrative employment.

It had all been a matter of simple logic—logic that had, in turn, prevailed over his more instinctive impulse to fling himself into the fighting as soon as he had reached his majority. This impulse was made even more difficult to resist as news of the Reign of Terror began to reach England in the form of French émigrés fleeing France to escape Madame Guillotine. It seemed that no one was to be spared the insanity of the mob. King Louis XVI was beheaded, followed shortly thereafter by his queen, Marie Antoinette. Reports were to reach England that, while sixty executions a month were being carried out in Paris, the Nantes tribunal had sent fifteen thousand persons to the guillotine in a period of three months alone. Nor had it helped to learn on his twenty-fifth birthday that British forces had been driven out of Toulon and only the British navy stood between the island nation and a French invasion.

The withdrawal of the British forces from Toulon had been the catalyst that had impelled him to a more active part in the war, that and the fact that his various personal projects were already well advanced. He had been one and twenty when the French mob stormed the Bastille and already an astute scholar of the intricate workings of politics and political institutions. Having come into a dukedom at the age of twelve, he had naturally acquired a knowledge of those forces that motivated the people around him as well as those over whom he exercised no little influence. In his maturity he had made a study of it. Considering his elevated position as a premier nobleman of the realm second only to royalty and his undeniably vast network of connections both at home and abroad, it had been practically inevitable that Traherne should be drawn finally into the political intrigue behind the scenes of war. But then, he had proved particularly adept at matters of intelligence gathering, analysis, and counterstrategies.

Six years later, he was only a little surprised when he was approached by Jean Duval, the former Comte d'Arbolet. Traherne had been sought out by agents of the government before with the intent of wooing him to exert his considerable influence on behalf of French émigrés with families still at peril on the Continent. Doubtless it had never been intended for him to place himself at personal risk by frequent forays into France itself. His lean jaw hardened at the remembered horror that had determined him on a course that was to plunge him in the end into a nightmare of suffering and near death.

His hand clenched about the silver head of the walking stick propped between his knees. God help him, he would have done it all again, suffered the wound, chanced death itself, had it meant he could expose those who traded in human souls for gold. It was his one failure—the single bitter drop in his cup—that he had not.

Feeling the throb of the long-healed wound in his left thigh, he deliberately unclenched his hand along with his despair. In the long weeks of delirium and pain, the feverish eternity of tormented dreams, he had gone over and over it in his head until he had been driven nearly mad with uncertainty. Had he been too arrogant, too bloody sure of his own infallibility? If he had trusted Duval with the twisted threads of clues he had uncovered, would things have turned out differently? The bits and pieces had been enough to quash the network of smugglers who had dealt in human suffering, but the evil genius who had dreamed up the horrific scheme had escaped. It would begin all over again—men, women, and children brutally murdered and cast adrift, some to wash ashore, as had Duval's young wife and daughter.

"The devil! It's over and done," Traherne muttered. Shutting his eyes tight, he leaned his head back against the squabs. "Bloody well time to forget the whole rotten mess."

He would find respite from his cursed thoughts, he told himself, in the seclusion of Briersly set in its sylvan glade overlooking the sprawling lake, the fells crouched all about like sleeping giants breathing clouds of mist.

Smiling to herself, Althea Wintergreen gave the huge pink bow a final adjustment, then stepped back to admire the delectably intriguing wooden box boasting a fanciful array of faerie figures and elves flitting over its enameled surface. Effie would love the soft velvet ribbon and the sprites. Althea could only hope the surprise inside would please the child equally well. She had stayed up most of the night to complete the final small touch-ups and now felt a tingle of anticipation at seeing her newest creation put through its paces.

Taking up the box, Althea let herself out of her attic workroom, careful to shut the door behind her, and made her way down the narrow wooden stairs to the house proper. Down the hall in the nursery, Effie would just be coming awake with the awareness that it was her birthday, thought Althea, wondering where the time had gone. Truly it did not seem possible that her little Effie was five years old today.

With a rueful grin, Althea thought back to that night when Effie had first made her appearance. Gazing down into that very human little face, she had realized for the first time what was meant by the term *miracle of birth*. It was indeed miraculous that anything so tiny and so fragile and yet so perfect in every detail could issue from a woman's body. Watching the wash of pink dispel the grayish color, which had made the infant appear something molded from wet clay, had been on the order of viewing creation in all of its mystery. And then to face the fear and wonder of the daunting responsibility represented by that fragile little form only just budding forth with life! It had come then to Althea that she had never been so uncertain of anything in her life before. Indeed, she had not known how she could manage all by herself.

But then, she had had Mattie to help her and dear Mrs. Fennigrew, who, like a gift sent from heaven, had presented herself at Althea's door one afternoon shortly after Effie's birth. In all the years following her father and the drum, Althea had never imagined that her own former nanny would still be in Glenridding seemingly waiting for the day when she might take up her old position again. Yet, there she had been, rather grayer and carrying not a little more bulk but still manifesting the same brusque competence that she had demonstrated at three and thirty. It had been Mrs. Fennigrew who resolved the problem of a wet nurse and Mrs. Fennigrew who, bullying and coaxing, had brought the child's ailing mama back to health. Together, the three had managed to nurture that tender bud of life that was Effie until she had grown into sturdy childhood.

And they would continue to do so, Althea told herself firmly, as she entered the breakfast room and set the gaily decorated box down on the breakfast table. Because Althea did not like to eat alone and because she enjoyed nothing more than to spend mealtimes listening to childish prattle, Effie had been allowed, since she grew out of the necessity for nappies, to take her meals with Althea rather than in the nursery. No doubt it was partly due to Althea's practice of talking to the child as if she were an equal and partly because Effie was an only child growing up among adults and without childhood playmates that the little girl exuded a maturity beyond her meager years. Had she paused to think about it at all, Althea would have undoubtedly attributed it to what she considered the child's natural precocity. She was unabashedly proud of her Effie and could not have been more pleased to see a great deal of herself in the little person growing up before her very eyes.

Inexplicably, a shadow darkened those eyes, the green-gold of a verdant glen in early autumn, as they came to rest on the exquisite china doll fitted out in purple satin, which lay on the table beside the enameled box. It was the gift

Althea's sister, Gloriana, had sent to Effie in celebration of this special occasion. Gloriana never forgot Effie's birthday or Christmas or Valentine's Day. Even Easter would see some little something arrive by post for Effie. A pity Gloriana could never bring herself to deliver the gifts in person. But then, Gloriana had made a splendid match. She was the Viscountess Winslade now, one of London's leading hostesses, the wife of a man who was distinguishing himself in the diplomatic service. It was one thing for Althea to take Effie to the unpretentious house in the unfashionable part of London for a short, secret visit with Althea's only sibling. It was quite another for Gloriana to invite scandal by openly coming to the Old Mill House to see the sister who had disgraced herself.

It was a fact of life with which Althea had long since come to terms, but it was the sort of cruel social absurdity that she abhorred. How could love or a child of love ever be a shameful thing? The act of love itself was an expression of a sublime passion, a rapturous joining of the universal masculine and feminine to achieve a wholeness for which every soul yearned. It was an inborn need, an irresistible force, an inescapable mechanism of nature and therefore, of itself, neither good nor evil. It was the superimposition of social customs on an essential human behavior that dictated a woman should be shunned for bringing a fatherless child into the world.

Althea's lips quirked in sardonic amusement. A "fatherless" child indeed. As if there ever could be such a thing. Anymore than there could be a "motherless" child. And how much greater the absurdity to visit shame upon the child of such a union. A child, any child, was by its very nature a creature of innocence and beauty, a never-ending source of wonder— a miracle of creation to be loved, nurtured, and treasured. And any set of social standards that dictated otherwise was not one she cared a fig for.

Indeed, it did not bother her in the least that she was

treated as an anathema, a pariah—a Fallen Woman, egad. She had Effie, and she had her attic workshop. What more could she really ask? The truth was, she was perfectly contented with her life. That was a deal more than most people could say, she told herself and dismissed the momentary pang of regret that Gloriana would not be here to see Effie's glee when the child first beheld her lovely new doll and the surprise waiting for her in the intriguing box. There would not be a cloud on this day, Althea vowed. She simply would not allow it.

Then, hearing the excited clatter of footsteps beyond the door, Althea turned, an expectant gleam in her eye.

There was, Traherne decided, propping his fowling piece over one broad shoulder, a decided bite in the air for late September. He took in with an appreciative eye the first faint sheen of red and gold among the press of beechwood and oak. There would be an early fall, followed no doubt by an equally unseasonable winter, he decided, aware of a small pang of regret that he would not be here to witness the full glory of autumn with its October pageant of brilliant colors. He had yet to experience a winter along the shores of Ullswater, something he suspected would be quite spectacular, if confining.

Following the course of a purling beck, Fitz, his Irish setter, at his heels, Traherne was sardonically aware of a new spring in his step, of a quickening of his blood. The crisp air sharpened his senses and cleared the cobwebs from his brain. It was not only the six months he had spent in and out of sickbeds, as he fought off infection and struggled to rebuild his strength, that made the keen scents of gorse and thyme and sorrel, wet with dew, even sweeter to his senses. Nor was it the sudden relief from the constant pressure of his numerous responsibilities that made him feel light and clearheaded as he had not felt for a very long time.

He had been engrossed in the matters of war for too long, he realized, until he had forgotten what it was to awaken with an appetite whetted by a chill mountain dawn, clean scented with pine and mist. He felt like a boy again, freed from the schoolroom for a holiday, he thought with cynical amusement, and for once was free of pain as he skirted through the furze with long, easy strides.

It was the magic of Briersly, he told himself, wondering that he had not thought to come sooner. Perhaps some deeper instinct than the impulse to avoid his uncle's censure had prevailed in bringing him back, he mused with a rueful twist of the lips—something deeper, even, than his aversion to the notion of encountering his prodigal parent someplace, sometime when he was least expecting it. Not that it would signify. The mother who had walked out of his life twenty-six years ago had long since ceased to exist for him. If they chanced to meet, it would be as strangers. There was the distinct possibility he would not even recognize her.

Traherne frowned, nettled nonetheless at having allowed even the thought of the dowager duchess's return to impinge on his pleasure in the day. It served to remind him, as well, of that other less than eagerly anticipated matter that awaited him—the courting of a new Duchess of Traherne.

But all that was for later, when he made his return to London. Now, the sun was burning the mist away, and before him, fringed with willows and gleaming silvery in the sunlight, lapped the waters of the lake. Beside him, the setter went suddenly still. Traherne, treading softly, eased into the thick cover of a stand of willows and peered out over a creek formed by a shallow fold in the hills.

The honk of wild geese brought the fowling piece to his shoulder, his finger, ready, on the trigger.

A rush of wings, a sudden body in flight. He raised the barrel and—

"NO-O-O!" shrilled across the silence.

His finger jerked and the gun discharged.

The feminine shriek that chilled his blood brought him spinning about, precariously off balance.

For an instant, Traherne stared, transfixed, into the gilt-green eyes of a wood nymph with glorious red-gold hair. Then he felt his boot slip on the wet, treacherous bank and, flinging up his arms to catch himself, plunged backward, full length into the water.

Chapter Two

Traherne came up out of the icy water gasping for breath—and was met with the sight of a tall, willowy young woman garbed in forest green, who was gazing anxiously down at him from the bank, a small replica of herself clinging tightly to her skirts.

"Thank heavens! Faith, how you frightened me," she exclaimed, apparently in no little relief to see the stranger surface. "Are you all right? Here," she said, leaning down to extend a slim shapely hand, "pray let me help you."

She was rewarded with a baleful look, robbed somewhat of its daunting effect by the deplorable state of its bearer's curly brimmed beaver, that, retrieved from the drink, the gentleman had clapped on his head. Once a proud example of its kind, its brim was now disreputably unfurled and, streaming water, drooped woefully about the man's ears.

"I believe, madam," pronounced the gentleman in no uncertain terms, "you have done quite enough. I shall thank you merely to step aside."

"But I feel simply dreadful," the impertinent female

insisted, an assertion, Traherne noted sardonically, that was immediately put into doubt by an unmistakable twitch at the corners of her lips in addition to a rather fixed immobility about the eyes. This gave the distinct impression that, now she knew he was safe, she was struggling not to give way to helpless laughter—the wretch! "You really must allow me to take you to my house to dry off. It is only a short distance from here."

"*No-o,* Althie," wailed the little girl, flinging her arms about the woman's legs. "I don't want him to come home with us."

Quickly, the woman knelt. "Hush, Effie. There's no need to be frightened—or uncivil. The gentleman means us no harm, I promise."

"He hurt Goosey Gander," sobbed the little girl, her pixie face streaked with tears turned accusingly to the man, who, unaided and wearing a thunderous brow, was making his way out of the water. "I w-want Goosey. He's my birthday present."

Traherne was feeling singularly unamused at his undignified plunge into the drink, especially before witnesses. He was even less gratified to learn he had apparently just shot out of existence a child's beloved pet—her *birthday* present, no less, egad.

Still clutching the fowling piece in his hand, he climbed, slipping and sliding, up the grassy bank until at last he stood over the wood sprite. Upon closer inspection, she was somewhat older than he had first imagined (certainly past the first blush of youth, but no more than twenty-four or five, he surmised) and even more strikingly beautiful than she had any right to be. There was about her a sylphlike quality, he mused, that was only partially due to her slender height. It whimsically occurred to him that, with her enchanting red-gold hair worn in a glorious riot of disheveled curls and trailing bits of twigs and leaves, she appeared some elemental creature who might vanish without a moment's notice into the air itself.

Then an icy shiver took him and he was jarred out of his reverie sufficiently to recall that the wood nymph, no matter how entrancingly lovely, was the cause of his present damnable circumstances.

"I beg your pardon, madam," he said, his chest heaving from his recent exertions, not to mention the effects of his unpremeditated immersion in chilly waters, "but I find myself in something of a quandary. Perhaps you would be so good as to explain to me what the devil possessed you to send up a shout at my back. Never mind that I take little pleasure in bathing in a damnably cold lake while fully clothed or that this just happens to be a Boutet fowling piece that you have unhappily caused to be immersed in water." Removing his ruined hat, he dashed it with enough force to the ground to make the wood nymph and her tiny sprite wince. "Hell and the devil confound it, woman, I might have *shot* you!"

At his first words, the little girl had gone quite still, her eyes wide in her small, piquant face. Now she gazed pensively up at the woman. "Althie," she said in a carrying whisper, her mien expressive of awe, tinged with something of an impish glee, "he said the naughty words. Is Mrs. Fennigrew going to pull his ear?"

Traherne, elevating an incredulous eyebrow, glanced from one to the other as he awaited "Althie's" verdict on that pertinent question.

"No, dear," he was no doubt relieved to hear, only immediately to suffer the uneasy premonition that he was on the verge of plunging once more into deep waters as gilt-green eyes, enchantingly set in an oval face remarkable for its creamy complexion, swept up to meet his in a rueful look. "In this instance, I'm afraid we must forgive the gentleman his lapse. As it happens, he has every right to be upset."

Far from deriving any pleasure in having thus been delivered from an ear tweaking at the hands of the unknown Mrs. Fennigrew, Traherne was made to suffer an unwonted twinge of conscience for his boorish behavior. Bloody hell, obviously he was in the presence of one of those females who had the unhappy knack of appealing to a man's better nature without even being aware of their insidious feminine power to do so. In addition, this sylphlike beauty, he decided, like all her supernatural kindred, was quite capable of luring an unsuspecting male into her net of enchantment and holding him there like a fly in a spider's web. Every instinct of self-preservation warned him to remove himself from her presence now, before she had the opportunity to work her spell on him.

Inexplicably, he found himself standing his ground as the woman, disengaging herself from the clutching hands of the child, rose to her feet to favor him with an apologetic smile.

"You are quite right," she said with disarming directness. "It was all my fault. I should never have cried out. But, really, I could not help myself. Surely you must see that. I daresay you would have done the same had you been in my position."

"Oh, indubitably," magnanimously agreed Traherne, who had not the smallest notion what the devil she was talking about and who, in any event, was hardly likely to give vent to a piercing scream at *any* time, no matter what the mitigating circumstances that might seem to call for it.

"But of course you would," applauded the wood nymph, considerably brightening. "In spite of my initial impression, I can see now that you are a man with a sympathetic nature."

Did she indeed? marveled Traherne, not in the least gratified at having risen a peg in her estimation, especially considering how low he must clearly have initially rated. Inexplicably, he felt an almost overpowering desire to crush the little malapert to his chest and kiss her unmercifully until she learned the Duke of Traherne was not a man to be taken lightly. The little girl's sniffling brought him to his senses. "On the contrary," he retorted, "I am a man who finds himself apparently in the unwelcome position of having been made the unwitting perpetrator of an Unforgivable Deed. I believe, at the very least, I am entitled to an explanation of the circumstances that precipitated it. And you, madam, have yet to answer my question."

For this astute observation, rendered in magnificently controlled accents, Traherne was awarded an assessing look in which there seemed to be an appalling lack of the woman's grasp of the proper gravity of the situation. The devil, he was quite certain he had detected in the arresting orbs a wry gleam of amusement, quickly hidden beneath the luxurious veil of her eyelashes!

"My, you are in a rare taking, are you not," observed the impertinent wench, all apparent solicitude. "And who could blame you? You must be chilled to the bone. Indeed, you are shivering. Pray don't deny it. Might I suggest again, sir, that it would be wise for you to change out of your wet clothing at once?"

"You may *not*," snapped Traherne, in no mood to be read a curtain lecture on what could not have been more obvious. "I shall thank you instead to mind your own business."

"And I shall thank *you*, sir, not to raise your voice in front of the child," the wood sprite did not hesitate to fling back at him. Her full but pleasingly firm bosom, which seemed tantalizingly designed to perfectly mold to the palms of his hands, heaved with rising indignation. "I cannot imagine what possessed you to come shooting today of all days. I daresay His Grace of Traherne would not be at all pleased to discover a gentleman trespassing on his grounds. You are fortunate he is not in residence at present. Poaching is a serious matter, as you must well know."

"Ah, but the duke *is* here, madam," Traherne announced with a cold air of triumph. "And you are quite right: He does *not* look with favor upon trespassers. I wonder if you are

prepared to explain to him who *you* are and what you are
doing here.''

From the sudden widening of her eyes in dawning comprehension, Traherne did not doubt that the lady had at last
been brought to an awareness of whose presence it was in
which she found herself. His Grace waited with sardonic
appreciation for her response.

Whatever it was that he had anticipated, however, it was
hardly to behold the indisputably bewitching eyes light up
with sudden and unmistakable mirth or to witness the irrepressible wood nymph clap a hand over her mouth presumably to stifle a wholly enchanting burble of laughter, which
bubbled forth nonetheless.

''Your-Your Grace,'' she exclaimed, her voice decidedly
unsteady. ''I do beg your pardon for not introducing myself
earlier. I am Miss Althea Wintergreen of the Old Mill House,
and this is my own little Effie.''

''No doubt I am pleased to make your acquaintance,''
observed Traherne, drawing certain inevitable conclusions,
not the least of which was that Miss Wintergreen displayed a
total lack of the self-consciousness one might have expected
from a husbandless female who laid claim to a child who
bore a striking resemblance to her. In spite of himself, he
felt his interest piqued. ''I was not aware that any Wintergreens had taken up residence at the Old Mill House.''

''There are only Effie and myself,'' replied Althea, wholly
unaware of the enticing picture of fallen womanhood she
presented with her bright smile and easy unassuming air.
''Certainly, I had no idea you were at Briersly. Faith, I dare
not imagine what you must think of me.''

What His Grace thought of her was to remain a matter
of speculation, as Effie chose that moment to draw attention
to herself.

''Look!'' she cried, tugging insistently at Althea's skirts.
''There's Goosey. I see him! I see him!''

Having been laboring for some little time under the unrewarding certainty that he had put a period to the child's beloved fowl, Traherne could not but be taken aback at the eager excitement engendered by Effie's discovery that Goosey must yet be miraculously afloat. After all, the unhappy recipient of a load of shot would hardly prove a pleasant sight for an infant not long out of leading strings. He was even more appalled to find Miss Wintergreen, who should have been perfectly aware of the unseemly state of the bird, had grasped his arm and was exhorting him to retrieve the thing.

"It's not too late, Your Grace," she declared, with every manifestation of one inordinately pleased at the prospect. "We can still get it back." Then, to the duke's mounting consternation, "Hurry, Fitz," she cried, pointing to the feathered object bobbing in the water. "Fetch."

The setter plunged into the lake as readily as if it had received its orders from the duke himself and proceeded straightaway to the downed quarry, a circumstance that brought Traherne's gaze hard to bear on the wood nymph.

"It would seem, Miss Wintergreen," he observed, "that you are well acquainted with my setter. Not only do you know his name, but he responds to your command as if you had had the training of him. No doubt you will pardon me do I confess I find that curious."

"I cannot imagine why you should," replied the unrepentant Miss Wintergreen. "Fitz and I are old friends. Tom, your gameskeeper, was pleased enough to have someone to exercise Fitz in your absence, and I was happy to oblige him. I beg your pardon if you think I have overstepped my bounds, Your Grace," she added, "but I really could not bear to lose Goosey now. Effie would never forgive me."

"Oh, naturally not," replied the duke, wondering what the devil the wench thought to do with the stricken bird. An image of Goosey Gander stuffed and installed in the nursery as a permanent fixture came hideously to mind, only to be summarily dismissed as being only slightly less

distasteful than the notion of serving the bird up on a platter
for little Effie's birthday dinner. Somehow he did not think
the wood nymph had either possibility under consideration.
Perhaps she intended to use her earthen magic to bring
Goosey Gander back to life, he speculated, his eyes on the
bewitchingly lovely profile.

He was to discover some moments later that the last
supposition most nearly approached the surprising Miss
Wintergreen's intentions, as Fitz, dropping the undeniably
mangled Goosey Gander to the ground at the woman's feet,
proceeded to scatter the unsuspecting humans by vigorously
shaking himself in their midst.

"Fitz!" Althea shrieked with laughter. "You ungrateful
dog, you."

Traherne, observing her animated visage with a bemused twist of the lips, took the dog by the collar. "Enough,
Fitz," he sternly commanded, pulling the dog a safe distance
away. "I believe I shall have to have a word with Tom
Sykes about you. Your manners would seem to leave a great
deal to be desired."

Effie, coming out from behind Althea's skirts, was the
first to reach Goosey Gander.

"Goosey!" cried the little girl, gathering the inert object
without hesitation to her breast in an ecstatic hug. "Don't
you worry. Althie will soon make you right again. Won't
you, Althie?"

"We shall know soon enough, dearest," replied the
woman, reaching to carefully extract the pitiful object from
Effie's grasp. "Just let me have a look. Well, now," she
murmured after a moment, her fingers prodding and probing,
"it is not so bad as it could have been. The exterior has, of
course, sustained some little damage. I daresay Goosey will
need some new feathers, and one wing will most certainly
require extensive repairs. These, however, are not insurmountable difficulties. If there is not serious internal damage,
I shall have Goosey on his feet again in no time."

Traherne, who had been expecting to hear something far different, received this pronouncement with no little sense of bemusement. Stepping forward to peer over the wood nymph's shoulder, he was given his first clear view of the goose that had caused the tranquillity of his morning to be so summarily disrupted.

His glance narrowed, then flicked to the wood sprite to hold with a curious intensity. Bloody hell, the last thing he had expected to see was a small trapdoor spring open where the goose's belly had ought to be or to glimpse, within, the small cogs, wheels, and levers of a cleverly wrought and astoundingly lifelike machine.

"Good God," he exclaimed in sudden enlightenment. "A child's toy!"

"Hardly just a child's toy, Your Grace," objected Althea, extracting an assortment of tools from a leather pouch slung over one shoulder in order to assay some minor adjustments on Goosey's interior workings. "As it happens, this is the prototype of my Animated Mechanical Goose, a member of my proposed Animated Mechanical Menagerie Collection, which I have designed for persons who, for one reason or another, cannot experience the joys of having a real live pet. It is my opinion that there is nothing that can give greater comfort to one who is bedridden or debilitated than to have a creature to fondle and shower with affection. And there are, of course, certain added benefits of a mechanical pet over a real live one: It does not bite, and one does not have to feed or clean up after it. There," she pronounced with an air of profound satisfaction and, appearing to wind a spring, rather like an oversized watch stem, she snapped the trapdoor shut and set Goosey Gander on his feet.

Immediately, the Animated Mechanical Goose appeared to come to life, its webbed feet moving with mechanical rigidity, but carrying the feathered creation nevertheless in a surprisingly lifelike goosey waddle. The beak snapped open and shut to emit a plaintive "Honk, honk," even as the head swiveled left and right and the tail feathers quivered. Effie squealed and clapped her tiny hands in patent delight.

"He may not be able to glide with a broken wing," Althea speculated, unaware that her lovely face was made lovelier still by a glow of delight in Effie's pleasure, "but he can walk and talk. Perhaps there is even the chance he can still swim."

"Please, Althie, can we try him on the water?" trilled Effie. Her small face suffused with eager anticipation, she flung her arms about Althea's neck.

"Naturally. I was just going to suggest that very thing. It is, after all, your birthday, and Goosey's too, for that matter. I think, however, in his present state, it would be better to confine him to something smaller—a tub of water, perhaps, or—"

"The fountain at Briersly?" suggested Traherne. Heartily weary of his sodden state, he yet felt an unexpected reluctance to see his unlooked-for adventure so soon at an end. No doubt it was only that he was curious to witness the final phase of Goosey's trial run, he told himself, his gaze fixed on the enchanting contrasting visions of feminine beauty presented by the slender woman and the little girl clasped in her arms. With a sense of having abandoned all rationale, he heard himself add, "Perhaps you and little Effie would care to take tea at the hunting lodge while I make myself more presentable."

Startled eyes lifted to his, then were as quickly lowered, but not before Traherne was given to glimpse a flicker of something in the gilt-green depths. Something like fear, he thought, or dread. The arrogant black eyebrows drew sharply together over the bridge of his nose. Hellfire, surely the absurd female did not think he meant to lure her to his lair to make unseemly advances toward her with the child in tow. His reputation for being dangerous where women were concerned was richly deserved, but he was hardly the sort to behave in a manner less than a gentleman in front of an innocent.

"You are very kind, Your Grace," began Althea, with a doubtful shake of her head, "but I—"

"On the contrary, I am never kind," interposed the duke before she could finish. "Nor am I prepared to accept no for an answer. It is only fair, after all. I may have started out as an unwitting participant in Goosey's maiden voyage, but now I am involved, I should at least be allowed to see how it turns out. I leave it to you, Miss Wintergreen," he added, turning with exaggerated solemnity to Effie. "As it happens, Mrs. Grant was just on the point of popping some fennel cakes in the oven when I left Briersly. I daresay they are baked to a golden brown by now. You see, I am not above resorting to bribery. What say you, *enfant?*"

Althea, who had hardly anticipated this particular maneuver on the part of the duke, suffered a wave of apprehension tinged with vexation as she watched Effie frown up at the tall figure who, despite its woefully sodden state, fairly exuded an air of command. Kept carefully sheltered from all but those who watched lovingly over her, Effie was hardly accustomed to the overtures of strangers, let alone one of the duke's compelling presence.

"I say I should like very much to have tea with you, Your Grace," replied the little girl, surprisingly, and dimpled in response to something she sensed in Traherne's grave manner.

"A young lady of discernment," applauded Traherne, offering the child his hand and waiting until she had placed her tiny member in it. "Splendid. I promise you will not regret your decision. Mrs. Grant is noted for the excellent quality of her fennel cakes. Come, Fitz," he added, turning in the direction of Briersly. "We shall discuss your defection at a later time."

Marveling at the ease with which His Grace had apparently won Effie's trust, Althea was left staring after their retreating forms with an odd sense that she had just witnessed something exceedingly rare and fine. The Duke of Traherne was hardly noted for his condescension to children, much less children of females without the benefit of a husband. His reputation, quite to the contrary, would have him harsh and cold natured, a man of arrogance and pride who held himself aloof from lesser beings. His triumph over Effie's earlier trepidation would seem to cast some doubt on such an assessment.

But then, she had been made acutely aware from the moment she looked into eyes, dark rimmed about the irises and the pale blue of an ice-covered lake in winter, that this was no common sort of man. Even in his absurdly drooping hat, his obviously well cut clothes shedding puddles of water about his sloshing boots, he had presented a compelling figure of proud masculinity. Indeed, she had felt an absurd heat pervade her limbs at the mere sight of his manly perfection. Marvelously broad shoulders that seemed uncommonly suggestive of strength, a deep chest tapering most satisfactorily to a narrow waist, and muscular thighs and calves that quite rendered ridiculous so much as the thought of buckram wadding—had all been displayed to magnificent advantage beneath his revealingly wet, clinging clothes. And, as if that were not enough to stimulate a plethora of feminine emotions she had not even dreamed she possessed, the stranger had to be blessed, as well, with the sort of sculpted features that put one in mind of a Celtic warrior-poet. Bold arrogant eyebrows were set in a high, wide intelligent brow, the long nose was finely wrought, and the wide well-formed mouth—the sensitivity of which he took obvious pains to conceal behind a cynical thin-lipped sternness—along with the firm stubborn jaw were made stronger yet by a decided cleft in the chin. He was just as she might have imagined the Cornish knight Tristram, who had died for love of King Mark's Iseult of Ireland, she mused. Add to that, coal black hair and the ice blue eyes of a piercing intensity, and it was little wonder that he had had a most peculiar effect on her equilibrium. Indeed, she had found herself more than once on the verge of succumbing to something resembling hysterical laughter. But then, *he* had been so comically determined not to give in to what perhaps understandably had shown every sign of being a truly magnificent rage.

It was not surprising he had triggered that unfortunate perversity in her character, which had ever manifested itself in an uncontrollable tendency to give into mirth at the most improper moments. Whenever her father had scolded her for some childish indiscretion, he had inevitably been met with a quivering grin that she could not for the life of her banish from her countenance, never mind that it had never failed to reduce her dearest papa to stuttering incoherence. In fact, it had driven him, finally, to abandon all attempts at directing her energies into channels considered proper for a female. She was Althea; and, woman or not, by gad, she was a free and independent thinker. Not even the fierce aspect of a member of Amir Khan's Pathan banditti, who had waylaid Althea one afternoon as she was taking her daily ride along the banks of the Saraswati where it met the Khan outside of Indore, had served to frighten her to a proper gravity. The truth was, she had come close to laughing in the astonished bandit's face, which, as it happened, was perhaps the only thing that had saved her from abduction and probably worse—that, and the pistol, of course, that she held aimed unerringly at the center of the villain's chest. Impressed with the memsahib's noticeable lack of fear, the fellow had bared white teeth in a wide grin and, bowing grandly, had allowed her to pass unmolested. She very much suspected, however, that the Duke of Traherne had not been similarly disarmed.

In fact, if anything, she judged His Grace was far more likely to have found her lamentable tendency to mirth more on the order of flaunting a red flag in his face. Had it not been for Effie, she doubted not the last thing he would have

proposed was an invitation to Briersly for tea, which was
obviously meant to make up to Effie in some small measure
for having unintentionally wreaked havoc on the child's
birthday present. It was clear he was a man of noble instincts,
and of kindness too, reflected Althea with a whimsical smile,
and never mind his claim to the contrary.

He was also a man who had stopped and turned to gaze
at her with an air of expectancy, she realized, jarred out of
her reverie.

"Well, Miss Wintergreen?" he queried with an imperious
lift of an eyebrow. "You do intend to join us?"

"Yes, of course, Your Grace," Althea called, never mind
that Briersly was quite possibly the last place she wished
to go, especially in the company of its new lord and master.
Clearly, the duke wielded a strange, irresistible power over
her rational thought processes, not to mention her physical
being, she reflected, ruefully aware that her heart was behaving in a most unseemly manner beneath her breast. "Only
give me a moment, if you will."

With a wave of the hand, Althea slipped into the willows
and hurriedly gathered up the paraphernalia she had left at
Goosey's launching site.

"I do beg your pardon, Your Grace," she said moments
later as she hastened up to the others. "I nearly forgot the
catapult. Although Goosey's first attempt at flight has proved
something less than successful, I have hopes the next will
go rather better. Goosey *will* fly, I am sure of it."

"Goosey did fly," Effie asserted with stubborn loyalty.
"He just got knocked down. It wasn't your fault, Althie."

"It wasn't anyone's fault, dear," Althea replied, smiling
fondly at Effie. "It was just one of those unfortunate inci-
dents. Still, just for a second or two, he did look like a real
live gander taking to flight, did he not?"

"You may be sure of it," agreed Traherne with only a
hint of dryness, as he recalled his fateful glimpse of the

feathered object hurtling through the air, wings spread and neck outstretched.

"Well, naturally *you* would say so, Your Grace," Althea retorted, comically crinkling her nose at the duke. "After all, you were fooled into taking a shot at him. I do so wish we could have seen him land. Just to see if his head came up and his wings folded to his body when he entered the water."

"Good Lord," exclaimed Traherne, wondering what new surprises this singular female had in store for him. "You were not sparing in your attention to detail, Miss Wintergreen. Next, I suppose you will say Goosey Gander was capable of laying eggs."

"That's silly, Your Grace," pronounced Effie with the utter conviction of one in possession of incontrovertible knowledge. "Goosey Gander's a boy. Boy gooses can't lay eggs."

"*Geese,* dearest," Althea emended. "Or more correctly, *ganders* do not lay eggs. Ganders are males and geese are females."

"Then why call him Goosey Gander?" queried the duke, his look of gravity belied by the gleam in his eye. "He cannot very well be a goosey if he is a gander, now can he?"

"Can he, Althie?" Effie demanded, frowning. Then, brightening with a new thought, "Does that mean he *can* lay eggs?"

"It does not," replied Althea, awarding His Grace a dampening glance. "He is named Goosey Gander because of the rather silly nursery rhyme about a Goosey Gander. And you are quite right, he cannot be both, which is precisely what makes the nursery rhyme particularly silly."

"Quite so," agreed Traherne, winking an eye at Effie. "In which case, I daresay it is as correct to say 'boy gooses' as it is to call the creature Goosey Gander. On the other hand," he continued before Althea could offer the retort that so plainly was on the tip of her tongue, "would it not have been easier, Miss Wintergreen, to confine your creation to rather simpler tasks? Merely having the appearance of a gander would seem to me enough to satisfy those looking for a surrogate pet to fondle."

A pucker furrowed Althea's brow. "I suppose I might have been a trifle overambitious," she conceded, considering the matter, "but once I conceived the idea of an animated mechanical goose, one thing just seemed to lead to another. If I could make a machine that could walk, then why not one that could honk like a goose? Or one that could swim, for that matter. And if I could solve the mechanics of walking, vocalizing, and swimming, then why not flight? Or, more precisely, gliding. I had every expectation the wings and neck would do just as I designed them to do. The force of the landing should have been sufficient to spring the mechanism to bring them into the proper position. The thing is, I could not be certain Goosey would not simply plummet headfirst into the lake, which obviously would not have done at all."

"But, thanks to me, that is precisely what he must have done," observed the duke, noting the manner in which Miss Wintergreen's entire countenance tended to grow animated when she was contemplating her mechanical creations.

"That, Your Grace, was one variable I failed entirely to consider in my calculations," Althea agreed, laughing. "You cannot imagine the computations with which I have had to struggle to resolve the problem of weight distribution, the proper angle of the wings in flight, the length of the wingspan, and finally, the method of launching. I was not at all certain the wingspan was sufficient to support the weight of the body, which had necessarily to be constructed of the lightest materials that could still be molded to the proper form. The mathematics of it would suggest I was on the right track. Still, I cannot tell you how many models I have attempted, only to discover the materials were not sufficient to my needs. The final and most difficult task was to create a lifelike effect using paint and feathers. Perhaps, Your Grace,'' she added with a chiding glance at Traherne, ''you understand now why I was moved to scream when I glimpsed you on the point of immolating what has taken me three years to achieve. I can only be grateful that I must certainly have misdirected your aim sufficiently to ward off a direct hit, else I daresay Goosey would now be in an utter shambles, and I should have to start all over again from scratch.''

''I believe it has become a deal clearer to me,'' admitted Traherne, who had been listening with a mounting sense of incredulity to Miss Wintergreen's account of the difficulties she had encountered in designing her Animated Mechanical Goose. Clearly, to have labeled the colonel's daughter as something of an original would have been to grossly understate the case. Miss Wintergreen was like no other female he had ever encountered. But then, there could not be many females who took up mathematics, engineering, and tinkering as chosen vocations, not to mention the artistry of replicating a goose's appearance to such a degree as to render her creation startlingly lifelike. No doubt the military could have used her unusual talents in any number of capacities, not the least being the engineering of war machines for the eventual invasion of France! ''I suggest the next time you launch one of your Animated Mechanical Geese over the lake, you do so in the spring or summer. No true sportsman would be contemplating hunting birds at such a time.''

''Why not?'' asked Effie, who thought it was not in the least fair that birds were hunted at any time of the year.

''Because, *enfant,*'' Traherne replied, ''it is in the spring and summer that boy and girl 'gooses' are busy building nests, laying eggs, and raising a family. It would hardly be sporting to bother them at such a delicate time. The young need their mamas and papas if they are going to survive.''

''*I* don't have a papa,'' the little girl pointed out solemnly.

"Neither do I," said Traherne with equal gravity, noting the flicker of consternation cross Miss Wintergreen's face.

"But you're old," Effie countered, frowning. "You don't need a papa."

"I daresay that neither do you, *enfant,*" said Traherne, smiling wryly at sight of Miss Wintergreen's suddenly flushed appearance. He was made unexpectedly aware of a hot stab of something like anger as it came to him for the first time to contemplate the man whom, in defiance of all convention, Miss Wintergreen had been persuaded to take to her bed only to find herself afterward with child and abandoned, a shunned and ruined woman. Whatever mistakes she had made in judgment, she had hardly deserved that from one who could only have been an out-and-out bounder. "After all," he added, his gaze holding Althea's, "you have your mama and Mrs. Fennigrew to look after you."

"And Mattie and Elias and Peg and Mrs. Crenshaw, who makes the most splendid plum pies," Effie added, brightening. "Still, I think I might like to have a papa." Eyes, remarkably similar to the wood nymph's, lifted to regard Traherne speculatively. "Do you have a little girl, Your Grace?"

"Effie!" Althea hastily interjected, dragging her eyes from Traherne's. Faith, she had always known one day Effie would come to her with questions about her father. She had hardly expected it to arise at such a time as this and under these particular circumstances. "I think that is enough of pestering His Grace. We shall discuss the subject of papas later—at home. Besides, here we are at Briersly."

They had been making their way through a thick wood of birch and rowan, the latter heavy with red berries. But now they stepped clear of the trees into a green glade at the edge of a pine forest with Briersly, a sprawling two-story house of red sandstone topped with a green slate roof and covered with clematis, basking serenely in the midmorning sunshine.

Unexpectedly, Althea experienced a sudden wrench at sight of the house in which she had been borne and which had been her home until her mama's death when she was just turned eight and her sister five. It had been the only real home she had ever known, and her memories, though clouded with the passage of the years, reverberated with childish laughter and the strains of songs her mama had used to sing in her sweet lilting soprano. It had been a happy house in those days, even with her papa away much of the time. His homecomings had been almost as festive as the Yuletide and certainly every bit as merry. Althea had been told often enough that she had inherited her looks and her love of laughter from her mama, but her stubborn sense of duty, she did not doubt, had come to her from her papa.

When Judith Wintergreen died in childbirth, the merriment had seemed to go with her, so that there had been only the colonel's duty to carry them from one posting to the next. Her fiercely independent nature, Althea reflected, must be uniquely her own. It had determined that she always make the most of her ever-changing circumstances while playing the role of surrogate mama to her younger sister. And it was undoubtedly the reason Althea Wintergreen now found herself a ruined woman, shunned by the good people of Glenridding and the dale.

She had not set foot across the threshold at Briersly since the day her papa had loaded his small family into the travel coach and started them on the long journey following the colonel and the drum over two continents. Knowing how she must inevitably be received by the household, she had little wish to step across that threshold now. To be treated with thinly veiled contempt in the one place rife with memories of her mama was, after all, hardly something to which she could look forward with anything approaching equanimity.

It came to her that it was not too late. She could still give her excuses and make a hasty retreat. After all, what did it matter if the duke formed a disgust of her for her boorish behavior? He would be gone in a week or two, and she would be less than a memory to him.

Then suddenly it *was* too late. The door had swung open to reveal the august presence of one of those rarities in the wilds of Ullswater—a very proper London butler. Taking Effie's hand, Traherne led the little girl through the doorway, leaving Althea little choice but to follow after them.

Chapter Three

Rupert Carstairs, one of those undeniably superior servants, an English butler, bowed the duke and his guests into the foyer. His bejowled face was as carefully impassive as if he were perfectly accustomed to beholding the Duke of Traherne in what could only be described as something less than his usual elegance.

"There has been a slight accident, Carstairs, as you can see," dryly announced Traherne, who, having known his butler for thirty-five years, saw through the stoic front.

"Indeed, Your Grace, and may I say it is gratifying that you appear no worse for the experience."

A look, sardonic from the duke and studiously inexpressive from the servant, passed between them.

"You may be certain of it," Traherne assured the butler. "And thank you, Carstairs."

Laying the fowling piece on a side table, Traherne peeled off his wet and bedraggled spenser and relinquished it to the butler.

"This is Miss Wintergreen and Miss Effie. Be pleased to

see they are made comfortable in the Rose Room. I beg you will excuse me, ladies,'' he added, turning briskly toward the stairway, ''while I make myself more presentable. I shan't be long, I promise. Oh, and Carstairs, kindly see that our guests are brought a tea tray sumptuously provided with Mrs. Grant's freshly baked fennel cakes. As it happens, today is a very special day. It is Miss Effie's birthday.''

''As you wish, Your Grace,'' replied the butler, holding the ruined garment, clasped gingerly between a thumb and two fingertips, a circumspect distance away from his immaculate person.

Traherne, however, had already reached the landing and vanished down the hallway, leaving Althea and Effie to the tender ministrations of one who exuded an awesome dignity, one who might have been the envy of the Sultan of Mysore himself, Althea reflected in sardonic appreciation.

Still, she had not traveled two continents in the company of her father's regiment for nothing, Althea firmly reminded herself. Not only had she performed the duties of managing her father's household from the tender age of fourteen, but it had fallen to her to play hostess to the colonel's officers on innumerable occasions as well. Carstairs might be the first English butler it had been her occasion to meet, but she had been in the company of soldiers the greater part of her life. Somewhere behind Carstairs's facade of starched spit and polish was a man, she was sure, and she would not be intimidated.

''Here we are, madam,'' said the butler a few moments later as he ushered them into a spacious withdrawing room done in paneled wall murals and made cozy with a fire crackling in the carved Gothic fireplace. The Rose Room elicited for Althea memories of Yule logs at Christmastide and snow spattering against the windowpanes, the attar of roses drifting in through the open French doors in summer and her mama doing needlework while Althea and Gloriana played jackstraws on the claret-colored Ushak rug. Save for the bric-a-brac, which had gone into barrels to be stored in the Old Mill House and which had been replaced with apparent relics of the duke's travels in the Orient, Traherne had not changed the room. Without conscious volition, Althea's fingertips found the nick in the rosewood occasional table, a casualty of her earliest attempts at employing a hammer, which she had stolen out of the groundskeeper's shed when she was four. Even the furniture, she thought, wondering what had possessed His Grace to leave everything as he had found it. But then, he seldom made time to visit what must surely have been one of his least significant holdings. Very likely, he had not deemed it worthwhile to refurbish the place.

"I was not aware His Grace kept a full staff at Briersly," observed Althea, her eyes questioning on the butler. "Indeed, I understood from Tom Sykes there were only Mrs. Grant, himself, and a few others to keep the place in readiness."

"Indeed, madam. As it happens, Lord Hilary Keene insisted on a full staff to insure His Grace's comfort. In light of His Grace's recent indisposition, I daresay he deemed it only prudent."

"Indisposition?" queried Althea, inexplicably suffering a sudden swift pang in the vicinity of her heart.

"Yes, madam." Then, "Tea will be served directly," Carstairs added with a ponderous dignity that made it plain the subject of the duke's health was not one upon which he intended to elaborate. "Will there be anything further, madam?"

"As a matter of fact, there will," Althea promptly answered, recovering from Carstairs's pointed rebuff, which had only been the proper butlerish thing to do (the duke's personal well-being, after all, was hardly any of her affair), and from her own startling reaction to the intimation that Traherne had apparently been exceedingly ill. His illness must have been serious enough to require his uncle to insist he be attended in the country by a butler of Carstairs's obvious remove, not to mention the noticeable additions of at least two maids and a footman. Faith, and she had caused him to be immersed in the chill waters of the lake! she thought with a terrible sinking sensation, a man who was just risen from his sickbed! Good God, it did not bear thinking on. The least she could do was try and make up for it in some small way. "I should like you to bring me His Grace's fowling piece," she said, "a metal rod, gun oil, and some old towels, if you would, Carstairs. There is nothing more detrimental to a firearm than moisture."

At a distinct, if muffled, rumble issuing from somewhere deep in the butler's throat, Althea impetuously reached out to touch his arm. "You needn't be concerned, Carstairs, that I shall damage the weapon. I am well versed in the use and care of firearms," she informed him. Then, when he still visibly hesitated, "It really will not do to allow a Boutet fowling piece to go to rust, Carstairs. You may trust me to know what to do, I promise."

"It's true," piped up Effie, peering up at the superior servant from behind Althea's skirts. "Althie knows all about how to fix things. Mrs. Fennigrew says she's a wizard."

"Does she indeed, Miss?" intoned the butler, his austere glance descending to Effie. "And what sort of wizard is that?"

Having brought the butler's attention down upon herself, Effie appeared visibly to contract. Still, she had not been reared in an atmosphere of free and independent thinking to no effect. Visibly swallowing, she blurted, "Mrs. Fennigrew says she can work magic with her hands. She fixed Mr. Treadwell's watch and the old grandfather clock and the kitchen stove that used to smoke and Mrs. Fennigrew's spectacles. She can fix anything if she has the tools for it. She made Goosey Gander from scratch for my birthday present," she added expansively, winding up the Animated

Mechanical Goose and setting it down to waddle, honking and twitching its tail feathers, across the room.

"Miss Wintergreen would indeed seem a wizard," intoned Carstairs, dispassionately observing Goosey waddle mindlessly past his feet straight into the Georgian ebonized, parcel gilt escritoire, only to continue to honk and waddle and twitch its tail feathers in seemingly gleeful ignorance of having reached an immovable obstacle. "It would seem, madam, in the face of indisputable evidence of your competence in mechanical matters, I may safely consign His Grace's fowling piece into your capable hands. And may I say," Carstairs added, bending down to retrieve the Animated Mechanical Goose, which, having run its course, had elapsed with a final twitch of the tail feathers into inanimate silence, "I wish you every happy return of the day, Miss Effie?" He extended the goose to the little girl, who, having taken refuge once more behind Althea, was regarding the butler's august presence with an obviously greater awe than that which had been inspired by the duke himself.

Wide-eyed, Effie gave a tug on Althea's skirts. "What do I tell him, Althie?" she whispered.

Again, that little growling rumble from Carstairs's throat.

"Tell him that he may say it and that it is very kind of him," Althea whispered back. "And thank him."

"But he already did say it," Effie pointed out with the daunting practicality of extreme youth. She gave the wooden-faced butler a searching look. Suddenly, her face lit up with a sunny grin. "And it *was* kind of you, Mr. Carstairs," she said, taking Goosey and hugging the mechanical creature to her breast. "Thank you very much."

"You are quite welcome, Miss Effie. And now if you will excuse me, I shall just go and attend to that other matter." Bowing, he retreated staidly to the door.

"He's nice, I think," declared Effie when the door had shut behind the exited butler, "even if he does try very hard to hide it. Why doesn't he want anyone to see that he's smiling inside, Althie?''

"Smiling inside, dearest?" queried Althea, running her hand over the lions' heads and swirls of fruit carved into the fireplace.

"It's not the sort of smile you can see. You just feel it." Then, before Althea could supply an answer to that observation, Effie puckered her brow up at Althea and launched into another, even more startling one. "Why does this room make you look sad, Althie? Is it because it doesn't have anyone to sparkle it up?"

"I don't know what you mean, Effie," Althea said, turning to regard the child with a bemused look.

"Sparkle it up," repeated Effie. *"You* know. Like when you wind up Goosey and make him come to life."

"Oh, indeed. I suppose it is something like that," Althea agreed, considering the matter. "But I am not really sad, you know. I am just feeling the memories. Gloriana and I used to live in this house with your grandmama and grandpapa a long time ago. We were borne here, in one of the bedrooms upstairs. Being here like this, after all this time, is a little like stepping into a dream of something that happened to someone else."

"It is? Why?" asked Effie.

"Because," Althea said patiently, "the things I remember happened so long ago. Time can blur one's memories, dearest, like looking at reflections in a foggy looking glass."

Effie frowned. "Why?" she asked.

"Well," said Althea, drawing a breath, "because you will find as you get older that your life tends to be so full of what is going on at the moment that what happened in the past just seems to fall farther and farther behind. You do not think about what happened a long time ago because you are too busy living from day to day, until something happens to make the memories pop up again. But by then, you are so far away from them that little bits and pieces are forgotten, and the colors and smells have faded somewhat. You recognize them, and they can still touch your heart, even make you laugh or cry, but they seem just a little bit like strangers with familiar faces.''

"That's silly,'' said Effie, pressing her nose up to the leering aspect of a jade monkey set on an occasional table. "How can strangers have familiar faces?''

"How can little girls have so many questions on their birthdays?'' countered Althea in fond exasperation. Launched on one of her endless bouts of "why's" and "how's," Effie could tax the patience of a saint, not to mention one's power to come up with satisfactory answers. She was relieved when a soft scratching on the door heralded the arrival of the tea tray, followed soon after by Carstairs with the Boutet fowling piece.

Soon Effie's mouth was happily too full of fennel cakes, baked to a golden brown, to allow for any more questions. And Althea, armed with a screwdriver from her pack, was too involved with dismantling His Grace's Boutet fowling piece to be troubled by the echoes of memories—or for that matter, by the fact that she was in the hunting lodge of a powerful nobleman with a reputation for being exceedingly dangerous.

No doubt if she had paused to consider that cogent particular, she would have dismissed it as being irrelevant. She had already determined for herself that Traherne was possessed of the sort of generosity that had prompted him to invite a child to tea to make up for having spoiled her birthday present, no matter how unintentionally. It simply did not occur to Althea that he might entertain designs on her own womanly virtue, which was, in any event, already tarnished beyond redemption. After all, she had already come to the conclusion, not without an unexpected twinge of regret, that she was hardly the sort to engage the interests of someone of Traherne's obvious distinction.

* * * *

What Althea had failed to take into consideration, however, was the potent effect of gilt-green eyes that tended to sparkle with impudent laughter. Like the sudden glance of sunlight through dew-drenched September leaves, Traherne found himself speculating whimsically, as stripped to the buff, he dried himself with a towel. Add to that a dazzle of personality, a quick intelligence coupled with what could only be described as a unique thought process, a charming vivacity utterly lacking in artifice, an engaging openness of manner that was neither coy nor coming, and a face and form to excite a man's lustier emotions—and one was presented with as intriguing a female as it had ever been his fortune to encounter.

That she was also neither an innocent nor a sophisticate of jaded sensibilities could not but add to her charm, even as it presented Traherne with the disturbing feeling that Miss Wintergreen was not precisely what she would seem to be. She was, in fact, he decided, contemplating his initial impression of fresh sylphlike beauty garlanded with bits of twigs and leaves, something of an enigma.

Who the devil was she, really? he wondered, or, more to the point, *what* was she? To know she was the elder daughter of Colonel Wintergreen told him very little beyond the fact that her mother had died when she was quite young and that her father had taken her and her younger sister abroad with him. Presumably she had been reared in the unlikely environment of foreign posts while following her father and the drum, which would undoubtedly account for her lack of self-consciousness in the presence of a stranger of the masculine gender. Having been reared among men, she would naturally feel at ease around them; and being more traveled than most of her feminine contemporaries, as well, would give her that sparkle of confidence he had remarked in her ready exchange of wits with him.

Suddenly, the handsome lips thinned to a humorless line as it came to him that there was an even more significant reason for Miss Wintergreen's ease with men. After all, she, it would seem, had engaged in the sort of intimacy that bred familiarity. The evidence was irrefutable. Miss Wintergreen had a child.

That he should find that inescapable fact vaguely disturbing brought a cynical twist to his lips. Who the devil was he to sit in judgment on Miss Althea Wintergreen? As it happened, he admired a number of things about her, not the least of which were her seemingly total lack of bitterness for what of necessity must be her exile from the world to which she belonged and her obvious devotion to the child who was the cause of her present circumstances. A young and eminently desirable female, she could not but regret that she was denied marriage and acceptance in the Society into which she had been borne. More than that, in all probability, she was spurned even by those beneath her station. In which case, it was little wonder that she filled her days tinkering with such oddities as her Animated Mechanical Menagerie.

Still, it was a bloody waste, he thought. Miss Wintergreen, in different circumstances, would undoubtedly have taken London by storm and not only because she was a cursedly beautiful woman. She exuded that rare sort of vitality that must inevitably set her apart from many another young beauty. Her very freshness and originality must naturally attract the notice of all who come within her sphere. It occurred to Traherne that he would have liked nothing better than to be the one to introduce the enchanting Miss Wintergreen into the fashionable milieu of balls, soirees, and dinner parties. Certainly, the fanciful notion held greater appeal than the actual Season he saw before him of paying his addresses to any number of ingenuous young misses in search of one who would not bore him to utter distraction. Miss Wintergreen, he suspected, would not soon prove boresome. Quite the contrary, he mused, recalling the mischievous imps of laughter in her eyes, she was far more likely to drive a man to distraction. Which might offer the sort of pleasant diversion he needed at the moment, a last fling, as it were, before he succumbed to the necessity of setting up his nursery, he reflected and immediately chided himself for a bloody fool.

If he were any judge of the matter, Althea Wintergreen was not the sort one dallied with and then easily forgot. In fact, his every instinct for self-preservation warned him to distance himself from her now, before he allowed himself to become too caught up in what must inevitably prove an unwieldy entanglement. Unexpectedly, he found that the last thing he could wish was to add to her hurt. The devil of it was he wanted her, and he had not wanted a woman in a very long time. Indeed, he had found he could think of very little else since he had had the misfortune to gaze into those damnably beautiful eyes.

He told himself it was only because it was some time since he had taken a woman to his bed. A circumstance due as much to the weariness of body and soul that had plagued him since his mission to France had ended in failure and near death, as to the actuality of his lengthy recuperation from the wound itself. Ruefully, he acknowledged that Miss Wintergreen would seem to have a unique gift for drawing him out of himself, even if it happened to be to rouse him to a state of unmitigated fury one moment only to engage him in mirth the next. She was undeniably the most fascinating woman he had ever met, not to mention one of the most desirable. She was, nevertheless, a temptation he could well do without. What he required at this stage of his life was not a mistress, no matter how intriguingly alluring, but a wife.

The devil, he thought, hardly aware of the tight-lipped ministrations of Greaves, his gentleman's gentleman. Having earlier greeted with horror the sight of the disastrous transformation from the sartorial perfection with which he had sent his employer out that morning to the scandalous state of ruin in which the duke had returned, Greaves was in the process of holding up a coat for His Grace to don. He would see the tea through and then he would send the enticing Miss Wintergreen on her way, Traherne firmly told himself, slipping his arms into the coat sleeves. And that would be the end of it.

"I'm afraid, Your Grace," said the valet as, with something resembling a sniff, he buttoned the duke's coat down the front, "I shall be hard-pressed to return the waistcoat to a semblance of its former appearance, let alone the breeches. Buff does not lend itself well to the removal of water stains. And the boots, Your Grace, I daresay, may never be quite the same."

"Quite so, Greaves," drawled the duke, in no mood for a fit of the spasms from his valet over the condition of his waterlogged Hessians, whose muddy exteriors indeed bore little resemblance to the normally unearthly sheen that only Greaves knew how to achieve. "I am well aware that I have put into jeopardy your unparalleled reputation for turning out a well-dressed gentleman." Straightening his cuffs, Traherne turned away from the looking glass. "It was, however, an unavoidable accident, and this is, after all, the country. I daresay word of the incident will never reach London." Reaching for the door handle, he added over his shoulder, "Try and see what you can do to salvage the boots and relegate all the rest to the refuse, if you wish. I leave it to you, Greaves. As for me, I have guests waiting."

With that breezy dismissal, Traherne left his scandalized valet to stare after him in open-mouthed astonishment. Ironically aware that he had treated his admittedly superior servant in an uncharacteristically cavalier fashion, Traherne suffered an unaccustomed twinge of remorse, which was quickly supplanted by an equally unwonted sense of pleasurable anticipation at the prospect of rejoining his guests. He would salve Greaves's wounded sensibilities later, he told himself, as he descended the stairway.

It came to him to wonder how Miss Wintergreen had fared in the familiar surrounds of her former withdrawing room. It could not but feel strange to find oneself a visitor in the house that had been one's family home, but to further discover it unchanged must make it all the more poignant. He considered the possibility that she might even be moved to resentment at what might be considered her reduced circumstances. After all, the Old Mill House clearly was not Briersly and all that the house must have stood for once.

Whatever he had expected to find when he entered the withdrawing room, however, it most certainly was not the sight of Miss Wintergreen, alone in the room and sitting cross-legged on the floor, her nimble fingers reassembling the various parts of his Boutet fowling piece with an expertise that might have put to shame a professional soldier. It was obvious she had not heard him enter, as he stood watching her progress in no little amazement.

"It would seem there is no end to the surprises you hold in store for me, Miss Wintergreen," he said a few moments later, when she was tightening the final bolt in place. "All this really was not necessary, however. As it happens, I have a gameskeeper who would have taken care of it for me. And where, I wonder, has Effie taken herself off? I had expected to find the birthday girl indulging herself in fennel cakes."

"Your Grace," exclaimed Althea, her lovely face lighting up as she turned her head to behold him standing behind her, his tall masculine presence compellingly handsome in a dark blue cutaway coat and dove gray trousers seemingly molded to his muscular thighs. Unexpectedly, she experienced at the sight of him a most peculiar queasy sensation in the pit of her stomach. "As it happens, your kitchen feline has a new litter of kittens, one of which Mrs. Grant has promised to Effie for her birthday. Carstairs has taken her to look them over."

"I must commend Carstairs and Mrs. Grant. I confess I had yet to come up with an appropriate gift, although it had occurred to me there might be something with which you might like to present her. Perhaps when she returns from her excursion to the kitchens, the two of you would allow me to show you upstairs."

Althea awarded him a dazzling smile, the effect of which was like potent wine to his senses. The devil, he thought.

"And I confess that I have been hoping for an excuse to see some of the rest of the house." Laying the assembled gun aside, Althea accepted his hands and allowed him to pull her to her feet. Upon which, Traherne found himself, to his growing bemusement, the object of an unnerving scrutiny.

"But you look simply splendid!" she pronounced with a profound satisfaction that brought a quizzical elevation of a ducal eyebrow.

"No doubt I am gratified to hear it," he replied with only the barest hint of irony. "You may be sure Greaves, my valet, will be ecstatic when I tell him. I might even go so far as to entertain the hope he will be so moved as to pardon me for ruining his earlier efforts."

If he had thought by this to bring the enchanting sparkle of laughter to her eyes, he was soon to be disappointed.

Miss Wintergreen, to the contrary, appeared unwontedly distracted.

"You cannot know how relieved I am that you appear to have suffered no ill effects from your drenching," she said, turning to pace a step, then coming back again. "I should never forgive myself were you to succumb to an inflammation of the lungs because of my-my—"

"Understandable attempt to save your remarkable invention from almost certain immolation?" supplied His Grace, smiling in sardonic appreciation of the enchanting Miss Wintergreen's poignant distress. Then, quietly, "Carstairs told you of my recent indisposition, is that it?"

Fascinated, he watched a slow blush stain her cheeks. "He merely mentioned it in passing, Your Grace, nothing more than that. You may be certain he was the soul of discretion."

"I *am* certain of it. He, like his father before him, has served my house with unwavering devotion since before I was in leading strings. Or perhaps I should say with a doggedness from which not even I could dissuade him," Traherne added with a peculiar twist of the lips. He was well aware that, while he had lain helpless in his bed, Carstairs had stood guard outside his bedroom door at night. Like a toothless mastiff in stubborn defense of its master, grimly reflected the duke. The devil only knew what Carstairs thought to have done had Meresgate's defenses actually been penetrated by would-be assassins. Yet, it seemed that everyone from the stablelads to the upstairs maids had been in league to protect their employer from his enemies. Even Greaves, while attending to Traherne's every need, had kept a loaded pistol hidden beneath a throw pillow on the settee. And they were about it still, thought Traherne grimly. "This is what comes of indulging my uncle's well-intentioned meddling," he said with a sudden impatience that gave an edge to his voice he had not intended. "You must not mind Carstairs, Miss Wintergreen. He tends to behave like an old woman where I am concerned."

"Does he?" murmured Althea, amused in spite of herself. "I cannot imagine why he should."

Traherne's gaze narrowed sharply on her lovely face. The impudent little devil, he thought. She was laughing at him again. "Nor can I, Miss Wintergreen," he answered, with an ironic curl of the lips. "As it happens, I am judged in most quarters to be more than capable of looking after myself. I should even go so far as to speculate that the world would be greatly surprised that anyone should think I am in need of coddling. I should warn you, Miss Wintergreen. I am, with good reason, thought to be both ruthless and dangerous."

"Are you, Your Grace?" said Althea, studying him with a noticeable lack of trepidation. How very odd, she thought, that a man of Traherne's obvious perspicacity should be utterly blind to the loyalty he inspired in those who served him, or, more important, to those qualities in himself that must elicit such devotion. She did not doubt he would have found the notion incredible that Carstairs and the others of the household might even hold him in something approaching affection. "But then, everyone, even dukes," she said, "must occasionally benefit from a little nurturing now and again. One cannot always be self-sufficient. Only imagine how very desolate it must be never to allow oneself to be cared for or helped by others."

Cared for or helped, egad, thought the duke. He had learned early on in life just how little one should rely on the caring of others! But then, Miss Wintergreen, he suspected, was not of the common mold. She, he doubted not, could never betray a trust. "Naturally, you would think so, Miss Wintergreen. It is what I should expect of you."

"Why?" she asked, aware of a sharp stab of disappointment at the thought that he could so easily judge her. "Because I am a woman? And therefore by my very nature must be expected to look to others for guidance and support?"

"No, Miss Wintergreen." Far from a wilting violet, she was, he did not doubt, every bit as stubbornly independent as himself. After all, she had embraced disgrace and ostracism rather than disavow her fatherless child. Furthermore, in the face of what he judged to be the greatest adversity, she had made a warm and loving home for that child. "As it happens, I have observed you with your little Effie. You stand condemned not of being a woman, Miss Wintergreen, but of having a loving heart. I daresay you could no more imagine not caring for others than you could stop breathing."

"And you could?" asked Althea, recalling to mind his reputation for aloofness. Surely, he did not believe that to give into the promptings of the heart was a sign of weakness. He did not seem the sort to give a tinker's damn what anyone might think of him. No, it was something else. Strangely, an image came to mind of a young lieutenant in her father's regiment who had had a gun go off in his face. The terrible wound had done more than disfigure him for life. It had served to freeze his emotions into a bitter hardness that would allow him to feel nothing. It had been his only defense against the horror and pity of others. Inexplicably, she found herself wondering what His Grace would do if she were to be so forward as to lay her palm against the side of his face. Immediately, she felt a sudden heat explore her veins, as it came to her that she was laboring under the impulse to do much more than that.

Something of her thoughts must have shown in her face. To her dismay, Traherne moved closer so that, in spite of her own generous inches, he seemed suddenly to loom over her.

"You will find, Miss Wintergreen," he said quietly, reaching up to untangle a willow twig from her hair, "if you come to know me better, that I make no claim to any of the softer human emotions."

Althea felt her heart behave in a most erratic manner beneath her breast. Indeed, she only just managed to refrain from running her tongue over absurdly dry lips. "No, I daresay you would not, Your Grace," she replied, reminded suddenly that he was a man of enormous influence and power, a man used to command—a duke. But a man, nonetheless. And what a strange man he was, to be sure, she thought, recalling a trifle giddily the ease with which he had won Effie over. He was, she judged, capable of great charm when he chose to wield it. Worse, he was the sort of man women would come easily to love. And *he,* by his own admission, was not prey to the softer human emotions! All at once she frowned. "Why is that? I wonder," she said, tipping her head back to look searchingly into his eyes.

A short bark of laughter seemed forced from him. The devil, he thought, acutely aware that her lips were a tantalizing few inches from his. He had forcibly to remind himself that she was not an innocent. She must know very well what she was inviting. And who was he to deny her? Deliberately, he lifted his hand to trail a fingertip lightly down the side of her face. "Do not make the mistake of imagining, Miss Wintergreen, that there is some dark terrible secret lurking in my past which has embittered me and hardened my heart. The truth is much simpler than that."

A faint smile twitched at the corners of his mouth as Althea's eyes widened on his.

"Is it, Your Grace?" she said in a voice hardly above a whisper. Then, as he continued his tantalizing journey down the graceful column of her neck and, farther, to the delectable entrance to the valley between her breasts where they pressed against the square neckline of her bodice, she drew in a shuddering breath and blurted, "What, pray, is the truth?"

She was adorable, was the little wood sprite, he thought, as he felt her tremble beneath his touch. If he did not know better, he might have believed she was reacting to his caresses with the ingenuousness of an untouched miss. But then, she could have found no surer way of arousing his interest. It would seem she was as clever at manipulation as she was at mechanical engineering. He could feel the swell of his desire against the front of his breeches.

"The truth is—" he murmured, slipping his arm about her slender waist. She made no move to resist, but stood perfectly still, her eyes, like deep emerald gems, staring unblinking back into his. Inexorably, he pulled her to him. "I am," he uttered thickly, lowering his head to hers, "a man who values logic above emotion."

The next moment his mouth covered hers.

Whatever his views on the superiority of logic over emotion, it was hardly reason that ruled his reaction to the feel of her lips parted beneath his or to the distinct groan that issued from somewhere deep within her as he thrust his tongue between her teeth. The long sigh that shuddered through her slender body did not arouse his intellect to a smoldering pitch of excitement. Nor was it his intellect that derived a keen appreciation in the indisputable fact that her arms had lifted to wrap themselves about the back of his neck and that her delectably feminine form seemed to mold itself to his larger, masculine frame. By God, she was all fire and generosity, was the little wood nymph!

He was swept with a burning impatience to savor her in all of her sweetness.

Only the certainty that the child must soon return to the drawing room impelled him to release her.

A smile touched his lips as he raised his head to behold her eyes still closed, her aspect distant, dreamy. With bated breath, he watched her eyelids drift slowly open to reveal the gilt-green depths of her eyes like unfathomable pools shadowed with mystery. Slowly, she awakened to him, to the clasp of his arms around her.

"Your Grace," she breathed, sudden awareness flooding her cheeks with color. "You-you kissed me."

A chuckle sounded deep in his throat. Gently, he brushed a stray curl from the side of her face. "I did, and how not? You are a beautiful, desirable woman. More than that, I find you delightful. Whom, I wonder, do you let care for *you*, Althea?"

Speechlessly, Althea stared back at him. It was not a question she had foreseen arising when she thought to instruct the duke on the subject of opening oneself to the caring of others. Nor did she think that was precisely what he had in mind with that particular question. It was, in fact, all too clear what he was asking. He had just kissed her. There could only be one interpretation for his query, one that she was not in the least prepared to answer at the moment.

Indeed, she could only be grateful to hear Effie's piping

voice issue from beyond the closed door. Hastily, she unclasped her arms from about the duke's neck and stepped back in time to meet the child's clamorous entrance.

Althea was acutely aware, however, that the question, left hanging, had only been postponed for the moment. Indeed, it was like a palpable thing between them when, some moments later, Traherne conducted Effie and Althea upstairs to show them something he thought perhaps they might find interesting.

If the Rose Room had brought back memories, the room at the end of the hall fairly reverberated with remembered scenes from Althea's childhood. As Traherne thrust open the door, it was like peering through a window in time to a past untouched by the passage of the years. The nursery, replete with all the mementos of the halcyon days of extreme youth, was just as she and Gloriana had left it all those long years ago. On the day their papa, informing them that they must leave behind the things of childhood, had bundled them from the nursery and into the coach that would take them seemingly to the ends of the earth.

"You had it kept this way, all this time," she said, lifting wondering eyes to the duke. "Why?"

He was watching her with a curious intensity, which had the unsettling effect of arousing a flutter in the pit of her stomach.

Traherne shrugged a single broad shoulder. "It suited me to have it preserved as I found it. No doubt you could attribute it to a whim, Miss Wintergreen. And now I think Effie should pick out whatever she would wish to take home with her. The rest I shall have packed up directly and sent over. What do you say, Effie?"

"May I, Althie?" said the little girl, her eyes wistful in her pixie face.

Althea smiled. "I believe His Grace intends this in the way of a birthday present. We shouldn't wish to be so rude as to refuse him, now should we?"

The little girl's face lit with an answering grin. "No, Althie," she agreed. Then, still afraid to believe in her good fortune, "May I really choose *anything?*" she asked, her eyes wide on the duke.

"Anything that tickles your fancy," Traherne assured her.

It came to Althea, watching the duke lead Effie into the treasure trove of dolls and dollhouses, tiny tea sets complete with china, books, kites, carved wooden horses, a hobby horse, fairy costumes, polished rocks, and a collection of shells from a summer spent at the seaside, among a wealth of other things to be devoutly desired by a five-year-old girl, that Traherne was deriving almost as much pleasure from Effie's blissful explorations as the child herself. What a strange man he was, to be sure, she mused, finding it difficult to pair the man, who had knelt on one knee to take the china doll Effie was holding up for his examination, with the duke, who had not hesitated to remind her that he had the reputation for being dangerous and utterly ruthless.

Suddenly, she found herself wondering which of the two had kissed her—the strong gentle man or the powerful duke? Or did it matter? Surely one was as dangerous to her peace of mind as the other, and whoever he was, really, he had asked her a question.

She would have to come up with an answer sooner or later—if not for Traherne's satisfaction, then at the very least to settle the unexpected turmoil he had introduced into her previously untroubled existence.

Chapter Four

"I'll see that Effie is kept busy in the nursery. You know you needn't fret about that, missy," Mrs. Fennigrew assured Althea with a distinct air of disapproval. "It's you I'm some worried about. You can feel it as well as I can—the weather is fixing to turn. Like as not there'll be rain long before you can get back from the foss. I'd give it a second thought before I went traipsing off over those boulders alone with the threat of a storm in the air."

"You worry too much, Nessie," said Althea, flinging on the faded moss-colored cloak she was used to wearing on her tramps through the forest and slinging the strap of her leather pouch over one shoulder. "If I'm caught out in a storm, I shall simply take refuge in the old woodcutter's cottage until it blows over." Seeing that her assurances had not eased the misapprehension from her former nanny's face, Althea reached out impulsively to touch Mrs. Fennigrew's arm. "Pray do not fret, dearest Nessie. The truth is, I simply cannot bear to remain indoors today. I have the fidgets. I shall most certainly go mad if I do not get some fresh air and exercise. I shall be fine, I promise.''

"See that you are,'' Mrs. Fennigrew returned with a sniff. "There's more'n yourself to think about, and you're looking pale about the gills. You're not sleeping well, are you, miss, which isn't at all like you. Like as not you're coming down with something.''

"Nonsense,'' said Althea, wanting nothing more than to escape the nanny's keen-eyed scrutiny. Agnes Fennigrew possessed the eyes of a hawk when it came to one of her charges, and Althea, despite her five and twenty years, might never have left the nursery so far as the old nanny was concerned. "You know I am never ill. Now, give Effie a kiss for me and tell her I shall come to the nursery to see her as soon as I return.''

Without waiting to hear any further remonstrances from the well-meaning woman, Althea fled out the door into the crisp September breeze. Nevertheless, an echo of words seemed to pursue her as she struck out with long, quick strides along the familiar path that followed the bank up the rushing beck: *"Whom do you let care for you, Althea?"*

A wry grimace twisted at her lips. *How dare His Grace turn her sentiments against her!* she thought, striding ever faster, as if she might escape the unfamiliar turmoil within her breast.

The Duke of Traherne had kissed her! Was it truly only yesterday? she marveled. It seemed she had been wrestling with the reality and the unspoken implications for weeks, even eternities. Had Effie not returned when she did, what answer would she have given to that tantalizing question? Indeed, how could she even be certain she had understood what he meant by it?

Mrs. Fennigrew, Mattie, Elias, Gloriana—they took care of her. But that was not the answer, surely, for which he had been waiting while his eyes, the winter blue of an ice-covered lake, seared her with sudden piercing flames.

Faith, what an *idiot* she was not to have seen it coming! She was not without experience in such matters. Neither was she naive. She knew what people would think of her—did think of her. She had even considered the possibilities herself, not in the way other women fantasized about love and marriage, but in a cold-blooded fashion of the only avenue for at least the pretense of love that was open to her. It had occurred to her in such moments that to be a man's mistress was not entirely without its merits, especially on the terms upon which she would insist. After all, she was assured of an income ample to her needs and consequently did not have to look to a man to provide for her and Effie. This gave her considerable latitude should she ever decide to pursue an illicit affair of the heart. It, in fact, allowed her to enter into such an arrangement as an independent and therefore equal participant, which she considered superior, in many respects, to the status of a wife. In marrying, a wife must bow to her husband's authority, and, in so doing, gave up the right to rule her own life, her fortune, and her independent thinking.

To Althea, who treasured her independence above everything, save for Effie, marriage had ever loomed as a pitfall she could well do without, which was why it had never weighed heavily with her that she bore the taint of a Fallen Woman. Those who spurned her for what they considered her transgressions were not worthy of her consideration. Those who would have spurned Effie were never allowed within the closely guarded circle of the child's existence. And when the child could no longer be contained within the confines of the Old Mill House and the surrounding dale, Althea would take her abroad to be tutored in the broader aspects of the world. Effie would grow up to be a beautiful and accomplished woman, one who would be capable of determining her own life and her own destiny. Althea was quite set on that.

It had all been laid out for Althea from the moment she

had looked down into the face of the infant who was to become dearer to her than life itself. It had little signified that, in dedicating herself to providing for Effie's needs, her own must clearly be sacrificed. She had never wanted anything beyond Effie's happiness—that was, until yesterday, when the Duke of Traherne had dropped out of nowhere into the unruffled tranquillity of her life and kissed her.

In spite of the freshening breeze, chill with the promise of rain, Althea suffered a fresh rush of heat through her veins at the mere memory of his touch, featherlight, against her skin. Taken wholly unaware, she had been rendered peculiarly immobile with the sudden flood of sensations engendered by that slow deliberate quest of his fingertip along her cheek and down to the very borderline of forbidden places. It had been rather like the time she had come face to face with a Bengal tiger and had stood, staring, transfixed in mute fear and fascination, at the animal's savage beauty and agile strength. Only, it had not been fear that held her powerless before Traherne, but something quite as potent.

The devil, she thought. She was very much afraid that she had failed to learn a thing from Effie's conception. Had she not sworn at Effie's birth and again in the long weeks of sickness and despair that had come after that she would concede to no man the power to rule her emotions! And the first time a man had tried, what had she done but turn suddenly all quavery inside! Faith, it did not bear thinking on. And yet she must think about it. Indeed, that was all that she *had* thought about since she had at last made her escape with Effie to the Old Mill House and a dinner that had remained practically untouched, followed by a sleepless night spent battling her pillows.

The devil take the duke! If his touch had rendered her weak willed and impotent, his kiss had seemed to strike fire from her very core—a swelling heat of emotion that had threatened to engulf her and then, having taken her utterly by surprise, had left her stunned, her head ridiculously reeling. It was bad enough that she had felt shaken to the depths by the discovery that, with a mere kiss, Traherne had swept away her every resistance and awakened her to a woman's passion. It was far worse to acknowledge to herself that, had it not been for Effie's timely interruption, she was not sure to what lengths that passion would have taken her. As it was, she had suffered a shameless pang of disappointment when he had released her, a feeling of loss so intense that she had experienced an acute sense of disorientation. And now what was she to do? It was all so damnably unexpected!

Obviously, her five years of self-imposed exile had served to distance her from the anger and consternation that had attended her first revelation that a child had been conceived in a moment of blind unruly passion. That any man could swear an undying love for a woman only to abandon her and his child to scandal and ruination without so much as a passing thought had taught her to guard her heart well. Unfortunately, she had hardly been called upon to maintain the walls of her defenses in the wilds surrounding Ullswater—until now. The years of solitude had led her to forget what it was to be in the presence of a man who, besides fairly exuding an air of command, was strong, intelligent, handsome, charming, and damnably fascinating. But then, she doubted there could be anyone else quite like the Duke of Traherne. He was certainly the most compellingly attractive male she had ever encountered, and growing up in the midst of her papa's regiment, she had met not a few strong virile men in her lifetime.

It was little wonder that she had been taken wholly off guard. After all, she had already been caught unaware by the discovery that the stranger she had caused to be immersed in Ullswater was none other than the new master of Briersly, the Duke of Traherne himself. She had hardly had time to recover from that unsettling revelation and her own unexpected feeling of overpowering attraction to him—not unlike the magnetic phenomenon demonstrated by iron particles in the presence of lodestone, she reflected whimsically—than he had further demonstrated his compelling magnetism by subjugating her will to his with naught but a touch of a fingertip.

It was clearly a manifestation of the natural phenomenon of irresistible gravitation between two opposite poles, the universal principle of the male-female compulsion to achieve wholeness through the rapturous joining of one with the other. Strange, that, while the intellect would seem capable of analyzing and defining the principle, the phenomenon itself was possessed of a far greater potency than that of the mind to contain and control it! But then, the very fact of Effie's existence should already have been proof positive of that without the need for further empirical evidence from His Grace of Traherne, she reminded herself.

Althea knew what answer she should give the duke; indeed, every tenet of logic pointed to but one rational conclusion. The empirical evidence left little doubt that, while in all likelihood Traherne would walk away, untouched and unscathed, from a brief liaison with Althea Wintergreen, she could not possibly be so fortunate. For him, it would be a thing of passion only; but for her, it must inevitably lead to love, and love was something she had never yet given to any man. Love, after all, for a Wintergreen was forever, as it had been for her dearest papa, who still pined for his lost Judith.

It was not logic, however, that had driven her from the comfort of her home and the morning spent happily tinkering in her attic workroom. Nor was it reason that impelled her now, despite the gathering storm, to continue on the more arduous climb past Aira Force to the Upper Falls. It was the insidious whisperings of her woman's heart that told her to fling caution to the wind, that whatever lessons Effie's conception and birth had served to teach, this was something on quite a different order. What she had experienced the previous afternoon with Traherne was like nothing she had ever felt before. Nor was she likely ever to feel it again. And if she lost her heart in the process, what did it really matter? At least she would have experienced the sort of love that came only to a very few, and it would not be the pretense that she had imagined was all for which she could ever hope.

"The devil," she gasped, her breast heaving from her strenuous exertions, as she came at last to a rocky outcrop overlooking the thunderous rush of High Force falling away through the great boulder-strewn chasm. She had always prided herself on being a woman of free and independent thought. If Effie had taught her to guard her heart against men whose promises of love were false, at least Traherne had made it plain that he promised nothing, and love least of all. Clearly, she risked nothing in the way of disillusionment with the duke. If she were to give him the answer he wanted, she would be going into the affair with open eyes and without expectations. If she came to love him, at least she would have experienced that which she had given up all hope of ever knowing. In which case, she would have gained far more than she risked losing. After all, that which mattered most in the eyes of the world she had given up long ago. She was a Ruined Woman.

It all seemed so very simple here, away from the Old Mill House and Briersly, with High Force hurtling away beneath her feet and the air crackling with the developing threat of a storm. It seemed that she could see far more clearly than ever before. It was not the act of love that she had feared, but the anguish of love proved false. With Traherne, she might give all of herself and fear nothing. He, after all, would never love her.

It was only with that stupendous revelation that she became aware of the gusting fury of the wind and, with it, realized that she had tarried overlong. The sky, glimpsed through the flailing branches of the trees, revealed the thickening of gray, roiling clouds overhead.

She felt a familiar wild elation in the sheer power of the elemental forces gathering around her, even as she began her hasty descent. She dared not think what Nessie would say when she came home drenched to the skin. Althea knew all too well how foolishly negligent she had been not to take heed of the warnings. A driving rain would render the climb down from High Force not a little hazardous. But then, she had had a deal to ponder, she reminded herself as, gathering her skirts above her knees, she slid down the side of a boulder. She was to remind herself as well, as the heavens opened up to unleash a torrent of rain, that she had known and weathered worse perils than a mountain storm. If, at the moment, she could not think of one of them, she did not pause to consider the lapse. She was far too occupied with making her way in the face of a driving rain, not to mention with the effort to keep her footing on the slippery path.

Consequently, it was hardly surprising that she failed to note the tall figure loom suddenly out of the trees directly before her. One moment she was ducking beneath the grasping branch of a pine, and the very next, straightening, she came up hard against an immovable object.

"The devil!" she gasped, as a pair of strong masculine arms clamped peremptorily about her.

"Miss Wintergreen," coolly acknowledged a voice with what might very well have been interpreted as satanic overtones.

"Good God," exclaimed Althea. "It is *you!* What in heaven's name are you doing here?"

"It is most assuredly I, Miss Wintergreen. And as it happens, I came looking for you," replied Traherne, his expression exceedingly grim, as he detected a shiver course through Althea's slender form. "You insane little fool," he growled. "You are drenched to the skin." Releasing her, he reached to undo the buttons at the front of his many-caped greatcoat.

Althea reacted in instant alarm. "Pray don't be absurd, Your Grace," she cried, stopping him with a hand on his arm. "There is not the least sense in our both being drenched. I suggest we make for the abandoned cottage with all haste. I am not like to die from a little wetting, I promise. I should, however, dearly love a dry shelter at the moment, and a fire."

Traherne bit off a curse. Hellfire, there would seem little point in wasting time in argument. Clasping Althea's hand in his, he turned and headed down the path.

Glancing up at his grim countenance, Althea felt an involuntary grin tug at her lips. Faith, but His Grace would appear to be in a rare taking. But then, she had not asked him to pursue her nearly to the top of High Force. Indeed, she could not imagine what had possessed him to do any such thing. Surely he had not been so keen on having an answer to his question that he could not wait another day or two, she reflected.

"How did you know?" she shouted above the fury of the storm.

"I beg your pardon?" he shouted back, glancing briefly down into her upturned face.

"How did you know where to find me?"

"Mrs. Fennigrew. I called at the Old Mill House with some of the things from the nursery. For Effie," he added, as if in the way of an explanation. "Mrs. Fennigrew was worried about you."

"Nessie is always worried about me." Althea gave a comical grimace. "I told her I should be fine. She simply will not accept that I am perfectly capable of taking care of myself."

"With good reason, it would appear," growled Traherne, apparently in a similar frame of mind as the fretful nanny. "No doubt you will pardon my curiosity, Miss Wintergreen, but I cannot help but wonder what the devil possessed you to climb all the way to High Force with a storm threatening?''

"That, I'm afraid, Your Grace, may be laid at your door," retorted Althea with an irrepressible gleam of laughter in her eyes. The next moment, having spotted the stone cottage through the trees, she pulled her hand free and dashed ahead, leaving the duke to stare after her, a thunderstricken look on his handsome face.

The abandoned woodcutter's cottage—apart from a rough cot laid with a worn mattress stuffed with straw, a rickety table and two chairs, an oil lamp, and a wood box supplied with logs for the convenience of wayfarers—was little better than an empty shell. It had been built, however, to withstand the vagaries of the weather in the fells. Its sturdy stone walls and shale roof afforded a dry haven for the two who burst gratefully through the rough-hewn door into the single room, which smelled of must and long disuse.

"Thank heavens," exclaimed Althea, flinging off her sodden cloak and slinging it over the back of one of the wooden chairs. Shaking out her hair, she set aside her leather pouch. "I daresay all we need is a fire to make this place a snug little lair."

"I daresay indeed," agreed Traherne with somewhat less enthusiasm, as it came to him to wonder how the devil she thought to achieve any such thing in the obvious absence of flint and steel. He could not recall that it had ever fallen to him to have to contrive to light a fire without the modern conveniences immediately at hand. Indeed, for the most part, there had always been servants for that sort of thing. He was aware of the scientific principles involved in making fire—the use of friction to produce heat sufficient to ignite dry leaves or wood shavings, for example, or even the use of a magnifying glass to concentrate the sun's rays on an inflammable substance (clearly an impossibility in their present circumstances deprived, as they were, of sunlight). Nevertheless, he was swept with a wholly unfamiliar feeling of inadequacy at the prospect of producing satisfactory results from anything so primitive as rubbing two sticks together. It was a most damned uncomfortable sensation, especially in the presence of a female whom he had undertaken to rescue from her own foolhardiness.

Miss Wintergreen, however, appeared wholly oblivious to the duke's dilemma. The redoubtable colonel's daughter was already busy laying wood in the grate.

"There," she said with no little satisfaction, as brushing her hands together, she viewed the kindling arranged neatly in a structure rather resembling a rough model of a log cabin. Wood shavings and dry pine needles lay at the center and larger logs were set across the top. "Now, if only I have not forgotten the last essential. I am quite certain it is in here somewhere," she muttered, reaching for her leather pouch and rifling through its contents.

Traherne watched in no little bemusement as a curious array of articles began to emerge from Miss Wintergreen's voluminous brown bag. There were no fewer than five screwdrivers of varying sizes, a small hammer, pliers, a penknife, and a file. Then appeared a hunk of bread and cheese, wrapped in oilcloth; a silver flask; a toothbrush, its wooden handle peculiarly encased in a brass cylinder with something resembling a wind-up key at the end; a small wooden box with what seemed to be tissue paper protruding out of a slit in the lid; and a number of curiously, though clearly deliberately, shaped pieces of wire, one of which had been slipped over the edge of several scraps of paper, presumably to clip them together.

"Ah, here it is," announced Althea, when the bag seemed nearly emptied, and withdrew her hand.

"Er—quite so," agreed the duke, eyeing with some reservations what gave every appearance of being a deadly

enough looking pistol, though it was hardly larger than the
feminine fist that held it aimed directly at his midriff.

"I suggest, Your Grace, that you stand back," warned
Miss Wintergreen, with a seriousness of expression that did
little to assuage Traherne's sudden birth of misgivings.

Good God, he thought, what was this? Surely it did not
stem from his having kissed the woman, an event which, at
the time, he had perceived as being as pleasurable to her as
it had been to him. Certainly, when he had awakened that
morning with the altogether enticing prospect of renewing
his brief contact with the enchanting wood nymph, he had not
considered the possibility that his overture of the previous
afternoon should have engendered feelings that might contribute to a murderous impulse. It occurred to him somewhat
belatedly that Miss Wintergreen, having been ruined and
abandoned to scandal by one unscrupulous member of his
sex, might very well have developed a hatred for all men
in general. Strangely, it was not fear of having a period put
to his existence by a deranged and bitter female that was
engendered by that cogent possibility, but a smoldering rage
at the blackguard whose unscrupulous treatment had apparently unhinged her.

"Softly, Miss Wintergreen," he said in tones, which in
the past had served to calm any number of spirited steeds.
"I assure you there is not the least need for . . ."

"But I assure you there is every need, Your Grace,"
interrupted the deranged Miss Wintergreen, apparently all
impatience to complete what she had started. "I do beg your
pardon, but I really cannot wait a moment longer. Pray be
so good as to keep your distance."

Traherne's lips parted to inform her that he had not the
least intention of imposing himself on her. Before he could
utter that assurance, however, Althea had turned and, aiming
the gun at the stone hearth, squeezed the trigger.

There came a distinct metallic whir of a notched steel
disk striking against flint, followed almost instantaneously

by a whoosh of flame from the gun barrel. A blue-and-yellow stream of fire appeared to leap out at the pile of tinder. Then just as suddenly as it had come, the flame vanished, leaving behind the smell of burnt ether and the crackle of pine needles ablaze.

"There, it is quite safe now," announced Althea, watching with no little sense of satisfaction as the fire in the grate leaped and spread to the kindling to lick with a deliciously growing warmth at the logs laid on top of the pile. "While I have spent some little time refining my automatic mechanical igniter, due to the volatile nature of unadulterated alcohol, I can never be quite certain how it will perform from one time to the next."

"Good God," exclaimed Traherne, eyeing Althea's serene expression with something approaching horror. "I daresay you are exceedingly fortunate the barrel did not explode in your hand."

"I wish you will not be absurd, Your Grace," Althea countered, awarding Traherne a comical grimace. "Here, see for yourself," she said, handing him her automatic mechanical igniter. "As it happens, I have taken safeguards by means of a wick extended through a cork stopper both to make certain the spark never reaches the actual store of fuel in the hollowed-out handle and to retard evaporation. The alcohol itself is absorbed in thick wads of cotton packed in the handle, which eliminates the problem of spillage. The steel wheel strikes against the flint, sending a spark down to ignite the alcohol-saturated wick. When the trigger is released, the douser automatically falls in place," she added, indicating a metal cap on a spring hinge covering the end of the barrel. "And, *voilà*." She shrugged, extending her hands out to the warmth of the crackling fire. "Actually, it is nothing so very new. Aside from some modifications in design, it is still, after all, essentially the same principle on which the old wheel-lock guns were fashioned."

Traherne's eyebrows swept toward his hairline as he

regarded Miss Wintergreen with something more than bemusement. Indeed, recalling his initial feelings upon finding himself apparently in the gunsights of a homicidal female, he could not but wonder what other surprises might be in store for him should his acquaintanceship with Miss Wintergreen prove of more than a fleeting nature. If nothing else, the little wood nymph, far from palling, was manifesting a complexity of character of the sort either to fascinate or to drive a man to contemplate wringing her bloody neck for her.

At the moment, he decided, finding himself contemplating putting his hands about that lovely throat, not for the relative merits of wringing Miss Wintergreen's neck, but due to the graceful line of that particular part of her anatomy, not to mention the exquisitely smooth texture of her skin, the creamy perfection of which was uniquely the property of the natural redhead. She was most definitely fascinating. Even with her glorious hair, hanging limp and streaming water, she was infinitely desirable. Indeed, he was visited with a tantalizing fantasy of Althea Wintergreen, in all of her glory, stepping out of her bath to him and the waiting embrace of a warmed bathsheet. Strangely enough, he found it equally easy to imagine himself taking no little pleasure in engaging her in conversation over morning coffee after a night spent exploring every magnificent inch of her lissome body. In that respect she was like none other of the numerous barques of frailty whom he had variously taken under his wing of protection. She was, in fact, like no other woman he had ever known; and that, in itself, was enough to compel his interest, not to mention arouse his more primitive instincts.

The little wood nymph had begun to loom as something in the nature of a *prima facie* case, which he felt compelled to try and disprove for his own peace of mind. Only in bedding her could he demonstrate she held no greater power over him than had any other woman before her. He would undoubtedly arise from *un fait accompli* no longer in her thrall. At the moment, however, he found that he was wholly captivated by the damnably intriguing female.

"On the contrary, Miss Wintergreen, your automatic mechanical igniter is nothing short of remarkable," he said in a voice that brought Althea's gaze up to meet his.

Inexplicably, she felt a slow heat pervade her cheeks at the look in his eyes. Indeed, she was made suddenly to realize that he had laid aside her automatic mechanical igniter and had closed the intervening distance between them without her being aware of it.

"Do you really think so, Your Grace?" she answered, her smile slightly awry. "For, truth to tell, I was not at all certain the thing would perform as it was supposed to do. It was all very fine in theory, but I have been hard put to work out all the little snags. I believe it still requires some small modifications here and there."

"Perhaps," replied the duke, marveling at the wood nymph's utter lack of awareness of how very exceptional she really was. "Naturally you would be the better judge of that than I. I believe I can safely say, however, I have never seen anything quite so extraordinary, save, of course, for its creator."

"You mean because its creator is a woman," Althea said, eyeing him doubtfully. She was not at all certain she liked being thought extraordinary, which, after all, might very well be only a polite term for eccentric.

"Precisely because you are a woman," affirmed the duke, who could not but be acutely cognizant of the fact that Miss Wintergreen's wet frock of pale yellow cambric was clinging provocatively to her feminine form in such a manner as to reveal that she wore next to nothing beneath it. He was equally aware of an instantaneous stirring in the region of his loins. "You may be certain I should not be experiencing anything remotely like what I am feeling at the moment if you were anything but a most desirable female."

"No, I daresay you would not, Your Grace," agreed Althea, who was equally certain that, were she in the exceedingly close vicinity of anyone other than the Duke of Traherne, she would not now be suffering a most peculiar fluttering in the pit of her stomach. Or a strangely exhilarating sensation not unlike the instantaneous quickening of one's heartbeat along with a tingling of nerve endings when one found oneself on the threshold of an extraordinary adventure fraught with a delectable anticipation of danger. She drew in a shuddering breath.

A smile flickered across Traherne's lips at the distinct heave of Miss Wintergreen's bosom. Egad, what a mistress she would make! She portrayed the image of unassuming innocence with a faultlessness that might have been the envy of that greatest of performers, Sarah Siddons, at the peak of her illustrious career. And yet she must be consummately aware that she stood all but revealed to him in all her womanly perfection. And she was truly magnificent, tall and slender, but with well-rounded womanly hips and a firm full bosom to entice a man to madness. Indeed, her nipples, delightfully peaked, thrust against the nearly transparent fabric of her bodice in a manner that he really could not ignore a moment longer. Miss Wintergreen was truly a forest sprite, a creature of nature. Unlike her feminine contemporaries, she chose to go unfettered by stays. But then, she had no need for artificial means of achieving the Grecian form, which was all the rage just then among the fashionable ladies of Europe.

"You are wet, Miss Wintergreen," he noted, provocatively running his hands over her shoulders and down her arms.

Althea, who could hardly deny the truth of that assertion, and who, indeed, wondered what, precisely, it might be leading up to, ran her tongue over suddenly dry lips. "Yes. I-I fear I must present a disgraceful sight."

Disgraceful, egad, thought Traherne, who could not but

think her "disgraceful" appearance wholly delectable. How very clever of the little wood nymph to point it out with such blushing artlessness. She was indeed a consummate actress. His hands paused with seeming deliberation in the proximity of her bosom.

"And cold," he added, touching a fingertip to one of her delectably hardened nipples.

Althea bit back a hysterical laugh. Good God, cold would not begin to describe what she was. She was ice seared by flame. "You would seem to have a gift for pointing out the obvious, Your Grace," she uttered, marveling in the circumstances that her voice had not risen from its normal alto to an operatic soprano. "I'm afraid, however, there is very little help for my deplorable state."

"You are quite right," agreed the duke. "As a matter of fact, I can think of only one solution to your problem."

Althea went suddenly quite still, as Traherne reached to undo the running string *en coulisse* at the neck of her dress. Indeed, it was all she could do to stifle a gasp as her bodice *à l'enfant*, released of its sole means of support, slid down over her shoulders to her empire waist below her bosom. "I suggest you would do better to remove your wet things and hang them to dry near the fire."

Traherne's eyes glittered in the firelight as though smoldering with a flame that was meant for her alone, a circumstance that Althea could not but find uncommonly stimulating.

"In-indeed, Your Grace," she agreed, swallowing. "I daresay it would not take longer than an hour or two before they must be put quite to rights again. Perhaps you would be so good as to undo the fastenings at the back." Turning, she stared straight ahead, as she added, "I seem to be all thumbs at the moment."

Althea, waiting, braced herself not to flinch at the anticipated touch of his fingers at the buttons of her dress. She had not prepared herself, however, for the brush of his lips against the nape of her neck as he worked the buttons loose, or for the shock of pleasure that shot through her to awaken an unexpected throb of heat in her nether regions. The gown slid, unnoticed, into a pile around her feet, leaving her clothed in naught but her shoes, her stockings, and her drawers; and Traherne, reaching around her, pulled her backside against him.

"How very beautiful you are," murmured the duke, his hands covering the soft swell of her breasts even as his lips spread a trail of kisses along the side of her neck to the exquisitely tender flesh at the soft curve of her shoulder.

"A-am I?" breathed Althea, experiencing no little difficulty concentrating on the gist of his words, as she was swept with a swelling tide of sensations, chief of which were a melting pang that spread outward to her extremities, a feverish torment that rendered her peculiarly breathless, and a compelling urgency to have His Grace continue his glorious manipulations.

Traherne gave a deep-throated chuckle. "You know very well that you are. I daresay you have been told by any number of gentlemen how very exquisite you are."

"Oh, indeed, Your Grace," gasped Althea, feeling about to be consumed by a conflagration, as Traherne, cradling her breasts, gently squeezed her nipples, already rigid with need. "By any number, I am sure of it."

Traherne thrilled to her keening sigh, to the suppleness of her back arching against him. Egad, but the little wood nymph responded with a ready passion. But then, she had been living in isolation in the Old Mill House since the birth of the child. No doubt she had need of a man after five long years of what amounted to a nun's celibate existence. The devil knew *he* had need of *her*. His groin ached to possess her. Releasing her, he reached to undo the buttons of his greatcoat.

"Your Grace?" Set suddenly adrift, Althea swayed.

"Softly, *ma mie*," Traherne whispered huskily. "You

may be certain I cannot wait to taste of your sweetness but not, I think, without the amenities of at least the facsimile of a couch.''

Shrugging out of the garment, he spread the heavy fabric over the bed of straw before turning back to Althea, limned against the firelight. Something in her stance occasioned him an uncomfortable pang of conscience.

The devil, he thought, and pulled her close. "I beg you will forgive me," he murmured, feeling her tremble against him. "This is not precisely how I imagined taking you."

"No, I daresay it is not at all what you are used to, Your Grace," replied Althea in a muffled voice. "I imagine your lights of love are more usually attired in flowing silk and set in surroundings of candlelight and fine damask. I, however, find a certain charm in our rustic environs, and, if there is not candlelight, we at least have the fire."

"Thanks to your automatic mechanical igniter." He laughed, a deep vibrant sound that went to Althea's head like rich wine. "I confess I hadn't the least notion how I was going to light the cursed fire."

"I am, if nothing else, handy when it comes to solving any number of mechanical problems, Your Grace," confessed Althea, smiling up at him. "I daresay I might even be adept at unfastening the buttons of your coat, if you will allow me. As it happens, I find I have an aversion to standing about half-naked in the presence of an elegantly attired gentleman. The very least you could do is join me."

Her hands lifted to begin demonstrating her adeptness at undressing an elegantly attired gentleman. Oddly, she was soon to discover that, while she could in the norm perform with ease any number of intricate mechanical tasks—from dismantling and reassembling a wide assortment of firearms to repairing clocks and creating animated mechanical ganders from scratch—when it came to undoing the Duke of Traherne's coat buttons, she was become suddenly and hopelessly awkward. But then, in the norm, she did not have the added distraction of the Duke of Traherne's hands trailing tantalizing flames over her bare shoulders, her back, and any number of other areas of an exceedingly sensitive nature. Long before she had finished undoing the last button, she was swept with a wholly unladylike urge to simply rip his coat open.

Apparently, His Grace was of a similar disposition. Without waiting for her to pull the coat down over his arms or to turn her attention next to his waistcoat and shirt, not to mention the intricate folds of his yard-long white linen neckcloth, Traherne bent suddenly and, clasping Althea behind the shoulders and knees, swung her peremptorily up in his arms.

"Enough!" he said, his eyes seeming to devour her. "I have known the pleasure of any number of mistresses, Miss Wintergreen, but none quite so magnificently accomplished as you in the art of arousing a man to an ungovernable passion. I congratulate you. I daresay I have seldom if ever been so thoroughly tested."

"Have you not, Your Grace?" replied Althea, no doubt attributing her dizziness to her sudden, swift change in altitude. "I-I daresay I should return the compliment. I have known many men, but in all truth I cannot recall ever having felt with any one of them quite as you have made me feel at this moment."

Inexplicably, that glowing assurance, far from gladdening the duke's heart, served instead to cause a wrench in the vicinity of his stomach. The devil, he thought. There had never been any question, of course, that Miss Wintergreen was not without experience in matters of intimacy. She, after all, had a child. Somehow, however, it had not occurred to him that there might be more than one illicit love in her checkered past. That she readily owned up to having known many men in her young life was not precisely what he had wanted to hear.

Immediately, he chastised himself for a bloody fool. What

the devil could it possibly matter how many men had come before him? It was not as if he wished to marry the wench. She was with him here, now, and she was damnably adept at the art of arousal. The devil, "adept" hardly did justice to what she was! She was a Fallen Angel of Seduction, a siren who had lured him on with a deceptively sweet air of innocence beneath which beat the heart of a practiced jade. Hellfire! He had never wanted a woman so much as he wanted Althea Wintergreen at that moment!

Carrying her to the makeshift bed, he laid her down and, kneeling, proceeded to divest her of her worn, but sturdy, brown leather half-boots that laced up the front.

Watching him, Althea could not but detect a subtle difference in his touch, not to mention his countenance, which had taken on an aspect of chiseled hardness. Unaccountably, she felt her heart sink.

"Are you quite certain, Your Grace," she ventured, staring up at him with doubtful eyes, "that this is what you want? Perhaps we are rushing things."

Rushing things, egad! he thought, acutely aware that in his present state he would be hard put not to disgrace himself with a precipitate ejaculation. "You may be sure, my *mie,* that I not only desire it, but I am far beyond the point of desiring anything else," he said, working her stockings down over her calves and off her feet. His smile, which was distinctly satyrlike, was hardly reassuring. "I shall allow you to tantalize and tease me to the point of madness at a later date. Indeed, I shall look forward to it with eager anticipation. Now, however, I'm afraid I really cannot wait to have you." Leaning over her, he reached for the drawstring at the top of her drawers.

Miss Wintergreen, he was soon to realize, was even more breathtakingly lovely than he had allowed himself to imagine. Indeed, it was difficult to conceive that the slender perfection of her willowy torso and firm flat belly had lent itself to the process of childbirth. Her breasts were firm and high and seemed perfectly molded to fit his hands. Her legs were long and slim, the skin possessed of a silken smoothness.

In a fever to possess her, he straightened and with hard swift hands rid himself of his coat, waistcoat, neckcloth, and shirt. His boots and stockings were to follow with equal dispatch, and at last, revealed in all his glory, he turned to the bed.

He paused at Althea's sudden low gasp, his glance piercing the shadows. Now what the devil? Her eyes appeared great luminous pools in the pale blur of her face. He stifled a groan, as he exerted himself to control his overpowering need to plunge himself into her soft woman's flesh.

Leaning down to her, his hands braced on the bed on either side of her shoulders, he pressed his lips into the curve of her neck. "Miss Wintergreen. Althea?"

"Your Grace?"

"No doubt you will pardon me if I observe you present the appearance of one in some little dismay. If there were something amiss, I trust you would feel free to tell me."

"Amiss, Your Grace? No. No, it is nothing like that. It is only that I believe I have never seen anything to compare to-to—well, to your anatomy. You possess a truly magnificent example of the male appendage, Your Grace, as I am sure you must be perfectly aware."

Something between a laugh and a groan seemed forced from him. Good God, she was priceless, was his little wood sprite.

"And you, Miss Wintergreen, are the inspiration that has made it what it is at this moment," pronounced the duke, spreading wide her thighs and inserting himself between them.

"Indeed, Your Grace, I am not entirely ignorant of the principles behind the natural mechanics of male-female physiological functions. As it happens, I am acutely aware of them at this particular time."

She was, in fact, in the grips of a rising torment of sensations generated by Traherne's lips caressing her nipples, first one and then the other, not to mention the quest of his hand over the small mound of her belly to the moist pulsating warmth between her inner thighs. A keening sigh breathed through her depths as he found the tiny pearl nestled within the swollen petals of her body and, no longer capable of coherent thought—let alone the practical observation of the natural mechanics of male-female physiological functions—she arched her body frantically against him.

Traherne groaned, marveling at the fullness of her response to his lovemaking. She was unfettered passion, was the little wood nymph, her body flowing with the sweet nectar of arousal. Experimentally, he inserted a finger into the moist warmth of her body. Egad, how small and tight she was!

"Your *Grace!*" gasped Althea, writhing beneath him in a mounting ecstasy of need. "I cannot bear it. I pray you will *do* something!"

"Softly, *ma mie,*" groaned Traherne. The sweat standing out in beads on his forehead and shoulders, he fitted the tip of his swollen shaft into her body's unguarded lips. She was ready for him, and the devil knew he could not wait longer.

Brutally, he drove himself into her.

Her cry of pain pierced his brain like a white-hot needle, and he went deathly still inside her, his mind frozen with awful realization.

"The devil!" he cursed. He had just bedded a virgin!

Chapter Five

Althea lay rigid with surprise beneath Traherne, her eyes squeezed shut and her legs clamped about his waist. The searing pain of his thrust through her maidenhead had subsided almost as quickly as it had come, and now she could not but marvel that he was snug within her. Indeed, at her first sight of his magnificent manhood, she had entertained no small doubt as to the probability of success in such an endeavor. But then, she had reminded herself that she had helped with Effie's birthing, and a man's male member, no matter how undeniably awe inspiring in its full-blown glory, could not compare, when one went right to the heart of the matter, with an infant's head.

Still, coming to an acute awareness of the man clutched between her thighs, she could not but feel a profound sense of awe at the physical mechanics involved in the accommodation by her feminine body of Traherne's noble dimensions. Truly, it was something on the order of a natural wonder.

The question now was, what was to happen next. As impressive as her present circumstances were, she could not but think there should be a little something more. Indeed, it struck her that there was something about Traherne's stiff immobility that was most distinctly odd.

Carefully, she unclenched her eyes.

And looked up to find Traherne staring back at her, his face a rigid mask of control in which his eyes shone, glittery, in the firelight. It came to her immediately that he was in no little discomfort. Indeed, sweat stood out in beads on his forehead, and his strong white teeth were bared in what gave every appearance of being a grimace of pain.

"Your Grace, what is it?" Althea exclaimed in instant alarm. "Are you all right? You look positively dreadful."

Traherne gave vent to a groan of laughter. "No ... Do I?" he gasped between clenched teeth. Miss Wintergreen would seem remarkably observant, he reflected dourly. "But then, it is not ... everyday ... I find myself buried to the hilt ... in an innocent whom I have just ... had the dubious honor of deflowering."

"Indeed, Your Grace, I'm afraid that you do," Althea answered, her lovely eyes filling with concern. "And I daresay you are right to blame me. I suppose I should have warned you, but, unfortunately, I am not greatly knowledgeable in the natural mechanics involved in male-female inter-actions, especially as concerns the physics of human procreation. I had no idea my maidenly state might be a mitigating factor. I fear that particular lack of information may have led you to grievously injure yourself."

Injure himself! Good God, thought Traherne. He had just ravaged a virgin, and she was afraid *she* had injured *him!* No doubt he must soon disabuse her of any such notions. Now, however, would hardly seem the time for a rational discussion of the physics of human procreation. Instead, it appeared a demonstration was not only in order, but, at this point, was most damnably unavoidable.

"*Hush,* Miss Wintergreen," he said, the muscles of his shoulders and arms standing out in ridges as he willed himself to maintain the status quo. He had broken the one rule upon which he had always been adamant, never to be lured into bed with an Innocent; and now there would seem to be only one sensible course open to him. Carefully, he moistened dry lips.

"Now, Miss Wintergreen," he said, striving for an impossible calm. "You have . . . only . . . to trust me to carry us . . . both through."

"But I do trust you," Althea hastened to assure him. "I daresay I should not be in the position I am in if I did not, Your Grace."

"Splendid," applauded Traherne, with no little irony. "However, I doubt either of us would be in . . . the position we are in . . . if only you had thought . . . to trust me with the truth."

"The truth, Your Grace," Althea did not hesitate to answer, "is that it could hardly have made any difference. You may be certain I thought the entire matter through last night and today. And I have determined we are in the sway of an inescapable mechanism of nature, rather like the phenomenon of irresistible gravitation between two disparate bodies."

"Egad," growled Traherne, hard put to maintain his equilibrium. "What the devil has physical science to do with our predicament?"

"Not 'physical science,' " Althea explained indulgently, "but 'natural law'—the universal principle of the male-female compulsion to achieve wholeness through the rapturous joining of one with the other. Given the unique circumstances of the time and the place, I daresay we could no more help ourselves than we could resist the forces of gravity."

"No doubt, Miss Wintergreen," pronounced Traherne, who was more inclined to believe in the superiority of reason over the mindless inevitability implied in natural law, especially as applied to human behavior. His error had been in giving into false assumptions based on untested empirical evidence. "Then you may comfort yourself with the knowledge that the worst is over. Try and relax. Leave all else to me."

Relax! Good heavens, she thought. Having been aware for some little time of a prickle of straw beneath her left hip—not to mention the novelty of her position with Traherne clasped between her thighs—Althea did not see how the devil she was to relax!

Cautiously, then, he began to move inside her, and any thought of endeavoring to heed his suggestion was lost in the duke's slow, rhythmic manipulations and the reawakening of the pleasurable sensations that had preceded his plunge into her. In a rising swell of blissful torment, she clenched muscles she had not even known she possessed.

"*Softly,* my girl," gasped Traherne, trying not to lose himself in the exquisite tightness that gripped his flesh. "There is nothing . . . to fear in what I am doing."

"I am not in the least afraid, Your Grace," Althea promptly informed him. And, indeed, fear was the furthest thing from her mind. "On the contrary," she continued on a rising note, "I find what you are doing quite-quite stim-u-*latING*. Faith! I pray you will not stop now, Your Grace!"

"You may be sure of it," gasped Traherne. Stimulated almost beyond control, he could not have stopped had he wanted to have done. "We are almost at the moment of realization."

"Faith, I am like to die of it!" Althea, transported into realms of sensation she had never imagined, was moved to sink her fingernails into the duke's shoulders. "Hurry, Your Grace, I pray you!"

"Soon, Althea. Soon," Traherne rasped in a voice rendered hoarse with his efforts not to give in to the fiery bliss of release. Wholly artless in her responses to his lovemaking, she had utterly abandoned herself to her woman's passion as none of his numerous accomplished mistresses had ever done. She was all sweet untutored generosity, was the little wood sprite, and she aroused him as no other woman had ever done. Egad, but she was magnificent, he thought feverishly, marveling at her supple beauty as she reached for the thing that only just eluded her. The devil! He could not put off the inevitable a moment longer!

Drawing up and back, he covered her mouth with his, even as he sought the swollen nub of her desire with his hand.

Althea, in a torment of exquisite anguish, felt herself rising on the crest of something more momentous than her first discovery of the account of Richard Trevithick's invention of the first high-pressure noncondensing steam engine. Indeed, she could not but feel an affinity for that invention as she felt herself on the verge of bursting her seams. A keening sigh broke from her lips as, in a frenzy of need, she arched against the duke. Then Traherne pressed the heel of his hand against the throbbing bud between her thighs.

It was too much.

"*O-o-oh,* Your Grace!" Althea gasped.

"Sweet Althea," groaned Traherne and thrust deep, spilling his seed inside her at the very moment Althea erupted in a rapturous explosion of release, which left her a blissful few moments later trembling and weak.

Together, they collapsed on the bed in a tangle of arms and legs, to lie sated and magnificently sapped of energy.

It came to Althea, lying wrapped in Traherne's arms some little time later, that she had never felt warmer or more deliciously languorous. Surely, there was nothing that could compare to the rapturous joining of two disparate bodies in an act of sublime passion, unless it was the exquisite sense of contentment one experienced in the aftermath. She had never imagined there could be such bliss in lying snug against a firm muscular male body. Of course, she had never before met anyone quite like the Duke of Traherne. He would seem to have a singular power to arouse womanly emotions in her she had never suspected she had, let alone experienced. But then, she had long been an advocate of the theory that a truly sublime passion came only to those who were uniquely drawn to each other in a multidimensional arena of compatibility encompassing chemistry, physics, metaphysics, and intellect. It would seem the only plausible explanation for the curious phenomenon of two people who, on the surface, seemed perfectly matched, but who, contrary to the dictates of appearances, felt not so much as a spark of passion for each other. Or why, on the other hand, two apparently ill suited persons should experience an instantaneous mutual attraction, which would seem wholly irrational, but which was fated to blossom, nonetheless, into an all-consuming love.

It was a subject to which Althea had given much thought over the years. She, after all, had the example of her own mother and father, not to mention that of her sister, upon which to draw. It had never been a secret that Judith Wintergreen had married beneath her station. The favored granddaughter of an earl, she had seemed destined for a brilliant match. Instead, she had fallen instantly head over ears in love with a young captain of the King's Royal Light Dragoons, who, as the son of lesser gentry, was clearly beneath her touch. Judith Wintergreen, however, had never shown the smallest regret for having eschewed the lap of luxury and the certainty of wedding a title in exchange for the modest income and obscurity of an existence as wife to a King's officer. Only a fragile constitution and the insistence of her dearest Nigel had kept her at home in England apart from her husband for months, even years, at a time. Neither time nor distance, however, had served to diminish their affections in the slightest. The colonel had been used to call his fairest Judith his polestar, which must ever guide him home; and in the eleven years of their marriage, he had never once faltered from his course.

Theirs had been, reflected Althea, unconsciously snuggling closer to Traherne's comforting warmth at her back, the sort of love one only dreamed about. She, herself, had long since ceased to believe it could ever happen to her. To Gloriana, perhaps, she had been used to tell herself, but not to Althea Wintergreen. She could not have foreseen, however, that she would meet the Duke of Traherne. Indeed, not in her wildest fancies could she have anticipated what had happened that afternoon in the abandoned woodcutter's cottage.

Immediately, she brought herself up short. But then, nothing had really *changed,* she reminded herself, frowning at where her thoughts had seemed to be taking her. She might have become enamored of the Duke of Traherne almost from the first moment she laid eyes on him, a condition that she suspected would very easily become a great deal more; but *he,* after all, had made it patently clear he was not prone to fall similar victim to the softer human emotions. It was the basis for her entire capitulation to events that had subsequently proved far more potent than she could ever have imagined beforehand. And even if Traherne could have been brought to feel more than a passing fancy for her, a possibility that must be considered remote in the extreme, it would have made little difference. In the eyes of the world she was a Ruined Woman, and a man of Traherne's rank and position did not align himself with a female who was steeped in scandal—save, of course, for a brief liaison of an illicit nature.

At least, she mused whimsically, she had had one small taste of what it might have been like to love and be loved. Somehow it would have to be enough. Indeed, since to have had it any other way would have meant never having had Effie in her life, she would not have altered the events that had brought her to her present circumstances even if she had had the power to do so.

She reminded herself that soon they must stir themselves

to rise and dress, and then it would be over and done. Tomorrow or the next day or the next Traherne would return to the world, and he would forget all about his brief fling in the country. It was just as well, she told herself. After all, she had Effie and her workshop and any number of projects that required her immediate attention. Really, there would seem very little room in her life for the complication of an affair of the heart.

Strangely, that acknowledgment brought her little comfort. Indeed, she was acutely aware of a hollow pang somewhere beneath her breastbone as she felt Traherne lift himself on one elbow.

"Althea." Althea caught her bottom lip between her teeth at the touch of his lips, featherlight, against the nape of her neck. "Althea, I believe it is time we talked, don't you?"

"Talked, Your Grace?" murmured Althea, staring straight before her at the merry leap of flames in the grate. "Really, there is nothing to say. You may be sure I know what is in your mind. Indeed, I understand perfectly. Pray, let us not spoil everything with needless words."

Needless words? thought Traherne. Having recovered his rational thought processes in the wake of what had proved to be an afternoon fraught—to put it mildly—with surprises, he could not but think there was a great deal in need of discussing. Indeed, for the past several minutes, as he had lain acutely aware of Althea's slender warmth clasped in his arms, he had been pondering very little else. "I see," he said. "I suppose it is natural that you might feel some reluctance to talk about what has transpired between us. I'm afraid, however, that it cannot be helped. It would seem we find ourselves in the devil of a coil. As it happens, I do not make it a practice to impose myself on Innocents."

"I did not suppose that you did, Your Grace," Althea answered, surprised that he was bothered at what must in the circumstances be considered a trifle. But then, she had known he was a man of generosity and kindness. No doubt he wished to make sure she understood that, despite what they had experienced together that afternoon, there could never be anything of a more lasting nature between them. "On the other hand, you did *not* impose yourself on me. Quite the contrary. I was, as I recall, a more than willing accomplice. And, while it is true you have unwittingly bedded a maiden, I should hardly consider myself an Innocent. In the eyes of the world, I am precisely what you believed me to be. Ergo, I fail to see wherein lies the coil."

"The coil, Miss Wintergreen," replied Traherne in ominously measured tones, "lies in the fact that, whatever the world may believe, I know the truth. And that, my girl, is the only thing that is really pertinent. Which leaves us with but one viable solution. We shall be married with all dispatch by special license, unless, of course, you prefer a trip to Gretna Green and the anvil."

"Good heavens," exclaimed Althea, hastily turning over on her back to look at him. "You are serious, are you not?"

"I daresay I have never been more serious. Pray don't look so dismayed, my dear," he added, his smile distinctly ironic. "As it happens, you have saved me a deal of trouble. I had already determined it was time to set up my nursery. Thanks to you, I shall be spared the onerous task of searching for a likely candidate to fill the role of duchess. I believe I am actually grateful to you."

At that startling announcement, Althea bolted upright on the bed.

"You are no such thing!" she declared, wholly oblivious to her unclad state or to the magnificent picture she presented, her breasts heaving in sudden swift agitation and her beautiful eyes eloquent with alarm. "I will not listen to such utter nonsense. No doubt I should thank you for the honor you would do me in making me your wife, but regrettably I must refuse, Your Grace. Indeed, it is preposterous even to suggest such a thing."

"Preposterous? Why?" countered Traherne, marveling at

Miss Wintergreen's singular thought processes. He did not doubt that any other female in similar circumstances, far from pointing out that he was hardly required to offer marriage to a woman whose reputation was already beyond salvage, would have been congratulating herself on *un fait accompli*. "Because you took upon yourself your sister's disgrace and now think to release me from my obligation to right the wrong that I have done you?"

Had he entertained any doubts as to the truth of his assertions, Althea's sharp intake of breath would instantly have dispelled them. But then, there could hardly have been any other explanation for Effie's remarkable resemblance to her self-professed mama or, for that matter, for Althea's having embraced exile and dishonor for a child who, clearly, was not hers.

"The truth, Althea," he said quietly. "Effie is your sister's child, is she not?"

Chiding herself for having failed to take into account the inescapable circumstance that Traherne must instantly arrive at the truth of Effie's birth, Althea rose from the bed and, gathering up her stockings and her drawers, clutched them to her breast before turning to face him once more. "You are mistaken, Your Grace," she stated unequivocally. "Effie is mine in every way that matters. And that is all I shall ever say on the subject."

"I see," murmured the duke, his eyes seeming to pierce holes through her. "It is not your secret alone, is that it? I do understand, Althea, believe me. Need I say you have my word I shall never reveal it?"

"Pray do not be absurd," Althea uttered gruffly. The devil, she thought. Why had Traherne to be so fine and understanding? His kindness battered at her defenses in a manner she had not thought possible. Hastily, she turned away, lest he see the tears start to her eyes. "It never occurred to me that you would. And now, I beg you will excuse me.

Storm or no storm, it is time I was getting dressed and heading for home. Nessie and the others will be worried.''

"Althea," sighed His Grace, made belatedly aware that the little wood nymph was going to prove far more difficult than he had previously anticipated, "come back to bed at once. You are shivering from cold."

"I am perfectly fine, Your Grace," insisted Althea, who was attempting with as great a dignity as she could muster to pull on a stocking while balancing on one foot. Worse, she was mortifyingly afraid that she was about to give into a fit of the vapors. "I was doing just fine taking care of myself long before I met you, and I shall continue to do so without your help."

Giving in to the inevitable, Traherne heaved himself off the bed. "No doubt you will pardon me if I say you have a curious way of showing it. You cannot possibly leave before your things are dry and the rain has stopped. Here, put this on." Tossing her his shirt, he reached for his own stockings and breeches. "I daresay you have been used all your life to looking after your younger sister, have you not?" he asked, sitting on the edge of the bed to dress. "Especially as you were deprived of your mother at an early age. Your sister, however, is grown and married." Standing up, he fastened the front of his breeches. "Do you not think it is time you thought of yourself?"

"I am thinking of myself, Your Grace," sniffed Althea, who, having put on her drawers and deciding there was little to be gained in insisting on donning her sodden dress was busy pulling Traherne's shirt over her head. "And of Effie and Gloriana—and of you, too. I must, since you seem to have lost all sense of reality. You know very well I should only bring scandal upon your house, and that I shall never agree to do. Any more than I should allow Effie to be exposed to a host of spiteful wagging tongues."

"If that is what you think, then you are even greener than I thought," declared Traherne, kneeling to add a log to the fire. He came to his feet and faced Althea. "Effie would have my name and the mantle of protection that goes with it."

At Althea's sharply indrawn breath, Traherne smiled ironically. "Come now, Althea. You cannot imagine I should marry you and not adopt Effie."

"I-I am not sure what I thought, Your Grace."

"Lucius, my dear. If we are to be married, surely you can bring yourself to use my name."

"I have not said I should marry you, Your Grace," insisted Althea, who felt a distinct heat pervade her limbs at sight of His Grace bared to the waist. Faith, she was very much afraid that at heart she was little better than a shameless wanton. Indeed, she was keenly aware at the moment of an exceedingly unladylike urge to run her hands through the mat of hair on his chest. Hastily she turned away that she might bring some order to her riotous thoughts.

She was not, however, to be given the respite she needed. She felt rather than heard Traherne's light step behind her. His hands, coming to rest on her shoulders, held her. His unsettling proximity pierced her defenses, as did his words, which painted an undeniably tempting picture.

"Effie is a bright and lovely child, Althea. You cannot keep her hidden away forever. Nor should you. She deserves far better than that. You deserve better than that." Deliberately, he turned her to face him.

Althea stared in helpless fascination as, his palms cradling her face, he looked deeply into her eyes. Really, he would seem to have a strange power to overrule her reason, not to mention her senses. Faith, how easy it would be to give in to him, to his words and the promptings of her own unruly heart! *Would it be so wrong?* whispered a voice insidiously in her ear. *Would it not be better for Effie?* Without conscious volition, she closed her eyes and tilted her head back.

Traherne smiled faintly to himself. How readily she responded to him. She was all sweetness and fire, was the little wood sprite. Strangely, he found the notion of taking her as his wife more appealing than he could previously have imagined.

"Only think, Althea," Traherne said softly, touching his lips to hers. "As my wife, you will find all doors opened to you—and to Effie. You need never again endure the whispers or the stares. You may be sure no one will slight the Duchess of Traherne. No one would dare to do."

It was a mistake. He knew it as soon as the words were out.

The spell broken, Althea's eyes flew open.

"The *Scandalous* Duchess of Traherne!" she gasped, pulling away from him. "It will never do, Your Grace. Not even if you adopted Effie—" She stopped, struck, suddenly, with the full extent of what he was willing to embrace for her in the name of honor. "Faith, what am I saying?" she exclaimed, turning on him with accusing eyes. *"Especially* if you adopted Effie. Surely you must realize that everyone would think Effie was yours and that-that you and I had-had—that-that we—"

"And have we not?" observed the duke, insufferably amused at her blushing confusion. "Furthermore, it is my heartfelt wish that we may do so again, repeatedly and often. Was I mistaken in thinking you were of a similar disposition?"

"Devil!" Althea retorted, awarding him a wry grimace. "I wish you will be serious. You know very well to what I was referring. It is one thing for you to have bedded an unwed mother of a child, but quite a different matter to have fathered a child on an unmarried woman. While the first must be considered at least marginally acceptable, the latter would most certainly sink you beneath reproach."

"And you think I should be concerned with what anyone might say of me behind my back?" countered the duke, his gaze enigmatic on Althea's animated features.

"I do," Althea answered without hesitation, "when I am

to be the cause for all the unpleasant speculation. Oh, do you not see, Your Grace? If it were just I, it would hardly matter, but I will not be the black mark on your name. I should never be able to live with myself."

"I see well enough," answered Traherne, much struck at the irony inherent in the young beauty's apparent determination to protect him from what she considered his imminent ruination. Obviously, Miss Wintergreen had not the slightest notion of the ignominy and scandal that were already attached to his house and his name. He, not to mention his mother and father, could hardly have been accused of living exemplary lives, nor would Althea Wintergreen be the first Scandalous Duchess of Traherne. And this lovely innocent was not only willing, but apparently adamantly set upon, refusing his title and his fortune in order to spare him scandal! "I see you are taking a great deal upon yourself," he said with a cynical curl of the lip, "and quite unnecessarily. As it happens, you would soon find my credit is sufficient to carry us both through. In any event, it hardly matters. People can think what they bloody well please, Miss Wintergreen. It has nothing to do with you or me."

"Naturally, you would say that, Your Grace," Althea declared with an eloquent wave of the hand. "Indeed, it is precisely what I should expect of you. It is, after all, only what I have said myself these past five years. There is nothing so comforting, is there, as thumbing one's nose at public opinion when one finds oneself outside the pale?"

"No, I daresay there is not," agreed Traherne with a grim hardening of his eyes. "On the other hand, there is nothing so forgiving as a fortune and a title second only to royalty."

Instantly, he was swept with the unsettling premonition that he had been deftly maneuvered into a trap of his own making.

"At last," said Althea, with a rueful air of triumph. "We come to the heart of the matter, do we not."

"The devil, Althea—"

''No, Your Grace. I *will* say it,'' interrupted Althea, with an unwitting jut of her delightfully stubborn chin. ''I should rather be your mistress and endure the slights and the stares, Your Grace, than carry the burden of knowing I had entrapped a duke in marriage. That was never my intention.''

''Pray don't be absurd, Althea. I never supposed that it was. If it had been, you may be certain we should not now be having this conversation.''

''No, but it will be said, nevertheless, by others. And whether it was what I intended or not, the results are still the same. You will admit, Your Grace, that, had I been a Fallen Woman in fact as well as in name, you would not now be proposing marriage.''

''Hell and the devil confound it!'' uttered Traherne, unable to deny it. However, while it was true it might not have been the marriage he would have chosen before he bedded Althea Wintergreen and discovered she was as good and as innocent as she was beautiful, it was the marriage upon which he was now determined; and it was time she was made to understand that. ''Whatever I should or should not have done is hardly relevant now. I am many things, Miss Wintergreen, but I am not the sort to rob a woman of her virtue and then abandon her to whatever fate might be meted out to her. Egad, there might be a child, *my* child, and I am damned if I should allow it to grow up nameless and without a father. That is one iniquity to which I refuse to lend myself. You will marry me, Althea Wintergreen. I will make up for the wrong I have done you whether you wish it or not. Of that, you may be certain. I shall not leave Briersly without you.''

''Shall you not?'' Traherne went suddenly still, his blood unaccountably leaping in his veins, as Althea lifted her hand tenderly to the side of his face. ''*You* could never do anyone wrong, Your Grace,'' she said softly, her smile misty. ''Nevertheless, I promise I will think about it. A fortnight. That is all I ask. Then, if you are still of the same mind, I shall give you my answer.''

"The devil you will!" His fingers closed about her wrist. Dragging her hand down, he held it between them. Ice blue eyes, which had made grown men quail before their chilly intensity, bored into hers. "Do not try me too far, little wood nymph. And do not make the mistake of misjudging me or my intentions. I warned you once before what I am. I shall have your word you will do nothing foolish, Althea. I am not without influence. Should you try and run from me, I will find you.''

He was immediately to note that, far from impressing her with a proper grasp of his harsh and dangerous nature, Althea demonstrated not so much as a quiver of trepidation. On the contrary, the look that met his served to take his breath away.

"You may be sure, Your Grace, that I should never mistake you or your intentions. As it happens, I am an excellent judge of character. I know precisely the sort of man you are. You, my dearest lord duke, are a man of rare integrity and honor; and though you try very hard to hide it, you are every bit as generous as you are kind.''

"The devil I am," growled Traherne.

"Indeed, Your Grace, you are." Any further protest was silenced by the touch of Althea's fingertips to his lips. "I promise I shall not try and run from you, but I cannot promise I shall change my mind about marrying you. You see, I have a conscience, too; and it tells me that, were I to accept your offer, I should be doing you a greater wrong than anything you have done to me. I, after all, derived a deal of enjoyment in being ruined by you. It was, I daresay, the single, most revealing experience of my life. Furthermore, it is doubtful it should ever have come to me had it been anyone but you who shot Goosey Gander and tumbled into the water. I believe I quite lost my heart to you when you clapped that ridiculous hat on your head and climbed out of the lake in such a fine fury.''

"Foolish child," rumbled Traherne, "you haven't the smallest notion what you are saying."

"You are mistaken, Your Grace," Althea countered, refusing to flinch beneath the fierce leap of his eyes. "I may be foolish, but I am hardly a child. And you may be sure I knew perfectly well what I was doing when I let you take me to your bed. I have had five years to contemplate the forces that lead one to abandon all rationale to an all-consuming passion. I have long since come to the conclusion that the act of love itself is a—"

"Rapturous joining of the universal masculine and feminine to achieve a wholeness for which every soul yearns. Yes, you have already told me. Though I haven't the faintest notion what the devil it has to do with your reluctance to marry me."

"But it is quite simple, Your Grace," Althea insisted, determined to drive her point home. "What you have just described is an inborn need, an irresistible force, an inescapable mechanism of nature, if you will, and therefore, of itself, neither good nor evil. So you see, any wrong that may be attached to it is purely a matter of external construction and therefore open to debate. As a freethinker, I choose not to accept that particular interpretation. Ergo, there can be no wrong in what we have done. Nor is there any need for you to sacrifice yourself in a marriage you cannot want. You, my dearest lord duke, are acquitted of any wrongdoing."

"And you, Miss Wintergreen, are as naive as you are misled if you think for one moment accountability does not go hand in hand with giving in to an act of passion, sublime or otherwise. You have only to look to your own motives in taking your sister's child to rear and to the disgrace that, unjustly or not, became yours with your noble sacrifice."

"It was never a sacrifice," Althea objected, "noble or otherwise. Effie has brought me nothing but joy."

"And exile from the society to which you were borne."

"Pray don't be absurd, Your Grace," retorted Althea. "I have never entertained the least ambition to enter Society. I daresay I should have been a dreadful failure had I attempted any such thing. I am not in the least fashionable."

Fashionable? thought Traherne, who did not doubt Althea Wintergreen would turn heads wherever she went. As the Duchess of Traherne, she would *set* the bloody fashion! "You cannot know how you might be received, since you have never put your fate to the touch," he observed. "There is not the least question that you would be judged an Incomparable, a diamond of the first water, an indisputable Original. You may take my word it could not be otherwise."

"It is not that I do not trust your word, Your Grace," replied Althea, her eyes twinkling with rueful amusement. "It is only that I am keenly aware how very determined you are to persuade me to your point of view. As it happens I have always known that I am too tall and far too thin to be judged a beauty of the first water. I have never learned needlework, nor do I play the harp or the pianoforte and may, consequently, be judged to be wholly lacking in any feminine accomplishments. I am, furthermore, hopelessly independent and used to blurting out whatever comes to my mind with little regard for the consequences. This, you will admit, is hardly the description of a lady of fashion."

"No, it is the portrait of a woman who not only has never really looked at herself in a mirror, but who has been too occupied with looking after others to indulge herself in more frivolous pursuits. Presumably you did what you did to save your sister from ruin in order that she might contract an eligible marriage. With the result that you have been made to suffer all the ignominy that must otherwise have been hers."

"And how should I not?" Althea countered with a shrug

of a slender shoulder. "Gloriana and Winslade had already come to an agreement before she learned she was increasing. She was seventeen. A child. What purpose would it have served for her to be deprived of her happiness because of a youthful error in judgment? I, on the other hand, was and have been perfectly content to remain a spinster. My sister is safely wed to a good man who loves her, and I have the best of both worlds—the freedom to live my life as I choose and a child who is more dear to me than life itself." Deliberately, she lifted her eyes to his. "I have never asked for nor wanted more, Your Grace."

"I am ruefully aware of that, Miss Wintergreen," said the duke, a curious glitter in his compelling orbs. "You may be equally certain, however, that I have every intention of amending that situation. You will marry me, Althea—willingly—before all is said and done. Never doubt it for a moment."

Chapter Six

Carefully smoothing Goosey Gander's feathers over the newly repaired wing, Althea was regretfully conscious of the fact that her attention was focused most distractingly on events proceeding outside in the small enclosed courtyard below her attic window. She had, in fact, been resisting the urge for no little time to give up the pretense of being too occupied with her numerous projects to participate in Effie's newly instituted daily riding lesson. A plague on the duke! she thought uncharitably, recalling Effie's patent delight in the marvelous Welsh pony Traherne had presented in the way of a belated birthday present only two days after the fateful afternoon spent in the woodcutter's cottage.

Good heavens, had it truly been only twelve days since she had succumbed to the error in judgment that would have the potential to change her life forever? It seemed that she could not remember a time when Traherne had not been a potent, disturbing presence in her life! Worse, he was fast becoming an indispensable factor in Effie's, which was undoubtedly precisely what he intended.

It would seem Traherne was not above resorting to any ploy which might gain him the advantage in his determined campaign to break down Althea's resistance to becoming his wife. He had even gone so far as to completely win over Agnes Fennigrew, who positively beamed with approval whenever he put in an appearance, an event which had become a daily occurrence. As for Mattie and Elias, they had given in to the duke's allure long before Althea's fateful encounter with Traherne on the shores of Ullswater. Consequently, they could not but view His Grace's undisguised interest in their mistress as something on the order of the heaven-sent answer to a prayer.

The devil, thought Althea, who knew all too well the devastating effect of Traherne's forceful personality. She had long since ceased trying to explain the power he had to render her weak and giddy with naught but the fleeting brush of his hand against hers or a sudden meeting of glances, which must inevitably linger until, fearing what he must read in her eyes, she looked away. Nor did she bother to deny that she found herself listening for his footstep every morning after breakfast when he was wont to arrive at the Old Mill House to engage her in a lively exchange as she lingered over her coffee. This was only the preamble to a day spent in long walks along the lakeshore or in drives to the various points of interest about Ullswater or in nothing more momentous than a picnic or an afternoon engaged in tinkering in her workroom while Traherne looked on with interest. Her ear seemed peculiarly attuned to catch the rumble of his voice in the foyer, as Mattie relieved him of his greatcoat and informed him where he might find Miss Althea and Effie. Worse, her heart had developed an unsettling propensity to behave in a most erratic fashion whenever she happened to catch sight of his tall elegant figure framed in a doorway or striding purposefully toward her with the controlled supple grace that was so characteristic of the man.

Traherne had become the focus of her daily existence.

More than that, he had awakened her to all that she had come to miss without being aware of it—intelligent discourse with an educated well-informed adult as well as meaningless small talk with an attractive man of wit and charm, news of the world at large and London in particular that was not contained in the *Gazette,* the newest fashions, the latest *on dits,* something so simple as the nonjudgmental acceptance of a friend. Faith, how she had had need of a friend! And how she would miss him when he was gone! Indeed, she did not see how she could sustain such a loss. And yet she must, she told herself, wishing that Traherne had never dropped into the quiet tranquillity of her life to open her eyes to how very small her world had become.

Nor were those the only iniquities of which he was guilty, she reflected wryly.

Setting Goosey aside, she allowed herself to be drawn to the window overlooking the courtyard. Below her, the pony walked daintily in its circle about Traherne, who held it on a lunge rein while Effie, a colorful splash of color on the pony's back, concentrated on staying in the saddle.

The sight of Effie, garbed in the bright pink velvet riding habit, which long ago had belonged to Gloriana and which Nessie had unearthed in a trunk that had been sent over from Briersly along with the things from the nursery, brought an unwitting lump to her throat. Effie might have been Gloriana all over again as she had been at age five on her venerable pony, Rufus. Only, the trim little mare Traherne had purchased for Effie, and which Effie had named Pegasus because she knew the pony must surely fly when put to her swiftest pace, was a far cry from the plodding Rufus.

Althea felt her heart constrict with anxiety as the pony broke from a walk into a canter. Effie clung to the mane, her small form bouncing precariously in the saddle. Althea's fingers clenched on the sill. She had weathered the colic and teething pains of Effie's infancy, had hovered over and chased after the child through toddlerhood's single-minded explorations of discovery, had sat up through seemingly endless nights as Effie lay in the fretful grip of one fever or another. Why had she not foreseen that there must be ever greater dangers lying in wait for the child as she grew and her world expanded to include new challenges? Why had Traherne to bring that oversight so dramatically to her attention? she fretted, watching with her heart in her throat as Effie, no doubt at Traherne's instruction, let loose of the mane and fought to keep from being jarred from the saddle.

Damn him! she thought, fumbling to fling open the window, as she saw Effie's foot come out of the stirrup.

She realized almost at once that she need not have worried. Traherne, seeing the child lose the battle, was there, one hand reaching to steady Effie in the saddle even as the other pulled the pony to a halt.

The hard knot in her stomach slowly unclenched, leaving Althea feeling vaguely ill. Weakly she leaned her head against the window frame. Traherne had been there to keep Effie from falling. Althea had only to say the word, and he would always be there for the child, a strong steadying influence, an impregnable mantle of protection that Althea, by herself, could never hope to provide. Would it be so wrong to give in to him, to the urgings of her own riotous heart? she wondered, and immediately flung away from the window.

There, she was doing it again, she thought, angry with herself for having let her guard down against the insidious voice of temptation. Or was it the voice of reason? she found herself asking. Certainly, there was no denying the benefits to be accrued from a marriage with the Duke of Traherne. She had been over them a hundred times in her head, always to come up against the one inalterable obstacle to such a union: The benefits were all one-sided. *She* would bring nothing to the marriage but a tarnished reputation and scandal—and the love that had been growing steadily inside her.

Faith, she could not deny it, not anymore, and most certainly not to herself. She loved Traherne with her whole heart and being. And how not? She had known from the very beginning that she stood not a chance against his compelling presence, not to mention the forces of nature that had drawn her to him almost from the first moment she had laid eyes on him. Nor had he helped to dispel this affliction of the heart. Far from it. He had instead demonstrated a relentless thoughtfulness, an unshakable patience, a kindness, which had come very near to lulling her into a false sense of tranquillity.

Not once in the days following the events at the wood-cutter's cottage had he mentioned what had transpired there. Not once had he reminded her of the promise he had exacted from her, not once tried to woo her with honeyed words or stolen kisses. Subtly, unobtrusively, he had fitted himself into the flow of her existence, augmenting and altering it until she could no longer conceive how she could return to the way she had lived before, with only Effie and the household with whom to share her thoughts, her hopes, her fears. He could have chosen no better way to break down her defenses. Worse, he had made her love him as she had thought never to love anyone, other than Effie. Really, it was too bad of him.

And now what was she to do? Marry him and make him the talk of England?

Strangely, that had not quite the force it once had possessed to deter her; indeed, had that been all to keep her from marrying Traherne, it might not have been enough. There were other, far more cogent reasons, which Traherne could not and must not ever know, that made such a match, indeed, *any* match, clearly out of the question. No, she had not altered in her resolve to spare him the scandal that must come to him if he took her to be his wife, but she had come by degrees to realize how truly little Traherne cared about the opinions of others. Indeed, while he had been about the business of winning her heart, she had been divining a great deal about the Duke of Traherne, not the least of which was that the reserve he affected for the rest of the world was naught but a front to hide what she very much suspected was a deep-seated loneliness.

It was not something she could quite put her finger on, this feeling that had come over her that Traherne, far from being devoid of the softer human emotions, was a man both of sensitivity and insight. She had sensed it at that first meeting on the lakeshore, and the feeling had grown stronger with each passing day.

It was not only in the way he treated Effie, with an ease of manner that was neither presumptuous nor patronizing, but characterized by humor, tolerance, and a respect for the child's individuality. If nothing else, he would one day make a splendid father. But it was more than that. It was many things—like Tom Sykes's encomium that His Grace "were a good master, never the sort to bullock them what served 'im or come the ugly, but always willin' to listen to a body." Or the way problems seemed to have of simply dissolving in his presence.

Sensible of the fact that the villagers viewed her something in the light of a pariah, Althea had done all that was possible to make the Old Mill House self-sustaining. A few goats, a milk cow, chickens, a hothouse, the small orchard, and a kitchen garden had gone a long way to establishing that goal. Coal, however, for the stoves and meat from the butcher shop, as well as oil for the lamps and a ready supply of candles, among other things, she had, perforce, to purchase from the village.

On her early trips to the village, shortly after Effie's birth, Althea had turned a blind eye to the snubs and the stares; but after a time she had not gone again, preferring to send Mattie or Elias or to have supplies delivered. It could hardly have been described as a satisfactory arrangement. The local tradesmen, while perfectly willing to accept her money, were not averse to slighting her in goods and services. Furthermore, other than the girl Peggoty—who was glad enough to find employment of any kind—and old Jake Turner—who, having served as Judith Wintergreen's coachman, had been glad to serve her daughter in the same capacity—there had been no one willing to do so much as odd jobs about the place. As a result, the old house had been made to suffer from neglect. The roof, which Althea believed had not been repaired since the Old Mill House had ceased to function in the capacity for which it had been built, was given to leak in the frequent storms that swept through the dale. Knowing it would be futile to protest, Althea had inured herself to the deliberate inconveniences and the intent that lay behind them.

Miraculously, within a few days of the duke's return to Briersly, it seemed that everything had undergone a swift and sudden change. Deliveries began to arrive on time, and rather than the poor quality of goods, which Althea had previously received, only the finest were brought to the service entrance to the Old Mill House. More than that, Althea had been startled awake one morning by the rumble of wagons in the drive. To her stunned disbelief, it seemed an army of men armed with tools and roofing slate had descended upon her. In short order, the roof had been rendered as good as new.

She did not have to be told who was responsible for these singular events. She had taken Traherne to task for placing her in his debt.

"Pray don't be absurd, Althea. It was never my intention to put you under my obligation."

"No," agreed Althea, "I am perfectly aware you did it because you realized immediately why I should have let the old place fall to rack and ruin." She paused, her eyes, troubled, on his. "You should not have interfered, Your Grace. Indeed, I wish you had not. We were doing just fine without your help, and now—"

"*Now* it will not be necessary for you to have recourse

to pots and pails whenever it rains, and you will no longer be forced to tolerate the inconveniences imposed on you by a lot of demmed impertinent tradesmen. If that is an imposition on my part, then so be it. I trust you do not expect me to apologize for it.''

Althea, gazing up into Traherne's maddeningly unreadable countenance, suffered a stab of shame at the paltry fashion in which she had thanked him for his thoughtful generosity. Impulsively, she laid a hand on his sleeve. ''If it was an imposition, Your Grace, it was one which was kindly meant. And I am grateful, truly I am. Still, I do wish you will stop doing things for Effie and me.'' She smiled to take the sting from her words, and dropped her hand from his arm. ''You will spoil us, my dear friend. And that will never do.''

''The devil it won't.'' Her heart had leaped to her throat as Traherne appeared suddenly to loom over her. Faith, but his light piercing eyes had seemed to penetrate to her very soul! ''I should have to be blind and a fool not to see what you have been made to endure here, Althea. The marvel of it is that you have managed to keep Effie from seeing it. That, however, changes nothing. You, my girl, are foolish beyond permission do you think for one moment I should stand by and do nothing.''

Confused and disturbed by something inevitable she sensed in him then, Althea had been robbed of a reply. Now she smiled twistedly to herself.

''You are quite right, my dearest lord duke,'' she murmured aloud to her empty workroom. ''I should have known precisely what you would do. And now I fear it is too late. I have come quite against my will to rely on you as I have never relied on anyone else before. I should rather die, however, than let you know that—or that I shall find it harder, from now on, to stand on my own.''

The sound of Effie's laughter and the clatter of footsteps on the stairs informed Althea that the riding lesson was over and that her privacy was about to be invaded. Hastily, she crossed to her worktable to pretend an interest in a new project, which she had only recently undertaken.

She did not have to turn and look, as the door was thrust open and Effie burst in the room, to know that Traherne had come in with the child. The sudden soft thrill through her midsection had already made her acutely aware of that fact.

"Althie," Effie exclaimed, her small piquant face flushed with excitement and the aftermath of her morning's exercise, "I wish you could have seen me. I rode Pegasus ever so swiftly. It was simply splendid even though I nearly came off. My foot slipped out of the stirrup and I thought I should fall, but Lucius caught me and set me back again."

"But I did see you, darling," Althea said, carefully avoiding Traherne's eyes as she clasped Effie's hands lightly in her own. "I was watching from the window. I must say I was terribly impressed."

"Were you, Althie?" queried the child, fairly bridling with pleasure. "Did you see me nearly fall?"

"I saw everything. I told you. And now I hear Nessie calling, dearest. Go and get cleaned up before tea."

She had spoken brightly, her lips smiling. There must have been something in her voice. The bloom of joy about the child suffered a sudden blight. Worse, Althea was suddenly acutely aware of Traherne's eyes on her.

"What's the matter, Althie?" said Effie, peering up at Althea with pensive eyes.

"Why, whatever do you mean, Effie? Everything is fine, I assure you."

"It's because you were afraid for me, isn't it?" Effie persisted, her face threatening to crumple. "Please don't be, Althie. Nothing bad happened. Please say you won't stop me from riding Pegasus."

Althea suffered a wrench at her heart. *Had* she been contemplating doing that very thing? she wondered.

Instantly, she sat down on her heels before the child. "No, dearest," she said, drawing Effie close, "I shan't ask that of you. Why ever should I? As it happens, I have been thinking lately that it is time I purchased a riding hack, just so we might ride together. Would you like that, Effie?"

"Indeed I should!" cried the child, her face clearing as if by magic. "I should like it above everything, Althie. Did you hear, Lucius? Oh, *did* you? Althie's going to go riding with us."

Althea vibrated to that childish appeal to Traherne, even as she shrank at the thought that she must soon disillusion Effie of the notion that the duke's stay at Briersly was to be of a lengthy duration.

"I heard, *enfant.* And if I am any judge, I should think she is a bruising rider. I suggest we put it to the test in the morning. I shall provide the mounts. I daresay the track along the lakeshore should not prove too arduous if the weather holds fine."

"Oh, may we, Althie?" breathed Effie, her eyes round in her face. "I promise I shan't be any trouble. I'll do everything you tell me."

"Splendid," laughed Althea, avoiding the duke's eyes as she rose to her feet. "Be sure I shall hold you to that. Now off with you," she added, giving the child a playful nudge toward the door, "before Mrs. Fennigrew comes looking for you."

Hardly had the door closed behind Effie than Althea became keenly aware that she was alone with Traherne and that a queer uncomfortable silence had fallen over the room.

"What? Again, Your Grace?" she said, with a helpless gesture of the hand. "I find myself falling ever deeper in your debt." When she received no reply, she drew in a deep breath. "I daresay I have seldom seen Effie so in alt. But then, Gloriana was always an avid equestrian. Indeed, all the Wintergreens are mad about horses. I suppose one might say it is a family tradition, the love of a spirited animal. In truth, I had not realized how much I missed . . .''

Coming about, Althea broke off, startled to find Traherne's tall masculine form directly before her.

''Your Grace!'' she exclaimed on a gasp.

''Althea.'' A wry smile touched the duke's lips and as quickly faded as he looked into her eyes. Frowning, he slowly ran the back of his hand down the side of her face. It was all Althea could do to keep from yielding to that featherlight touch, and all the while he studied her face with a piercing intensity that quite robbed her of the power of speech. ''You are angry,'' he said at last, ponderingly. ''Why? Because you feel I was taking chances with Effie's safety today, is that it?''

In the grip of disturbing sensations, not the least of which was a growing lump in her throat, Althea could only close her eyes and shake her head.

The muscle leaped along the hard line of Traherne's jaw. The devil, he thought, recalling his glimpse of her white face framed in the attic window. ''You must know I should never allow anything to happen to Effie.'' His breath caught as her eyes, like deep pools of anguish, opened to engulf him.

''I do know it,'' she said. ''Even if I had not seen you with her, I should have known it.'' Afraid, then, that if she remained where she was, she would soon find her unruly arms lifting to encircle his neck, she pulled away. ''I daresay that is what has set me on end.'' She laughed a trifle shakily. ''Absurd, is it not? But I confess it had never occurred to me before today that the time might come when I should be powerless to keep Effie from harm. It was your misfortune to be the one to open my eyes to that unsettling prospect, when really I wish you had not.''

Traherne's gaze narrowed sharply on Althea's averted profile. She was lying, he thought. Or at least she was not telling all the truth. How unlike his straightforward Althea to avoid his eyes! It came to him, not for the first time, that he wished she could bring herself to trust him.

"I wish you will not talk flummery. Not to me, my girl. No parent can hope to protect a child from every hurt. Nor is it in the least desirable. Egad, think how stifling that must be. But then, I trust you know that as well as I do. There is something else troubling you, Althea."

"Indeed, Your Grace?" gasped Althea, with a sense of incredulity that he could not know what tormented her. "What could I possibly have to trouble me?"

Althea's heart leaped to her throat as the duke clasped her by the arm and turned her to face him.

"Lucius," declared Traherne, as close to losing his patience with his maddeningly elusive wood nymph as he had ever come. "Surely we have progressed far enough in our acquaintanceship for you to employ my given name. Effie does. Why not you?"

"Effie is a child," Althea reminded him. "And you gave her your leave to call you by your name. I saw no reason to complicate what to her must seem perfectly natural. You know very well she has become exceedingly fond of you."

She thought she must swoon as Traherne's eyes bored into hers. Indeed, she could not meet that look. Soon it must all come out, she knew, and then how was she to bear it?

"I thought perhaps you might have, too, Althea," said the duke quietly. "Or at least that you might have developed a certain tolerance for me. You have not seemed indifferent to me."

At that, she did look at him, her eyes filled with dismay. "Pray do not be absurd. I *have* grown fond of you. You know very well I have. You are my very dear friend. Faith, my only friend. But that does not alter my awareness of-of who you are. Or what I am. I cannot overlook the inalterable fact that Althea Wintergreen must be considered far beneath your touch."

Althea winced beneath the savage tightening of his grip

on her arm. She felt her strength flagging, her defenses crumbling, as he bent his head to peer at her. "The devil, Althea, what nonsense is this? Your mother was the granddaughter of an earl. Your father was borne to gentility. You might have taken your place in society and married as high as you pleased."

"Yes, but I did not, Your Grace," returned Althea, eloquent of face. "And now I never shall. How should I? I love you—far too much ever to wish to bring shame to your house."

There. It was out, thought Althea, telling herself she could not have put it off another day, let alone two, to end the charade. Indeed, in her present state, she did not see how she could have borne the waiting.

She was hardly prepared for the fierce leap of the duke's eyes.

Traherne, in the sway of a powerful emotion, stared at her. Althea had said she loved him! Sweet, noble-hearted Althea, who was like no other woman he had ever known. He had not thought to hear those words from her. Still, he reminded himself, she had in the same breath refused his offer of marriage for the very reason that she did love him. Hellfire! How like the wood nymph to create a paradox out of what should have been simple and straightforward. She loved him too much to marry him! Egad. And yet, it was only what he should have expected of her. The question was how to resolve the dilemma of a woman's sense of honor—a woman like Althea who had already sacrificed all for the sake of a beloved sister. He knew her too well to suppose she could be coerced or cajoled into overcoming her bloody scruples. Nor, it would seem, would it serve to appeal to her heart. Indeed, he had only to look at her to realize that the very nature of the love to which she had confessed had brought her to the resolve to give him up. Traherne resisted the urge to laugh at the irony. The greater her love, the greater must be her determination to preserve him from what she perceived to be his imminent ruination. Hellfire. It was a riddle worthy of the bloody Sphinx!

Traherne, however, had neither the time nor the inclination to indulge in a lengthy pursuit of a resolution to the riddle that Althea, in her mistaken notion of noble self-sacrifice, had created for him. On the other hand, if her discovery that she loved him had fortified her determination to refuse him, it had served as well to sweep away any last vestige of doubt he might have entertained for the course he had chosen for himself.

He wanted her for his wife, and he would bloody well have her if he had to marry her over the anvil!

Hardly had that thought crossed his mind than all his old cool command reasserted itself, along with the certainty that he would be a fool at this point to rush his fences.

Althea Wintergreen had confessed she loved him. With that assurance, he could be content for the moment—he must. Indeed, to do anything else might hasten events to a most damned unwelcome conclusion.

Deliberately, he loosed his hold on her.

"It would seem, lest my ears deceive me," he said coolly, "that you have given me the answer which was to wait for a later day. As it happens, I am not inclined at the moment to accept it. You did, after all, ask for a fortnight, did you not? Unless my grasp of mathematics fails me, I have two days left to dissuade you from your present decision."

"Two days, Your Grace, will change nothing," said Althea, battling opposing sensations of relief that Traherne had not immediately to disappear from her life and the terrible dread that two days more of blissful torment must surely see her fail in her resolve to do what she must. Steeling herself against the voice of temptation, she hastened to burn her bridges behind her. "It is, at any rate, patently unnecessary. Last night I made certain you need have no further concern for me. You will be happy to learn I am not increas-

ing, Your Grace. You do not have to marry me. There is
not going to be a child.''

It came to Traherne with blinding clarity the instant before
she told him—the reason she had demanded the fortnight.
Hell and the devil confound it, he should have known at
once. But then, while he was indeed relieved that she was
not breeding—if there was to be an heir, there must be no
question of the child's legitimacy—he was not in the smallest deterred from his fixed resolve to marry Althea Wintergreen. He was, in fact, if anything, more determined than
ever to have her for his wife.

And how not? The past several days spent in Althea's
company had, if nothing else, served to make him keenly
aware of just how singular a female Fate had put in his way.
It was not only that she was, by nature, warm, passionate,
and giving. Egad, she had responded to his lovemaking with
a sweet generosity, the mere memory of which was enough
to make him wish to take her there and then and damn the
consequences! But she was a patient loving mother, as well,
to the child whom she had taken to her heart. Furthermore,
she was spirited without being headstrong. She was possessed of a wholly captivating, if unnerving, tendency to
laugh in his face. And he knew without a doubt that she
would never prove boring. But more than all of these was
her unshakable sense of loyalty to those fortunate few to be
admitted into her small circle of loved ones. It was that
quality in her which had aroused in Traherne all the primitive
male instincts to possess and protect. Most maddening of
all, however, he had come to know Althea Wintergreen as
a woman of quiet, but determined, strength who valued
above all things her right to direct her own life and who
would have scoffed at anyone who tried to tell her she
needed a man to help shoulder her burdens. He had seen
from the beginning that therein lay his greatest obstacle.

He was not certain when the impulse to alleviate some
of Althea's more obvious discomforts had changed to a

personal mission, fueled by a slow burning rage to put an end to the blatant injustices to which she was subjected. One afternoon he had watched her make a game of catching spills from the roof in a wide assortment of vessels spread about her precious attic workroom. She had included Effie in it, laughing as they raced to empty one vessel and hurriedly replace it with another. It was only when the child had been sent down to the nursery for her nap that he had seen past the charade to the true state of affairs. Blowing into hands cupped against the chill in the room, Althea had moved instinctively to the coal hod beside the small cast-iron stove, only to stop with a small sigh of resignation.

"Dear, I quite forgot. Mr. Jessop is late in bringing the coal. I must suppose his cob has gone lame again. Well, it would seem there is nothing for it but to remove to the parlor. At least, thanks to Elias, we need never want for firewood."

Traherne's first grim suspicion that Althea had been left to live in a state of near penury had led him to discreetly question old Mattie and Elias. It had been made quickly apparent to him that Althea's difficulties did not stem from a lack of the ready. She was, in fact, possessed of a sizable competence which had come to her from her maternal grandmama. It had followed, then, that Althea was being made to suffer the bitter fruits of disfavor.

No doubt the last thing Thomas Jessop could have expected was to have Tom Sykes of Briersly show up on his doorstep early one morning with an invitation to step into the Duke of Traherne's closed carriage. Certain it was that Jessop could not but have been taken aback upon discovering inside the carriage no less a personage than the duke himself. Stranger still, and far more gratifying, was the gradual realization that His Grace was favoring him with a confidence of no little importance. The duke, it seemed, finding himself in the obligation of one Colonel Wintergreen, had undertaken as a personal favor to see to the well-being of the colonel's older daughter. Naturally, a man of Jessop's obvious understanding must perceive that anyone who took special care to ensure that Miss Wintergreen received every consideration was someone who would stand high in the duke's favor. Similar visits to Atticus Leach of Leach's Emporium and to Thaddeus Elright, proprietor of the local butcher shop, had yielded immediate results. It was, in fact, to be noted that Jessop's cob demonstrated a remarkable recovery and that deliveries of coal began to arrive at the Old Mill House on a regular basis, the quality of cuts from the butcher shop improved dramatically, and lamp oil and candles were henceforth never in short supply.

It was little enough, thought Traherne, who would have preferred to relieve Althea of all her burdens, if only she would let him—if only she would swallow her pride and agree to marry him! Somehow, without his knowing it, she had become the only woman he could conceive in the role of his duchess. Not that he could ever bring her to believe that. *She* remained convinced that his sole motivation for pressing his marriage suit was a misplaced sense of honor— or, far worse in his mind, a highly developed sense of altruism. Egad! He was aware of a mounting frustration with the maddeningly elusive wood sprite. It was bloody well time he disillusioned her of the notion that he was anything but in deadly earnest.

"Naturally, I must be relieved that you are not increasing, Althea," he said, with only the barest hint of irony. "When you bear me a child, I should prefer it to be within the bonds of matrimony."

"When I bear you a child!" breathed Althea, her face going a pearly white. "Lucius, you cannot mean to pursue this further. I have told you there is no need for you to marry me."

"But I have every intention of pursuing it," Traherne did not hesitate to inform her. Deliberately, he took a step toward her. "The fact is, this news changes nothing." Althea, mistrusting the glint in his eye, backed before him. "After all, you did say, did you not, that we were in the sway of incontrovertible natural forces?"

"Lucius," gasped Althea, coming up with her back against the wall, "pray be reasonable. We cannot possibly . . . you really cannot mean to-to—I cannot allow you . . ."

Whatever it was, however, that she could not allow was silenced as Traherne planted his hands firmly against the wall, one on either side of her shoulders. "Like two disparate bodies, you said, drawn together by an irresistible gravitational attraction," he continued, as if she had not so rudely interrupted him. His eyes, glittery beneath hooded eyelids, moved over her face, deliberately probing, until a shadow of something like bafflement flickered in their depths. "The devil, Althea," he said, his voice strangely husky. "I have been exceedingly patient. More so than I should ever have thought possible. I am not, however, disposed to wait indefinitely." Lowering his head, he kissed her brow, then her eyes, the tip of her nose, and at last, hungrily, her mouth.

Caught in the throes of emotions over which she had no control, Althea parted her lips to him. Traherne's tenderness was far more than she could possibly withstand. It unleashed all the terrible longing in her heart, all the love that she had sought to keep hidden away inside. Really, it was too bad of him. She could no more resist him than she could stop breathing. Lifting her arms about his neck, she forgot everything. Pride, honor, resolve—all were swept away in sweet mindless surrender.

Feeling her melt against him, Traherne clasped an arm about her waist and crushed her to him. His breath sounded harsh in his throat. "The devil, Althea, I have wanted you— more than I had thought ever to want anyone."

"Then you will have me, Lucius," Althea whispered, turning her face into the strong curve of his neck. "I shall happily be your mistress."

Traherne went suddenly still, his hard lean body rigid

against her. Deliberately, then, he pulled her arms down from around his neck and put her from him.

Suddenly bereft, Althea swayed on the edge of bewilderment. Traherne stood away from her, his face seemingly chiseled in stone. "Lucius?"

Traherne ignored the flutter of her hand. "I'm afraid, Miss Wintergreen, I shall have to ask you to postpone our ride. I am called away for a day or two. Pray give my excuses to Effie. Tell her I shall expect her—and you—to be ready to accompany me on the lake track the day after tomorrow. Shall we say immediately after breakfast? I shall call for you at nine sharp."

Crossing to the door, Traherne paused, his hand on the door handle. "I have no need for a mistress, Althea." He turned his head to look at her. "I want you for my wife. Two more days, Miss Wintergreen. Need I remind you that you gave me your word? I shall expect you to be here, awaiting my return."

Then opening the door, he left her to stare after him.

The Duke of Traherne was noted for many things, not the least of which was his practice of keeping a string of his own blooded cattle along the posting inns from Meresgate in the north of Cumbria to London. Those who did not know him well were moved either to accuse him behind his back of blatant extravagance or to reluctantly admire him for his bloody demmed arrogance. Had anyone bothered to ask Traherne why he went to the expense of maintaining two dozen grooms and four dozen prime bits of blood along what comprised nearly the entire length of England, he would undoubtedly have replied that it was merely a matter of practicality. Speed of travel was not merely a luxury he could well afford, it was in business, as in war, an indispensable adjunct to any successful enterprise encompassing time and distance.

Little more than fourteen hours after taking his leave of Althea, Traherne stepped down from his travel coach and strode briskly into the foyer of his Town House.

"A tolerable journey, Roberts," he replied to the greeting tendered by Carstairs's understudy as the servant relieved him of his hat, gloves, and greatcoat. "I trust something in the way of a cold collation may be garnered from the kitchens. I find I am devilish sharp set."

"And little wonder, Your Grace," observed a dry masculine voice from the stairway. "I daresay you did not take time for so much as a pint at one of the posting inns. It was one of your passages made with Caesar speed, was it not."

"You may be certain of it, Edward," smiled Traherne, coming around to regard the berobed figure of his private secretary, who was observing him with a distinct air of expectancy. "I was and am in something of a hurry. Had you sought your bed, Edward? I should hate to think I am about to disturb your rest."

Taking in the lean countenance of his employer, the eyes rapier keen and compelling, Phips felt the man's immense energy like electricity in the air. It was the Traherne he had come to know in the nearly dozen years of his service to the duke, the Traherne he had feared was gone forever in the wake of the terrible wound and the long struggle to recovery. Something had happened in the wilds of the Lake District, something of moment. Suddenly, he grinned. "I was merely relaxing with a book, Your Grace. I am, as ever, at your service."

"Excellent. Then you will not mind joining me in a late supper in my study. I will hear what news you have to impart and then there is a matter we must discuss."

The late supper of cold chicken, cheese, thick slices of bread, and strawberries covered in cream was garnished with a discussion of the latest market reports, the French occupation of Hanover, the end of the false peace of Amiens, and news of the expected fall of Sindhia of Gwalior to the forces of Arthur Wellesley.

"Wellesley is the man to watch in the coming months," predicted Traherne, standing with his back to the crackle of flames in the Adams fireplace. "British ships cannot win this war alone. It will take our soldiers in a campaign on French soil to defeat the tyrant. Wellesley may well prove the man to lead them. That, however, is not what has brought me to London." He crossed to the grog tray and, pouring two glasses of brandy, handed one to Phips. "I have decided to marry."

Phips froze with the glass halfway to his lips as he digested that startling piece of information. So, a woman was responsible for the duke's remarkable transformation. Curiouser and curiouser. Then, recovering his equilibrium, he raised the glass in tribute. "With your permission, Your Grace," he said, smiling with genuine pleasure for his employer, "a toast to you and your future bride, and my heartiest congratulations."

"Congratulations may be somewhat precipitous," the duke observed dryly. "The lady has thus far obdurately refused my suit. I thank you, however, for the sentiment, Edward."

"*Refused* your suit, egad." Phips stared in stunned incredulity at Traherne.

"Quite so," drawled the duke, taking a sip of brandy and rolling it over his tongue before swallowing. "A woman who, far from desiring either my title or my fortune, adamantly refuses to wed the Duke of Traherne—it would seem to defy belief, would it not? And the crowning touch is that she would do so because she loves me."

In mute fascination Phips watched the flicker of a smile play about Traherne's stern lips, then vanish.

"It does not signify, however," said the duke. "I have no intention of letting Miss Wintergreen slip through my fingers. I require you to do something for me, Edward, with all dispatch, as I intend to be back at Briersly by nine o'clock of the morning the day after tomorrow.''

"You have only to name it, Your Grace," asserted Phips, at least part of the puzzle resolved. Miss Wintergreen could only be a daughter of the Colonel Wintergreen from whom Traherne had purchased Briersly. There could be little doubt as to which daughter, since the younger was already wed to Viscount Winslade. Vaguely, he seemed to recall some years before there had been some talk going the rounds concerning a Miss Wintergreen. The memory escaped him, however, at Traherne's next words.

"In the morning you will retrieve the family jewels from the bank vault. I shall have need of a ring that belonged to my grandmama. After that, you will call on the Right Reverend Whipple and inform him the Duke of Traherne requires an audience with him here no later than ten.'' At a slight cough from his private secretary, Traherne elevated a ducal eyebrow. "Come now, Edward. Pray cease to squirm in your chair. The bishop may protest, but he will come. As it happens, he owes me a favor or two.''

"Naturally, Your Grace," Phips replied with only the hint of a smile. "I fear for a moment I forgot with whom I was speaking.''

"You are impertinent, my dear Edward," drawled the duke, gently swinging his quizzing glass back and forth on its riband. "I wonder why I put up with you.''

"I'm sure I could not say, Your Grace.''

"It occurs to me that I am not working you hard enough," observed the duke. "An oversight which I shall immediately rectify. While I am away, you will occupy yourself with discovering the present whereabouts of Colonel Nigel Wintergreen. And while you are at it, I should not view it amiss if you found out what you can about the Viscountess Winslade. Something tells me if I am to be successful in my present endeavor, I may have need of any information you can uncover. Oh, and, Edward." Traherne's hooded gaze rested gently on his private secretary. "I know I do not have to remind you to be discreet."

"Indeed not, Your Grace. You may be certain I strive ever to be the soul of discretion. Was there anything in particular you wished to know about Lady Winslade?"

Traherne turned to contemplate the fire in the fireplace. "I am not sure, Edward," he said slowly, after a moment. "Perhaps it is merely a feeling I have."

The feeling, whatever it was, was still with Traherne when, half an hour later, he repaired to his sleeping quarters.

He was immeasurably weary after his long ride, and yet he felt a reluctance to undress and seek his bed. Sinking down into the overstuffed wing chair before the fire in his sitting room, he was visited with an image of Althea, white faced, her lovely eyes anguish filled and shadowed with secrets. The devil, he thought, imbued with a sudden impatience to be away from London and on his way back to Briersly, back to the wood nymph who, having cut up his existence, had come to occupy his every waking moment.

The growing conviction that he had been mistaken ever to leave Althea was become a driving sense of urgency long before he had finished the business that had brought him to London. Indeed, not even the certainty that he had taken the only course Althea had left open to him was enough to assuage his inexplicable feeling that all was not well at the Old Mill House. The return journey, even at Caesar speed, was rendered interminable.

Forced to contain his burning impatience, Traherne found little comfort in the fact that the passage was achieved in a record thirteen hours and twenty-two minutes. Hardly had the coach come to a clattering halt in the cobblestone drive before Briersly at precisely a quarter till nine on the morning of his promised engagement with Althea and Effie than he was issuing orders to have two horses saddled and brought immediately around.

Ten minutes later, he was astride and, leading the riderless mount, riding at a canter along the track to the Old Mill House.

He was ruefully aware of a quickening of his heartbeat as he sprang from the saddle and tethered the horses. Egad, he displayed all the symptoms of a moonstruck cub about to engage in his first assignation with a beautiful woman, he thought with wry amusement at himself. Then, with long purposeful strides, he had reached the door and was sounding the knocker.

Mattie opened the door as always, Mattie, who had ever a broad smile of welcome for His Grace. A hard fist clamped down on the duke's vitals. The elderly housekeeper was not smiling now.

"You came, Your Grace," said Mattie, wringing her hands. "Miss Althea said you would. Dear me, if only you'd been sooner. Left in the middle of the night, she did. And taken Effie with her. Said she'd not be comin' back an' I was to tell you she was sorry she couldn't keep to her word."

"Her word." Traherne stared at the woman, a blank space opening up somewhere inside him.

Somehow, all the way from London to Briersly, even driven nearly to distraction with the feeling that something was damnably amiss, he had not thought she would break her promise to him. He grappled with the reality.

Althea was gone, and he had not the first clue where to find her.

Chapter Seven

Althea, feeling more than a little out of sorts after a night spent battling her pillows, flung aside the counterpane and slid out of her bed. The shock of the chill air after the snug warmth of the bedclothes sent her scurrying across the room to throw fresh kindling and a log on the smoldering embers in the fireplace. Then seeing the flames leap, she made a dive for her covers.

Sitting with her knees to her chest, the blankets pulled to her chin, she was reminded that it was approaching the middle of October. Another month would see the trees shedding their leaves. Elias, ever practical, had already set in a sizable store of firewood. There were all the signs of the approach of winter, and she was ruefully aware that for the first time since her return to Ullswater, she felt an unwonted reluctance at the thought of the long weeks of being confined to the house—something else she could lay at the door of the Duke of Traherne, she doubted not.

Traherne, in two short weeks, had wreaked havoc on all the plans she had so carefully mapped out for herself and for Effie. She had always looked forward to the time when the snows came to cut the dale off from the rest of the world as a time when she need not worry about outsiders penetrating the remote fastness of the little haven she had created for herself and for Effie. She could rest, snug in the knowledge that her dearest Effie was safe. That she should now suffer this sudden discontent with the very thing that had made Ullswater and the Old Mill House the perfect sanctuary was unthinkable.

Nothing had changed, she reminded herself sternly. While she could be grateful the past five years had not been disturbed by the appearance of strangers in the dale inquiring about a woman and a child, she must not fool herself into believing the need for vigilance was past. She would be worse than a fool if she allowed herself to forget the desperate measures she had been compelled to undertake to remove herself and Gloriana from Madras and the man who had sworn a terrible vengeance on them both. She could only be grateful the colonel had never learned of the circumstances that had precipitated their flight from India. She had no illusions as to what he would have done in such an event. It would have meant the end of his career, ruin for all of them. At least this way, when the day came for him to discover the existence of his eldest grandchild, there would be both time and distance between him and the event of Effie's conception. Furthermore, with Gloriana safely married, Althea did not doubt the colonel would see the folly of pursuing a course that would bring the entire unhappy episode into public notice.

Still, she could not deny that she was relieved the colonel, who was to have been sent home for a brief stay in England, had apparently been diverted to Alexandria. It was not that she could not bear the thought that she must stand before him accused of having failed to live up to his expectations of her. Had Effie been truly her own, she would have felt no shame in facing her father. How could she, when Effie was everything she could have asked for in a daughter? It would have meant being ashamed of Effie, and that she could never be. Besides, as one who adamantly professed to be a freethinker, she could hardly be expected to adhere to the proscriptions of traditional precepts. Nevertheless, freethinker or not, she could not relish the notion of lying to the colonel, which was what she was committed to do to preserve Gloriana in her father's eyes.

The devil, she thought, stifling a groan. How much less must she rejoice in having to lie to the man who had won her heart! And yet that was precisely what she must do. Indeed, to do anything else must certainly be to bring peril not only to him, but to herself and Effie as well. She could not be sure, after all, that she was not still being pursued. She was terribly certain, however, what Traherne would do if he knew she was living in dread of a man who was perfectly capable of hurting her and Gloriana through Effie.

Traherne would spare no effort to hunt the villain down and put a period to his existence, and that she could not allow. It was bad enough that he had already set his mind to marry her out of some mistaken notion of honor. She would not have him taking up the cudgel in her defense as well, especially for something that not only was clearly none of his concern, but that must inevitably plunge him into dark and perilous waters. It simply was not to be thought of. Besides, she was the colonel's daughter. She had never before asked anyone to fight her battles for her, and she certainly had no intention of beginning now.

The devil, she thought, flinging the blankets aside in sudden irritation with her less than felicitous mood. What in heaven's name was the matter with her? In spite of her never-ending vigilance over Effie, not to mention the extensive measures she had taken to make the old house secure from intruders, the truth was she had not thought about the possibility of pursuit for months. Why it should suddenly rise up out of the blue to cut up her existence—now when she had other, more pressing concerns to occupy her, not the least of which was the imminent return of a certain gimlet-eyed nobleman who had made it plain he had no intention of abandoning his resolve to make an honest woman of her, whether she wished it or not—was outside of enough.

Now, more than ever, she should be grateful for the approach of winter, she told herself sternly. Indeed, she *must* be. After all, it must inevitably bring an end to her bittersweet torment. Traherne was a man of enormous responsibilities and influence. It was inconceivable that he would take the risk of being trapped at Briersly for weeks at a time. No, with the prospect of winter before him, he would have little choice but to admit defeat. He would go away, taking her heart with him, and that would be the end of her brief dream of happiness—as well it should be.

Crossing to the washstand, she splashed water from the pitcher into the basin and, gritting her teeth, took a measure of perverse satisfaction from her cold ablutions. A pity she had been unable to bring herself to ask Traherne for the use of his hired roofers to install the system of copper water pipes she had designed, along with her own version of a gravitational pump. Coupled with a hypocaust of Roman tradition, she might now be enjoying the luxury of hot and cold running water.

For a moment she lost herself in computing the savings in time and labor that would have been afforded by her relatively simple innovation for bringing water to the upstairs bedrooms. Then, taking up her automatic mechanical toothbrush and applying her own special mixture of tooth cleanser to the brush made of boar's bristles imbedded in a smooth wooden handle, which was in turn encased in a brass cylinder, she turned the wind-up key. No doubt she could attribute her present state of mind, she reflected, oblivious to the cranking of the brush, up and down, against her teeth, to the fact that only the day before she had received one of her sister's exceedingly rare missives. How like Gloriana to cross and double cross her lines so that it had required a full thirty minutes to puzzle out the intended message, she mused with sardonic appreciation.

Thinking of that cryptic hodgepodge of seemingly random observations, Althea stood for a moment or two, unaware that the coil in her toothbrush had wound down and gone suddenly inert. There had been something exceedingly odd about Gloriana's scribblings, which had seemed even more given to aimless ramblings than was usual for her scatter-brained younger sister. Frowning, Althea rewound the stem and continued her daily rite of oral hygiene. Perhaps what had first seemed gibberish—all the references to what Althea had supposed to be little Lord Guilmore's proclivity for dangling by his feet, but which subsequent deciphering had revealed to be the eighteen-month-old heir's having been denied of late a paternal knee upon which to dandle in childish glee—was but a reflection of some deeper concern of Gloriana's. In retrospect, Althea was given to speculate that all might not be well between the viscount and viscount-ess, that, indeed, some external influence threatened to drive a wedge between husband and wife. Perhaps not the ''gnaw-ing worm of disintegration,'' which Althea had at first been given to apprehend from Gloriana's chicken scratchings, but Winslade's ''growing mark of distinction'' in his diplomatic pursuits was responsible for absenting him from his wife and young son and daughter with ever-greater frequency. In addition, and perhaps most significantly, though it had not seemed so at the time of her first reading, there was passing mention of Gloriana's having been visited with a ''reminiscence,'' which had occasioned her thoughts to turn most longingly to her ''dearest, most loved sister and Effie.''

It came, then, to Althea that it was that final reference to a remembrance of the past, especially as applied to herself and Effie, that must have awakened the old slumbering feelings of unease. How unlike Gloriana, who shrank from the least unpleasantness, to dredge up memories of a past that had held nothing but pain for her! That she had felt compelled to write was evidence of how greatly she had been affected by it.

Althea suffered an unwonted twinge of annoyance at her sister. Anyone but Gloriana would have known better than to toss vague hints into a letter without bothering to tell the whole of it. Surely, had she thought at all, she must have known Althea would be left to imagine any number of dire possibilities to explain that offhanded comment. Reminiscence, indeed, fumed Althea, rifling through her wardrobe for a gown to wear. But then, it could have been something perfectly innocuous—like coming across an old piece of jewelry or a pressed flower, a book, or some other little thing from their days in Madras—that had triggered Gloriana's sudden nostalgia for her big sister and the daughter she could never acknowledge. Unlike the ever-practical Althea, Gloriana had always been possessed of delicate sensibilities. The tiniest thing could have set her off.

Botheration, thought Althea, snatching a brown serge gown from the wardrobe. She was undoubtedly making a great deal out of nothing. Surely, if there had been anything about which Althea needed to concern herself, Gloriana would have told her straight out. Far more immediate than any shapeless fears generated by her sister's cryptic letter was the unavoidable reality of the duke's return on the morrow.

He would come. Of that she had not the slightest doubt. And very likely precisely at nine, just as he said he would. She hardly knew what was worse—the wholly irrational racing of her heart at the mere prospect of seeing him again or the equally powerful sense that to be in his presence, even for the length of one more day, would be to her utter downfall.

She was sorely tempted to pack a trunk and flee with Effie to London. After all, would it not be better to stand condemned of having broken her word than to fail in her resolve and bring ruin on the Duke of Traherne? The bitter terrible truth was she did not want to go; indeed, she could not bear the thought of losing those precious few last hours with her dearest friend.

An hour later, fully dressed and having finished a breakfast of coffee and toast, Althea made a desultory attempt to lose herself in her latest project, an automatic mechanical clothes washer powered by a waterwheel similar to the one that had run the mill, save on a considerably smaller scale. She had already perfected—at the cost of innumerable shredded garments and Mattie's avowal that pigs would fly before any self-respecting housewife would consent to use a contrivance clearly inspired by the devil for the promotion of idle hands—a model with a manually operated crank. Being Althea, however, she could not be satisfied until she was able to contrive a machine that was fully automatic. One day, she did not doubt, there would be automatic machines to do every sort of manual labor. The working classes, freed from drudgery, would find time and opportunity to improve their lives in employment better suited to human beings. All that was needed was a cheap dependable source of power to stimulate the creation of an infinitude of automatically operated machines.

Lost in contemplation of harnessing the energy contained in the oceans' currents and tides or transforming sunlight into a usable mechanical power source or even domesticating the raw power of electricity, not to mention capturing and utilizing the energy potential of the earth's molten core as demonstrated in volcanic eruptions as well as hot springs and geysers, Althea was oblivious to the passage of the time. It was not until the rumble in her stomach alerted her to the fact that it was time for nuncheon that she became aware, not only that the morning was gone, but that Effie had not come bursting in on her to disrupt the morning's work with a myriad questions or pleas to leave off whatever Althea was doing and play with her, as was the child's usual practice.

Althea suffered an immediate sinking sensation in the pit of her stomach. Faith, how could she have gone the whole morning without once missing Effie, especially as only the night before they had had one of their exceedingly rare head-to-head confrontations? Upon being told that her riding lessons would have to be curtailed until the duke's return, Effie had demonstrated most dramatically that, when thwarted, at least in something that was dear to her heart, she had inherited her mama's potential for going into high fidgets.

"It isn't fair. You *promised,* Althie," declared Effie, ominously screwing up her face.

"It is only for a couple of days, Effie," said Althea, trying the diplomatic approach. "Until His Grace returns and until I can purchase a riding hack. I have already asked Elias to inquire about the dale for a suitable mount. I feel sure we shall hear of something very soon."

Far from being reassured, Effie had crossed her arms and stomped her foot. "I don't believe you. You want to take Pegasus away. But you daren't. Pegasus is mine. Lucius gave her to me."

It was then Althea, unprepared to have the duke flung in her face and momentarily caught off guard without a calm reasoned reply, took recourse in the age-old parent's last resort. "Effie Marie Wintergreen. I shall thank you not to use that tone with me. You will not ride Pegasus until I say you may, and that is the end of it."

It was, of course, a grave error in tactics. No doubt it gave incontrovertible evidence as to how little Althea was accustomed to speaking to Effie in such terms. The results were practically inevitable. For the brief space of a heartbeat, Effie stared at Althea as if she had just been delivered a slap in the face. Then, her face crumpling, she burst into tears.

"You're mean and-and hateful. And-and I don't like you

anymore," she gasped, between sobs. "I shall run away and live with Auntie Gloriana. *She's* never mean to me."

"*Effie!*" In her childish innocence, Effie had stumbled upon the one sure way to wound Althea to the quick. No doubt sensing something of this in Althea's astonished utterance, Effie gave Althea a look of anguish mingled with fright and fled.

Althea had not gone after her. She had been too shaken to deal rationally with the child then. It was not until later, after an hour spent pacing her sitting room and mulling over the unhappy incident, that she stole softly into the nursery to peer down at Effie, wrapped in what gave every evidence of being peaceful slumber.

Faith, what a ninny she had been to let the child's unfortunate outburst pierce her skin, thought Althea, leaving her workroom to go in search of Effie. It had been nothing more than a childish fit of temper bred of disappointment, behavior that, of course, could not be tolerated; but hardly the sort of thing to set a rational being in a spin. She, after all, was an adult, who should have known better than to relinquish control of the situation to a five-year-old. Nor was it any excuse that she had been feeling a trifle off balance in the wake of that unsettling few moments with Traherne earlier in her workroom. If nothing else, the incident had opened her eyes to feelings she had not known were festering inside her, chief of which was a sense of guilt that Effie was being made to live a lie.

It was one thing to keep the truth of the child's birth a secret from the colonel and the rest of the world, but quite another to deny Effie the knowledge of who her real mother was. Until now, Althea had allowed herself to believe that they had done the best thing for the child's welfare, that to tell Effie the truth about her mother would only do the child irreparable damage. After all, how was a child to understand how it was that her real mother could know and love her, yet never acknowledge her as her own? How could anyone expect Effie to believe in herself if she were to learn she had a half sister and a half brother who enjoyed all the benefits of being recognized as legitimate offspring?

Althea had vowed the child would be spared that final devastating truth, even as she had pledged herself to do all in her power to mold Effie into a woman of unshakable confidence and independent thinking. It was the only weapon she could think to give Effie, the only buffer against the injustice of a world that would seek to revile and judge her for something that was not her fault. It would be difficult enough when Effie was old enough to realize what it meant to be a love child, without the added burden of knowing her mother had given her up and why.

Or would it? wondered Althea, descending the attic stairs. Was a lie ever justified?

Suddenly even that disquieting question was forgotten, as she met Nessie, panting and heaving from apparent exertion, her normally stolid front expressive of grim misgiving.

"Nessie, what in heaven's name—" Althea began, only to break off in sudden dread certainty. "Dear God, it is Effie. Tell me at once. What has happened?"

"I should never have let her talk me into leaving the nursery, even for a second," declared Agnes Fennigrew, as close as the redoubtable nanny had ever been to giving way to despair. "I could tell there was something working on her, quiet as she was all morning. Oh, she was a clever one, she was, promising as how a dish of hot chocolate would make everything right as rain with her again. No sooner was my back turned, than she took herself off, heaven only knows where. I've looked everywhere I can think of, Miss Althea. There's not a sign of her to be found." Blowing her nose lustily in a plain muslin handkerchief, Nessie blurted, " 'Tis no one's fault but my own, Miss Althea. I shan't ever forgive myself if something has happened to that child."

"Pray cease at once to torment yourself, Nessie," Althea said with a calm at sharp variance to her racing thoughts, not to mention the sudden churning in her stomach. "We shall find her. She cannot have gone far. Did you look in the stables?"

The sudden dawning of hope in Mrs. Fennigrew's troubled countenance was answer enough.

"Wait here, Nessie, in case Effie comes back. I shan't be long, I promise."

Picking up her skirts, Althea hurried from the house. Faith, why had she not foreseen that Effie might try to ride her beloved pony on her own! The child had all of the Wintergreen obstinacy and not a particle of fear in her makeup. Still, it would seem exceedingly far-fetched to suppose that Effie could saddle and bridle the pony all by herself. Perhaps she had merely thought to slide down on the mare's back from the stall partition, in which case, she might be lying on the ground even now, her tiny body trampled by a frightened animal.

The hard knot in Althea's stomach was scarcely eased by the sight of the stable door standing ajar. Elias would hardly have been so remiss as to leave it open. Flinging through the doorway, Althea made her way down the aisle between the stalls. The coach horses, Ned and Jack, nickered at her, no doubt hoping for a cube of sugar. Her heart hammering beneath her breast, Althea hurried past them to the last stall at the far end of the stable.

Althea had faced the certain prospect of an ambush by a heavily armed band of Amir Khan's Pathan banditti with greater fortitude than that with which she peered over the half-door into the stall occupied by the dainty mare. For a moment, she thought surely her knees must give way beneath her, as she was met with what gave every appearance of being her worst nightmare made a reality.

The pony stood, quietly feeding, seemingly oblivious to the small crumpled form at its feet.

It was a moment or two before Althea could summon the wits to make her limbs do as she bid them. "Softly, Pegasus.

Easy, girl.'' With infinite care not to frighten the animal, Althea eased through the stall door.

The hard fist clamped on Althea's vitals gave way with sickening suddenness as Pegasus, snorting, lowered her head to nudge that small inert body with her nose. Effie stirred, her eyes fluttering open.

"Pegasus. You woke me up," said the child accusingly and, stretching out her arms, gave vent to a yawn.

The next moment, Althea was kneeling, her arms reaching to gather Effie to her breast.

"Althie, you found me," observed Effie with childish seriousness. "I was hoping you would. Did you see them, too? Is that why you came looking for me?"

"See them. See whom?" said Althea, only just recovering from the overwhelming wave of relief that had swept over her upon discovering Effie safe and unharmed. She had no little difficulty in making sense of the child's seemingly disjointed utterances.

"The two men," Effie shrugged. "I saw them from the window. I didn't think they looked in the least friendly. I was afraid for Pegasus."

Good God, thought Althea, a great deal made suddenly, frighteningly clear. Left alone when Nessie had gone to the kitchens to make hot chocolate, Effie had seen two strange men on the grounds. Faith, she had come to the stables to be with her beloved pony! It came to Althea with terrible certainty that there could only be one reason Effie should have felt afraid for Pegasus. "You saw them where, Effie?" she said, feeling a prickle of nerve endings at the nape of her neck.

"They were here. I saw them, but they didn't see me. Mayn't we go now, Althie? I'm dreadfully hungry."

"Yes, dear. Nessie will have your chocolate ready for you. We must not let it grow cold, must we? But, first, I think we shall play a little game. Would you like that?"

"What kind of a game?" replied the little girl doubtfully.

"A game of pretend, dearest." Lifting Effie to her feet, Althea stood and took the child's hand in her own. "We shall pretend that you are a circus performer, and I am the Ring Master. You are the daredevil lady bareback rider, and Pegasus is your prancing steed. You must cling very tightly to her mane to stay on. Indeed, you must not let go no matter what. Do you think you can do that?"

"Yes," Effie said, regarding Althea with frowning eyes. "It's because of the men, isn't it? You're afraid of them, too, aren't you, Althie?"

"I don't know, Effie," Althea replied truthfully. "I know I dislike the notion of strangers near the house, where they have no business to be." She paused, not wanting to frighten the child. "You should not have left the house alone, you know. You gave us all a terrible fright. What if something had happened to you?"

Effie screwed her face up in contemplation. "Like what, Althie?"

"Any number of things. You could fall and hurt yourself. You could twist your ankle and not be able to walk home again. This time, you might have found yourself shut up in the stables and unable to get out. What if I had not thought to look for you here? You might have been in the dark and the cold all night. And then what would Nessie and Mattie and I have done? We should have been frantic with worry, Effie."

"I didn't mean to worry you," declared the child, her eyes clouding with tears. "I had to see if Pegasus was all right. I *had* to. I didn't mean to fall asleep."

Kneeling, Althea pulled the little girl close. "I know, dearest, but you did fall asleep and we *were* made to worry. You should have come to me, Effie. You should have told me about the men."

"I couldn't, Althie. You wouldn't have let me come to see Pegasus. You were ever so mad at me. I didn't think you liked me anymore."

"Effie! Sweetheart," exclaimed Althea, mortified at what her hasty tongue had wrought. "I should never ever stop liking you. And there is nothing you cannot tell me. If I should ever get mad at you again, you must promise to remember that I never stay mad for very long. And it does not mean I don't like you. It could never mean that. Promise me, Effie. Promise you will always come to me when there is anything that troubles you."

"I promise, Althie," said the little girl solemnly. Then, flinging her arms about Althea's neck, she cried, "I didn't mean it, Althie. I don't hate you. I should never wish to live with anyone but you."

"I know, dearest." Her heart full, Althea held Effie close. "I know." At last, feeling the child grow quiet, Althea put Effie from her. She smiled and smoothed the child's tousled curls. "It is time we returned to the house," she said. "Are you ready?"

Effie nodded vigorously.

"Good." Taking the lead rope down from where it hung, coiled, on a peg in the wall, Althea attached one end to the pony's halter. Then, looping the other end over the mare's neck, she tied it to the halter as well. It was a poor substitute for a bridle and reins, but it would have to do, she thought with a sickening sensation in the pit of her stomach at what she intended. She had never known such fear for Effie as she felt then, and yet she could not see that there was anything else to be done. At last, lifting Effie, she set the child astraddle the pony's back. "Remember," Althea said, watching Effie grip the long tufts of hair in tight little fists, "hold to the mane and grip as hard as you can with your legs. Don't let go."

With a last pat for Pegasus, Althea led her from the stall. Then giving the child a reassuring smile, she started cautiously down the walkway.

The stable was steeped in silence, disturbed only by the clip-crop of the pony's hooves on the cobblestones and the low hoot of an owl nesting in the beams overhead. The spill of sunlight through the open door at the far end of the stable danced hazily with dust motes. Indeed, Althea reflected, there would seem to be little about the peaceful environs to hint of danger. Perhaps the men had been nothing more than vagrants passing through, and were already long gone. The countryside was littered with lamed derelicts from the army and wounded sailors cast ashore without hope of further employment. In London, she had given coins to not a few of them. In the dales, however, removed from the sea and hemmed in by high fells, such castaways would have been rare indeed.

Still, it was not an impossibility, she told herself, as she approached the tack room near the stable exit. While able-bodied males employed as shepherds were granted exemptions from serving, there were not a few young men from the dales who had volunteered to fight, like Mattie and Elias Treadwell's son, Jonas, who had signed on to serve as the colonel's batman. Perhaps these men were sons of the Lake District making their way home to mother or sister or wife. Whatever the case, only a few more steps separated Althea and Effie from the door. Once outside, they would have an unobstructed run to the house, a distance of no more than a hundred feet. It was what might be awaiting them as they stepped through the door that made Althea unconsciously tighten her grip on the pony's halter.

The mare's ears flicked suddenly back. From behind came the muffled thud of a step. Althea turned her head, caught a glimpse out of the corner of her eye of a hulking shape. Leaping aside, she brought the flat of her hand down hard on the pony's hindquarters.

"*RIDE, Effie!* Don't look back!"

Startled, Pegasus bolted for the gaping doorway, the child clinging with all her might to the pony's back.

Althea beheld a second masculine figure leap into view, arms flailing to ward off the mare. Too late. Frightened and enraged at that unwonted slap on the rump, Pegasus lunged past the intruder into the open.

Only then was Althea rudely reminded of her own immediate danger, as a burly arm clamped without warning about her throat. In no mood to be throttled, let alone endure a mauling, Althea clutched the offending arm with both hands and, ramming her hip into the villain's midsection, dropped her weight forward. A howl of pain and surprise was torn from the villain's throat at finding himself flying, head over heels, over Althea's shoulder. Hardly had he landed with a resounding thud flat on his back, than Althea planted a foot solidly across his throat.

"No doubt I should beg your pardon for tossing you over my shoulder," she said solicitously. "However, you really should not have put a hand on me. And now you will be pleased to tell your friend to stay back, or I shall not accept the blame for the consequences." Carefully, she applied enough pressure to cause the man's eyes to roll in alarm. *"At once,"* she added, acutely aware that the second villain, having caught sight of his cohort's sudden turn of affairs, had started toward them.

" 'Old it, mate. She means t' crush me gullet for me."

The other would-be assailant came to an abrupt halt. Nervously, he glanced over his shoulder, then back at his felled companion. Upon which, apparently deciding retreat was the better part of valor, he turned tail and ran.

Hardly had he vanished around the corner than it was made immediately apparent what had determined him on his precipitous flight.

A masculine voice, reassuringly familiar to Althea, hailed the stables. "Miss Althea? It's Tom Sykes. Elias sent for me. Are you in there?"

"*Effie,* Tom," Althea shouted back. "Is she—"

"Mattie has her. You needn't fret about her, miss. Effie's fine. I'm armed, and I'm coming in now. Are you alone?"

Nearly faint with relief at the news that Effie was safe

and unharmed, Althea only just summoned the wit to answer him. "It is quite safe, Tom. Please, do me the favor to wait just outside. I promise I shall join you directly."

Althea could almost feel the gameskeeper's hesitation, but at last he answered her, "I'll be right here if you need me, Miss Althea. Just give me a shout."

"It would seem you are all on your own," Althea pointed out to the villain. At the announced arrival of reinforcements for Althea, he had gone limp with resignation. Carefully, she removed her foot from his throat and stepped back. "I should warn you that Mr. Sykes is a crack shot. There is not the smallest chance he would miss you if you were so foolish as to try anything rash."

"I guess I knows when I'm stumped. What I'd like t' know is how'n hell did a mite of a female toss Jack Weems over her head like he were no more 'n a rag doll."

"It is a simple matter of leverage, Mr. Weems," Althea replied, "with my hip as the fulcrum and your torso as the lever. Anyone versed in the practical application of physics could have done the same. That, however, is neither here nor there. I suggest, if you have any wish of leaving here in one piece, you tell me who sent you and what you thought to accomplish here today."

"Why not," growled the felon, heaving himself into a sitting position and wryly rubbing his throat. "I got nothin' t' lose by it. We was promised ten quid t' snatch the girl. I doesn't know who hired us. Th' bloke never told us 'is name. We was to bring her to the Lion's Head Inn after dark to get our blunt. I doesn't know anything else."

"You are lying," Althea declared flatly. "At the very least, you know what this villain looks like."

"Only that he were a gennelman. I swears it. I never laid eyes on 'im afore today. Wore fancy clothes and sported a walking stick with a falcon's head made o' gold."

Althea felt cold fingers explore her spine. "A gold falcon's head. Are you certain?"

"Couldn't've mistook that," darkly asserted the felon. "Shoved it in me face, 'e did. Said 'e'd bloody well cut me 'eart out if'n I breathed a word of what'd been said between us. And now I told you everything. How's about lettin' Jack Weems take a walk? It wouldn't do anyone any good to 'ave that bloke outside cut me stick for me."

"I shall do better than that. Do you swear to leave the dale and never come back again, I shall give you your ten quid, Mr. Weems. Only swear you will go nowhere near the Lion's Head Inn. I shall know if you break your word, Mr. Weems, in which case I should not hesitate to turn you over to the local magistrate. Is that understood?"

Mr. Weems, who could not but apprehend that his prospects, even without the promise of ten quid, were considerably improved over what they had been only a few moments earlier, hastened to assure Althea that he would rather cut his own throat than place himself within ten miles of the bloody Lion's Head Inn. "You didn't see the look in 'is eyes, miss. An' if'n you was to've done, you'd not worry that Jack Weems won't keep to his word."

Little more than an hour before midnight, after pressing a good-size roll of the flimsies on Mattie and Elias with the assurance that there would be a quarterly sum at their disposal as soon as ever she could make the arrangements, Althea bade a reluctant farewell to the Old Mill House and its tearful inhabitants. Then joining the sleeping Effie, who lay bundled up in a quilt with her head nestled on Mrs. Fennigrew's lap in the travel coach, Althea instructed Jake to set the team in motion.

She could not like having to steal away from her home like a felon in the middle of the night; indeed, she had not wished to leave at all. The attempted abduction of Effie, however, had left her little choice in the matter. She did not fool herself into thinking there would not be other attempts if she stayed. The only sensible course was to spirit herself and Effie away.

Being Althea, she had long ago laid her plans for just such a contingency. They would go first to London, not by way of Penrith, as she had originally thought to do, it was true, but by way of Patterdale and the Kirkstone pass to Windermere and on south to Manchester before bearing east again. She had no wish, after all, to risk a chance meeting with Traherne on the road, which would be all too likely were they to take the faster, more direct route. At any rate, a more leisurely, rather meandering journey better suited her purposes. Like the zigzagging, backtracking fox, she hoped to confuse her pursuers.

Once in London, she would go to the house her sister kept for her; but only for a day or two, until she could make arrangements for letters of credit on her bank and book passage on a ship to the Americas. In the New World she and Effie could assume new identities. In the Americas they could begin life afresh, free of the taint of scandal and most certainly delivered from the dread of pursuit. Not even Traherne could find them in the newly formed United States. Even his influence did not reach beyond the bounds of the British Empire.

Somehow the thought brought her little comfort. Indeed, she was aware of the birth of an aching emptiness somewhere deep inside her. In truth, she had not known such grief since the untimely demise of her mama. But she had survived even that sorrow, she sternly reminded herself. After all, there had been Gloriana and the colonel depending on her to keep their spirits up. This time she had something far more precious to see her through: She had Effie.

She was to discover in the four-day journey to London that her responsibility for Effie was become a mixed blessing.

The child slept through that first night, hardly even stirring when Althea carried her to her bed in the inn on the outskirts of Kendal shortly before dawn. She was, in consequence, fully rested by nine in the morning, while Althea, having enjoyed little more than three hours of sleep, was feeling something less than her usual self when she was awakened by the child, demanding to know where they were and how they had got there. It was bad enough that Effie had opened her eyes to unfamiliar surrounds, but that she had done so without even the benefit of a lucid memory of having been carried from her nursery bed and placed in a coach had served to unsettle and disorient her. She most adamantly did not like leaving home under havey-cavey circumstances. Indeed, she did not like leaving home at all, and nothing Althea could say could change her mind about it, especially when it came to her to realize that Pegasus had had to be left behind.

"I am sorry, dearest," said Althea, who had indeed been dreading this moment of unhappy revelation. "Truly, I am. But you must try and understand that it was utterly impossible to bring Pegasus with us. She will be happier at home with Elias to look after her."

"But what good is it to have a pony if I am not there to ride her?" Effie insisted with infallible logic. "Please, Althie, I don't want to go to London. We shall miss Lucius. He was bringing you a hack to ride. It will hurt his feelings if we're not there. Althie, he won't like us anymore."

"Of course he will, Effie. I asked Mattie to tell him why we could not be there. You may be sure he will understand that it simply could not be helped."

Effie was silent for a long moment, apparently digesting that information. It was soon to be made clear that she had grasped a deal more of their situation than Althea could possibly have realized.

"We shan't ever see him again, shall we, Althie?" she stated with perfect conviction, her eyes filled with childish wisdom. "We shan't ever see Pegasus again either. Or Mattie and Elias."

"I don't know, Effie," Althea answered truthfully. "Never is a very long time."

Althea was not certain whether she was relieved or sorry that the child appeared to accept the sudden changes that had been forced on her without any real explanation. Effie asked no more questions. Indeed, she appeared to withdraw into herself, something that she had never been prone to do in the past. When the horses had been rested sufficiently to take up the journey again, she made no protest, but sat in the corner, peering out the window, or slept with her head cradled in Nessie's lap. She was a silent and brooding figure whom no amount of cajoling or coaxing could reach.

Long before the coach approached the busy outskirts of London, Althea was plagued with doubts. And yet, she could not see what else she could have done. Had things been different, it was doubtful she would ever have taken Effie away from all that she had come to know and love before she was old enough to understand the necessity for it. Had there never been the kidnapping attempt, she would have been content to allow Effie to bloom and grow in the protected environment of the dale until, with Effie on the threshold of blossoming into womanhood, it was become time to introduce her to the broader world. As it was, Althea found herself sorely lacking in the wisdom necessary to breach the shell of despondency that Effie had erected about herself.

Indeed, tormented by her inability to reach Effie and worn to the nub by the endless miles of silence, Althea felt a mere shadow of herself by the time the coach pulled up in front of the modest house on Plover Street. Night had fallen, and, save for the lamp in the foyer, the house loomed, dark and unwelcoming. No doubt the skeleton staff who were kept on to maintain the house in a constant state of readiness for Althea had long since retired to bed. It would be a pity to wake them, she decided, as she climbed stiffly from the coach and, turning to take the sleeping Effie from Mrs. Fennigrew, instructed Jake to rouse a stablelad to help bring in their things. Not wishing to attract attention by hiring a coach to carry any additional luggage, they had brought little enough with them. Even Goosey Gander had had to be left behind, along with the entirety of Althea's various projects and her precious tools.

"Nessie, be so good as to look through my reticule for the key. It will save time if we simply let ourselves in."

Effie, allowed this once to sleep in her shift, was soon installed in her bed in the nursery with Nessie to sleep in the room adjoining.

At last Althea, after dropping a featherlight kiss on the little girl's forehead, let herself out in the hall with the flicker of a candle to light her way. She could not recall when she had felt quite so tired or so utterly dispirited. On the morrow, she must make a determined effort to rouse her fighting mettle. Really, this was no way for the colonel's daughter to begin what was to be a great adventure. It was, in fact, quite utterly unlike her.

The stablelad, looking rumpled and sleepy eyed, was waiting in a spill of moonlight with her trunk and bandbox outside the door to her rooms.

"Just set them inside, Toby," said Althea, opening the door to let him pass in ahead of her. "And then you may return to your bed. I am sorry to have dragged you out in the middle of the night."

"Not at all, miss. Shall I light the lamp for 'ee?"

"Thank you," smiled Althea tiredly, wishing only to be left alone, "but I am sure I can manage."

"I'll just be going then," said the stablelad. "Good night, miss."

"Good night." Althea closed the door behind the boy and, setting the candle on the mantelpiece, thankfully slipped out of her green leather slippers. Then reaching up to slide the strap of her leather pouch off her shoulder, she let the bag come to rest on the lowboy.

Suddenly, she froze, a prickle exploring the nape of her neck.

For a moment she stood quite still, her every sense attuned to the quiet of the room, to the shadows, impenetrable beyond the faint circle of the candlelight. Carefully, she slipped her hand inside the leather pouch.

"Who is there?" she demanded, her hand emerging from the pouch. "I warn you I am perfectly prepared to defend myself."

"So I have been informed."

Althea's breath caught as a man's tall form unfolded itself from the wing chair and stepped free of the shadows.

"Not, I think however, with that," he added, indicating the object clutched in Althea's hand. "I am hardly the sort to be fooled twice by a gun that is in reality an automatic mechanical igniter, Althea."

"Lucius!" breathed Althea and, dropping her automatic mechanical igniter to the floor, stepped into his arms.

Chapter Eight

Traherne, who had expected something quite different from the maddeningly elusive Althea, folded her instinctively in his arms. Now, what the devil, he thought, acutely aware of her tightly clinging embrace.

It came to him with grim certainty that he could have no surer evidence of the strain she had been under for the past several days. But then, Tom Sykes, despite his reluctance to say anything that might have disputed the word of a lady, had finally been brought grudgingly to declare that there had been more, to his way of thinking, than what had been made to appear a mere incident of a child on a runaway pony. Furthermore, if it were true the fellow who had come out of the stable with Miss Wintergreen was a handyman hired to do a few odd jobs about the place, Tom Sykes did not know a candidate for Jack Ketchum when he saw one.

Something had happened to upset the redoubtable colonel's daughter sufficiently to send her into a precipitate flight from her home in the middle of the night. For the first time in the four days since he had arrived at the Old Mill House to discover Althea had broken her promise to him, Traherne felt a lessening of the hard knot of bitter certainty that she had been fleeing from *him*.

His impossibly stubborn and maddeningly independent Althea had a deal of explaining to do, and this time he would not be put off with a parcel of nonsense about loving him too much to impose on his good nature—good God. His well-developed instincts were all sounding a warning that Althea was in danger, indeed, that whatever trouble she had got herself in had played more than a minor part in her refusal to marry him. He knew her far too well to suppose she could ever bring herself to ask for his help. Anything so patently logical would have meant, after all, making him a part of whatever had spurred her into flight, and that she would never willingly do—never mind that he was far better equipped than she to deal with any possible threat to her or Effie.

That sort of nonsensical logic, however, would all end tonight. He was bloody well damned if he would submit to going again through so much as a single day resembling the last four of living in dread of what might have come to Althea and her Effie outside the mantle of his protection. He would bring Althea to trust him, he vowed, no matter what it might take. Indeed, this time he would settle for nothing less than the whole truth.

In the meantime, however, he was keenly aware that Althea, in an exceedingly rare moment of vulnerability, had turned to him as a source of strength and comfort. For the moment, he was content to hold her, his eyes grim, as he waited for her to recover her composure.

Althea, oblivious to everything but the sustaining warmth of Traherne's arms about her, when she had been so utterly certain she would never see him again, did not care for the moment that she had given herself away. She could not recall ever having felt so despondent in body and spirit as she had upon arriving at the house in London. To have

Traherne appear suddenly out of the very air, it seemed, was simply too much for her. How natural it had been to walk into his arms! And how easy it would be to allow him to take all her burdens upon his broad capable shoulders! That, however, was simply out of the question. She was not so lost to all sense of self-respect as to wish that on him— or on herself, she thought, acutely aware that her ability to fend for herself and Effie was at risk. Rather the way a muscle tended to atrophy from disuse, so, too, must her self-reliance be weakened by becoming too much accustomed to dependence on the Duke of Traherne. She really must take herself in hand, at once, she told herself. But she was made immediately aware that perhaps the last thing she wished at that moment was ever to feel Traherne's embrace lifted from around her.

No doubt it was due to some perversity in her character that that realization made it utterly impossible to remain a moment longer where she was.

Raising her head, she favored Traherne with a rueful grimace. ''You are determined, are you not, to place me in your debt. Really, it is the shabbiest thing that just when I was feeling particularly downpin, you should appear to give me comfort. What are you doing here, Your Grace? How in heaven's name did you find me?''

''Are you surprised?'' queried Traherne with the arch of an arrogant eyebrow. ''I did warn you what would happen if you tried to run from me, Althea.''

Acutely aware of Traherne's nearness, Althea felt, in spite of herself, a slow heat pervade her veins. He had apparently been waiting some time for her arrival as was evidenced by the disturbing fact that he had earlier discarded his coat. Furthermore, his waistcoat was unbuttoned and hung open in front, his usual impeccably tied neckcloth was missing entirely, and his raven hair bore a disheveled look that suggested he had repeatedly run his fingers through it. Unaccountably, she found the duke's unwonted state of deshabille far more disturbing to her presence of mind than was in the least good for her equilibrium.

"That does not answer my question," she said, putting a more comfortable distance between her and Traherne's tall masculine form.

A mirthless smile flickered at the corners of Traherne's mouth. Patently, the barriers were up again. More important, his bewitching wood sprite was manifesting every sign of a female who was struggling against irresistible natural forces. "As it happens, I employ a highly competent private secretary who is adept at performing any number of tasks," he said, carelessly propping an elbow on top of the mantelpiece, "not the least of which was discovering that the Viscountess Winslade has been known on occasion to visit a house in an exceedingly unfashionable part of Town. Upon further investigation, he was able to learn that the lady, curiously enough, had taken out a lease on that very house a little over four years ago."

"That is impossible," Althea objected, wondering which of Gloriana's servants Traherne's secretary had managed to bribe for that telling tidbit of information about Gloriana's visits to Plover Street. "I made sure Gloriana leased the house under an assumed name."

"But of course you did," agreed Traherne, gently mocking. The wretch! thought Althea, biting her lip to keep from giving into an hysterical burble of laughter. "Still, I cannot but wonder if it was your idea or Lady Winslade's to employ the alias of Miss Judith Anne Pomeroy?"

"Oh, good God," groaned Althea in instant enlightenment. "How like Gloriana to use our mother's maiden name. One must suppose your exceedingly efficient private secretary had little difficulty in making the connection."

"For Edward, it was, I fear, a matter of child's play," Traherne admitted with an apologetic air. "Still, you might have saved me a deal of trouble, Althea, had you simply informed me you preferred to meet in Town for our promised engagement. I am not in the least accustomed to being stood up.''

"Faith, what a whisker," gasped Althea, turning away from him in chagrin. "You know very well I had no intention of keeping our engagement—in London, or anywhere else, for that matter. As for having stood you up, I do most sincerely beg your pardon. Unfortunately, it simply could not be helped."

"No," he conceded, recalling with a singular lack of amusement his initial reaction to discovering his wood nymph had broken her word and fled. "When I had time to think about it, I was sure it could not. After all," he added, watching her from beneath drooping eyelids, "you were not running from me, were you, Althea."

It was not a question, but a statement, offered in the infinitely gentle tones of utter certainty. Inwardly, Althea groaned.

"I thought we had already established that particular point, Your Grace. I broke my word. I ran from you," declared Althea, ruefully aware that a tide of color flooded her cheeks at the falsehood. But then, it was not all a lie. She *should* have been running from Traherne. Instead, what had she done, but fling herself at the very first opportunity into his arms! Faith, it did not bear thinking on. Nor was that all or the worst of it. If he had found her so readily, then she must suppose that others could as well.

"The devil, Lucius, what are you doing here?" she exclaimed, struck at last with the full significance of what the duke's presence must mean to her. In a sudden fit of exasperation, she flung away from him. "Why could you not have just stayed away? Have you the least notion how unsettling it is to find you here waiting for me, when I have taken such particular pains that you would not?"

"No, did you? My poor Althea. You might have saved yourself the trouble. There was never any question that I should find you."

"Nor is there any question that others will, too. Thanks to you, it is now quite impossible for me to remain in London for so long as a single day. I cannot think how I shall tell Effie. It has been hard enough on her, finding herself uprooted, and then with the added burden of having to leave Pegasus behind—" Recalled suddenly to another iniquity that could be laid at Traherne's door, she turned to flay the duke with accusing eyes. "Oh, *why* did you have to give her a pony, of all things, Lucius? I did try and tell you not to interfere in my affairs, but you would not listen, and now see what it has bought us. Faith, I shudder to think how close I came to losing Effie because of her attachment to that pony. And now she is sunk in a slough of despond at having to leave it behind. She blames me. She will go the rest of her life blaming me, and who is to say she is wrong? Perhaps I have been deluding myself all these years," she went on, knowing she was treading on dangerous grounds and yet somehow unable to stop herself.

"I told myself everything I did was for Effie's best interests, but perhaps I was doing it for myself—because I could not bear the thought of ever losing her affections. And now, because of all I have done, I came closer than I had ever thought to losing her in reality. Faith," she exclaimed, in bitter anguish, *"why* did we not stay in Madras and face things once and for all rather than flee and leave the door open for . . ."

Suddenly she stopped, acutely aware of how close she had come in her distraction to blurting everything out. Worse, Traherne was looking at her in the way he had of making her feel as if he could see straight through into her heart. "The devil," she uttered on a shuddering breath. "I cannot think what has got into me. I seem most uncommonly prone to rip up at you, Your Grace, when the truth is you have been nothing but kind to Effie and me. And now I suppose you will not be satisfied until I have given you an explanation for what must seem my exceedingly odd behavior. Really,

I wish you will simply go away and leave me to contrive what I must do next.''

''But that is obvious, surely,'' observed Traherne, with unnerving certainty. ''The first order of business must be to remove Effie to a place where she will be beyond the reach of those who tried to abduct her—''

''Abduct her. I never said anything about—you could not possibly know—''

''And who you obviously believe will try again,'' continued the duke, as if he had not been so rudely interrupted.

''But that is absurd,'' Althea objected, determined to bluff her way out of the trap into which she had foolishly blundered. ''You are indulging in nothing more than fantasy. There can be no possible reason to suppose anyone is after Effie.''

''Come, Althea. There is no point in trying to deny it,'' countered Traherne in no mood to humor her. ''Pray give me credit for at least a modicum of intelligence. Everything you have said and done points to the inescapable conclusion that just such an attempt was made.''

''Gammon,'' Althea retorted, consigning Traherne without remorse to the devil. The last thing she could wish in her present state was to be subjected to a Spanish Inquisition. ''I have never once doubted your intelligence, Lucius.''

''No doubt I am gratified to hear it,'' Traherne said with sardonic appreciation that she had evaded the pertinent question. ''In which case, you cannot really expect me to believe you would allow Effie to ride bareback, when only the day before you were unstrung at the merest possibility that she might sustain a fall. I saw your face, Althea. You were clearly on the point of putting a period to Effie's riding career. Am I now supposed to credit that you underwent a complete change of heart in little more than twenty-four hours?''

''I am sure I cannot be responsible for anything you might

think,'' Althea replied bitterly. ''The truth is Effie stole out to the stables without telling anyone.''

''Whereupon she managed to contrive a bridle out of a halter and lead rope? Is that what you are trying to tell me?''

Althea's head came up, her eyes flashing glorious gilt-green sparks of defiance. ''And why not? You said it yourself. Effie is exceedingly bright.''

''She is also an infant,'' Traherne odiously persisted. ''I cannot but wonder how she managed to retrieve a rope that hung from a peg clearly beyond her reach.''

Althea gave vent to an impatient gesture of the hand. ''Faith, how should I know how she managed it? I daresay she must have stood on something.''

''Indeed, there is always that possibility, one must presume,'' agreed Traherne, frowning, as Althea unconsciously rubbed her hands up and down her arms against the chill in the room. ''Unfortunately, there was nothing in the stall to support that particular theory, or Effie, for that matter.'' Bending to retrieve Althea's automatic mechanical igniter from the floor, the duke knelt to light the fire already laid out in readiness on the grate.

''The truth, Althea,'' he said, coming to his feet to stand looking down at the leap of flames, ''is that you took down the rope and fixed it to the halter.'' He turned his head to look at her. ''You put Effie on the pony's back and led her out of that stall.''

''No, did I?'' said Althea, wondering a trifle hysterically if there was anything Traherne had failed to determine for himself. ''But then you would seem to be in possession of all the facts, would you not?''

''Enough to know how desperate you were ever to risk Effie on a runaway horse.'' Traherne saw her flinch and had forcibly to restrain himself from going to her. Hellfire, there was no other way, he grimly reminded himself. For her sake and Effie's, he would have the truth from her. ''The devil, Althea,'' he said harshly. ''Do you think I am unaware you could never have done it had you not been convinced the danger to Effie inside the stable far outweighed the chance you would be taking sending her out on Pegasus? You were fortunate Mattie had earlier spotted two men on the grounds and, assuming they were poachers, thought immediately to send Elias to fetch my gameskeeper. He arrived, after all, in the nick of time to intercept Pegasus.''

Hugging her arms to her breast, Althea turned away, sickened by the memory of the terrible chance she had taken, of the rending terror she had felt for Effie.

Consequently, she failed to see the sudden leap of muscle along the hard line of Traherne's jaw or to detect the bleak look in his eyes. When she came back around, the grim look was gone from his stern features, replaced by the impenetrable mask of the Corinthian.

''For that, I shall always be grateful to Tom,'' she said with the quiver of a smile. ''Effie was in alt at her little adventure. *She* had not the smallest doubt in her ability to stay on Pegasus.''

''In that, I daresay she takes after you,'' observed the duke, who had little difficulty surmising that, in her driving concern to save Effie, she had never once considered her own danger. His blood ran cold at the certainty that she had faced the child's would-be abductors alone, with never a thought of making her own escape. She, after all, was the colonel's daughter. She had stayed behind to serve as a diversion—to give Effie her one chance at escape. ''How, by the way,'' he said, reminded of one of the missing pieces of the puzzle, ''did you manage to subdue the felon you tried to pass off as a handyman, let alone send his friend flying to all appearances for his life?''

Althea shrugged, all too aware that the time for evasive tactics was regrettably past. Traherne had already guessed most of it. There would seem little point in withholding the few remaining details. ''I merely gave them a lesson in the basic principles of a fulcrum and lever,'' she submitted wearily. "Mr. Weems made the mistake of trying to throttle me with his arm about my throat, a circumstance to which I took immediate exception. I'm afraid it was a matter of pure instinct to propel him bodily over my head."

"Naturally," agreed the duke, much struck at the image evoked by the slender wood nymph's offhanded account of the event. "How exceedingly unwise of Mr. Weems. And the second fellow?"

"Oh, him." Again Althea shrugged, as if it were a matter of even lesser import. "Tom's fortuitous arrival served to frighten him away. And now that you have all the facts of that regrettable incident, will you not be satisfied to leave it alone, Lucius?"

The instant incredulous lift of the duke's eyebrows put to immediate rout that remotest of possibilities. "All the facts, Althea? It occurs to me that we have yet to scratch the surface. I am perfectly aware that you would like nothing better than to consign me to the devil rather than confide in me, let alone turn to me for help."

"And how not," said Althea in bitter accents, "when this is none of your affair, Lucius. I will not have you involving yourself in something that I have wrought for myself. Especially as I am perfectly capable of dealing with the likes of—of anyone who thinks to impose himself on Effie or myself."

"Yes, no doubt," murmured Traherne, who had not failed to note with a deal of interest that near slip of the tongue. "Unfortunately, you have not the slightest hope of dealing in a like manner with *me*. You will accept my help, Althea, and my protection for you and Effie. You are far too caring a mother to refuse and far too intelligent a woman not to realize I can do the one thing you could not do for yourself."

Althea gave Traherne a wary look. "And what, Your Grace, is that?" she asked, feeling herself teetering on the edge of an abyss and yet compelled to take the fatal plunge.

"The freedom to act against your enemies." He paused,

his eyes glittery in the firelight as he waited for her to grasp the significance of what he was about to suggest. "*I* can provide Effie with a safe haven."

Feeling her knees threaten to give way beneath her, Althea sank weakly down on the edge of the wing chair that Traherne had only recently vacated. Faith, but it was all so incredibly simple. Indeed, she could not imagine how she had not thought of it long ago herself. But then, always, from the very beginning, everything she had done, all the decisions she had been compelled to make, had been determined by the need to protect. First, it had been Gloriana. Desperate with the knowledge that she was increasing and frightened with the realization that—in her willful flaunting of what she had resentfully seen as her sister's assumed authority over her—she had involved herself with a man who was as unscrupulous as he was dangerous. Gloriana had come to Althea, as she had always done when she landed herself in a scrape. Althea would know what to do. Althea always knew what to do. And, afterward, when it was too late to change the course they had chosen, there had been Effie.

Traherne had seen at once what Althea, in her preoccupation with providing a safe and nurturing environment for a growing infant, had failed to comprehend. The only sure way to rid herself of the need for constant vigilance was to turn and face her enemy. But then, that was hardly something she could hope to do so long as she had Effie with her. What Traherne was offering was the means of freeing Althea from the role of protector. With Effie safely tucked away, Althea could go after the man who would remain a threat to the child until he had achieved his nefarious purposes or was stopped once and for all.

At last she lifted shimmering eyes to Traherne. "Where?" she asked. "Who?"

Traherne, who could not but realize that he had at last

breached Althea's formidable defences, did not pretend to misunderstand her.

"I daresay my cousin Eleanor's house outside of Reading will do nicely," he answered, having had some little time to contemplate the problem as he had sat the entirety of that evening awaiting his elusive wood nymph's arrival. "Her husband, the Earl of Leister, gives every evidence of one exceedingly tolerant of children. He has, after all, fathered seven of them, five of them girls with whom Effie will no doubt deal extremely well. You may be sure no one would think to look for her there."

If he had expected to win her immediate and unqualified approval for his choice of a suitable haven for Effie, he was soon to be exceedingly disappointed.

"No, good God, what are you saying?" exclaimed Althea in tones of one who obviously thought him mad. "I thought you meant one of your estates or-or the home of a trusted retainer. But the Countess and Earl of Leister! Surely, you must be jesting." In sudden agitation, she bolted to her feet. "Even if your cousin could be brought to take Effie in, I could not possibly agree to such an arrangement. You must see how impossible it would be for-for Effie, indeed, for all concerned."

"I understand well enough," said Traherne with a sudden coldness she had never felt from him before. Indeed, she almost quailed at the terrible leap of his eyes. "You, my dear, are a snob, and the worst sort, at that. You would trust Effie to paid servants, thinking that they, perhaps, would not dare show contempt. The Earl and Countess of Leister, however, must certainly be depended upon to look down their aristocratic noses at an Innocent borne out of wedlock. What, precisely, do you think they will do to her? Order her to keep her distance from the other children? Confine her to the servants' quarters? Read her a daily curtain lecture on the unfortunate circumstances of her birth? They, after all, have their position to maintain, do they not?"

"And is that so far from the reality?" demanded Althea who had lived far too long under a pall of censure to entertain any illusions concerning the world into which she had been borne.

"The devil, Althea, you have an odd notion of my character do you think for one moment I should subject Effie to hurt and humiliation. My cousin Eleanor will take her in gladly because I ask it of her and because she has a generous disposition However, you do not have to accept my word that Eleanor and Leister would provide her with a caring environment. You may trust that Effie will be treated with the same consideration as would be accorded any child whom I have taken to be my legal ward."

"Your . . . ward," Althea repeated in faltering tones, as she struggled to comprehend this new and unexpected turn of events. Faith, what had Traherne done? What in heaven's name was happening? She felt her control over her own existence being ruthlessly stripped away from her by this man who had won her heart and Effie's. It would seem to make little sense in light of all that she had come to know and love in him. But then, he had said he would have her as his wife, whether she willed it or not; and he was a man of power and influence—a duke. Had he not declared he lacked any of the softer human emotions? Indeed, had he not taken care to warn her that he was both ruthless and dangerous? Was there anything he would not do to attain what he wanted, even to go so far as to take Effie away from her in order to break her to his will?

"It was the most logical solution, Althea," said Traherne watching her with eyes the opaque blue of a winter lake and suddenly just as lacking in the depth of soul with which she had credited them. "The papers have been drawn up, and Prinnie himself has authorized them. Effie is legally under my protection."

"Your protection!" Althea's face went suddenly white Indeed, she was gripped with the terrible reality that Traherne had betrayed her. "By what right, Lucius? Effie is mine! I will not submit to have her taken away from me, not even by you. How dared you presume to usurp my authority?''

"Now you are being absurd," observed Traherne with dampening calm. "It was never my intention to take Effie away from you, and, if you were not worn to the nub, not to mention driven to distraction, you would realize that all I have done is provide Effie the shelter of my name and all that goes with it.''

Althea stared at him out of eyes that were unnervingly blank.

"Hell and the devil confound your blasted pride, Althea," thundered Traherne, hard put not to give into the impulse to shake her. "It is done, and there is nothing you can do to change it. You may at least rest easy, knowing Effie is safe under my aegis, while, together, you and I do whatever is necessary to ensure she is never threatened again.''

"You and-and I? We . . .''

Traherne, a man of keen insight, could not but be aware of the manner in which his fiercely independent Althea might have been expected to receive the news that he had taken the matter of Effie's protection into his own hands. He was hardly prepared, however, to have her sink down on the wing chair as if her legs could no longer sustain her or to behold her bury her face in her hands. In consternation, he beheld her shoulders start to shake.

Silently, he cursed himself for an unfeeling boor. He had meant to overcome her resistance to the notion of accepting his help, not to break her reserves and reduce her to tears.

"Althea!" Instantly, he had crossed to her and, reaching down, was attempting to draw her to her feet. "No one will take Effie from you, least of all, I. Good God, you cannot believe I should do anything to hurt you or Effie.''

It was only then, as Althea's hands came free of her face, that he was met with the sight of her lovely countenance convulsed in what gave every evidence of being helpless paroxysms of laughter.

''No, of-of course you w-would not,'' she gasped, wiping tears of laughter from her cheeks with the back of her hand. ''Faith, I beg your p-pardon. It is only that I was made suddenly to realize how ridiculous I was ever to think any of the dreadful things I—''

Abruptly, she broke off at sight of the expression on his face, her mirth giving way instantly to chagrin. ''Lucius, my dearest lord duke, pray forgive me. I should have known you could never do anything so ignoble as to use Effie against me. Really, it is simply too absurd, but for one dreadful moment it occurred to me that you had gone to the lengths of making Effie your legal ward for the sole purpose of coercing me into marrying you.''

''The devil you did,'' growled Traherne, a dangerous light leaping to his eyes. ''I am like to do far worse than that. You, my impossible girl, stand in danger of being throttled to within an inch of your life.''

''Dear, I have upset you, have I not?'' said Althea, aware of the sudden onset of a peculiar queasy sensation in the pit of her stomach, not at the prospect of having the life throttled from her, but at the almost overpowering urge welling up inside her to press her lips to the throbbing vein at the side of her dearest Traherne's neck. A scarlet wave washed over her at what could only be construed as her wanton nature. Flinging up her head, she made herself continue. ''And who can blame you? It was horrid of me to doubt your motives. Obviously, I was not thinking clearly. I do see now, however, that everything you have done was for Effie's sake. My dearest friend, please say you forgive me.''

Finding himself treated to the full entreaty of Althea's spellbinding orbs, Traherne could not but suffer a stab of guilt at the knowledge that she had not been far from the truth in her accusation. Making Effie his legal ward had been only the prelude to officially adopting her, a step that would now undoubtedly have to wait until he had dealt with the trouble that plagued Althea. Cynically, he wondered what his little wood sprite would say if she knew there resided in his coat pocket a special license to marry her issued by the bishop himself. Had Althea been at home to receive him at the Old Mill House four days ago, she would now be the Duchess of Traherne, and he would not be in the damnable position of playing the bloody hypocrite!

Still, it could not be helped, not with a pall of menace hanging over Althea. He knew Althea too well to suppose she could be persuaded to marry him now, when she felt her dearest Effie was in danger. It was one of the things he adored most about her—her selfless devotion to Effie. That it had subsequently proved to be one of the most nerve-racking aspects of her character as well, promised fair to make his immediate future a deal less than tranquil. He felt a hard fist clutch at his vitals at the mere thought of Althea alone against a pair of murderous felons. Indeed, his blood ran cold whenever he was brought to contemplate how things might have turned out had Tom Sykes failed to make a timely appearance. And now, it would seem, her fiercely protective nature was to be a stumbling block in his concerted effort to make sure of the one woman who he no longer doubted was essential to his future happiness.

The devil, he thought. He would wait to make her his bride, but he was damned if he would wait to claim her for his own. *That* he had put off for far too long.

"Lucius? Lucius, what is it?"

Althea, calling his name, brought him to the awareness that he had been staring for no little time into her lovely countenance, the unbearable pressure in his chest at the thought of how close he had come to losing her giving way to a burning need to possess her.

"Lucius, you have been looking at me so strangely. Are you ill?" Instinctively, her hand went to his forehead. "Faith," she exclaimed, her lovely eyes darkening with quick concern, "you are quite warm to the touch. I fear you have taken a fever. You should have a tisane to bring it down. Indeed, Lucius, we must get you to bed at once.''

''The sooner, the better,'' agreed Traherne. While he could not but take exception to the merest notion of imbibing anything quite so loathsome as a dose of barley water, he found her final suggestion an object to be devoutly desired. ''Allow me to relieve you of your pelisse.''

''But, Lucius,'' objected Althea, as Traherne began purposefully to undo the buttons down the front of that particular outer garment, ''I meant *you* must be got to bed.''

''And so I shall be,'' Traherne did not hesitate to reassure her, ''as soon as ever we have rid you of your undeniably attractive carriage dress.'' Having divested her of her velvet pelisse, he enclosed her in his arms, presumably to begin the process of unfastening the plethora of tiny pearl buttons down the back of her dress. ''Have I ever told you how well forest green becomes you?''

''No, Lucius, I cannot recall that you have,'' submitted Althea.

Having found the delectable curve of her neck placed conveniently close at hand, Traherne availed himself of the opportunity to press his lips to it, while Althea experienced what she could only suppose must be the first indications that the duke's fever was highly contagious.

''Well, it does.'' Traherne slid his hand beneath the fabric of her bodice. ''You were wearing forest green the first time I saw you. I knew then you were a wood sprite of uncommon magical powers.''

''Now you are bamming me. Indeed, it is too bad of you,'' said Althea, who found the duke's hand running sensually over and down her back not a little distracting, not to mention stimulating. Indeed, she was having the greatest difficulty focusing on the threads of his conversation.

''It is true, nonetheless,'' asserted Traherne, kissing the exquisite tender flesh beneath her right earlobe. ''I assure you that was the moment you cast your spell over me.''

"But that is preposterous, Lucius." Feeling compelled to protest that, as an advocate and practitioner of scientific methodology, she could hardly give credence to the existence of mythological creatures possessed of magical powers, Althea started to add, "It is naught but a figment of your imagination, induced by—" Upon which, Traherne inserted his hand beneath the waist of her drawers and found the crevice between the twin mounds of her buttocks. "Your *fever,* Lucius!" Giving vent to a startled gasp, she arched against him. "Oh, God, I fear you are delirious."

"You may be sure of it," groaned Traherne. Acutely aware of the hot leap of blood in his veins, he did indeed feel in the grips of a magnificent delirium the likes of which he had never known before. Impatient to have more of her, he worked the gown off her shoulders and over her arms, until it slid down her lissome form to lie, forgotten, in a pile about her feet. A flame leaped in his eyes as the full swell of her bosom in all of its infinite perfection was bared to him. The nipples, already hardened with arousal, stood out like twin berries, ripe for the plucking. "Bloody hell," he uttered, cupping his hand beneath the firm mound of a breast and rubbing his thumb over the peaked nub of her desire, "I am afire with wanting you!"

Althea, who, had been aware for no little time of a melting heat radiating upward from her nether parts at Traherne's manipulations, now felt it manifest itself in something like a hot flash shooting the entire length of her body. *"Faith, Lucius!"* she gasped, sinking her fingernails into the duke's broad powerful shoulders, presumably to keep from succumbing to the sudden onset of weakness in her knees. "You-you cannot know how re-relieved I am to hear it. When you l-left me, I was sure you had t-taken me in aversion."

In aversion, egad! thought Traherne, in the throes of an irresistible gravitational attraction. Supremely conscious of the taut bulge at the front of his breeches that was fast approaching the level of torment, he fairly yanked at the drawstring at the waist of Althea's drawers, which allowed the unmentionables to fall down around her ankles. Indeed, it occurred to him that he could not withstand the power of the wood nymph to arouse him to an ungovernable passion longer than it would take him to get her to her bed.

"You could not have been further from the truth, Althea," Traherne did not hesitate to inform her. "You are, in fact, about to discover just how thoroughly I am in the grips of the male-female compulsion to achieve wholeness through a rapturous joining." Reaching both hands behind her, he grasped her beneath her delectably rounded posterior and lifted her bodily to him.

"LUCIUS?" No doubt it was purely instinct that prompted Althea to clasp her legs about his waist and her arms around his neck, as Traherne bore her purposefully across the room to her bed. "I cannot think this is at all wise. Your fever, Lucius. You might harm yourself with extreme exertion."

"The fever be damned," growled Traherne. In an agony of desire, he could not but think he would be exceedingly unwise at this point to cease what he was doing. Harm him? Hellfire, he did not doubt it would do him irreparable damage if he did not finish what he had started! "Pray don't concern yourself, Althea. I could not stop now if I wanted to. I'm afraid I really must have you. Say you want me too, Althea. Tell me you cannot wait to have me."

"I do want you, Lucius," replied Althea, with a fervor that quite took Traherne's breath away. "I have wanted you for ever so long and never more than I want you now."

"Sweet, generous, fiery Althea," breathed Traherne. Planting his knee on the bed, he dropped Althea down amid the billowy softness of the eiderdown comforter. Then in a fever of impatience, he flung out of his waistcoat and stripped off his shirt, followed equally swiftly by his boots, stockings, and breeches.

At last he leaned over her, a hand propped on the bed on either side of her. His eyes, feverish in the firelight, drank in her fresh loveliness. How gravely she returned his gaze! "Tell me how much you want me, Althea," he commanded, swept with sudden unreasoning doubt. "Show me you need me, little wood sprite."

"I need and want you, Your Grace," declared Althea on a tremulous breath as she reached slender arms about his neck. "so much, my dearest lord duke," she confessed, in the throes of emotions over which she had no control, "that, even if you had not come after me, I think I should not have found the heart to leave England." She drew his head down to her and kissed him with all the sweet unbridled longing that she had kept locked away in her heart. Then releasing him, she smiled mistily into his eyes. "And now I know I cannot. Not ever, Lucius, not so long as you want me."

"Althea," uttered Traherne, his breath harsh in his throat. Good God, she set his blood on fire. In her innocence, she had breached his defenses as no other woman ever had or ever could. She touched his soul with her earthen magic. He had never thought to desire a woman as he desired the impossibly stubborn, maddeningly independent, wholly captivating Althea Wintergreen; and she had told him she could not leave him!

That confession filled him with a sudden fierce elation that was as surprising as it was unexpected. Althea loved him, and being Althea, she would never prove false. He had never thought to find a woman like his magnificent wood sprite.

His hunger, a gnawing thing inside him, he held her face between his hands while he devoured her with his eyes—until at last her lips parted in silent entreaty.

"Althea," he groaned. Then, covering her mouth with his, he thrust his tongue between her teeth to taste of her exquisite sweetness.

Carried on the rising swell of a passion, the likes of which she had never dreamed possible, Althea arched and writhed beneath Traherne. Never had she felt such a storm of desire in her dearest lord duke. Gone was the man of steely restraint who had treated her with patience, biding his time until he had won past her defenses and made himself an indispensable part of her life. In his place was a man driven to possess her.

With savage tenderness, he devoured her with his lips, aroused her with his hands. And when at last he drove himself into her, her only coherent thought was that she wished he could love her, if only a little. Then even that was lost as she was carried away in a rapturous explosion of release and Traherne, covering her mouth with his, spilled his seed inside her

Chapter Nine

"His name is Merrick," said Althea, lying on her side facing Traherne, her head cradled in the crook of one arm, while the fingertips of her free hand wandered absently through the mat of hair on the duke's chest. "Or at least that is what he called himself then. Evelyn Merrick. Faith, how I loathe that name! Unfortunately, you may be certain he has long since discarded it for another."

"You may be equally certain," observed Traherne, capturing her hand and carrying it to his lips, "that even that will not save him. Whatever name he is hiding behind, we will find him." A gleam flickered in his eyes. "I did mention, did I not, that I employ a highly efficient private secretary."

"Indeed—Mr. Phips, is it not?" smiled Althea whimsically. How easy it was, she marveled, to tell Traherne the things she had kept so long to herself. But then, she had always, save for that one moment of madness, sensed that Traherne was a man to be trusted. Her smile faded as she returned to a contemplation of Evelyn Merrick. "Mr. Phips will, however, have his work cut out for him. Merrick is as slippery as an eel, and he is wholly devoid of scruples, something I could not impress upon Gloriana, no matter how hard I tried or how flagrantly Merrick scouted every code of human decency.''

''It has been my experience,'' murmured Traherne with an air of bemusement, ''that there is nothing quite so difficult as trying to convince a Wintergreen of anything, once she has made up her mind not to be persuaded.''

''Wretch!'' Althea choked on a helpless burble of laughter. ''I have only been trying to save you from having us foisted on you, along with all our baggage, when there was never the slightest need for it.''

''A hideous prospect,'' agreed the duke, relieved to see the shadows banished from his wood nymph's eyes, if only for the moment. ''No doubt I should thank you for it, never mind that I am perfectly capable of deciding for myself what is best for me. But for now, tell me more about Merrick.''

''Merrick, indeed,'' Althea said with a grimace. ''When he first started to pay marked attention to Gloriana behind the colonel's back, I began to make inquiries. Merrick was, to say the least, enterprising. I daresay he amassed a fortune in 'gifts' from various native princes, not to mention village chieftains, in exchange for the Company's protection; indeed, he must have done, for he lived in the lavish style of a Nabob. I know for a fact that he was exceedingly generous in the goods he allotted to his own private business enterprises to the detriment of his employer. Worse, I had evidence he was involved in the opium and slave trades as well. I dare not think how many girls and young women, not to mention boys of a comely appearance, were bought and sold to add gold to his coffers! And even that was not enough to satisfy his overweening ambition. He would have the younger daughter of the Governor of Madras to add to his laurels as well, never mind that she was not yet turned seventeen at the time.''

Traherne closed strong fingers about the captive hand in

his. "You did not expect the knave to set his sights on you, did you, Althea?" he said quietly. "I have known his sort before. A wolf goes after the lamb, not the tigress. The lamb is by far the easier prey."

"Tigress, good God! I was a witless fool, blinded by my own selfish pride to the truth. Merrick was a serpent, and Gloriana should have been better protected. I failed her, Lucius. At the moment that she needed me most, I looked away."

At her first outburst of anguish, Traherne pulled Althea strongly into his arms and held her. His hand moved slowly over her hair and his face grew grim with the realization that, all those years, she had been blaming herself for her sister's folly—Althea, who had never done anything false or base in her life!

"You are many things, Althea," he said after a moment, "but you are hardly witless or a fool. Furthermore, I sincerely doubt that you could ever be accused of selfishness. Think back, wood sprite, to the way things were for you and your sister. You could not have been much more than eighteen yourself at the time. Does it not occur to you that there was nothing you could have done to avert what happened, short of locking your sister in a cellar?"

The thought of Gloriana locked in a cellar startled a choke of laughter from Althea. "Good heavens, if only I had *had* a cellar!" she exclaimed, much struck at the possibilities. Tilting her head back to look at him, she smiled ruefully.

"After I fled Madras with Gloriana, I made sure Merrick's duplicity and corruption were exposed to his superiors in the East India Company. It could not make up for what he had done to Gloriana, but I hoped it might put a period to his lucrative trade in human souls. How naive I was!"

"It was determined Merrick had done nothing in violation of the Company's charter," the duke surmised. "They would hardly frown on his having accepted gifts from the native princes. Lord Clive himself was exonerated from blame for it. It is done all the time, as is the practice of agents involved in private trade. It is tacitly understood to be one of the compensations for a man's incurring the risk of leaving his home and undertaking to live in a hostile foreign environment. As for the other, the opium and slave trades have been practiced in India for time immemorial and, as such, are considered a part of the fabric of the culture. The Company itself is not averse to exploiting their existence to its own profit when it suits its purpose.''

"How well you have grasped the situation!" Althea exclaimed with a wry grimace. "I was thanked for my concern, misplaced though it obviously was, and was politely informed Mr. Merrick was considered one of the Company's most trusted agents. Had it not been for an accident of fate, I daresay he would still be in Madras, and I should not now be here in your arms.''

No, reflected Traherne sardonically, she would be in his bed at Meresgate and she would be his wife. But then, there had been certain compensations, he reminded himself. Althea had said that she could not have brought herself to follow through with her plans to leave England. Indeed, she had said she could never bring herself to leave him for so long as he wanted her!

"And what accident of fate was that?" he asked, little knowing whether to thank or damn the powers that be.

"Something so seemingly insignificant as a clerical error," replied Althea with a bemused quirk of her lovely lips. "It seems shortly after our arrival in England, one of those princes who was so generous to Merrick requested the escort of a company of the colonel's sepoys for a caravan coming to him from a neighboring province. Unfortunately, the clerk apparently got it backward. Imagine the prince's chagrin when the company of sepoys arrived at his palace expecting to ride guard on a caravan that had already been lost to Pathan banditti for lack of an escort. Unfortunately for Merrick and the prince, the caravan was carrying tribute that must have been worth a king's ransom. From what the colonel wrote, Merrick was lucky to escape India with a whole skin, while his fortune remained forfeit in the hands of the disgruntled prince.''

''And now he is in England and reduced, it would seem, to plotting to abduct the colonel's granddaughter,'' mused Traherne. ''Why, after all these years, would he come after Effie, and to what possible purpose?''

''He *is* Effie's father,'' offered Althea. ''That is the really dreadful thing. When Gloriana turned seventeen, I persuaded the colonel to bring her out. I thought, in the excitement of her first Season, she would forget all about Merrick. And, indeed, for a while it seemed to be working. She was happy, vibrant. No doubt being the center of a bevy of eligible admirers went a little to her head. However, it was not long before it became obvious a young captain had won her affections. I was sure he would offer for her. And then something happened. Gloriana broke it off with him. Worse, she began to openly take up with Merrick, even going so far as to flaunt it before everyone. When I tried to take her to task for her behavior, she laughed at me. There was a terrible scene, and I'm afraid I took snuff. I washed my hands of her.''

''And consequently have heaped blame upon yourself ever since. It was not your fault, Althea,'' he said, gripping her arm. ''It is time you let go of it and began to think of yourself.''

Swallowing, Althea shook her head. ''I should have seen she was only acting out of desperation. When she finally came to me, it was too late. Merrick had had his way with her. She was terrified of him. He had threatened to kill her young captain if she married him. She was convinced Merrick would have us all murdered one night as we lay in our beds if she did not do exactly as he told her.''

''As he told her?'' queried Traherne, his glance narrowing on Althea's face. ''You mean marry him.''

"Hardly." Althea gave vent to a bitter laugh. "It seemed he had never the least intention of doing the honorable thing. He made that clear enough when I went to him to demand he leave Gloriana alone."

"*You* went to him!" Good God! thought Traherne, marveling that the colonel's daughter, with her unnerving propensity for charging into danger, had managed to survive to adulthood. It was a facet of her character that boded ill for his future peace of mind.

"Well, naturally, Lucius, what else was I to do?" replied Althea, as if there was never any question that an exceedingly young, unmarried female should brace the serpent in its lair. "Clearly, it was imperative to sever Merrick's hold on Gloriana. Unfortunately, he did not prove to be of a reasonable frame of mind."

"No, did he not?" Traherne commented with an incredulous arch of his aristocratic eyebrows. "And what, precisely, did Mr. Merrick do?"

"He laughed at me. Then, when I threatened to inform the colonel that I knew Merrick had been in league with Amir Khan's Pathan banditti, indeed, that I had evidence he had sold them guns—which was only a stab in the dark, but apparently was closer to the truth than was comfortable for Merrick—he came at me with every intention, I doubt not, of doing me bodily harm. He left me little choice in the matter. I shot him."

"You shot him," echoed Traherne. "But of course you did. I can only wonder how it is that he is still alive."

"I am a very good shot, Lucius," Althea replied with perfect candor. "The colonel insisted on that. I did not shoot to kill Merrick, though perhaps I should have done, considering all the trouble he has caused. As it was, I only wanted to incapacitate him long enough for me to make an exit. I shot him in the foot, a circumstance for which he was not in the least grateful. As a matter of fact, he promised any number of dire fates for me, my sister, and the brat she carried. So, you see, he has a very good motive for trying to abduct Effie. I daresay he must view it in light of icing on the cake. Had he succeeded in getting his hands on Effie, you may be sure Gloriana would even now be in possession of a ransom note demanding a princely sum for Effie's return and for ensuring his silence about Effie's parentage.''

"Only, you believe Merrick would not have been inclined to return the child," Traherne speculated darkly, "even if the viscountess paid the sum."

"It has been my darkest, most enduring nightmare," confessed Althea. "Certainly, he could find no surer way of mortally wounding my sister and me."

"The devil, he meant to keep Effie hidden away somewhere, while he bled you and your sister dry."

"And when we could no longer pay, he would most assuredly have sold her into slavery. He has, after all, done it innumerable times before with other poor souls. And that is why I have been willing to do anything to keep Effie hidden, even flee to America with the intention of forever vanishing from sight, which was my intention until you found us, Lucius. Indeed, now that you know the nature of the trouble that is pursuing me, I should understand perfectly if you decided to separate yourself from any further involvement. I do wish you will think about it, Lucius. I should never forgive myself if anything happened to you because of me."

For Traherne, a great deal had been made suddenly, exceedingly clear, not the least of which was why Althea remained adamantly opposed to marrying him. He felt a cold fist clamp down on his vitals at the realization of how close he had come to losing her forever. Althea had not only been planning to leave England. Egad, she had meant to lose herself and Effie in the vast wilds of the Americas! He experienced the birth of a slow burning rage at thought of the man who could drive the indomitable colonel's daughter to such desperate measures.

Watching him, Althea felt a cold chill explore her spine at the look in his eyes. Then he was drawing her close.

"There is nothing to consider, Althea." Lightly, he pressed his lips to her hair. "It is settled. Tomorrow we shall take Effie to Reading, where, she will be delighted to discover, Pegasus has already taken up residence."

"Pegasus—!" Althea pulled away to stare at Traherne with startled indignation. "The devil, Lucius, how dared you be so sure of yourself!"

"Rather say I was certain of you, wood sprite," he emended, a twitch at the corners of his mouth. "You are, after all, a female of uncommon logic. Presented with the proper criteria for making a judgment, you were sure to arrive at the only conclusion possible in the circumstances."

"Wretch!" declared Althea, made to feel little better at the lowering thought that she was so entirely predictable to the odious duke. Upon which, a wave of tenderness welled up inside her at this further evidence of his thoughtfulness. How much easier must Effie find it to adjust to new and strange surrounds with a dear friend on hand to welcome her!

"If I am predictable," she said, favoring Traherne with a look that threatened to bring on an immediate recurrence of his earlier fever, "then you, my dearest lord duke, stand convicted of being exceedingly kind. And pray don't deny it."

"Althea—" Traherne uttered in tones of protest, only to be instantly silenced.

Althea, lifting her arms around his neck, kissed him full on the mouth.

"Thank you, Lucius, for Effie and myself," she murmured some moments later, when rendered breathless by Traherne's unreserved response to her gesture of gratitude, she pulled away to draw in a shuddering gasp of air. "And I am sorry to have been the cause of so much trouble. I am well aware you have been thinking I should have, from the very first, turned the entire matter over to my father, who must seem to you by now a remarkably indifferent parent.''

''It has occurred to me to wonder why, thus far, you have failed to mention him,'' confessed Traherne, who at the moment could not have cared less about the absent colonel. But he sensed, nonetheless, that his wood nymph felt the need to explain her apparent oversight. ''Or his part in all of this. Having come to know his remarkable elder daughter, however, I suppose I assumed he had long since come to rely on you to handle all of the household matters. And you, being who you are, never thought to burden him with the onset of your sister's unruly pubescence. My poor Althea. You were only a girl yourself. The responsibility for Gloriana should never have devolved on you.''

''She was my sister, Lucius, and our mama was gone. And as for the colonel? Well''—Althea shrugged—''he is the Colonel. In his own way he has always done what he thought was best for us. I'm afraid it never occurred to him to interfere in our lives, for which I have always been grateful. I am, after all, hopelessly independent and pride myself on being a freethinker. It is, perhaps, an aspect of my character that you have failed to consider, Lucius,'' she added, an irrepressible imp peeping out of roguish eyes. ''No matter how hard I might try, there is every possibility I should never make a conformable wife. As a mistress, however—''

''You should soon find yourself out in the cold, my girl,'' growled Traherne, rolling over on top of her, the better, presumably, to impress upon her the error of her thinking. ''A man,'' he continued, pressing his lips into the curve of her neck, then lower, to the ivory perfection of her shoulder, and lower still, to the valley between her breasts, ''expects his mistress to pleasure him, not only in his bed . . .'' Greatly pleasured by his momentary detour to the rosy bud of a nipple, Althea was moved to arch her back and tangle her fingers in his hair. ''But in her demeanor, as well,'' rasped the duke, marveling at the supple beauty of her.

Flinging back the bedcovers, the better to continue his instruction, he inserted himself between her thighs. "She is subservient to his whims." Giving into sudden whimsy, he brought her knees to her chest. "His desires, his every mood." His desire manifesting itself in his magnificently erect member, he found himself in the mood to drive them both to a frenzy of passion. "And should she fail to conform to his expectations of what is pleasing"—he spread her knees apart—"she may expect to find herself—" He leaned over her to press his swollen member against the petals of her body. Flinging her arms above her head, Althea opened to him, her eyes, dark with sublime passion, pleading with him. "In the lurch!" he gasped and drove himself into her in long slow forays of discovery.

"Lucius!" Althea cried, in the grips of incontrovertible natural forces, not the least of which was an insurmountable yearning to achieve the universal principle of male-female wholeness. Good God, she was like to explode with it! "I do love you, Lucius. Indeed, I cannot help loving you."

"Althea!" gasped Traherne, lifted to new heights. Then feeling her reach for completion, he thrust deep, spilling his seed inside her.

Moments later, lying sated beyond her wildest imaginings, Althea could not but reflect that the irresistible mechanisms of nature were truly wonders of Creation. Indeed, she doubted not that there could never be an automatic mechanical machine to compare to the marvel of the rapturous joining of two disparate bodies to achieve a mystic oneness.

"Lucius," she said in awe-stricken tones. "Does it occur to you that, in my entire life, I can never hope to invent anything quite so magnificent as what you and I have just fashioned between us? And the truly marvelous thing is that we can re-create it again and again *ad infinitum,* seemingly out of the air itself and whenever we like, rather like a machine set into perpetual motion."

Traherne, who had collapsed facedown on the bed beside

Althea, an arm flung over her waist and his breath coming in ragged gusts while he willed his heart to return to a semblance of its normal rate, could only receive that sublime observation with something less than his unqualified agreement. Patently, his indefatigable wood nymph was prepared to indulge in a perpetual orgy of excursions into the realm of the natural mechanism of human procreation! Ruefully he acknowledged he was far from feeling equal at present even to contemplate such a gargantuan task as that must be. Indeed, his greatest ambition at the moment was to sink into a blissful state of undisturbed torpidity. Still, he reflected, summoning the strength to heave himself over on his back to better draw Althea into the cradle of his arm, he could not but find such a proposition potent with intriguing possibilities.

"I suggest, rather than a perpetual motion machine, it is more realistic to employ the metaphor of a feast," he submitted reflectively. "A feast whose tables are ever spread with savory offerings just waiting for us to drop in and gorge ourselves, which we shall do with the frequency of dedicated gluttons. In which case, you, my adorable wood sprite, would do much better as my duchess than as my mistress."

"Oh, I should, should I?" queried Althea, propping her chin on the back of her hand laid on his chest and gazing speculatively into his eyes. "For the life of me, I cannot see why. Surely the appetite of a mistress is no less than that of a wife."

"Precisely, my sweet," applauded Traherne, apparently pleased that she had so easily grasped the obvious. "However, even a glutton, presented with the prospect of feasting with a wife *and* a mistress of equal appetites, especially if you are the gauge, must soon be made to founder. You had better marry me, my ravenous little wood sprite. Duty requires I take a wife, and feasting with you, it seems, will require my every ounce of strength."

Noting the distinct droop of his eyelids, Althea could not

deny that her dearest lord duke would indeed seem at the moment inordinately drained by their recent gorging. How strange that she, who had felt weighted down with fatigue and something very nearly approaching despair only a few hours earlier, should now feel imbued from head to foot with a rich, warm inner glow of vitality.

Truly, the natural mechanisms of human procreation were marvels of an ingenious design!

"But, Lucius," she said, pressing her lips tenderly to Traherne's muscled chest, "besides bringing scandal to your house, I am hopelessly set in my ways. Really, my dearest lord duke, you should have a wife who is young and malleable, one whom you can mold to suit her exalted position."

"Egad, what a dead bore that must be!" declared Traherne, sufficiently roused from the lethargy into which he had been deliciously sinking to correct anything so utterly erroneous as Althea's absurd supposition. "I neither require nor remotely desire a conformable wife. The unenticing prospect of wedding a green girl only just out of the schoolroom is precisely what has kept me from falling to Parson's Mousetrap—until now. The thing I like most about you, my absurd little wood nymph, is that you are fully formed and are, most assuredly, not in need of any molding from me. You may be equally certain, I should never ask you to be anything but yourself."

"Would you not?" queried Althea, much struck by such an assertion from Traherne. She turned her gaze to the flicker of the fire lest he see the sudden mist of tears in her eyes. "For if you must know, Lucius, I was not sure that you liked me at all. After all, I have been nothing but trouble for you from the very first instant that we met. You can hardly overlook the fact that it was my fault you fell into the lake. And, certainly, matters have hardly improved since. I confess I . . ."

Whatever Althea had been about to confess, however, was to remain forever in the realm of speculation, as she was interrupted at that very moment by the soft, but unmistakable, susurrus of a snore issuing from her dearest lord duke.

A tender smile twisted at her lips, as she raised her head to gaze at Traherne's dearly beloved face. How young he appeared, wrapped in slumber, a rebellious raven lock falling in abandonment across his forehead and the stern lines about his eyes and mouth all but vanished in peaceful repose! Carefully, she lifted herself away from his chest and, easing off the bed to gather up the bedclothes, covered him against the chill in the room. Then, filled with a strange sense of restlessness, she retrieved her nightdress, dressing gown, and bed slippers from her trunk and slipped them on. At last, taking up a candle, she lit it and let herself out into the hall.

The house—a three-story Georgian brown brick, which undoubtedly had been designed, like those on either side of it and lining the block along both sides of the street, to house a moderately successful tradesman and his family—lacked the homey charm of the rustic Elizabethan mill house on Ullswater. Nevertheless, it was solidly and comfortably built and had been well maintained, at Althea's expense, to afford a pleasant haven on her infrequent visits to the City. Besides Miss Stoddart, the housekeeper, who also performed the duties of cook, the household was comprised of Mary Crenshawe and Sally Higgens, the upstairs and downstairs maids, respectively; Mirabel Jones, the scullery maid; Toby Heath, the stablelad; and Dick Turpin, the groundskeeper. In the four years of their employment, they had assumed the closely knit fabric of a family, which Althea did not hesitate to attribute to the fact that they were seldom bothered by the presence of their employers. It was a circumstance that afforded them the greatest sort of independence while providing a very respectable income along with a more-than-decent roof over their heads. Althea had hoped the pleasant arrangements would ensure their loyalty; indeed, she had come in time to believe no one in the house would ever betray her by word or deed if for no other reason than that it would cost all of them their positions.

Now, however, it would seem she had been living in a fool's paradise, Althea reflected, as she made her way down the hall to look in on Effie. The truth was, she had never been safe in this house. There had always been the distinct possibility that Merrick would find it, just as Traherne's Mr. Phips had done. No doubt that realization was what was keeping her from her bed and the waiting bliss of Traherne's strong arms, she told herself, and knew immediately it was more than that.

She very much feared that she had slipped more than a cog or two in her own estimation. Indeed, she was perilously close to betraying every tenet she had ever set for herself. But then, Traherne had made it utterly impossible for her to continue as she had been, indeed, as she had thought always to do. He had taken the reins out of her hands, and, certainly, he had been right about one thing: She could not possibly have gone on refusing his aid. His way offered the only hope of making sure once and for all of Effie's safety. The question was, What was she to do after the thing was done? When they found Merrick and put an end to his evil schemes, what then?

Obviously, Traherne foresaw only one possible conclusion to their impossible situation. He fully expected her to become his scandalous duchess. Why else should he have gone to such lengths to involve himself in her troubles? If she was wrong to agree to marry him for a baseless notion of honor, then how much greater would her wrong be to refuse him after he had helped to save her from her enemies—even going so far as to gladly place himself at risk for her and Effie!

Really, it was too bad of him! she thought, as she let

herself into the nursery and tiptoed across the room to gaze down at the sleeping child. The sight of her dearest Effie, locked in innocent slumber, served to bring home with awful clarity the impossible coil in which she found herself. Blowing out the candle and setting it aside on a table, she sank down into the rocking chair beside Effie's bed.

It was not enough that she must love Traherne with her whole heart and being. Now she must find her own sense of integrity in direct opposition to the yearning of her heart. She could not, no matter how greatly her happiness might depend upon it, marry Traherne out of gratitude! Faith, what sort of foundation would *that* be for a marriage? The irresistible forces of nature, which had been the cause of the dilemma in which they now found themselves, could not indefinitely sustain a marriage in and of themselves. Even a marriage blessed with a mutual, all-consuming love, such as the one her mama and papa had known, had been beset with difficulties, which must have seemed at times insurmountable to the two involved. What possible hope could there be for a marriage entered into for all the wrong reasons and in which the love was all one-sided?

In the end, Traherne must surely come to despise the pact he had made. Indeed, she doubted not that he must inevitably come to loathe the wife he would never have chosen for himself had not circumstances dictated otherwise, and that she simply *could* not bear.

And yet, what other choice had she? she wondered, wrapping her dressing gown more firmly around her and leaning her head against the chair back. It came to her, feeling her eyelids drift irresistibly down over her eyes, that she was far too tired to think at all clearly. Indeed, she doubted not tomorrow would be soon enough to sort things out.

The dream came with frightening clarity. She was in the house in Madras. It was the dead of night, and she was in the room she shared with Gloriana. Something had awakened her—a step in the dark, the rustle of the wind-tossed curtain, a sense of impending danger, which had reached through to her even in slumber. In mounting horror, it came to her that she was held in the grips of an immobilizing force that rendered her powerless. Somehow she knew with terrible certainty that something—*someone*—had entered the room. Indeed, she sensed, rather than saw, the shadow of a man bending over the bed, bending over Gloriana! Assassins! Good God, she thought.

And suddenly she was free of the paralysis, freed by the terrible sense of need to protect Gloriana.

Only it was not Gloriana, but Effie! Althea was awake, and the shape was real—a man. He was scooping the sleeping child into his arms!

"Stop!" Althea flung herself out of the chair and hurled herself at the intruder, her hands clutching at Effie. *"Lucius, help me! Lucius, he is after Effie!"*

It seemed, then, that the room erupted in chaos. Effie, startled into wakefulness and finding herself in the arms of a stranger, began to scream in terror. Mrs. Fennigrew lumbered into the room with a lamp in one hand. Taking a single look at the scene being enacted before her, she set the lamp aside and snatched up the nearest weapon to hand, in this case a child's pink parasol, which she wielded, poking and jabbing, with a telling efficiency that might have won the admiration of a fencing master. The besieged felon gave a bellow of pain and rage and swung a backhanded blow at Althea, striking her on the side of her jaw with enough force to send her reeling backward into the rocking chair. Upon which, clutching the shrieking Effie in one arm to his chest, he spun on the ferocious nanny.

"Enough!" Traherne's single utterance, couched in steely accents and accompanied by the cold touch of a gun barrel to the felon's temple, was sufficient to freeze the villain where he stood. "Yes, that is better," Traherne murmured

with velvety softness. "I suggest, however, you remain exceedingly still." With his free arm, he reached for the child. "Effie, come to me, *enfant.*"

The child, casting a single frightened glance at the duke, ceased her wailing and, with a shuddering sob, flung herself at Traherne. "Softly, *enfant*," said Traherne, holding her tightly in his arm. "Althea!" he uttered sharply, never taking his eyes off his captive.

Althea, who had never been so glad to see anyone as she had been to see the duke suddenly appear, clad only in his breeches, his eyes glinting sparks of steel, made a valiant attempt to rally her flagging senses. "Y-yes, Lucius. I am-am fine. Only a trifle shaken."

Something exceedingly grim eased slightly from the chiseled hardness of Traherne's features. "Mrs. Fennigrew, you will kindly take Effie to your room."

"Indeed, Your Grace. There, there, child," crooned the nanny, quick to take the weeping little girl from Traherne. "There's nothing to fear now."

Effie, however, was not to be so easily comforted. "Althie," she sobbed, reaching outstretched arms to Althea. "Althie!"

"Yes, dear." Althea, who had already shoved herself to her feet, to stand swaying dizzily, lurched to the side of the bed. "Everything is fine now, dearest," she said, assaying a reassuring smile. "You needn't be frightened. Go with Nessie. I must stay and help Lucius for a moment, but I shall come to you directly. I promise."

"Is Lucius going to stay with us, Althie? He won't leave us, will he?" The child clutched tightly to Althea.

"No, Effie. Lucius will not leave us. He is going to stay. You need not be afraid." Gently disengaging herself from the little girl's clinging hands, Althea nodded to Nessie to take Effie away.

Hardly had the door closed behind the nanny and the

child than Althea turned to face the villain, standing staring morosely at the flower design in the Aubusson carpet.

"And now," she said, feeling suddenly and immensely weary, "perhaps you will explain yourself, Dick Turpin."

"I am not so much surprised at Turpin's defection," Althea said, no little time later as she stood watching the first blush of dawn beyond her bedroom window, "as I am saddened by it. I had no idea he was the sort to engage excessively in games of chance. But then, I really do not know him—or the others of the household—all that well. I fear I simply took their loyalty for granted. Faith, how many good men have been ruined by gambling!"

"He knew what he was doing, Althea," Traherne observed coldly. Far from sharing Althea's sympathy for the man who had betrayed her to the extent of striking her in the face in an attempt to abduct an innocent child for the sake of a gambling debt, Traherne would have had the miserable cur transported to the penal colonies. Instead, he had found himself acceding to Althea's wishes in the matter. Clearly, he had taken leave of his senses. But then, the little wood sprite would seem to have that sort of unsettling effect on him.

"You do not approve of my method of handling the situation." It was a statement, not a question. She turned her head to look at Traherne over her shoulder. He was fully dressed. Save for the distinct shadow of a beard along the lean jaw, which served only to accentuate his compelling masculinity, there was little to betray that he had been up most of the night or that, behind the facade of steely composure, was contained a cold burning anger.

"What? Allowing the man to stay on here and even going so far as to give him the wherewithal to pay his gambling debts? In exchange for what, Althea? Do you really think you can trust him not to betray you again? He sold his soul to the devil once. You may be sure he will find it even easier to do so again in future.''

"Perhaps," Althea conceded, the image of Turpin, falling to his knees in tearful contrition and gratitude, seemingly etched in her brain. She had believed him when he said he had not meant to strike her, that it had been an unfortunate accident. That did not, however, excuse him for what he had intended for Effie. Still, he had been convinced he was doing nothing more than uniting a father with his long-lost daughter. No doubt Turpin had felt there was nothing wrong in that, perhaps that there was even a measure of justification in it. It hardly mattered now, she thought, feeling unutterably weary in the wake of the night's events.

"On the other hand, I had to try," she said. "Turpin is our only link to Merrick. If Merrick contacts him again, there is at least a chance Turpin will send word to your Mr. Phips. Besides," she shrugged, turning again to gaze out the window, "it hardly signifies. He can pose no further threat to Effie. In which case, there would seem little to be gained from a punitive action and a great deal to be lost. He is promised to marry, did you know that? To Sally Higgens, one of the maids. You must have noticed how upset they all were. I believe it was shame for what Turpin had done."

"You may be sure of it," said Traherne, who would gladly have consigned Turpin and all the others to the devil if it meant it would banish the pain and disillusionment from his wood nymph's eyes. Althea had been right about one thing, however. It would precipitate a deal fewer complications to simply turn Turpin loose. The last thing he could wish was for Althea and himself to be involved in a trial, even one as summary as would have been Turpin's merit. The mere mention that the Duke of Traherne had been called as witness in a case of the attempted abduction of a child would have brought everything out in the open and into the public notice. Not that he had ever contemplated a trial for the wretch. It had been his intention to put Turpin in the way of one of the navy's press-gangs. It was exceedingly doubtful he would ever have been heard from again.

Only, Althea, being Althea, had insisted on dealing with Turpin in her own inimitable way.

Coming up behind her, he clasped her lightly by the shoulders. "Be that as it may, however, you do know you cannot stay here. The sooner we are away, the better."

"Away?" Reaching up to cover his hand with one of her own, she leaned her weight against him. "Yes, of course, to Reading. In all the excitement I had almost forgot. I wish it had not to be so soon. Effie needs time to recover from her fright. How can I possibly leave her in a strange place with unfamiliar people so soon after all that has happened?"

"Obviously, you cannot. But then, we are not going to Reading. Not just yet. First, there is the little matter of our nuptials, followed by a lengthy honeymoon at Meresgate. I regret that it cannot be the south of France or the Swiss Alps, or even a walking tour in Scotland, but—"

"But that is impossible!" exclaimed Althea, jarred out of her momentary feeling of apathy.

"Quite so, my dove," agreed Traherne, without missing a heartbeat. "There is the small inconvenience of the war on the Continent, and clearly this is not the best time of year to visit the Highlands. I should say late spring or summer would be far more congenial for our purposes."

"No, how dare you pretend to misunderstand me!" objected Althea, coming around to face him. "I mean it is impossible for me to marry you."

"It not only is possible, but, in light of present circumstances, it is become wholly unavoidable." Clasping her firmly by the arms, Traherne held her where she was. "Althea, think. You said yourself Effie must have time to recover from last night's traumatic events. She will do much better with us for the time being. You may be sure Merrick will not penetrate the defenses at Meresgate. Not even the Scots were able to do that. You and Effie will be safe.''

''Safe, Lucius, but at what cost?'' demanded Althea. ''If I could not accept your offer before, how much less can I now in exchange for my safety and Effie's?''

''You can because it *is* for Effie's safety and because I have no intention of accepting no for an answer.''

''But Merrick—'' Althea insisted, feeling her defenses crumbling before Traherne's determined assault. ''He must be returned to London soon. He might be here even now. How can we possibly conduct a search from the borders of Scotland? And I must see Gloriana, to warn her—''

''Winslade and the viscountess have removed to Blydesdel for the winter and will not return to Town until the Season. You must have known that, Althea. And as for Merrick, he will keep. You may be certain I shall have men out looking for him. In the meantime, we shall have bought time for Effie and time to rally our forces. When we return to Town in the spring, we shall know how to proceed.''

''In the spring,'' echoed Althea, struggling to gather her wits about her. Everything was happening so fast. She wished only for time to think. And then at last it hit her: Traherne meant to bring her back to London for the Season. Good God, he meant to present her to the *ton*—faith, to all the world—as his wife, his duchess; and he would do so, knowing Merrick would hear of it. ''The devil, Lucius,'' she exclaimed, turning on Traherne with accusing eyes. ''You intend to draw Merrick out by offering yourself up as the bait!''

''And how not, my dove?'' conceded Traherne, with a chilling smile. ''I daresay Mr. Merrick will find the temptation of my name and the fortune that it commands exceeds his wildest dreams of avarice.''

Chapter Ten

Restlessly, Althea turned away from the sitting-room window overlooking the rolling grounds of the Campden Hill district, bristling with trees only just bursting out in foliage, and resumed her pacing before the fire laid out in the white Adams fireplace.

It was the end of March, and the Duke and Duchess of Traherne had taken up residence in Town. Faith, the whole world was about to be made aware of it! thought Althea, feeling slightly giddy at the realization. It hardly seemed that it had been five months since she had stood up with Traherne before the bishop and spoken the marriage vows. It felt more like only yesterday; indeed, she had yet to actually convince herself she was no longer simply Althea Wintergreen, the colonel's daughter, but in truth the Duchess of Traherne. The months at Meresgate had slipped by, like a dream of something that was happening to someone else— a sweet, magical dream in which she had been drawn closer than she could ever have thought possible to the strong, complicated man who was her husband.

Her husband! A fiery blush spread upward, flooding her face with color. How strange that a simple ceremony and a slip of paper could make such a difference! That first time they had lain together as husband and wife, he had made love to her with a fierce tender possessiveness, the mere memory of which was enough to suffuse her entire being with a wondrous warmth. Truly, it was something beyond the mere natural mechanism of human procreation! There had been something added—a new dimension of awareness, which owed itself to the knowledge that they were inextricably joined. It had manifested itself in a burgeoning new relationship, a relationship of the intimate sharing of themselves. She had first noticed this singular new phenomenon occurred after passion had spent itself, leaving them physically and emotionally sated, but singularly open and unguarded, vulnerable even to a deeper sort of emotion, which might express itself in a silent contented touching, devoid of that other breathless passion, or in quiet talk about things of a personal nature.

It was in one of these quiet moments of shared intimacy that Traherne had first broached the matter of his mother's elopement with an itinerant actor. No doubt it had been instigated by Althea's own revelation that she had met the duchess briefly in Madras only weeks before Althea had fled with Gloriana to England.

"I have been wondering, Lucius," she said, as she lay on her side facing him, "why you have never mentioned her."

She had sensed at once that she had touched on a topic that was not entirely of a felicitous nature. But then, a woman of keen observation, she had not failed to note that the ancient pile demonstrated a singular lack of the least thing that could be attributed to the influence of the previous duchess—not even so much as a portrait of her in the otherwise well populated picture gallery. It had naturally piqued her curiosity, but more than that, it had, strangely enough, touched a chord of memory: That day, in the withdrawing room at Briersly, Traherne had drawn her into his arms to kiss her for the very first time, even as he warned her that he laid no claim to the softer human emotions. It had struck her as singular even then.

"Nor have you," murmured Traherne, taking the opportunity to brush a delightfully rebellious curl from her forehead. "And you find it strange in me. Yes, naturally you do. No doubt I should myself if I had not long ago ceased to think about her at all. I must suppose no one has told you yet about my esteemed mama. But of course no one has. After all, it is a subject my father forbade to be mentioned in this house, an order I simply have never bothered to rescind. You, however, have a right to know about the family into which you have married. The bald facts are that my mother eloped with a traveling thespian twenty-six years ago and I have never seen or spoken to her since."

"How very singular of her," commented Althea. Exceedingly adept at mathematics, she had suffered an immediate pang in the vicinity of her breastbone for her dearest Lucius. Indeed, it occurred to her that there must have been something very greatly amiss for a mother to run away from her home and leave behind her nine-year-old son. "And you have had no contact with her since? But, why, Lucius?"

"Why?" echoed Traherne, to whom the answer had patently been self-evident.

"Dear, am I being obtuse?" Althea queried guilelessly. "I do beg your pardon. It is only that I was just turned eight when I lost my mother, and I have always thought how wonderful it must be if only I could see her one last time. You know, merely to hear her voice again and to tell her how very much I have missed her all these years. Perhaps we might even have time to catch up on all the news. I know she would dearly have loved to know of Effie and little Lord Guilmore and Baby Alice and to have heard all about the weddings of her two daughters. Unfortunately, I have had to accept that I can never see my mother again in this lifetime.''

''While I, on the other hand, must consider myself fortunate that my mother is still alive,'' observed Traherne, his handsome features maddeningly unreadable. ''Sweet Althea! I deeply regret that you had to lose your mama when you did. From what I have sensed of her lingering presence at Briersly, I believe she must have been a remarkable woman. Not unlike her elder daughter, I should imagine. I'm afraid, however, that I entertain none of the sentiments for my long-absent parent that you obviously still do for yours, anymore than I mourn the death of my father in a duel over his mistress of fourteen years when I was twelve. My mother ceased to exist for me long ago, and I have no intention of resurrecting her at this or any other time in my life.''

''No, I daresay you do not,'' submitted Althea, her heart going out to him. How deeply he must have been hurt by his mama's defection! And then to have lost his father in a duel little more than three years later, and under circumstances that could hardly have been easily understood by a youth of such tender years! Faith, it was little wonder he had deliberately suppressed all the softer human emotions, even going so far as to hold himself aloof from anyone who might try to get too close to him. ''And, indeed, who can blame you? You would naturally feel no little reluctance to chance opening old wounds. You may be sure I understand perfectly why you have never made the smallest attempt to contact your mama, never mind that she is not growing any younger. But then, of course, she may never return to England. In which case, it would naturally be exceedingly difficult merely to find her, let alone ever sit down with her to discuss what must have prompted her to do something so desperate as to run away from home.''

''She did it presumably for an all-consuming passion for a man whom she had known for less than three days,'' pronounced the duke in ominous tones. "And far from being beyond finding, she is even now residing in the Chesney Hotel in London with her lover of twenty-six years. So do not imagine, Althea, that I have spent all this time brooding over her possible motives. The truth is, I no longer care enough to know why she might have done it to ask her."

"No, of course you have not been brooding over it," Althea readily agreed. "You have been far too busy building a financial empire, not to mention a reputation for being a man utterly devoid of the softer human emotions, to give much thought to something that happened a very long time ago. I daresay she must have been exceedingly young when she married the duke, and he very likely was a man of mature years."

"She was, as a matter of fact, seventeen, and the duke was five and thirty, the same age as myself." Thinking no doubt to distract her, Traherne began a trail of light kisses along the inside of her wrist to the bend in her elbow. "I trust you do not hold my age against me?"

"Pray don't be absurd, Lucius," replied Althea, who could not but think thirty-five the ideal age for a husband, at least for a mature woman of twenty-five. "But then, I am a deal older than your mama was when she married. Still, such age differences are not uncommon among those of your station."

"*Our* station, Althea," interjected the duke gently. "Need I remind you that you are now of a rank second only to royalty?"

"Only by marriage, Your Grace," Althea did not hesitate to point out to him. "And while I was not quite on the order of a commoner, I have not been so high on the social ladder that I do not feel a little at this moment as if I have been yanked by the hair to my present elevated position. Which is why it occurs to me that it is quite possible it was as difficult for your father to know how to deal with a very young, inexperienced bride as it was for your mama to find herself suddenly not just the wife of a man much older than herself, but the wife of an exceedingly powerful duke, who was obviously in love with his mistress.''

"She was the daughter of a marquess, Althea," said Traherne repressively, patently wishing to terminate the discussion. "She was reared to marry a man of position, one might even go so far as to speculate that she was trained all her life to do her duty."

"Still, she was little more than a girl. You will admit theirs was hardly a marriage that gave promise for a warm and enduring affection between them. Has it never occurred to you to wonder, Lucius, what it must have been like for her in the nearly ten years that she strove to do her duty by a husband who openly favored another woman over her? It is possible she was never made to feel in the least comfortable with your father, that she might very well have seen herself more on the order of a prisoner in this castle than its chatelaine. In which case, it would not be at all extraordinary that she might feel compelled to effect her escape with a man who offered her the opportunity to travel the world and experience any number of grand adventures."

"Splendid," commented the duke, rolling over on his back in apparent defeat. "No doubt I am exceedingly glad for her. Now, since it would seem you have all the answers, perhaps we can relegate the entire matter to oblivion, which is where, in future, I should prefer it to be."

There had been not the smallest doubt that he meant that as a permanent end to any discussion of the subject of his mother. Althea, however, had known as well as he that there had been left unanswered the single most pertinent question. How could the duchess have brought herself to so thoroughly abandon her only son as not to see or speak to him for twenty-six years?

Furthermore, while a great deal that had puzzled her about her dearest lord duke would seem to have been clarified, there had remained another mystery surrounding Traherne, which he refused to discuss at all.

Althea hugged herself against a sudden chill at the thought that she had twice lain with Traherne before they were married and both times failed to notice the terrible scar on the outside of his left thigh. But then, she smiled ruefully in reminiscence, she had had a great deal to distract her on those two first excursions into the realm of the natural mechanics of human procreation, and they had been performed in dark environs.

She shuddered again at the memory of her first sight of the scar and the horror that had gripped her as it came to her how close she had been to losing her dearest Lucius before ever she had had the chance to meet him!

Even with what Althea was sure were unaccustomed stops to accommodate the needs of a five-year-old child, the journey to Meresgate had been accomplished in a single day in what Traherne's Mr. Phips had warned her would be Caesar speed. They had arrived in the dead of night, with Althea too weary to do more than see Effie and Mrs. Fennigrew safely settled into the nursery before Traherne had ushered her to the Duchess Suite and, kissing her lightly on the lips, had ordered her to bed. She had not seen him again until the following afternoon, when he had come in search of her in the conservatory, where she and Effie were enjoying tea among the tea roses and potted palms.

Dressed in buff riding breeches and a riding coat of olive drab, he had borne with him the scent of the outdoors. Indeed, he had presented a magnificent picture of virile manhood that had inadvertently brought a warm rush of blood to her cheeks, a reaction that did not go unnoticed by His Grace. Althea had the distinct impression that, despite his attentiveness to Effie, who manifested a positive delight in what she apprehended to be her and ''Althie's'' sudden change of circumstances (*that,* of course, being that they were to live forever after with Lucius, since he and Althea were now married), Traherne was biding his time until Mrs. Fennigrew should arrive to take Effie for her nap in the nursery.

She had not been wrong in her assessment. Hardly were they alone, than Lucius had availed himself of the opportunity to pull her into his arms and kiss her with a thoroughness that left little doubt he was fully prepared to make up for their postponed wedding night. Nor was he in any case to wait longer than it took to disrobe her in the privacy of the banana trees, which a previous duke had caused to be imported from the Orient and among which a chaise longue, wicker chairs, and a table were conveniently placed. Not that they had had any use for the wicker chairs or the table, Althea reflected, with a bemused smile. The chaise longue had suited their purposes very well. With an eagerness that should have put her to the blush, but which had seemed wholly appropriate at the time, she had not waited for Lucius to undo the fastenings at the front of his breeches. She had done it for him. Nor had she been satisfied only with releasing his magnificently erect male member. She had insisted upon removing his boots and stockings, as well, after which she had slid his unmentionables with a provocative deliberation down over his muscular thighs and legs.

It was then she had been given for the first time to view the scar in all of its terrible significance. His was not the first wound she had seen. Indeed, she was, after all, the colonel's daughter. She had helped tend the sick and wounded among her father's regiment, never mind that females were thought too delicate to view the terrible aftermaths of battle. The puckered tissue, still livid, gave mute evidence of Traherne's harrowing battle against infection. It was a marvel he had lived without the loss of his leg, a circumstance that could no doubt be laid to the efforts of a surgeon of superior talents. Still, she could not doubt his had been a lengthy siege of sickness and pain; and, indeed,

Carstairs, that first day at Briersly, had made mention of His Grace's "recent indisposition."

He was the Duke of Traherne, one of the most powerful men in England. Where and how the devil had he got a bullet wound in the leg?

She had not asked him then, though the question had been in her eyes for him to read as he lifted her to him. Indeed, it had trembled on her lips to be left unspoken as he covered her mouth with his. And later, when they had lain, spent with passion, she had known instinctively that it was not something about which he would willingly talk. After all, she was a soldier's daughter. She had learned early on in life that men who might tell any number of fabulous tales of the battles they had known often proved peculiarly reticent when it came to the least mention of wounds received. Perhaps it was a matter of a soldier's honor, as the colonel had claimed. Or perhaps it was the superstition of men who must go out and fight again. Althea was of the opinion that it had more to do with a reluctance to share with anyone the remembered horrors associated with the event than with anything else.

With Traherne, she sensed a dark secret kept locked away inside, the memory of which was bitter gall to him. She had glimpsed it at times in his eyes—a swift blur of pain, quickly gone. Or in the hardening of his lips with some unspoken thought.

It had come to her that she wished he could bring himself to trust her with it, as she had trusted him. But then, he was Lucius Keene, the Duke of Traherne, a man who kept his own counsel, she thought with a bittersweet sense that she was powerless to do more than woo him out of his dark mood if one should fall upon him.

She had become singularly adept at distracting him with cheerful small talk and lighthearted badinage. How strange that he seemed to enjoy her mundane prattle over the breakfast table! Small things about what Effie had said or done the previous day or Althea's attempts to find her way about the great pile with its numerous wings honeycombed with halls and twisting corridors—not to mention her determined efforts not to disgrace herself before the host of servants— he listened to it all with every manifestation of amused attention. At times he threw his head back in rich deep laughter, which had ever a curious effect on Althea's equilibrium.

Nor was that all they had come to share, Althea reflected in no little bemusement. Traherne seemed inordinately interested in all of her ideas for new automatic mechanical machines for the improvement of day-to-day living. Indeed, she could not but be gratified to have found someone who not only demonstrated a ready grasp of the designs that she was forever sketching in sketchbooks, but who maintained an open mind concerning their feasibility, practicality, and utility. He had even gone so far as to surprise her one morning with the sudden materialization of her former workshop in one of the attic rooms, complete with all of her old tools, half-finished projects, and Effie's very own Goosey Gander, all of which he had had transported intact from the Old Mill House. The gesture had touched her more deeply than she could ever have thought possible.

Far from the marriage of convenience she had anticipated, Traherne had made her in all ways his wife. He was in truth the most thoughtful and generous of men. Still, she could not but wish in her heart that he could love her, if only a little. Then perhaps it would not weigh on her so that he had married her out of his own peculiar sense of honor. Perhaps then it would not matter so much that she had, in all but intent, entrapped him.

That thought, besides occasioning Althea a sharp pang in the vicinity of her midsection, served to remind her of the more pressing matter at hand. Traherne had kept his word. Three days ago, they had seen Effie safely installed with Traherne's cousin Eleanor in Reading, an arrangement that had proved far more felicitous than Althea could ever have thought possible before she met the Earl and Countess of Leister.

Leister, a bluff nobleman of ample girth, discerning blue eyes, and a disposition that lent itself to joviality, had left little doubt in what vein he had received the news of Traherne's marriage. It was, he declared, pounding the duke painfully on the back, glad tidings. Glad tidings, indeed, and especially so, now that he had been given to see the bride. It was then Eleanor, Lady Leister, had stepped forward, taking Althea's hands in hers and admonishing her to pay no heed to the roaring of her dearest Leister. It was only his way of saying they could not be happier for Lucius's good fortune. Eleanor was, Althea had seen at once, everything that Traherne had promised she would be. Certainly, Effie had been put immediately at ease by the countess's gentle manner and warm friendly interest. The child had, in fact, been happily ensconced in the nursery with five of the earl's seven hopefuls when Traherne escorted a reluctant Althea from the house to the waiting coach.

He had brought her directly to London to initiate the search for Merrick. Thus she presently found herself alone and prowling about the Town House sitting room rather in the manner of a caged animal. Phips, it had been made readily apparent, had managed to discover little of a current nature concerning the former East India agent. Three years earlier, Merrick had sailed for England aboard the East Indiaman *Bristol Maid.* He had disembarked six months later at Billingsgate and then had seemed to vanish without a trace, until he had apparently surfaced in Glenridding where, if Althea was right in her assessment, he had bargained for the services of Messrs. Jack Weems and Thomas Meeks in the attempted abduction of Effie.

Still, it was only Althea's supposition that the man who had engaged a room in the Lion's Head Inn under the name of Phineas Wake had been in truth Evelyn Merrick. The innkeeper had been rather less than helpful. He claimed he never actually set eyes on Mr. Wake, as the room had been taken and paid for by the gentleman's servant. Furthermore, the two who might have corroborated Althea's suspicions, Jack Weems and Thomas Meeks, had been traced to Barrow, where they had run afoul of a press-gang. No doubt they were even then on a British man-of-war doing blockade duty somewhere off the French coast.

It had had to be Merrick, Althea told herself, not for the first time and with the same utter conviction. Weems had described the cane with the gold falcon's head in vivid detail. It had been one of Merrick's affectations, along with prematurely white hair worn shoulder length, a great emerald ring adorning the little finger of his left hand, and a manner of dressing and speaking that simulated the air of an aesthete. Faith, he had had the cane in hand on the memorable occasion of Althea's one and only visit to his palatial house in Madras. He had come very near to bludgeoning her with it, which had precipitated the event of Althea's discharging a pistol ball into one of his lower extremities.

Where the devil was Merrick? she fretted. And why had she ever allowed Lucius to persuade her to remain in the Town House while he went off alone to question Dick Turpin? In retrospect, it would hardly seem to signify that Merrick might have the house on Plover Street under observation, save, perhaps, to further the possibility that the villain could be persuaded to come after her. That was, she thought, the real purpose in advertising the fact that she was now the Duchess of Traherne and that, further, she was openly in residence in the Campden Hill district. Surely, she would have been quite safe on Plover Street in Traherne's company.

No, there had been some other reason Traherne had not wanted her along. It occurred to her that perhaps he intended to use a more forceful means of persuasion with her grounds-keeper than Althea would have permitted had she been present. Or perhaps Phips had had something new to impart, which, for his own reasons, Traherne had preferred to investigate on his own, the most probable motive being that he had apprehended the possibility of danger. She would be hard put to forgive him, if that turned out to be the case. It was one thing to accept her dearest lord duke's help in tracking down her enemy. It was quite another to be excluded from the hunt merely because Traherne's particular code of ethics would not allow a woman to be exposed to peril!

If only there were *something* she could do to further the investigation on her own! she fumed, flinging herself down in an overstuffed chair. She was heartily weary of being confined to pacing a hole in the carpet. Indeed, she did not doubt she would soon wear herself to the brink of a sharp decline if she had to spend one more hour staring at the same four walls. Not that it would help to stare at four different walls, she reflected sardonically, reminded that the Town House offered a wide variety of choices in rooms in which she could carry on her perambulations. What she needed was to get out of the house. Indeed, she wished most ardently to be able to talk to the one person who knew Merrick better than anyone. She wanted to see and talk to her sister.

Really, it was too bad of Gloriana to have postponed her return to London yet again, never mind that Baby Alice was apparently in the process of teething or that little Lord Guilmore had proved on the previous trip to Town to be an exceedingly poor traveler. Other than what Althea did not doubt was a sincere outpouring of well wishes for her recent nuptials, this was the only information contained in the viscountess's one letter to her elder sister since before Althea had fled the Old Mill House.

Indeed, Althea could not but feel an additional uneasiness at the noticeable lack of correspondence from Gloriana. Not that her sister had ever been an avid letter writer, but Althea had thought the news that circumstances of an unhealthy nature had necessitated the immediate removal of herself and Effie from the Old Mill House would elicit some sort of response. And if Gloriana had somehow failed to correctly interpret the nuance of meaning in those cryptic passages, surely the warning that Althea had recently been visited by an old acquaintance from Madras, one who was unlooked for and unwelcome as a reminder of their last unhappy days in the Orient, should have sounded an alarm. Naturally, in a letter that might come to Winslade's notice, Althea could not state plainly that Merrick had made an attempt to abduct Effie or that they had been forced into flight for Effie's safety. The viscount was not privy to the secret surrounding Effie's birth.

Still, Gloriana must surely have understood and felt no little concern for her eldest borne. If there was one thing Althea had never doubted, it was that Gloriana loved her daughter. Why, then, this incomprehensible silence concerning recent events? Why had she put off, seemingly indefinitely, coming to London when she must know Althea most particularly wished to learn if there was anything she could remember that might lead them to Merrick?

The devil, thought Althea, coming out of the chair. Fitfully, she started to pace once again. There must be *someone* in London with whom she had been acquainted all those years ago in Madras, someone who had known Merrick and perhaps something of his ties in England. One of her father's officers, perhaps, or a clerk retired from the Company to England, or someone of the numerous female contingent with whom she had enjoyed a measure of friendship, or—

Abruptly, she halted in midstride, a peculiarly arrested expression in her lovely eyes.

"Or someone who had the particular distinction of having been entertained numerous times in his own home," she said aloud to the empty room. "Even feted and fawned over, if my memory serves correctly. Merrick was the very worst sort of social climber. Faith, why did I not think of her before!"

Without pausing to give the matter or, more particularly, its possible repercussions, any further consideration, Althea reached for the bellpull.

She would take a few moments to change her gown and freshen up, she told herself as she waited for Carstairs to respond to her summons. She would even allow Grayson, her newly acquired abigail, to apply a few finishing touches to her hair, she decided, turning at the muted scratch at the door. And of course she would have to take Mr. Cutler, the man Traherne had insisted accompany her whenever she left the house. Calling for Carstairs to enter, she smiled roguishly to herself. After all, one should be at one's best when calling on a duchess, especially if the duchess just happened to be one's very own mama-in-law!

"I shall require the carriage, Carstairs," she announced to the butler, as if she had been in the habit all her life of giving orders to servants of Carstairs's exceedingly superior remove. "You may inform Mr. Cutler. I shall be down in twenty minutes."

Traherne stepped lightly down from his curricle before White's and, ordering the groom to "walk 'em," strode into the hallowed environs of London's most prestigious private club. Relinquishing his many-caped greatcoat, curly brimmed beaver, and tan kid gloves to a servant, he glanced casually about. At three in the afternoon, there was a subdued, almost staid air about the paneled lounge in which various gentlemen sat in overstuffed leather chairs reading newspapers or dozing. The gaming rooms would not begin to fill until after the dinner hour, around nine or ten, but there could usually be found any number of young bloods in the billiards rooms or at the bay windows ogling passersby in St. James's Street below.

Nodding here and there to acquaintances, Traherne made his way directly upstairs, where he made an immediate impression by his mere unheralded appearance at what, for him, was a wholly unprecedented hour.

In the brief sudden hush, followed almost instantly by the casual resumption of activity, an elegantly appareled gentleman in his middle-to-late forties sauntered forward. "Traherne, by gad. Never thought to see you here in the middle of the day. Come to think of it, don't recall having seen you here at all for a considerable time. Buy you a drink, Your Grace?" Giving a glance over his shoulder, he gestured for a waiter.

"Nothing for me, thank you, Alastair. I shan't be staying long. I was in hopes of finding Lord Branscombe at his customary pursuits. It seems, however, I am out of luck."

"Traherne out on his luck? Egad," commented Alastair, apparently much struck at the notion. "Don't suppose you would care to sit down to a game of piquet while you're at it? No, didn't think you would. Branscombe, eh? Haven't laid eyes on him, Your Grace. But then, the latest *on dit* has it that the young Adonis has taken himself a new lover. Occupies all his time these days."

"To the exclusion of all else?" drawled Traherne with the arch of a single aristocratic eyebrow. "Damme. His lordship must be smitten, indeed. Someone we know?"

"Haven't the slightest idea who it might be. If you're curious, however, his lordship is throwing one of his galas tomorrow night. A masquerade ball, I understand. Daresay you would have little difficulty obtaining an invitation. As a matter of fact, doubt there would be need of one. Can't think that anyone's ever been turned away from one of Branscombe's bacchanalias."

Some minutes later, Traherne having taken his leave of the loquacious Alastair, was driving his matched team of grays at a splitting pace through the London traffic. It had been a long shot that had taken him to White's in search of the Earl of Branscombe, an offhanded remark made by Phips to the effect that the dissolute young nobleman had come into a sudden windfall sufficient to stave off his creditors and save the family pile from going under the gavel. More pertinently, however, had been his secretary's pointed observation that rumor had it Branscombe had paid his shot with a handful of particularly fine diamonds. It was, in fact, all the talk among the local tradesmen.

Perhaps Traherne would have made nothing of it, had he not found on his return to Town a letter waiting for him— newly arrived from Alexandria.

One of Traherne's first duties, upon wedding his wood sprite, had been immediately to write to her father to inform the colonel of the event and to make him aware of the marriage settlements, which had been exceedingly generous, as clearly behooved a Duchess of Traherne. He had as well taken pains to assure his father-in-law that he meant to provide in every way possible for the future happiness of the colonel's daughter, whom he held in the greatest possible affection. After no little consideration and because he was not fully aware of the extent of the colonel's knowledge concerning the events surrounding Effie's birth, he had omitted adding that he promised to ensure the welfare of the colonel's eldest granddaughter, Effie Marie Wintergreen, whom he was already in the process of legally adopting. No doubt that information could wait until the colonel's eventual return to England. Indeed, Traherne did not doubt it would be better coming from Althea.

He had ended by appending a brief note of inquiry concerning a former East India agent, a Mr. Evelyn Merrick, who had been in the Company's employ during the colonel's tenure in Madras. Providing as an explanation for the inquiry the suspicion that the man was currently involved in activities in England of a questionable nature, Traherne had left it to the colonel's discretion to supply whatever information he might consider pertinent.

The answering missive had been both eye-opening and thought provoking. The colonel had replied in the vein of a man who entertained a considerable affection for his daughter, but who had long since given up any thought of directing her life for her. There would seem little purpose in it, after all, since Althea had always known her own mind better than anyone else could ever have hoped to do anyway. In which case, the colonel did not doubt that she had chosen a husband who, not only was worthy of her, but who was strong-minded enough not to be threatened or intimidated by a free and independent thinker on the order of his exceedingly unique Althea. Giving the marriage his blessing, the colonel had, with what would seem a characteristic brusqueness, applied himself next to the matter of Mr. Evelyn Merrick. He had fallen to disgrace in an incident involving a local prince and the loss of a caravan to Pathan banditti. Forced to flee Madras for his life, Merrick had, nevertheless, managed to avail himself of a sizable fortune in diamonds, which had been intended for the Company's coffers. It was a coup that had made him one of the Company's most sought after individuals. Should His Grace happen to run across Mr. Merrick, there was, in fact, a rather significant reward being offered for the villain's capture.

The colonel had ended by wishing Traherne and his daughter happy and by apprising them that he hoped to be ordered back to England as soon as ever the matter of the transfer of the Rosetta Stone into British keeping was completed. He hoped without the stone's destruction by the disgruntled French who were not averse to seeing it broken into pieces before ceding its loss to the enemy.

The letter had been interesting, not only for its personal import, but clearly for what it would seem to provide in the way of a most peculiar coincidence. While there would appear to be little or nothing on the surface to suggest a connection between the Earl of Branscombe and Evelyn Merrick, the singularity of diamonds in each case would seem too remarkable a possible common denominator for Traherne to ignore. Especially as it would seem the only other link to Merrick's possible whereabouts had apparently vanished off the face of the earth.

The duke's brief visit to the house on Plover Street had served to ascertain little more than that Dick Turpin had left the premises to partake of a tankard of ale at the nearby tavern two months previously and had not been seen or heard from since. Sally Higgens, the tearful bride-to-be, who had sent to Phips the news of her promised's disappearance, had been most adamant in her belief that her dearest Dick had been the victim of foul play. Traherne had hardly been prepared to dispute the distinct possibility.

It was one reason he had preferred to leave Althea behind in the safety of the Town House. He had little doubt that, once apprised of this new turn of events, his redoubtable wood nymph would not have hesitated to insist on beginning an immediate personal investigation into Turpin's disappearance. Traherne was sure she would even go so far as to blatantly visit the tavern in question, a process that would not only have failed to turn up any relevant information, but would have served instead to draw unwelcome attention to herself.

Arriving at his Town House in the Campden Hill district, better known as the "Dukeries" because its numerous landed mansions housed only the very highest ranks of society, Traherne acknowledged ruefully that he was in a devil of a quandary. His well-honed instincts fairly shouted that the man who had tried to abduct Effie was no common felon, but a man of deep and dangerous designs. The villain would stop at nothing, even murder, to achieve his nefarious ends.

The very thought of his redoubtable duchess setting out in pursuit of such an enemy was sufficient to make Traherne's blood run cold in his veins. Still, he had come to know Althea far too well to suppose he would not lose her should he do anything so fruitless as try to keep her from it. He had promised they would seek Merrick together, and he was honor bound to keep his word, no matter how little he might relish it. The question was, How the devil to do it and keep his duchess safe?

Had anyone told Traherne only six months before that the entirety of his future happiness would reside in a slender slip of a girl who was managing, stubbornly independent, and possessed of the unnerving ability to see into his very soul, he would not have hesitated to call that person mad. That, however, was before he had met and fallen under the spell of a wood sprite endowed with an earthen magic, not to mention a discerning heart as generous as it was boundless in its capacity for love.

Althea had broken through all his well-maintained defenses, even going so far as to bring him to an awareness that there still lingered in some dark recess of his soul feelings that he had long since thought forgotten. But then, no doubt they had been better so. After all, what use was it to recall moments from a childhood that had ended twenty-six years before? He was long past the age of needing his mother. Furthermore, far from regretting the early unlamented demise of his father, he could recall only having experienced a chilling sense of relief that he no longer had to dread the infrequent visits of his harsh and vengeful parent, who had taken perverse delight in pointing out the faults and frailties of a boy who had too much resembled his mother in looks and manner. Still, Althea had unerringly presented a picture of his mother that even yet lingered to haunt him with the possibility that he, no less than his father, was guilty of a harsh and pitiless vengeance against a woman whom he had never allowed so much as the courtesy of defending herself.

A frown darkened his brow at that final thought, opening the door, as it did, to unwitting wisps of memory. He had believed a blurred image of a sweet face, young seeming, the eyes sad until the lips parted in bubbling laughter, was all he had left of her. All, that was, save for the lingering impression of a cool hand to his brow when he had suffered the mumps in his extreme youth and the distinct memory of the scent of lavender whenever she had walked into a room. Now, unwanted and uninvited, images of her reading to him at night or of the two of them perched side by side before the piano, as she tutuored his fingers to a lively piece, were resurrected, or of her leaning down to kiss him good night—always first on one eye and then the other and then at the corner of his mouth. There had been long walks, too, through the deer park or along the beach below the castle overlooking the sea.

Suddenly he cursed, aware of a blight on his mood. The devil take his mother and her memory. She had walked out of his life twenty-six years before. Her return now was hardly pertinent, a minor irritant he would rather do without. *Especially* now, when he was faced with the greater prospect of having to preserve his wife against her own dauntless disregard for self.

Conscious of an eagerness to see his duchess, he strode quickly into the house.

"Carstairs," he said, relinquishing his outdoor garments and accessories to his butler, "kindly inform the duchess I require a word with her in my study. And be pleased to fetch a fresh decanter of brandy."

"I should, indeed, Your Grace. The duchess, however, is not within. Her Grace departed in the carriage some little time ago and has yet to return."

"Did she indeed?" murmured Traherne, absently fingering the quizzing glass dangling down his front on its black riband. "You astonish me, Carstairs. And where did Her Grace say she was going?"

"I believe I overheard mention of the Chesney Hotel, Your Grace. Though I daresay I might have been mistaken." Carstairs paused, his features studiously impassive. "Shall I fetch the brandy, Your Grace?"

Traherne, appearing to come out of a brief distraction,

avored his butler with a look that was distinctly without
umor. "Be sure of it, Carstairs. I shall be in my study.
nform me when the duchess returns."

"As you wish, Your Grace," intoned the butler, turning
o dispose properly of the duke's greatcoat, hat, and gloves.

Traherne, however, did not hear him. Mounting the curved
taircase two steps at a time, he disappeared into his study.
The door shut firmly behind him.

Chapter Eleven

Entering the foyer of the Chesney Hotel, Althea stood for a long moment, undecided how best to proceed. She was not at all certain by what name to inquire for Traherne's mama. In Madras, Her Grace had made a grand presence as the Duchess of Traherne with the ever-present Mr. Xavier Praetorius, like an aging, but still elegantly graceful Apollo, at her side. In London, with her son, the duke, in close proximity, perhaps she would have chosen to present herself in a fashion less calculated to draw scandalous attention to herself. There was every possibility she was not availing herself of the title at all, in which case, Althea most certainly could not wish to spoil things for her by asking for the Duchess of Traherne.

Althea was equally uncertain in what manner to introduce herself. She found the notion of announcing herself to the Duchess of Traherne as the Duchess of Traherne somehow absurdly redundant, not to mention smacking not a little of puffing off her own consequence. Still, she could not wish to present herself under false colors. She was married to the

Duke of Traherne, and she was acutely aware that Olivia Traherne had not been invited to the wedding. In fact, the ceremony had consisted of no one other than the bride and groom, the bishop, and Mr. Phips and the bishop's wife to serve as witnesses. She did not doubt the dowager duchess would see the omission for what it was—a cut direct from her only son.

Still, she could not stand indefinitely in the hotel lobby without beginning to attract a deal of unwanted notice. She had just made up her mind to brave the desk clerk, when a voice at her elbow instantly resolved most of her immediate difficulties.

"Why, Miss Wintergreen, is it not? Miss Althea Wintergreen, formerly of Madras? Perhaps you do not recall—I am . . ."

"Mr. Xavier Praetorius!" exclaimed Althea, happily extending her hand to the still-handsome gentleman past middle age. Garbed in the height of fashion in a purple double-breasted cutaway coat, canary waistcoat, and crimson unmentionables, his imposing figure was only just beginning to reveal a telltale bulge around the middle. "Of course I remember you. As a matter of fact, I have come in the express hope of calling on you and Her Grace." At the gentleman's perceptible hesitation, she quickly added, "It is a matter of some importance, sir. Her Grace will not regret that she has condescended to speak with me, I promise."

"Well, then, I daresay Olivia will not mind that I have broken her rule not to receive callers before afternoon tea. Come, my dear," he added, gallantly offering her his arm. "Never let it be said Xavier Praetorius disappointed a beautiful woman."

"You are too kind, sir," smiled Althea, prettily laying her hand on his wrist. "Are you glad to be back in England, Mr. Praetorius?" she asked, as he led her to the stairs.

"I am glad to be anywhere that pleases my lady love, and for the present, at least, that happens to be merry old

England. And should I find occasionally that the blessed isle should pall, I am not averse to having recourse to sordid pleasures in seamier environs. My lady understands. My dearest lady always understands. And you, Miss Wintergreen, do you find that you miss the exotic lands of the Orient?''

''Occasionally, perhaps,'' Althea answered reflectively. ''Mostly I miss the colonel, whom I have not seen since I left Madras over five years ago. Otherwise, I find I am not discontent with a quiet existence in the English countryside. Unfortunately, it has not been so peaceful of late as it was, which is why I now find myself in the never-peaceful City.''

''Ah, the teeming metropolis, the pulse and throb of the empire.'' Praetorius halted before a white paneled door. ''And this unhappy disturbance in the country, my dear. Is that what brings you to the duchess?''

''In part, sir,'' Althea replied honestly. ''It is, however, a business that does not touch Her Grace. She will not be harmed by it, I promise. I wish only to inquire about a mutual acquaintance from your visit to Madras. And to ask her blessing in another separate matter, closer to her heart. I have, you see, only just recently wed her son.''

''No, by gad, have you?'' exclaimed Praetorius, his entire face appearing to light up. ''And now you have called to make yourself acquainted with your mama-in-law. By heaven, you are a gel after my own heart. I hope you will forgive that I must ask you to wait here while I step inside. It will be only for a moment, I assure you. I must make certain Olivia is ready to receive. She'd have my head on a platter if we caught her in her curling papers.''

''I understand perfectly, Mr. Praetorius. I really should have sent ahead to warn you of my intentions. I was, I fear, prey to sudden impulse. I hope you and Her Grace will forgive what must seem a gross impropriety.''

''Hardly that, my dear child—er—pardon me—Your Grace,'' emended Mr. Praetorius, presenting an elegant leg.

"Only a trifle inconvenient perhaps. But never mind. All shall soon be put to rights."

It was soon made apparent that Her Grace, far from being in anything so inelegant as curling papers, was fully dressed in what could only be described as the first stare of fashion. Indeed, Althea could not but reflect that Olivia Traherne, in a rose jaconet round gown with goffered ruffles at the throat and puffed sleeves tapering to embroidered cuffs, presented a far more striking example of what a duchess should appear than did Althea Traherne in her plain morning gown of bronze shagreen. In her early fifties, with the same blue-black hair that she had bequeathed her son as yet unmarked by gray, she retained the delicate bone structure and finely molded features that had made her a noted beauty in her day. And if the onset of middle age had served to blur the clean line of her jaw and to sketch tiny wrinkles at the corners of her eyes and mouth, and if the ivory purity of her complexion had lost the fresh glow of youth, she was yet a strikingly attractive woman.

Her eyes, Althea noted, were not only of a darker hue than Traherne's, but they were regarding Althea with a peculiar hungry intensity the source of which, Althea could not doubt, was the unspoken desire for news of her son.

"Your Grace," murmured Althea, dipping the older woman a curtsy. "Thank you for agreeing to see me."

"Olivia, please, my dear. And I shall call you Althea. Otherwise we shall be 'Your Gracing' each other into a royal headache."

"It does seem a trifle awkward, I own," laughed Althea, recalling that she had liked this woman very well all those years ago. Now it was easy to remember why she had done.

"Please, won't you come and sit here beside me," said Her Grace of Traherne, indicating a dimity sofa near the fire. "There is so much that I should like you to tell me. Lucius—the duke, is he well?"

"He is very well. I daresay you would find him a man

of which any mother would be proud. He is tall and well knit; and, despite a certain hardness about the eyes and mouth, you would find he is exceedingly well to look upon. More than that, he is a kind and generous husband, who promises fair to be a good and understanding father.''

''Father. But then, my dear, am I to understand that you—?''

''*No.* No, forgive me. I meant Effie, my little girl.'' Unwittingly, Althea blushed. ''Naturally, you could not have known.''

Althea bolted to her feet in sudden consternation. ''I'm afraid, Your Grace,'' she blurted, ''I am not at all the sort of wife you would have chosen for your son. Indeed, I did try and dissuade him from what can only be considered a ruinous course, but he is the most stubborn of men when he makes his mind up to a thing, and he would have me for his wife.''

''No, would he?'' interjected the dowager duchess, apparently much struck at this unforeseen side of her son's character. ''And, having made up his mind on this particular thing, one must presume he pursued it with a single-minded dedication.''

''You have no idea,'' exclaimed Althea, flinging up her hands in a fit of distraction. ''For a man of superior intellect who prides himself on his logic, he behaved like a man possessed. All because of a ridiculous code of honor, which, in any case, obviously did not apply, since I was already a Ruined Woman beyond all hope of social redemption.''

''Clearly, he had abandoned all sense of reason,'' the older woman agreed, exchanging a quizzical glance with Mr. Praetorius, who responded with the lift of an eloquent eyebrow. ''My poor dear, you were sorely pressed, were you not? Especially, as you were desperately in love with him almost from the very start.''

''We were drawn together by an irresistible gravitational attraction; indeed, you might say we found ourselves in the sway of incontrovertible natural forces,'' Althea admitted, ''which I knew, if he did not, must inevitably lead me to love him. I told myself I had nothing to fear from it. After all, he had already made it plain that he was impervious to any of the softer human emotions. I knew he could not— indeed, never shall—bring himself to love me.''

Clasping hands over the back of the sofa, the Scandalous Duchess and Mr. Praetorius smiled in what gave every manifestation of a conspiratorial understanding. ''No,'' said Olivia Traherne, ''I daresay no one could imagine from your description of his behavior that my son was in any way influenced by that particular all-consuming passion.''

''No, you may be sure of it. Not that it deterred him one iota in his determined campaign to bring me to his way of thinking, for it did not,'' Althea continued, resolved to get everything out in the open. ''And while I repeatedly refused his suit, even going so far as to run away at last in the hopes that he would never find me, he proved far more resourceful than I. He was, in fact, waiting for me, when I arrived at what I presumed to be my unknown sanctuary in the City.''

''How very clever of him,'' said the dowager duchess.

''Really, it was too bad of him!''

''Yes, of course. That, too, my dear,'' conceded his mama.

''And then what must he do but save Effie from being abducted.''

''Clearly, he was having a busy time of it,'' observed Olivia to Xavier.

''A veritable milieu of golden opportunity,'' suggested Xavier back to Olivia, who smiled, her eyes twinkling in shared amusement.

''He insisted that only by marrying him could I hope to keep Effie safe from further attempts, which, of course, I could not deny,'' said Althea, who, in her agitation, had failed to take proper note of that little byplay. ''Anymore than I could deny that what he needed was a wife, not a mistress, in order to set up his nursery, or that gorging oneself at a feast of the senses with a mistress *and* a wife was asking too much of a man when either one or both is given to practically insatiable appetites. Indeed, I doubt not he was right to point out it could very well lead to an early demise, and naturally I could not wish that on him.''

''No, of course you could not. Anymore than you could have lent yourself, when it came right down to it, to stealing the food from the mouth of a dutiful wife.''

Althea's eyes flew to meet the dowager duchess's with sudden, perfect understanding. ''Indeed,'' she said, ''I daresay I should never have forgiven myself if I had ever been made a party to any such thing. In any case, Lucius had already made Effie his legal ward, and though I cannot think he would really have stooped to taking her from me if I had not agreed to marry him, I can never be actually sure now, can I, Your Grace? After all, I did marry him by special license before the bishop himself, and now I shall be known as Traherne's Scandalous Duchess, when all I ever wanted was to save him from disgrace.''

''I daresay if he had wanted saving, my dear,'' said Olivia, smiling a little, ''he would hardly have gone to so much trouble to persuade you to marry him. Perhaps having a scandalous Duchess of Traherne does not weigh quite so heavily with him as you seem to imagine.''

''Oh, but I am sure it does not,'' Althea asserted bitterly. ''He does not care a fig what anyone will say. He has made that more than plain. And no doubt I should not take it so much to heart myself, if it were not for the fact that I am not the wife he would have chosen had circumstances not dictated otherwise. Or that in marrying him, I have brought him a deal of trouble. For, if you must know, he has pledged himself to vanquish my enemy, who is a man utterly devoid of scruples. Worse, he has gone in search of the villain alone, leaving me to pace a hole in the carpet, when he distinctly promised he and I should deal with this together.

Which is the other reason I have come to see you, Your Grace.''

"Olivia, my dear," corrected the duchess. "Remember? Now, tell me: How, precisely, may I help you?"

"By telling me anything you can recall that might give us some clue as to where we might find Evelyn Merrick. As you must know, he was driven in disgrace from Madras shortly after my sister and I left to return to England."

"Evelyn Merrick," exclaimed Mr. Praetorius. "Good God! Is that the man you are after?"

"Yes, he was the Company agent in Madras when you arrived. You do remember him, Mr. Praetorius, I can see that you do."

"Remember him, I should say I do. Indeed, I should find it difficult to forget him. Especially as I happened to run into him night before last in the Cock and Bull."

"The Cock and Bull, Xavier. Really," commented Olivia, gazing fondly at her aging Apollo.

"A delightful tavern, my dear, peopled by the most unsavory lot of cutthroats, thieves, and Jezebels—and, as it happens, former East India agents."

On the drive home, Althea was lost in contemplation of the remarkable interview she had had with her mama-in-law, whom she could not but find utterly charming, and Mr. Praetorius, whose predilection for low haunts had provided the first solid evidence that Merrick was indeed in London. Nor was that all he had had to impart. Merrick, it seemed, had been in the company of a woman, a full-blown beauty whose patent desire to remain unremarked in the murky shadows of a corner table had provoked the curiosity of the enterprising Mr. Praetorius.

Feigning the reeling aspect of a man deep in his cups, Praetorius had staggered into close enough proximity to the table occupied by the former East India agent and the intriguing Lady Incognita to overhear the woman hiss a scathing oath made even more vituperative by the distinctly French accent that colored it.

''Whoreson! Devil's pimp! How dare you threaten Jacqueline Marot! Beware, Monsieur Develin. I will be tempted to cut out your heart for you.''

It was all he had been allowed to overhear. Merrick, glancing up, took note of the slouched figure hovering within hearing distance, and Praetorius had determined upon a judicious retreat. Indeed, he had confessed with his engagingly rakish grin he had been exceedingly grateful he had long since formed the habit of donning the wig, moustache, and beard, not to mention the less than elegant raiment of one of the scaff and raff, when he embarked on one of his excursions into London's seamier dens of iniquity. He had always made certain to go unrecognized to protect Olivia, his lady love. Althea could be equally certain, Praetorius had assured her with a wink, Mr. Merrick or Develin, as he apparently now was called, had not seen anything in the filthy nondescript fellow at the Cock and Bull to connect him with Xavier Praetorius, the world-renowned Shakespearian actor.

Althea was still congratulating herself on her good fortune when, bidding Carstairs a cheerful good afternoon, she stepped past him into the Town House foyer.

Her mood was not in the least blighted when Carstairs, helping her out of her velvet pelisse, carefully informed her that His Grace had requested a word with her in the study immediately upon her return. She had, on the contrary, been hoping to find the duke at home. Indeed, she could not wait to tell him all that she had discovered.

Picking up her skirts, she fairly flew up the stairs, leaving Carstairs to stare after her, his normally impassive features giving expression to a curious gleam of satisfaction.

''Lucius!'' exclaimed Althea a few moments later, flinging through the door without so much as bothering to knock.

"You will never guess where I have been or what I have found out."

"On the contrary, my dear," drawled Traherne from the high-back leather-upholstered chair behind the great oak desk, "you have just come from the Chesney, where you undoubtedly paid a call on my esteemed mother and quite possibly the gentleman who styles himself rather fancifully as 'The Great Praetorius, World-Renowned Elocutionist and Player *Extraordinaire.*' "

"He does, doesn't he?" Althea said, her delicious laughter gurgling forth. Heedless of the ominous crease between the duke's bristling black eyebrows, she plopped, in her enthusiasm, across his lap, one arm around the back of his neck, and her legs propped in an exceedingly unladylike manner over the arm of his chair. "I had forgotten that. How delightfully like him. And your mama, Lucius, I daresay she is not at all what she has been painted."

"No, I doubt not she is a paragon of virtue," observed Traherne in tones that could hardly have been interpreted as encouraging.

"Actually, I cannot think *paragon* is quite the right term to describe her," Althea rejoined, the tip of an index finger pressed to pursed lips as she considered how best to express what the dowager duchess was. "She is beautiful, of course, and charming and quite utterly delightful. But she is also blessed with a superior understanding. Perhaps one might best describe her as a vital personality."

"Yes, I daresay she is that," pronounced Traherne. Disentangling himself from Althea's arm, he lifted her bodily from his lap and set her on her feet, then rose from the chair.

Taken aback, Althea watched him cross to the grog tray and pour himself a brandy. Faith, but he was in a rare taking, indeed, was her dearest Lucius; and all, she did not doubt, because she had done what he could not bring himself to do. She had gone to his mother. Worse, she had come back championing her to him.

"Lucius, I wish you will try and understand. When it *came* to me, the one person other than Gloriana who had known Merrick in Madras, I had to go see her. There was every possibility she might recall something that would lead us to him—a family member or acquaintance, someone or someplace he might have mentioned. Perhaps it was grasping at straws, but I felt it was worth giving it a try."

"And you did not think to wait to consult me on this matter before rushing off on your own?" queried Traherne, setting the stopper back in the decanter. "No, why should you? If you had, I might have been given to inform you I have left implicit instructions there is to be no contact between this house and the duchess save through Phips." He turned to look at Althea. "In future, I trust you will remember my wishes in this regard."

"You may be sure I shall give it my full consideration," Althea retorted, a dangerous sparkle in her eye. How dared he apply pressure to the bit to bring her back in line! "Still, I wish you might change your mind, Lucius," she added, feeling that she had to make one last attempt to bring him to reason in regard to his mama. "I know you must have been terribly hurt when your mother ran off with Mr. Praetorius, and perhaps it was very wrong of her to abandon her husband and child. On the other hand, do you not think you owe it to yourself to hear her side of the story? You might be surprised to discover you like her very well, that you can even understand why she did what she did, even if you cannot bring yourself to accept it."

"But I do accept it," Traherne replied with infuriating dispassion. "I am content to allow my mother to lead her own life in any manner that she sees fit—so long as I am not required to be a part of it. And now that we have dealt with the issue of my mother, I have another matter to discuss with you. I'm afraid, Althea, Dick Turpin has gone missing.

He left the house two months ago and has failed thus far to return.''

''I don't understand,'' said Althea, considerably taken aback. For Sally Higgens's sake, she had been in hopes of Dick Turpin's total rehabilitation. ''Whatever could have happened to him?'' Only then did the awful truth hit her. ''Lucius, you do not think Merrick has cut his stick for him?''

Traherne's lips thinned to a grim line at the dawning horror in his wood nymph's eyes. Without remorse he wished Dick Turpin to the devil for having been the cause of it. ''It is, unfortunately, a distinct possibility, especially if he had been foolish enough to go to Merrick with the tale of his failed attempt on Effie. Merrick would hardly be the sort to leave loose ends hanging. However, thanks to Phips, I may have discovered another link to Merrick. I should suggest you do not set your hopes too high, Althea. It is only a dark horse that may prove to be nothing more than a chimera.''

''But you do not think so,'' interjected Althea, feeling a pang of conscience at her earlier less than complimentary thoughts concerning his seeming abandonment of her. Her dearest Lucius had obviously been trying to spare her the pain of disappointment. More than that, however, he was being perfectly open with her, when she had expected something quite different from him.

''I think, *enfant,* that there is no such thing as pure coincidence. I have received a letter from the colonel. I shall give it to you to read directly. I shall tell you now, however, that I wrote your father before we left for Meresgate.''

''You did? But why?'' exclaimed Althea, a sinking sensation in the pit of her stomach. The last thing she could wish was to have the colonel learn from someone other than herself about Effie's existence and Merrick's part in it. ''Why did you never tell me?''

Traherne shrugged a single broad shoulder. ''I assumed you would realize it was my duty to inform him of our marriage and how I meant to provide for you.'' Wryly, he noted the flush that came to his wood sprite's cheeks. The marriage settlements had occasioned their one and only heated exchange during the sojourn at Meresgate. Hell and the devil confound it, he had had almost to twist her arm to persuade her to sign the bloody papers! Indeed, he doubted not she would have consigned them to the fire had Effie not burst in upon them. ''I merely appended a brief inquiry concerning Merrick.''

''Good God, Lucius,'' exclaimed Althea, going suddenly pale. ''What did you tell him?''

''You needn't worry that I was indiscreet,'' Traherne assured her in exceedingly dry accents. ''I explained that there was some suspicion that Merrick might be involved in questionable activities here in England. The important thing is that the colonel relayed significant information of which we had previously been unaware. Merrick managed to smuggle a considerable fortune in diamonds out of Madras, diamonds that rightfully belonged to the Company. You may be sure his former employers are as eager as we to discover Merrick's whereabouts.''

''Lucius, have they?'' Althea queried eagerly. ''Found him?''

''I am sorry to disappoint you, wood sprite. You may be sure if they had, he would even now be in Newgate.''

''Then I do not understand,'' declared Althea, sinking down on the leather-upholstered sofa. ''How is this information pertinent to our own search?''

''It is pertinent,'' said Traherne, wondering if he should have waited to tell her until after he had something more solid to offer her, ''perhaps because a number of diamonds have recently turned up under somewhat peculiar circumstances. It seems someone has paid off his considerable debts with diamonds, someone who, only days ago, was well known to be on the rocks.''

''And that is the coincidence that you have found pertinently questionable," said Althea, who had little difficulty making the same connection that Traherne had done. "Who is he, Lucius? Pray tell me you know his name."

"He is the Earl of Branscombe, a young ne'er-do-well whose sole recommendations are a predilection for excess in his pursuits of pleasure, a face and form that have earned him the fanciful sobriquet of 'Adonis,' and a reputation for providing lavish entertainments of a voluptuous nature. He has managed to carouse his way through his entire inheritance in little more than five years. Unfortunately, I have as yet to determine if he has any possible connection to Merrick."

"Oh, but you may be sure that he does, Lucius," declared Althea, hiding a smile at Traherne's obvious distaste for anyone who could choose to conduct himself in the style of a sybarite. "Perhaps it is a mutual acquaintance. Could he by any chance keep a mistress? A full-blown French beauty, perhaps, by the name of Jacqueline Marot?"

If she had hoped to win a reaction from her maddeningly imperturbable husband, she was soon to be gratified beyond her wildest expectations.

Traherne's eyes beneath drooping eyelids pierced her through like rapiers. *"Jacqueline Marot,"* he said, the French pronunciation fairly rolling off his tongue with the ease of one who was fluent in the language. "Where the devil did you hear that name?"

Inexplicably, Althea suffered a sickening spasm through her midsection. Despite her unfamiliarity with the green-eyed monster, she had little difficulty in recognizing the feeling as a distinct stab of jealousy. The devil, she thought. She was not a simpering miss, but a woman of five and twenty who had always prided herself on being a freethinker. She was perfectly aware that Traherne was noted for the long line of barques of frailty he had variously taken to his bed. That this Jacqueline Marot might have been one of them should hardly occasion her the least surprise, let alone so much as a twinge of dismay, she told herself sternly, and was not in the least comforted by her own advice.

"As it happens," she answered, pleased that she should sound perfectly calm and collected, when inside she was struggling to subdue the green-eyed demon, "Mr. Praetorius, who enjoys an occasional evening in the seamier haunts of London, saw our Mr. Merrick in a tavern called the Cock and Bull only the night before last. He was, furthermore, in the company of a striking female who was taking great pains to remain incognita. Fortunately, however, Mr. Praetorius was clever enough to eavesdrop long enough to hear her call Merrick 'Monsieur Develin.' More than that, he learned the woman's name. It was Jacqueline Marot."

"If *she* was the woman, your Mr. Merrick would seem to enjoy a strange fellowship, indeed," said Traherne, who could not but think matters surrounding his wood nymph had taken a decidedly unsavory turn.

"Why, Lucius?" asked Althea, noting the crease had etched itself once more between the duke's eyebrows. "What do you mean? Obviously, you know the woman. Who is she?"

"The whole world knows Jacqueline Marot," Traherne replied in cynical accents. "Or knows *of* her. She is a French aristocrat who fled France to escape Madame Guillotine, or at least that is what she claims to be."

"You, however, entertain reservations concerning the validity of her story?" queried Althea, who could not but sense that her dearest lord duke would seem suddenly uncommonly distracted.

"I find her claims suspect." Appearing to shrug off his momentary abstraction, Traherne picked up his forgotten drink and absently swirled the amber liquid around the sides of the glass. "She arrived in London without any visible means of support other than a few jewels, which she immediately sold." Sampling the aroma of the brandy, he sipped experimentally. "Still, she has managed to live exceedingly well as the mistress to a succession of wealthy men of influence.'' A mirthless smile flickered about his hard lips. ''She even had ambitions to set herself up with the Duke of Traherne at one time.'' Lifting the glass, he sipped again.

''If that is the case,'' said Althea, favoring Traherne with a demure look out of the corners of her eyes, ''then I think it is pertinent to know if she succeeded, do not you?''

She was rewarded with a startled bark of laughter from her dearest Traherne. ''You may be sure she did not,'' drawled the duke, thinking the little minx had never looked more desirable than she did at that moment with twin imps peeking out of her all-too-fascinating orbs. ''Though I shall not deny the woman possesses a certain seductive charm, as it happens, I prefer to set out my own lures. Promise me, Althea, should you feel an irresistible impulse to call on Jacqueline Marot, you will consult with me first. Believe me when I tell you that it would not be wise to see her alone.''

''No, I daresay she is not at all a pleasant person. Mr. Praetorius heard her threaten to cut out Merrick's heart for him. I suspect she is the sort of scheming female who lures unsuspecting males to her bed with the intention of bleeding them dry afterward, in which case, Lucius, I cannot think it would be at all wise for you to see Jacqueline Marot without me to make sure she tries none of her tricks on you.''

''Little devil,'' said Traherne, in keen appreciation of the masterful way in which she had turned his words back on him. ''You may be sure I am perfectly capable of dealing with the likes of Jacqueline Marot.''

''No more than am I, Lucius,'' Althea did not hesitate to inform him. ''I wish you will cease to think of me as some wilting violet. Or, worse, as a green girl who has not the smallest notion that the world can be a dangerous place. I have been looking out for myself for a long time now, and just because I weakened on one crucial issue and gave in to the temptation to marry you does not mean I am prepared to be kept shut away in an ivory tower while you ride out to slay my dragons for me. You promised we should do this together, Your Grace, or had you forgotten?''

Forgotten? Egad, thought Traherne. His cursed promise had kept him awake at nights with the unwelcome prospect before him of discovering a way to keep his redoubtable wood nymph safe while keeping his word to her. And now that Jacqueline Marot would seem to be a part of the dark plot that threatened Althea, he was even less enamored of the promise he had made to her.

The truth was Jacqueline Marot was as calculating as she was dangerous. That she had been seen in a tavern of obvious ill repute with an adventurer like Merrick was more than curious. While she might not be accepted at Almack's or in the best of houses, she was a well-known figure at the opera, was invited to any number of balls and soirees, and could be seen tooling a spirited pair of matched bays in Hyde Park on any given day at the fashionable hour of five. She would, in fact, undoubtedly be present at Lord Branscombe's masquerade ball the very next evening, grimly reflected Traherne, a fact of which he vastly preferred his enterprising little wood nymph remain in ignorance. Not only would the ball be wholly unsuitable for a young woman of refinement to attend, but he much preferred to deal with Jacqueline Marot on his own; indeed, the last thing he could wish was to have Althea drawn to the attention of the French woman.

''You may be sure that I have forgotten nothing, Althea. Least of all our pact to take Merrick down together. I beg your pardon if it seemed that I had taken measures into my own hands while leaving you to seethe in impotence in your ivory tower. The truth is, I went to White's in the hopes of finding Branscombe at his usual pursuits.''

''White's? In the middle of the afternoon?'' said Althea in no little incredulity.

"I could not agree with you more, my dear," murmured Traherne with only the merest trace of irony. "Still, whiling away the afternoon at billiards or ogling the passersby in St. James's might to some appear a worthwhile existence. Unfortunately, the earl would seem to have a new lover who occupies all of his time these days. He failed to put in his usual appearance."

"But I daresay that might be a good thing, Lucius," postulated Althea, who could not but feel a trifle chagrined at having so clearly expressed her doubts in Traherne's veracity. Naturally, he could not take his wife into the sacrosanct environs of London's most prestigious private club for men. Not even the Duke of Traherne's credit would be sufficient to have carried off anything so blatantly unacceptable as that would be. "Especially if the earl's new lover is in fact Jacqueline Marot."

"I'm afraid you may be jumping to conclusions, Althea," Traherne judiciously observed. "In fact, our every supposition concerning Branscombe is based purely on conjecture."

"You are right, of course," agreed Althea, who was already occupied with devising a way to meet the earl and his newest inamorata. "Still, it is at present all that we have. It is a pity you were unable to speak to Branscombe. I don't suppose you would have any logical reason for taking your wife to pay a morning call on his lordship?"

"I'm afraid I am not intimately acquainted with the earl," replied Traherne, who had little difficulty divining the object of his wood nymph's fertile thought processes. "It occurs to me, however, that you and I have yet to make a public appearance together. Naturally, we shall be expected to give a ball to introduce the new Duchess of Traherne to the *ton*."

"A ball, Lucius, good God!" exclaimed Althea, her eyes flying to Traherne's in no little consternation at such a prospect.

"That, however, can wait for the time being, possibly

until after your sister's arrival. For now, I was thinking more in terms of the theater this evening.''

"In the norm, I should like nothing better, Lucius," Althea said, still wrestling with the notion of giving a ball to introduce herself to the *Beau Monde*. "Indeed, I have always wished for the opportunity to see the theater, but tonight . . . I'm not sure—''

"You are feeling up to it?" Traherne finished for her in tones of apparent sympathy and understanding. "A pity. While Branscombe has deviated from his normal practices, there is every possibility that Jacqueline Marot will not. She, I believe, has never missed a Season's opening performance at the theater. However, if you are truly feeling out of frame—''

"Devil!" pronounced Althea, awarding the duke a fulminating look out of glorious gilt-green eyes. "You know very well I am feeling perfectly fine and that I was only hedging because I thought we should be about the business of discovering who Branscombe's lover is and how Merrick and the earl can possibly be connected. How dare you tease me!"

"I dare, my beautiful wood sprite, because you were so obviously planning how you were to steal from the house to do what I have expressly asked you not to do."

"And how not, my dearest Lucius," retorted Althea, "when you are so plainly keeping something from me."

A wry smile twisted at the duke's handsome lips. "It would seem, my enterprising little dove, that we find ourselves at something of an impasse."

The following night, standing with his arms held somewhat out from his sides in order to allow Greaves to buckle the sword belt about his lean waist, Traherne was still contemplating with a feeling of unease the repercussions that might accrue from that final admission to his wife.

He did not doubt that Althea would find it exceedingly difficult to forgive him when she discovered he had deliberately kept her in the dark about Branscombe's masquerade ball, even going so far as to attend without her. But then, he vastly preferred to incur her displeasure than to court disaster by exposing her to the earl's bacchanalian excesses. Indeed, he found very little to recommend in the thought of having his wife ogled, not to mention made the object of lurid advances, by an orgiastic lot of tosspots. Furthermore, he entertained a decided distaste for meetings at dawn, which, he did not doubt, would be the inevitable issue of having the Duchess of Traherne put in an appearance at Branscombe's cursed masquerade ball.

Fortunately, he had thought to prevail upon his uncle to make certain Althea was occupied for the evening. Despite Hilary's initial, ill-disguised horror at the wife Traherne had chosen for himself, he had had only to meet Althea to fall immediately under her spell. Indeed, Traherne had not had to tell Hilary Keene that Althea had been more sinned against than sinning. He had come to that conclusion himself within twenty minutes of engaging her in lively conversation. Perhaps Ophelia, who had borne her doting husband five girls, had had something to do with Hilary's final and total capitulation. It had been her considered opinion that the new Duchess of Traherne was worth any ten of the quizzes and tittle-tattlers who would take delight in bandying Althea's name about. One had only to see Traherne with the girl to know she was good for him. And to Ophelia, who had taken the twelve-year-old duke into the bosom of her family and reared him like the son she had never had, that was all that really signified.

Althea had, in short, found instant and powerful allies in Lord Hilary Keene and his dearest wife, who, at Traherne's request, had invited the duchess to dinner that evening. Assuming that Traherne was intended for White's, Althea had seemed loath to go. Indeed, still angry with him in the wake of her first appearance in public as the new Duchess of Traherne at what she considered his heartless sin of omission, she had undoubtedly been happy to be spared his company.

The devil, cursed Traherne to himself, as he clapped the wide-brimmed pirate's hat with its ostrich plume on his head and descended to his waiting carriage. He was cynically aware that the evening at the theater had been less than an unmitigated success. He had known it was doomed the moment he stepped into his private box and was made instantly and acutely aware that an immediate hush had fallen over the entire theater and every head had turned to regard him with an air of scandalous anticipation.

No doubt he should have felt a measure of relief that it had not been his wife who was the object of the whispers and stares. On retrospect, he doubted not it was too soon for the rumors to have gone the rounds concerning Althea's checkered past. Still, he could hardly congratulate himself on having attended a play without having first made himself aware of what should, in the circumstances, have been of the greatest significance to him: He had not thought to discover what play was being performed or, more important, what players were acting the roles.

It had come to him, even before the surreptitious nudge of his wife's elbow, the real cause of his glaring discomfort. But then, of course it could hardly have been anyone other than the one person he foolishly had least anticipated meeting—the Dowager Duchess of Traherne. It was, in fact, practically inevitable in view of the full extent of the farce that the Fates had perpetrated against him.

Hardly had he made the pertinent discovery that his mother occupied the box next to his than the curtain went up, a circumstance for which he had been exceedingly grateful until, well into the first scene, which he had immediately recognized as the opening scene of Shakespeare's *Hamlet*, he had been visited by the vision of a ghost—the ghost of Hamlet's father, in the form of his own mama's lover. Egad!

It had been exceedingly doubtful from that moment on which drama being enacted occupied the attention of the audience: the one involving the Prince of Denmark's agonizing over the betrayal of his father by the prince's uncle and mother, or the one in the private box involving the imagined torment of the son of a powerful duke who had suffered abandonment and betrayal by an errant wife for a lover who was even then parading about on the stage.

No doubt, under different circumstances, Traherne would have appreciated the irony of his situation. Being forced to sit through the first three acts of a tragedy that circumstance had transformed into his own personal comedy, however, had not appealed to his usually keen sense of the absurd. He had signaled an end to his participation by leaving in the middle of the fourth act. Thus he had spoiled the pleasure that should have been Althea's at seeing her very first play in a London theater, not to mention their ostensible purpose for attending—to observe Jacqueline Marot and any of her acquaintances who chose to visit her in her box directly across the way.

Worse in Traherne's mind, Althea had been given to glimpse how the *ton* treated those who were the victims of scandal. He had known, even if she had not, that in a few weeks' time the event would be all but forgotten and she, as the Duchess of Traherne, would find herself the undisputed Arbiter of Fashion. It could not be otherwise. He had made sure of that when he gave her his title and all that went with it. Indeed, when he had legally adopted her acknowledged daughter.

No doubt the greatest irony was that had he but condescended to acknowledge the woman seated in the box next to his, he would have brought to an end as well his mother's exile from the society to which she had been borne.

It had needed only a gesture from Traherne, and that he

had not been willing to give. He did not doubt it had been that circumstance to which Althea had unreasonably taken exception, even going so far as to claim a headache rather than share her bed with him!

The devil, thought Traherne with sardonic appreciation for this unexpected turn of events. If he could find little to comfort himself in the fact that his refusal to demonstrate to the world his approval of his prodigal parent had engendered a coldness between himself and his wife, he could at least be grateful that it had spared him the necessity of openly lying to her. She had kept to her bed and taken her meals in her room until it was time to descend to her waiting carriage. Then she had done little more than bid Traherne a chilly good-bye.

No doubt he could console himself with the one profitable outcome of the disastrous events at the theater: There had been established an irrefutable link between Merrick and the Earl of Branscombe. Branscombe, had been present with Jacqueline Marot in the box directly opposite Traherne's, a fact that the duke had purposely omitted to point out to Althea.

The Earl of Branscombe's Town House presented every manifestation that a full-fledged orgy was in session. Gracile milkmaids, bewinged fairies, and plump Bacchae arrayed in provocatively scanty costumes were boisterously pursued by an improbable host of masked highwaymen, berobed sheiks, belled jesters, and buffoons. Attired in pirate costume complete with brown leather breeches tucked into black Marlborough bucket boots that reached over the knees, a white shirt with full flowing sleeves, and a wide leather belt about the waist—as well as a broad leather strap draped across the chest from one shoulder to the opposite hip, a pistol thrust through his belt, and a mask tied over the upper half of his face—Traherne had drawn more than one alluring glance from the attendant dusky-eyed wenches. Drawn by the strains of music, he made his way through the press to the ballroom draped fantastically in transparent flowing silk meant, no doubt, to depict an Elysian paradise.

It came to Traherne, disengaging himself from the clinging hands of an Arabian harem girl, that he would have been better served to spend his evening at home exerting himself to make up with his fulminating wife than trying to penetrate the multitude of disguises to find Merrick, Branscombe, or even the full-bodied beauty, Jacqueline Marot.

Hardly had that thought crossed his mind than his attention was caught by the solo performance of a Gypsy dancing girl, weaving and gyrating with sinuous grace at the center of the dance floor to the enthusiastic appreciation of a growing circle of oglers. The willowy figure was exotically costumed in a shimmering emerald green bodice, which left her midriff bare and had long full transparent sleeves and a plunging décolletage that drew provocative attention to the soft swell of her breasts. A full ankle-length skirt of vermilion gauze hemmed with gold braid showed purple drawers beneath, as well as bare legs, not to mention bare feet thrust into Spanish slippers that revealed golden toe rings and toenails painted an enticing vermilion to match her skirt. Despite the purple veil arranged to hide all of her face save for a pair of magnificent flashing eyes, he knew her at once. Indeed, she might just as well have stood barefaced before him. Good God, he thought. Althea!

Chapter Twelve

Shivering in the chill of the evening, Althea pulled her heavy cloak more firmly around her as she settled back against the red velvet squabs of her mama-in-law's private carriage. She hardly dared to think that very soon she must discard the cloak and parade herself before a host of people in what could only be described as a wholly indecent costume. Indeed, she doubted not she was about to sink herself quite utterly beneath reproach.

How odd that she felt none of the trepidation that she should have done. Instead, she was conscious of a delicious tingling of nerve endings not unlike what she had felt when, at the age of ten, she had stood poised on the third-story terrace wall of her father's house in Fort St. George in preparation of making her first test flight of her trapeze-flying-kite. A pity she had failed to consider the variations in wind currents as affected by the narrow alleyway bordered by tall houses on either side, the intense heat of the day, and the pressure of a storm building. The kite had flown magnificently for all of ten seconds with her clinging to the trapeze hanging beneath it, until what she assumed had been a sudden unexpected falling away of the wind, like a fist driving downward, had plunged her ignominiously into a heap on the ground. Fortunately, while her trapeze-flying-kite had suffered total annihilation, she herself had escaped with only a sprained ankle and a badly grazed knee.

Still, she was acutely aware that she risked a deal more than a bruised knee with this evening's adventure. Very likely, if her identity were discovered, she would find herself relegated to the castle dungeon on a diet of bread and water for an indeterminate length of time by her disenchanted husband.

The devil, she thought, deliberately fanning the flames of resentment against her dearest lord duke, who had broken his word to her. He had all but issued her a challenge when he admitted he was deliberately keeping something from her, and she had never run from a challenge in her life!

No doubt fortune had played into her hands. Returning from freshening up before dinner, she had overheard Ophelia Keene taking Lord Hilary to task for lending himself to a plot to keep the young duchess occupied while her husband of only five months availed himself of the opportunity to attend a masquerade ball at, of all places, the home of the Earl of Branscombe, who everyone knew was a dyed-in-the-wool libertine. Really, Ophelia had thought better of Lucius. Indeed, she could not imagine what had come over one who had never before demonstrated the smallest inclination to hedonism. Althea, seething with self-righteous enlightenment, was hardly soothed by Lord Hilary's assurances to his wife that it was not the orgiastic excesses that had impelled the duke to attend Branscombe's masquerade ball, but the hope of discovering Althea's enemies that he might bring their evil machinations finally to an end.

Pleading a headache, Althea had begged to be excused after only the fourth remove. In the face of Ophelia's whole-hearted championing of her dinner guest, Althea could not but feel a twinge of conscience for the lie. Even worse, she had not hesitated to abandon poor Mr. Cutler. Returning into her host's house ostensibly to retrieve his mistress's forgotten ivory-handled fan, he had been left behind when Althea immediately ordered the coachman to drive on.

Althea was very much afraid that she had discovered previously unexplored depths of depravity in her character. Indeed, she could not but wonder to what lengths she would be willing to go to teach her arrogant managing husband that she was not one to be manipulated and lied to. How dared he go to an orgy without taking her with him! Really, it was too bad of him.

Naturally, she had immediately thought to go to her mama-in-law. After all, there really was no one else who would be not only willing but able to provide her with a costume as well as discover the address of the Earl of Branscombe's Town House. Indeed, it never occurred to Althea that Olivia Traherne might find anything to object to in helping her son's wife attend a masquerade ball given by a man who prided himself on providing entertainments of an orgiastic excess. Nor had she been mistaken in her assessment.

Upon learning the purpose behind Althea's determination to attend uninvited the Earl of Branscombe's gala, the dowager duchess had appeared to fling herself wholeheartedly into the effort, even going so far as to suggest Althea send the duke's coach home and avail herself of Olivia's own newly purchased carriage. After all, it would never do to have anyone identify the Duchess of Traherne from the ducal coat of arms emblazoned on the side of her conveyance. Nor had she scrupled to press a small hand pistol on her daughter-in-law, advising she conceal it somewhere about her person where it might be conveniently reached. One never knew when one might find it necessary to discourage unwanted advances, especially in an environment of bacchanalian abandonment.

At last, disguised, armed, and ready to mount her mama-in-law's carriage, Althea had been given one final example of Olivia's thoughtful generosity. Garbed in the dashing striped jeweled turban, red jamal with a decorative sash, white trousers, and pointed-toe gold leather shoes of a Moghul lord, Mr. Praetorius stepped forward to give her an arm up before he himself, placing a buss on his lady love's cheek, climbed in after Althea.

"She is quite fond of you, you know," observed Praetorius, who had been watching the interesting play of emotion cross the young duchess's face. "Olivia, I believe, sees something of herself in you, a kindred spirit, as it were."

Althea smiled. "I'm sure I could not be more flattered. I find much to admire in Her Grace, most especially what would seem her utter self-assurance, not to mention her adventurous spirit. I do so wish Lucius would at least talk with her."

"Perhaps one day the lad will relent, though I fear I am something of a deterrent in that regard," mused Praetorius. "Especially as Olivia and I have never gone through the formality of a marriage ceremony. I daresay he views me in the light of an adventurer, who must live off his mama's largesse. And who can blame him? In his eyes, I cannot appear to have much to offer a woman like the duchess. In truth, I have never understood what it is that she sees in me."

"Could it be, Mr. Praetorius, that she sees a man who adores her? A man who delivered her from an existence she found intolerable and who has ever since filled her life with rich wonderful experiences and given her companionship of the sort she had previously ceased to believe would ever be hers to know. You have made her feel complete, Mr. Praetorius. With you, she is made to feel a whole woman."

"No, Your Grace," said Praetorius, an oddly bleak look in his normally twinkling eyes, "not quite whole. I'm afraid I could never fill the empty space created by the loss of her son. No one could ever do that. But then, here we are," he added brusquely, indicating the street lined with waiting carriages, and the moment was broken. "Are you ready, my dear? Whatever happens, I shall be somewhere nearby should you need me."

Finding herself some moments later in the Earl of Branscombe's foyer, Althea could not but be grateful for that final assurance, as she was treated to her first sight of an orgy in full progress. It occurred to her, observing a rotund beauty, scantily clad in the diaphanous gown of a Dionysian handmaiden, spilling wine from a ewer into the gaping mouth of a Roman gladiator sprawled on the floor, that there might not be a great deal to recommend in total orgiastic abandonment. She did not doubt the earl's magnificent Oriental rug would never be quite the same in the wake of it. Nor could she think there was anything in the least attractive in seeing a grown man bent, retching and heaving, over a potted palm. And, despite the aroma of burning incense, she was moved to wrinkle her nose against the stench of sour wine, perspiring bodies, and other even less pleasant odors, which she did not care to identify. Indeed, for the first time it came to her that Traherne might have had a perfectly valid reason for having schemed to deny her the dubious pleasure of witnessing the licentious behavior of the alleged genteel in various less than dignified postures of bacchanalian revelry.

It was with some relief that she discovered the ballroom exuded a certain otherworldly charm with its silk drapes fluttering beneath the ceiling at odd variance with the rollicking strains of a country dance just then in progress. It seemed, too, that here the revelers, perhaps benefiting from the exercise, were less under the grape's debilitating influence. They were hardly less restrained, however, in their pursuit of lascivious pleasure.

Had Althea ever entertained the wish to feel herself an irresistible object of desire, finding herself suddenly at the center of a pack of half-drunken fawning wolves must certainly have cured her of it. Worse, somehow she had become separated from Praetorius, who seemed to have simply vanished. Still, she had not lived all her life among soldiers for nothing. Holding in reserve as a last resort a demonstration of the basic uses of the fulcrum and lever, she took recourse in evasive tactics.

Holding her concealing veil firmly in place, she began to weave and sway out of the way of pawing hands in what she was sure must have resembled an amateurish rendition of Salome's dance of the seven veils. It was, however, proving effective in allowing her to maneuver through the press in the direction of the nearest exit. It was, at any rate, until twirling to evade the grasp of a besotted friar, she became entangled in her swirling skirts and, stumbling, came up hard against an immovable object, followed by the clamp of a hard muscular arm across her chest.

Feeling her veil come loose, Althea reacted instinctively. Clasping the forearm in both hands, she prepared to fling her weight forward.

"*Softly,* my girl," whispered a voice in her ear. "I haven't the least desire for a demonstration of the fundamentals of leverage at the moment, enlightening as it might prove to be. Perhaps at a later date in some more congenial place."

Althea stiffened, struck with joyful relief. "*Lu—,*" she gasped, only to be instantly silenced by demanding lips covering hers.

How strange that, even in the midst of the jeering revelers, the world should seem to spin and whirl away, leaving Althea and Traherne alone in a universe all their own. She had the peculiar sensation of melting in his arms. She was deliriously sure her knees would not hold her were she to withdraw her arms from about his neck. Then just as suddenly the world came crashing back again.

"You! Captain Buccaneer!" called the loud raucous voice of a burly fellow incongruously attired in the purple doublet, green-and-white-striped trunk hose, and gold-embroidered shoes of one of Shakespeare's gentlemen of Verona. "You've had your taste of honey, and that was more than you were entitled to. My friends and I had our sights on the wench. Either share her favors or unhand her.''

"Indeed, Captain. She's a lively piece,'' piped up a spindly legged jester in motley and bells. "Plenty enough to go around. No call to be miserly.''

"Here, here,'' agreed a brown-robed friar. "We saw her first.''

Hastily readjusting her concealing veil, Althea felt Traherne's strong frame stiffen. Then to her stunned amazement, he bent down to catch her behind the knees and, rising, slung her ignominiously over a broad powerful shoulder.

"I'm afraid you will have to wait your turn, gentlemen,'' announced the duke, bringing the flat of his hand down in what was meant to be a possessive slap on his duchess's firm rounded rump, but which landed with enough force to bring both her head and her feet up with a jerk. "I prefer to dine alone.''

"OH!'' squealed Althea, in mingled pain and outrage. "You, *devil!* How dare you—''

"Silence,'' commanded Traherne in brutal tones, "or it will be all the worse for you. And now I must ask you to excuse us, gentlemen. The wench and I have an assignation with a whip and a pair of manacles.''

Someone twittered in obvious titillation at the image evoked by that assertion. Althea, wondering with some alarm if Traherne had partaken of something more potent than the intoxicating fruit of Bacchus's vines, went suddenly stiff with incredulous disbelief, even as Traherne started forward in what gave every appearance of impatience to consummate his anticipated pleasures.

He was stopped by a rude hand on his arm.

"One bloody moment,'' objected the owner of that hindering member, whom Althea had little difficulty in identifying as the thickset gentleman of Verona. "You're taking a lot on yourself. What if we're of a mind to object?''

"Then, my friend," said Traherne, pulling the pistol from his belt and pointing it with an unnervingly steady hand at the fellow's bulging midriff, "you will be the first to taste this."

Good God, groaned Althea. Finding little to applaud in her present undignified position and far from relishing being made the unwitting cause of what suddenly loomed as an imminent and unavoidable slaughter, Althea was heartily wishing the entire male population at Jericho, when she glimpsed the approach of a striking newcomer to the scene.

Althea knew him at once. After all, his lithe, well-knit form gracefully appareled in a flowing white chlamys and Ionic chiton, his countenance unencumbered by a mask, he presented the sort of rare masculine beauty that put one clearly in mind of an Adonis. More than that, she had seen him only the previous night in the theater box directly across from the one occupied by herself and Traherne. The devil take the odiously deceitful duke! How dared he fail to mention that the gentleman was the Earl of Branscombe—or that in all likelihood the raven-haired beauty who had shared his company and whom even then Althea glimpsed slipping away through the throng of dancers was none other than Jacqueline Marot! Indeed, despite the Venetian half-mask of white lace, there was no mistaking the voluptuous figure arrayed in the costume of an Egyptian queen.

The earl presented a compelling presence of calm in the midst of threatening chaos.

"For shame, gentlemen," said his lordship, gently chiding. "Is this how we celebrate Bacchus—with guns and harsh words?" Deliberately he placed himself between the bristling gentleman of Verona and the pirate captain's steely menace. "Pray, calm yourselves. Put away your weapon, Captain. None here will dispute your claim to the woman. Rather shall we eat, drink, and raise our voices in blissful song. Come, let us to the feasting table go."

To Althea's relief and no little amazement, the throng

surrounding them appeared visibly to relax and then break up, gradually to drift away, until even the disgruntled gentleman of Verona relented to the friar's gruff urging that the Gypsy wench was not the only female available for the taking.

"I suggest, Your Grace," Branscombe said quietly, "that it will be safe to set the lady down now, if you wish. I daresay she has taken little pleasure in being treated in the manner of a leg of mutton." At Traherne's incredulous arch of an eyebrow, Branscombe shrugged. "I am a keen observer of men, Your Grace. There was no mistaking the way you carry yourself. And now perhaps you would both care to join me in a small libation before I must return to my other guests. Purely in the way of an apology for this regrettable incident. I trust you would not object, Your Grace, to an excellent spot of brandy?"

"At the moment, my lord," said Traherne, setting his burden down on her feet, "I believe I should like nothing better."

"Splendid." Penetrating brown eyes fixed speculatively on Althea. "And perhaps tea for our enchanting Gypsy dancer?"

"A touch of sherry perhaps. Unlike some I might name," added Althea, awarding her piratical husband a fulminating glance over the concealing fabric of her veil, "you are all graciousness, my lord."

"Not at all, my dear lady." The earl, gathering the folds of his chlamys over one arm, ushered them courteously through a nearby exit, which gave access to a private corridor. "As host of this gala in celebration of all that is most bestial in God's fairest creation, I must be gratified that the Duke of Traherne has chosen to honor us with his presence. It is well known that any social gathering must be judged a *success fou* if His Grace but chooses to make an appearance." Pausing before a white beveled door trimmed in gilt, his hand on the door handle, he smiled gently at Traherne.

"What a pity no one shall ever know of it." Opening the door, he stood back to allow his guests to step past him. "But there you have it."

The room into which Branscombe introduced them gave the appearance of a private sanctuary devoted to the contemplation of beautiful things. Indeed, Althea could not but think the air of refinement reflected in the carefully chosen *objets d'art* was in decidedly sharp contrast to the tasteless display of excess being enacted beyond the serenity of the chamber's four walls. The handpicked selection of paintings, sculptures, and various musical instruments arranged with simple elegance for their pleasurable enjoyment would seem to portray a sensitivity that she would not have ascribed to his lordship only fifteen minutes earlier. But then, in his late twenties, with his lustrous brown eyes and his fair hair clustering in short curls about his head, he was not precisely what Althea had expected. Faith, despite his air of worldly experience, she sensed in him a fine intelligence coupled with a gentleness of disposition that she could not but find curiously disarming. Strange that she did not fear him, a man she did not doubt was in some manner allied with Evelyn Merrick. Clearly, the Earl of Branscombe was something of an enigma.

"No doubt you will pardon me, Your Grace," said the earl, giving the bellpull a yank before filling two glasses from a decanter on a magnificent silver grog tray and a third from a bottle of what gave every appearance of being a fine amontillado, "if I confess to some surprise at your presence at one of my entertainments." Inclining his head, he presented Althea the sherry glass. "While, naturally, I could not be more pleased at the condescension," he continued, his gaze lingering for the barest instant on Althea's veiled face before he turned back to the grog tray, "I had heard you were recently married. I believe, in fact, I had the pleasure of seeing your lovely wife only last night at the theater." Handing Traherne a glass, Branscombe lifted his own in graceful tribute. "May I extend to you my sincerest congratulations and say that I wish you both exceedingly happy?"

Meeting the earl's eyes over the brandy glass, Traherne smiled faintly in perfect understanding. Branscombe, having penetrated the disguise of the Duke of Traherne, had had little difficulty in guessing the identity of the lissome Gypsy wench. He was right, after all. Although the Duke of Traherne might be well known for the barques of frailty he kept, his reputation did not extend to indulging in debaucheries on the order of a bacchanalian love-fest. Never mind the additional peculiarity of undertaking to pit himself against a score of drunken revelers for the dubious honor of claiming the favors of a nubile young beauty he presumably had never seen before. No doubt his lordship could find but one explanation for his uninvited guest's exceedingly odd behavior: Obviously the duke, contrary to appearances, was not unacquainted with the wench. Indeed, she could have been no one other than the only woman for whom a man of the duke's remove (the previous Duke of Traherne notwithstanding) would have dared risk his life and his reputation. She was, of course, his duchess.

"My lord," murmured Traherne, raising his glass in acknowledgment of the earl's perspicacity as well as what would seem the man's peculiar sense of integrity.

The earl had made it plain the duke's secret would never leave the room.

Traherne found himself forced to revise his opinion of one whom he had previously dismissed as a wastrel and a decadent. Obviously, there was more to Branscombe than that for which Traherne had given him credit. Still, his irrefutable association with a man of Evelyn Merrick's stamp, not to mention the likes of Jacqueline Marot, would seem to condemn him. Either he was exceedingly deep or he was a pawn in a game of which he was kept in ignorance.

Either way, he had generated a host of questions that Traherne would have given a great deal to have answered.

A soft scratching at the door announced the arrival of a servant in answer to the earl's earlier summons.

"It has been a pleasure, Your Grace," murmured Branscombe, setting his empty glass aside with a subtle air of finality. "But alas, I fear the duties of a host await me. My servant will be pleased to conduct you to a room upstairs where your lovely Gypsy dancer may freshen up if she so desires." He paused with a meaningful air. "Might I suggest, Your Grace, that you lock the door against any possible intrusions?"

With a final admonishment to treat his home as their own, Branscombe, bowing, left them to the ministrations of the servant, who conducted them by a private stairway to the floor above.

Some moments later, the Duke and Duchess of Traherne found themselves alone at last in a spacious chamber. Though tastefully appointed with fine furniture, rich Oriental carpets, and damask drapes, the room exuded an air of long disuse.

"Faith, Lucius, he knew!" exclaimed Althea, as soon as the door had closed behind the servant. "What a strange creature he is, to be sure. How do you think he was able to see through our disguises?"

Turning the key in the lock, Traherne came around to regard his wood nymph with a singular lack of amusement.

"I cannot speak for mine," he said, taking in the undeniably alluring sight of his duchess garbed in what could only be described as scandalous attire. He was made instantly aware of a distinct stirring in his loins. Hellfire! he cursed silently. "Yours, however, would seem particularly designed for transparency. What are you doing here, Althea? And where the devil did you come by that costume?"

"You know very well what I am doing here, Lucius," replied Althea, removing her veil to sip at her sherry. Unable to sample it earlier without revealing her face, she had had perforce to bring it with her. "The same thing that you are doing here. As for the costume, I'm afraid that must remain my secret." At last she looked at him, her gaze accusing. "We all have our little secrets, do we not, Lucius? Or are you going to try to tell me you did not see Branscombe and his lady friend at the theater last night? Or that you had not planned all along to come to his orgy without telling me a word about it? An orgy, Lucius, to which you would rather come alone! Really, that was too bad of you.

"Or will you try to convince me, for that matter, that you did not enlist Lord Hilary's connivance in keeping me safely out of the way while you went about breaking your word to me? Poor Lord Hilary. I daresay his dearest Ophelia will never forgive him for that—or me for having perforce to claim a headache, when I was feeling perfectly fine. And then there is the unfortunate Mr. Cutler, whom I had little choice but to abandon. I very much fear I am become a wholly depraved character, Lucius, and all because you could not bring yourself to trust me."

Good God, thought Traherne, who was chiding himself for a bloody fool for ever having believed he could trust anyone but himself to keep an eye on his enterprising duchess. On the other hand, if it was an orgy his little wood nymph wanted, he was most damned willing to oblige her!

Deliberately he took a step toward her.

"And if I had told you all the truth, would you have agreed to stay out of it, Althea?" demanded His Grace, in no mood to be made the villain in the evening's near-disastrous events. "Never mind that you came to within an inch of instigating a Donnybrook Fair or that you very nearly were given an object lesson in the finer aspects of bacchanalian revelry. A lesson, which, while undoubtedly enlightening, would hardly have proved felicitous to your peace of mind, never mind mine. The fact remains tonight's entertainments are not in the least suited to a female of quality. You, my girl, are lucky I do not take you over my knee and beat you.''

"I believe, Your Grace, that you have already taken that liberty,'' said Althea, standing her ground as she was recalled to his earlier iniquitous behavior. "How dared you strike me when I was in no case to defend myself. And what in heaven's name was all that about a whip and manacles? Really, Lucius, I am beginning to wonder about you.''

"As well you should,'' declared the duke, a dangerous glint in his eyes. "If you do not swear to me that you will never again pull a stunt like this, you are very likely to discover precisely what use I had in mind for those particular items.''

"Very well, Lucius,'' Althea replied without hesitation, as she set her empty glass aside, "I promise.''

Traherne, who had expected something quite different from his stubborn, maddeningly independent duchess and who, further, had as yet to find ease from the pressure in his chest, reacted as if he had not even heard her. "The devil,'' he growled, taking her by the arms. "I will not experience another moment such as the one I went through upon arriving to discover the Gypsy girl performing a dance of seduction at the center of a circle of drunken bacchanalian revelers was my wife.''

"Indeed, it must have been a terrible shock for you,'' agreed Althea, meeting the fierce glitter of his gaze with a look of perfect understanding. "My poor Lucius, I should never have been so headstrong as to suppose you did not have a perfectly good reason for not wishing me to attend Branscombe's ball. Unfortunately, it was already too late by the time I came to that realization.''

Traherne's black eyebrows fairly snapped together over the bridge of his nose. "The devil, Althea, do not think you can talk me out of this. This time you have gone too far.

Egad, there was not a male in that ballroom who had not conceived the notion of carting you off to the nearest bedchamber to have his way with you. Hell and the devil confound it! Have you any idea how close I came to shooting an unarmed man in order to prevent just such an occurrence?''

"You may be sure I am perfectly aware of it, Lucius," declared Althea, who suffered a chill down her backbone at the mere thought of it. "Indeed, I shall not soon forgive you for having put yourself in that position, when it really was not necessary."

"Not necessary," said the duke, drawing back to look at her. "You astonish me!"

"Yes, I am aware of that," Althea observed with perfect equanimity. "As it happens, however, I was perfectly prepared to defend myself. If a demonstration in the fundamentals of leverage had not been sufficient to discourage any unwanted advances, I feel certain a shot in the air would have done. You must not think I was so remiss as to come tonight without taking the precaution of arming myself."

"Egad, a sobering thought," reflected Traherne, who was even then envisioning his duchess holding at bay an entire room of belligerent bacchanalians with a single-shot pistol.

"No more sobering than the prospect of having the Duke of Traherne on trial for murdering an unarmed man," Althea observed in a practical vein. "Which does not alter the fact that everything that happened tonight was entirely my fault. If I had stayed at Lord Hilary's as you wanted me to do, you would not have been placed in the position of feeling you had to defend your wholly scandalous duchess. Be sure that I understand perfectly what motivated you, and whether it was necessary or not, given your highly developed masculine code of honor, not to mention the natural mechanism of a male's instinct to protect his mate, the outcome was inevitable. I most sincerely beg your pardon, Lucius. I should have considered all the factors in play before I gave into the irrational dictates of emotion."

"You should, indeed," agreed Traherne, who perversely found little to recommend in the lowering notion that Althea had taken all the blame on herself for the evening's near-catastrophic events for the sole reason that she should have realized her husband was ruled by natural laws and instincts over which he apparently had no control. Good God! As if reason had had nothing to do with assessing the odds ruling the probable outcome of the scene with which he had been greeted on entering Branscombe's ballroom! "On the other hand," he heard himself saying with a distinct sense of having abandoned all rationale, "we cannot rule out the possibility that, had I been wholly honest with you from the very beginning, we might have been able to reach a reasonable compromise that would have obviated the necessity for independent action. In which case, the entire unhappy affair could have been avoided."

Struck anew at her dearest lord duke's generosity, Althea was impelled to fling her arms about his neck in gratitude for his attempt to exonerate her for her unfortunate lapse in judgment, which had resulted in placing him in a wholly untenable position, not to mention in peril of his life. "How very good you are to me, Lucius, when I have done very little to deserve your understanding! I'm afraid, however, that is hardly sufficient grounds to excuse my behavior. Even if you had confided the entire matter to me, you must see it would, in this instance, have changed very little. It is clear you would never have agreed to bring me to an orgy of major proportions anymore than I, never having seen one before, should have been content to allow you to come without me. I daresay, in retrospect, there was simply no avoiding our present circumstances."

Althea, leaning against her tall husband's powerful frame, tipped her head back to gaze quizzically up at him. "In which case, Lucius, would it not seem a shame to waste this perfectly golden opportunity? After all, this is my very first orgy, and it does not appear that we are going to discover anything of any significance here concerning Merrick. I should not like to think all the trouble we have been to to get here was totally for naught. Would you think me terribly depraved were I to confess I find the idea of making love in the midst of a bacchanalia strangely exciting to the senses?''

''Depraved in the extreme,'' pronounced Traherne. Having been given to view his scandalous duchess only twenty minutes earlier perform an exotic dance of seduction, in addition to having been acutely aware ever since that she was attired in a wholly provocative state of dishabille, the duke was, in point of fact, a deal closer than she to giving in to unbridled moral turpitude. Flinging off his hat with the ostrich plume, he caught her ruthlessly in his arms. ''A condition,'' he said, ''which you may be sure I intend to exploit to the fullest.''

''You cannot know how pleased I am to hear it,'' confessed Althea, who had been exceedingly cognizant of the fact that there was something inordinately stimulating about Traherne, garbed in tight leather breeches, which seemed singularly designed to draw attention to his muscular thighs and legs, not to mention his pleasingly firm derriere. Clasping her arms about the back of his neck, she gazed up at him out of doubtful eyes. ''For if you must know, it had occurred to me you might have found something to disgust in my attire. You have not seemed to have so much as looked at me, Lucius, since you rescued me from that ridiculous Gentleman of Verona.''

Not looked at her? Good God, thought Traherne, acutely aware of Althea's supple body pressed against his. He had been wondering, purely as a matter of academics, where in the devil his wood sprite could possibly have hidden a gun on her person. A man would have to be either blind or a blithering fool not to *look* at her! ''You may be sure that everyone who came within your sphere of influence tonight looked at you, wood sprite. It would be exceedingly difficult not to do.'' Hungrily, he lowered his head to taste the exquisitely tender flesh beneath her right earlobe while, with his hands, he initiated a tantalizingly thorough search of the likeliest hiding places for a single-shot pistol.

Althea, shuddering with pleasure, melted deliciously against him, one leg entwined about the back of his as she pressed into him. Egad, but she was all sweet fire and generosity, was his incomparable duchess. She had breached his defences as had no other woman before her. With Althea, he would never be bored. More than that, with Althea, he would never feel alone.

At last, impatient to taste her sweet delights, he lifted up her skirts and, undoing the string at the waist of her unmentionables, slipped them down over her hips and legs, a maneuver that left little doubt where she had thought to hide her pistol.

Indeed, his scandalous duchess presented a wholly provocative picture of wantonness in her transparent vermilion skirt with nothing on beneath it, save for a gun the size of her automatic mechanical igniter thrust through a black lace garter about one shapely leg well above the knee.

"Egad," uttered Traherne, envisioning the mitigating circumstances under which his wood sprite might have had occasion to retrieve her sole means of self-defense from a place that in the norm must surely have proved nigh unto impossible to reach in any sort of haste. The devil, he thought. He wanted nothing more than to take her—now— in just such a fantasized scenario.

Releasing her, he yanked at the wide leather belt girded about his waist.

"I never . . . dreamed, Lucius," breathed Althea, clinging to him, as she pressed hungry kisses into the strong column of his neck, "that a feast . . . of the senses . . . could be so . . . wondrously enhanced . . . by the . . . wearing of . . . disguises."

"I should say that depends on the disguise," rumbled Traherne, who found little to recommend at the moment in skintight leather breeches, let alone Marlborough bucket boots that reached over the knees. Grasping Althea by the wrists, he pulled her hands down from around his neck.

Suffering a pang of loss at the interruption, Althea swayed toward him. "Lucius?"

"A moment, wood sprite," he groaned and kissed her on the lips before pulling away.

Impatiently, he divested himself of the sword, which was proving a cumbersome impediment to his freedom of movement, and then his pistol, which he laid judiciously on a nearby occasional table. "If Greaves is correct in assuming this is the representative garb of that lusty breed of Englishmen who plundered and pillaged Spanish shipping two centuries ago, then I do not doubt female captives did not run the immediate risk of being ravished," he postulated, keenly aware of the painful bulge of his manhood against its leather confines. "It was the devil's own work to get into the cursed things."

"Dear, it never occurred to me—the difficulties inherent in achieving a successful orgy," observed Althea, immediately apprehending his difficulty. "I daresay there might be a distinct advantage to a Highland kilt at the moment or something on the order of Branscombe's Ionic chiton. Have you ever considered," she added, watching Traherne tug at the recalcitrant fastenings at the front of his leather breeches, "how much easier it would be if there were some sort of contrivance that would allow one to simply rip articles of clothing open and then, conversely, seal them back again? Something on the order, perhaps, of intermeshing steel teeth, like interlocking cogs sewn into the fabric, or—"

Whatever other possibilities she had envisioned for her contrivance for ripping apart and resealing the openings of clothing, she was not allowed to finish. Having won release of his magnificently erect male member—and in no case to struggle with the removal of his leather breeches, let alone his Marlborough bucket boots—Traherne dropped without preamble onto the armless Louis XV walnut prie-dieu chair with spiral carved columns, conveniently situated near at hand, and pulled Althea, standing, astraddle his thighs.

"*Lucius?*" gasped Althea at finding herself suddenly in a posture fraught with startling possibilities. Instinctively, she braced her hands against Traherne's chest to keep from falling forward.

"Excellent," Traherne applauded, his eyes glittery embers between slitted eyelids. "I believe you already have a firm grasp of the matter before us."

"Indeed, Lucius," agreed Althea with a roguish grin, "it would seem rather obvious, would it not?" Gathering her skirts to her waist, she set a knee on either side of his hips on the chair.

Traherne's smile more resembled a grimace of pain. "You did say you wanted an orgy, my girl," he reminded her. Running his hand along her inner thigh, he took the precaution of disarming her before clasping her waist between his hands to guide her to the pinnacle of his desire. "And I, as it happens, am poised and ready."

Althea had never before imagined making love while almost fully dressed, let alone while mounted on a Louis the Quinze prie-dieu chair, her beloved magnificently posed under her and between her thighs to receive her. She could not but think there was something to be said for a private orgy between oneself and one's lover. She was certain no woman had ever a more generous husband than her dearest Lucius. Despite having every reason to be displeased with her, he was yet prepared to broaden her education in the finer aspects of licentious behavior. It came to her as she fitted the head of his shaft against the swollen lips of her body that she had never loved him more than she did at that very moment.

That was her last coherent thought as Traherne, in no case to put off the lesson for so much as a moment longer, pulled her down on top of him, burying his shaft inside her.

She was to reflect some little time later that she must clearly have been taken over at that point by some hitherto unsuspected natural mechanism of human procreation. How else could she explain her utter wantonness of behavior, which had led her to lift herself off her dearest Lucius and then fill herself with him again and again, even going so far as to arch her back in an ecstasy of her own woman's power to tease and tantalize, to drive herself and him to a frenzy of need, and at last to bring them both to a blissful explosion of release?

She had never felt so gloriously sated as she did when it was all over and, blissfully aware that Traherne yet resided within her, she rested with her arms clasped behind his neck and her face nestled against his cheek. Truly, orgies with her dearest Lucius were events to be savored. Indeed, she could not but wonder if in time she might be able to bring him to love her, if only a little. For in truth he did not seem totally indifferent to her. Surely she could not be mistaken in thinking that he enjoyed their feasts of the senses every whit as much as did she. In which case, might not what had begun as an irresistible gravitational attraction between two disparate bodies develop into something deeper and longer lasting? Might not the marriage on paper become a true wedding of souls? she wondered, her heart behaving in a wholly erratic manner at a notion that must surely be as fantastical as it was impossible. And yet she could not still the tiny voice somewhere deep inside her that whispered it could happen, given enough time.

If only they had not a pall of danger hanging over them! she thought with a pang. And if only she had not had to involve him in the lie she had perpetrated for Gloriana's sake!

Hardly had that thought crossed her mind than Traherne stirred and pressed his lips to her forehead.

"Little as I care to disturb this moment," he said, his voice tinged with dry humor, "it occurs to me that, the earl's hospitality notwithstanding, we should do better not to overstay our welcome."

"I suppose we should be going," Althea agreed with no little reluctance. "After all, it is unlikely we shall find what we came to discover."

"Althea," Traherne gently prodded some seconds later, when his wholly scandalous duchess had made no discernible effort to remove herself from her present position. "Should any of Branscombe's besotted guests take a notion to invade our privacy, I'm afraid they would find me at something of a disadvantage."

"You should have considered that particular *before* you thought to introduce me to the exquisite pleasures of orgiastic excess," murmured Althea, snuggling closer. "Besides, it's all hollow. No one is likely to break down the door to Branscombe's private quarters. And in case you had failed to notice, we are presently ensconced in what could only be the countess's chambers. If there were a countess, which I presume there is not, since, from all appearances, the room has not been used for some little time. Nevertheless, you may be sure the door behind us connects to the master suite."

"Very astute of you, I do not doubt," applauded Traherne, dropping a kiss on the top of his duchess's head. "On the other hand, you may be sure our host does not anticipate our spending the night next door to him. Up with you, my girl."

"Devil," chided Althea with a moue of displeasure. Suffering a pang of loss as Traherne's now-flaccid member slipped out of her, she stood and, reached for her discarded purple drawers. "At least it would seem probable that Jacqueline Marot is indeed Branscombe's new lover, since she was here with him tonight.''

''The devil she was,'' said Traherne, who, having risen from the memorable Louis XV prie-dieu chair with spiral-columned legs, was occupied with putting himself back to rights. A shiver coursed down Althea's spine at the look he bent upon her. ''You saw her?''

''I saw her slip out of the ballroom just before Branscombe dispersed the angry pack around us.'' Finished tying the string at the top of her drawers, Althea slid the pistol in her garter and, covering it, let her skirts drop. ''I had the distinct impression she wished to be away before the earl delivered us out of our dilemma.''

''You may be sure of it,'' Traherne grimly concurred, ''if she recognized me. At the very least she would know I was not here for the entertainments. I'm afraid we may have alerted her to—''

At the distinct sound of footsteps in the corridor, he broke off, a warning finger to his lips. Hastily, he reached for Althea's hand before dousing the lamp.

Acutely aware of the hard clasp of Traherne's hand on hers, Althea vibrated to the click of a latch and the sound of a door opening and closing. A familiar masculine voice, notable for its cultured accents, penetrated the thick pall of darkness.

''Come, my dear, must you be unhappy with me tonight, of all nights? I have been disconsolate these past two days without you. Can we not simply rejoice that we are together again? After all, we are alone at last, and it is a night of celebration.''

''Do not start with me, Sinjun. You know I cannot stay. I should not have come at all tonight had it not been for the French woman. I should never have involved myself with that cursed she-devil. Jacqueline Marot will be the ruin of me yet!''

Althea, who had uttered an involuntary gasp at the first

of that utterance, stood stiff with horrified disbelief. Even after six years, there was no mistaking that voice—or the significance of that singular exchange between the two occupants of the adjoining room.

Good God, she thought, her mind reeling with the stunning realization. Branscombe's lover was Evelyn Merrick!

Chapter Thirteen

Gratefully, Althea felt Traherne's arm slip around her shoulders to draw her to him in the darkness. It was not the realization that Merrick and Branscombe were Roman in their pursuits that had made her knees go suddenly weak beneath her. She was not so green as not to know the ways of the world. It was the resounding implications of that revelation that had set the room to spinning around her.

Merrick and Branscombe were lovers! seemed to reverberate through her mind like a question with no answers. How could this be?

Merrick was Effie's father. Or was he?

Certainly, the unmistakable sounds of a lovers' quarrel issuing from the other side of the door would seem to cast some doubt on that previously unquestioned assertion. Not that a man whose preferences ran to other men could not father an infant on a woman. She knew that it was not an infrequent occurrence. Still, for the first time since Gloriana had weepingly confessed the tale of Merrick's seduction, which presumably had led to Effie's conception, Althea found herself questioning her sister's veracity.

Merrick was not above using a schoolroom miss to further his own interests. The question was what had those interests been? What a fool she had been not to have asked that pertinent question before, thought Althea. Traherne's arm was all that kept her from walking through that door and confronting Merrick, as the Earl of Branscombe called him to task for having taken up with a woman who would seem to offer more in the way of inducement than himself.

"I am not inclined to share you with anyone, my dear," said his lordship, "least of all a French tart with a deplorable lack of appreciation for anything that does not reek of the gutter."

"Pray do not play the maudlin fool, Sinjun," came Merrick's rejoinder couched in tones heavily laced with sarcasm. "It hardly becomes you. You know I have no personal interest in the French harlot. She has proved useful to me in the past, and I have need of her at present. It is purely a matter of business."

"Business, yes, of course. But whose business? Yours or hers? She was here tonight looking for you, Evelyn. Worse, she availed herself of my box at the theater last night, though she has not the smallest grasp of Shakespeare."

"She likes to parade herself before her betters," sneered Merrick. "It flatters her vanity to be seen by those who would not spit on her in public, but who keep her purse well lined out of fear of what she could reveal of them."

"In that case, no doubt you will understand if I feel little gratification that she chose to display herself with me. I know not what you have got yourself into with the Queen of Tarts nor do I wish to know. However, I strongly suggest, even implore, my dear Evelyn, that you divorce yourself from her as soon as is possible. I may be a libertine and a wastrel, but I am, to the regret of my esteemed forebears, the Earl of Branscombe, and I mislike the notion of anything that smells of treason against King and country.''

''Treason! In hell's name, Sinjun, what are you ranting about? What the devil did she tell you?''

''Evelyn, my dear,'' came chillingly to Althea's ears, ''you know my views on violence. Unless, of course, you intend this as preliminary to an act of intimacy, I must request that you unhand me. I should not wish to have to ask you to leave my house.''

''Your house?'' Althea winced at the sound of Merrick's laughter, harsh and mocking. ''Perhaps you might recall that it was my largesse that kept it and everything else you possess from going under the gavel.''

''You have been generous with your money, Evelyn, for which I have expressed my gratitude. Your largesse was, however, a gift and, like my love for you, freely given. You did not purchase me with it, my dear. I thought you, of all people, understood that.''

''I understand *you,* my beautiful Adonis. You are a vain, arrogant exceedingly expensive trinket, who would do anything to keep this house and all that goes with it. Do not talk to me of ultimatums. Now tell me what the French woman said to you.''

''Only that the viscountess is back in Town and that you would know how to proceed. The French tart wished you to understand that time is running out. It seems her buyers for the merchandise will not wait longer than a fortnight more.''

''There, you see,'' said Merrick. ''That was not so difficult, was it? And now we can forget this ever happened. Return to your ball, Sinjun. This will all be over very soon now, and we can go back to the way it was before.''

''Be careful, my dear,'' came Branscombe's voice in the wake of the door's closing at Merrick's departure. ''Winslade is an important man in the government. I cannot think it is the viscountess who interests Marot. Indeed, I am afraid the game you are playing is far more dangerous than you realize.''

''Branscombe is right, Lucius,'' said Althea some ten minutes later, as she and the duke, letting themselves out the service entrance, made their way around to the front of the house and Traherne's waiting carriage. ''Whatever it is Jacqueline Marot is after, it surely cannot be ransom money for Effie. Gloriana's quarterly allowance would hardly be sufficiently tempting to a woman like Marot. Even my sister's jewels would not bring in enough to warrant the French woman's involvement in Merrick's scheme, whatever it is. I feel it. Besides, I cannot think Effie is the 'merchandise' to which Branscombe referred. The devil, Lucius. *Why* did you stop me from confronting Merrick? We had him within our grasp, and you let him slip away again.''

''And what do you think would have happened had we barged in on Merrick and Branscombe—without proof of any wrongdoing other than our suspicions? You do not imagine, do you, that Merrick would have invited us to sit down to chat about his nefarious dealings with Jacqueline Marot? No, I can see that you do not. More pertinently, do you really believe Branscombe was not perfectly aware that we were on the other side of that door listening to every word that was said?''

Althea's eyes flew to Traherne's in sudden consternation. ''Branscombe instructed his servant to take us there. Good heavens. He knew what we would do. He was counting on it.''

''The earl, it would seem, has his own game,'' said Traherne, berating himself for a cursed fool for having played so easily into the hands of his enemies. He had sensed a trap from the moment Phips had so conveniently stumbled across the enticing tidbit about the diamonds that must inevitably lead him to Branscombe and the masqued ball at which his disguise had been readily pierced. His appearance at Branscombe's Bacchanalia had hardly been a surprise. On the contrary, he had obviously been expected. Everything from the moment he had arrived back in Town had been carefully orchestrated, and he had been too focused on what he had presumed to be Althea's peril to see the truth. "Until we know what the game is, I suggest it would be wise to proceed with caution. I find little to amuse in being made a pawn to another's purpose, especially if England's enemies are made to benefit by it."

"Branscombe's comment about treason against King and country!" Althea clasped Traherne's arm. "Faith, Lucius, you think Branscombe was trying to warn us. Jacqueline Marot is a spy, and Merrick is her accomplice!"

"I think, my love, that, if Jacqueline Marot has any part of this, then you may be sure there is more at stake than the attempt to abduct Effie. It is time, moreover, that we paid a call on your sister."

"Now, Lucius? Tonight?" exclaimed Althea. Though she would like nothing better than to put some pertinent questions to her little sister with as little delay as possible, she could not relish the thought of calling on her brother-in-law in the guise of a scantily clad Gypsy dancing girl. Really, that would be asking too much of the viscount, who had as yet to even meet his wife's scandalous sister. "It must be well after midnight. If they are even at home, they must surely be in bed by now."

"I'm afraid it cannot be helped, wood sprite," replied the duke, as he assisted Althea into the carriage. "I have the feeling we dare not let it wait for morning. Charles," he added to the coachman, "Number Three Grosvenor Square with all haste, if you please."

"As you wish, Your Grace, and, begging your pardon, but a foreign gentleman asked to leave a box inside for Her Grace. I hope I did right in letting him. The gentleman was most insistent."

"You did precisely as you should, Charles," called Althea, who could not have been happier to discover, packed away neatly in a bandbox, her white velvet pelisse, her green sarcenet evening dress, cut in the style of a frock with short puffed sleeves and a square décolletage. The bandbox also held her satin slippers, dyed to match her dress, her elbow-length white kid gloves, her diamond earrings and matching necklace (which had belonged to Traherne's grandmama), her reticule and other accessories—all of which she had last seen strewn around the dowager duchess's bedchamber at the Chesney Hotel. Faith, her dearest mama-in-law, not to mention the dowager duchess's aging Apollo, had thought of everything!

She could almost forgive Praetorius for having abandoned her at the first sign of trouble. No doubt he had been distracted by the insurmountable temptations of the bacchanalia going on around him, and who could blame him? She, after all, had found a great deal to distract *her* at Branscombe's orgiastic celebration of the senses.

"A foreign gentleman?" queried Traherne a moment later, as he settled on the seat next to his duchess. Having taken the precaution of lowering the shades, Althea was even then in the process of divesting herself of her concealing veil.

"Apparently," shrugged Althea, avoiding the duke's eyes as she busied herself with wriggling out of her borrowed vermilion Gypsy skirt. "Strange, is it not?" Turning her back to Traherne, she added, "Would you be so kind as to undo my buttons?"

The four-story brown brick at Number 3 Grosvenor Square was bathed in darkness, save for a single lamp in the foyer, presumably left burning in anticipation of the return of the principal residents. It hardly presented a promising aspect, reflected Althea as, fully dressed in garb more suitable to calling on her sister and brother-in-law, she alit from the carriage. Consequently, she was no little surprised that Traherne's determined assault on the door knocker drew an almost immediate response. She was even more surprised to realize the considerably disheveled figure who flung open the door with what appeared a singular eagerness, which was quickly doused, was no less a personage than the viscount himself. Far more startling than anything else, however, was Althea's instant stunned recognition of the brother-in-law whom she presumably had never met.

"Good heavens!" she gasped, staring at the viscount's handsome visage—the brown curls considerably tousled and the lean cheeks showing the faint shadow of a beard—as if he were an apparition. "It is *you!*"

Viscount Winslade, far from demonstrating a similar astonishment, gave every evidence of one inordinately pleased to see her.

"Althea!" he exclaimed. "By all that is marvelous. Thank God you are here! Pray come inside at once."

"Although we have been formally introduced, Your Grace," said Winslade to the duke, as he ushered his unexpected guests into his private study, "it has been several years ago. I daresay you do not remember me."

"*I* remember you, my lord," Althea interjected in ominous tones. "Only you were not Winslade when I knew you and championed your cause to my sister Gloriana. You were Captain Jack Travers, as I recall, and you may be sure there is nothing wrong with my memory. I find it exceedingly strange that all these years no one thought to inform me that the viscount Gloriana married was the captain with whom she fell in love at Fort St. George. What else, I wonder, have I not been told?"

"No more than I, apparently," replied his lordship, reaching for a glass and decanter set out on the mahogany desk, indisputable evidence, had Althea needed it, that Winslade had been making deep indentures. "Brandy, Your Grace?" he queried of Traherne.

"Thank you, no. I have a feeling that one of us will require a clear head before this night is over."

"Meaning mine is already muddled," laughed Winslade, lifting his glass in tribute to his guest. "You are quite right. I am downright obfuscated with drink and plan to be more so before this night is through. And why should I not at the moment my life lies in ruins about me and my career will soon be in a shambles? It would seem, I have fathered a child on your wife, Your Grace, while mine has taken it in her head to leave me. I call those grounds for a drunken spree. In the circumstances, are you sure you will not join me, Your Grace? No? Well then."

Swaying on his feet, Winslade tossed off his drink in a single long swallow, which had the effect of throwing him off his already precarious balance.

"The devil," he muttered. Reaching a hand to his forehead, he buckled forward at the waist.

"Steady, my lad." Traherne caught Winslade and, easing him down on the chair at the desk, availed himself of the glass and decanter ahead of his reaching lordship. "I think not, my lord. It would appear you have exceeded your limits."

"The devil I have. Who are you to say?" Squinting up at His Grace out of bleary eyes, he frowned in sudden concentration. "I say, you've a queer look about you. Dressed like a bloody demmed pirate, aren't you?"

"How keen of you to notice," observed His Grace in sardonic appreciation. "Merely one of my wife's quirks. Has a fetish for men dressed as pirates. You must not mind it."

"Fiddlesticks," declared Althea, awarding Traherne a comical moue of displeasure. "I pray you will not listen to him, Jack. The truth is we have just come from a masqued orgy. Traherne was giving me my first lesson in the finer aspects of licentious behavior. Which is all beside the point. More important at the moment, where is Gloriana?''

The viscount's dark eyes, blurred with pain, swept up to meet Althea's. ''I told you. She has left me, without so much as an explanation. Unless, of course, you take this note to be one.'' Slinging a crumpled sheet of paper across the desk at Althea, Winslade propped his elbows on the desk and sank his head into his hands. ''I have always accounted myself a reasonably intelligent man and a loving husband. I believe I have even made a doting father. I find, however, I cannot make head or tails of what is apparently meant to be Gloriana's confession of wrongdoing. Egad, Althea, I should be ever so grateful if you could tell me what I have done to estrange Gloriana's affections. No doubt you will think me a coward do I confess I cannot contemplate a life without her.''

''I'm afraid that may take a moment, Jack,'' said Althea, peering at her sister's chicken scratchings, made even more obscure than normal by the addition of blurry splotches, which must surely have been teardrops.

''It would, indeed, seem to be something of a confession,'' observed Traherne, reading over Althea's shoulder. ''Does she write she 'stole a white horse for the sake of forbidden lusts'? Good God.''

''It does appear so,'' agreed Althea, frowning. ''However, I believe it more accurately reads, she 'stole out of the house to partake of forbidden love.' Yes, it would seem to make sense in the context of the rest of the paragraph. Merrick, it is obvious, had been exploiting her innocence to gain secret information from the colonel's private papers. Gloriana never understood to what use he might put that sort of thing. It was a game to her, an adventure to break the monotony of a schoolgirl's existence. And then Jack came into the picture. She told Merrick she was through playing childish pranks. She was going to marry Jack.''

"Naturally, Merrick took exception to the notion of losing his secret source of information concerning troop movements, trade agreements, paid informants, any number of things that might have greased the wheels of his own private interests," Traherne speculated. "No doubt he actually did threaten to put a period to the captain's existence if she did not break it off with him. That part of her earlier story was very probably true."

"Yes, she says as much here," agreed Althea, indicating a smeared passage. "She did break it off with Jack, that much is certain. Upon which Jack, in a final attempt to bring her to her senses, informed her that he was being ordered home. Faced with a life of unrequited love, she stole out of the house to partake of forbidden passion. Which resulted, it would seem, in the conception of a child. Merrick is not Effie's father, Lucius. Jack is. At last a great deal is made suddenly clear."

Indeed, it would all seem to make perfect sense. With her dearest Jack ordered back to England upon the untimely demise of his elder brother, Gloriana had been afraid to tell Althea and her father the truth for fear they might force Jack to marry her. That she simply could not have countenanced, not when she knew Jack was no longer plain Captain Travers, but Viscount Winslade, heir to his father, the Earl of Bradmoor. She made up the story about Merrick, knowing her father would never press such a marriage. And then, Althea had come up with her plan to take all the blame upon herself. Gloriana, used to having her sister clean up her messes for her, had been too weak to refuse. And after Jack, the new Viscount Winslade, sought her out in England and begged her to marry him, she was too ashamed to tell him the truth. Now, however, she could no longer keep her silence. Indeed, she had been left no recourse but to leave him. It was the only way to save him from scandal and herself from an act that would forever damn her in the eyes of all whom she held dear.

"Merrick is up to his old tricks again," announced Althea, lifting her eyes to Traherne's. "Only this time he is demanding something of Winslade's. Lucius, what are we going to do?"

Drawing Althea to her feet, Traherne pulled her into his arms. "Find her and bring her back. You know her as well as anyone, Althea. Where would she go?"

"The house on Plover Street!" Pulling away from Traherne, Althea gripped his arms in sudden dread. "She is unaware that Merrick knows of it. I dared not tell her in a letter of the events that occurred there for fear Winslade might read it."

"What events?" demanded the viscount, lifting his head. "What bloody house?"

"I'm afraid there is not the time to explain," said Traherne, his face exceedingly grim. "Suffice it to say, if you wish to see your wife again, we must leave at once."

The drive to Plover Street was passed in grim silence, save for an occasional groan from Winslade. Feeling the effects of his recent debauchery, he was struggling not to disgrace himself before the Duke and Duchess of Traherne.

Althea could not but pity him, though she found it difficult to forgive him or her sister for having left her in ignorance of the pertinent fact of his identity. Faith, it was little wonder Gloriana had never brought Winslade to meet Althea and Effie at the house on Plover Street. How the web of lies she had woven must have pressed in on Gloriana, thought Althea, wondering that she herself had been so accepting, so blindly unquestioning. But then, she had had her own burden of guilt to bear: She had caused Effie to live a lie! Worse was what she very much feared was her own selfish wish to keep Effie to herself.

Still, to be perfectly honest, she had to acknowledge her motives had not been all self-actuated, not so long as she

ad believed Merrick was Effie's father. Indeed, she did not
ee how she could have told Effie her father was the sort
f man who would stoop to anything, even abducting his
wn child for ransom.

Merrick, however, was not Effie's father. With that revela-
ion it seemed all the lies had come toppling down, leaving
ut a single truth: Effie must be told who her parents were.
t came to Althea that, deep down, she had known all along
he day would come when she must destroy the child's faith
n her. No doubt that was why she had ever been "Althie"
nd never "Mama" to the child. It had been the one hypoc-
isy to which Althea could never lend herself.

And now what was she to do? Where was she to find the
vords to tell Effie the truth?

Lost in contemplation, Althea had all but forgotten she
vas no longer alone in her dilemma. Traherne's hand, clos-
ng over hers in the darkness of the carriage, brought her
ead up, her eyes seeking his in the fleeting light of a
treetlamp. She felt her heart swell as, wordlessly, he raised
er hand to his lips.

A man of powerful intellect and keen insight, Traherne
ad read her thoughts. Indeed, he must surely have been
hinking along the same lines. How could he not, when he
ad already set into motion the steps that would have made
Effie his adopted daughter! Faith, how had she not thought
o consider his probable feelings in the matter? She knew
s plainly as if the words had been spoken aloud. Whatever
he decided, she was not alone. Traherne, always and from
he very beginning, had pledged his strength to her and Effie.

Grimly, Traherne noted the house on Plover Street, unlike
he houses neighboring it, was lit from within, giving mute
vidence that the household had not taken to their beds.
ittle desiring to alert the inmates to their arrival, he ordered
he coachman to halt short of the house. He would have

liked nothing better than to order Althea to remain behind
with the carriage as well. On the other hand, the mere prospect of surprising Merrick and his henchmen within, without
knowing what his redoubtable duchess might be about at
any given moment, was not one to contribute greatly to his
peace of mind. It was undoubtedly better to have her where
he could keep his eye on her, he reflected, helping Althea
to alight.

It was evident that Winslade's training as a soldier was
standing him in good stead, as the viscount, white faced
and grim but surprisingly steady, stepped down from the
carriage. It was obvious, as well, that he had been thinking
on the drive from Grosvenor Square to his present rather
unprepossessing environs, Traherne mused, noting the glint
of moonlight off the barrel of a pistol held in the viscount's
hand.

"You have yet to tell me what all this is about," Winslade
shrugged in response to the duke's speculative glance. "I
did, however, hear you mention the name Merrick. I have
not been gone from Madras so long that I have forgotten
him or what he is capable of doing. What do you intend,
Your Grace?"

"I believe a rear action is called for in this instance, do
not you, Captain?" spoke up Althea and was met with a
sudden telling silence. "Botheration," she said, as she found
herself impaled by two pairs of masculine eyes. "I *am*
'Your Grace,' too, after all, and I am not entirely without
experience in strategic planning. I have been through three
major battles and a siege in the company of the colonel."

"If we are to grant you that, my girl," odiously drawled
Traherne, "I think it is pertinent to know who won those
engagements."

"Devil!" pronounced Althea with no little feeling. "You
know very well who."

"Well, then, I suppose your plan has merit," Traherne

was quick to counter. "As it happens, little termagant, *I* was going to suggest we enter at the rear of the house."

"With a diversion to draw attention away from the direction of the actual assault," agreed Winslade with a mirthless grin.

"I suggest the sudden appearance of the lady's irate husband at the front door should do nicely," Traherne speculated, observing the shadow of a figure move across the yellow glow of the downstairs parlor window. "It occurs to me that our intruders, if intruders they are, are awaiting Merrick's arrival."

"But of course," exclaimed Althea, "why else would they still be here? No doubt Merrick thinks to frighten Gloriana into returning home to do whatever it is that he wants of her. In which case, we may be sure that she is as yet alive, Jack, and unharmed."

A shadow of emotion flickered across Winslade's lean hard countenance and was immediately banished. "That is a deal more than can be said for Merrick," he said coldly, "if ever I get my hands on him."

"A pity we haven't someone to stand guard outside," mused Traherne, little liking the distinct possibility that Merrick might arrive while they were occupied inside the house.

"I'm afraid we shall just have to chance it," Althea said, frowning. "I know Gloriana. She is not acquainted with you, and she is liable to fly into a fit of hysterics when she sees Jack. If she is inside, she will need her sister."

"I'm afraid Althea is right," Winslade wryly interjected. "Gloriana is the most lovable creature, but she is possessed of exceedingly delicate sensibilities."

Traherne, who had had the dubious pleasure of trying to decipher the lady's letter of confession, could hardly deny that his own impression of the viscountess had hardly been of a female of strong inner reserves, let alone steady nerves. He did not doubt she was the sort to fly into high fidgets.

"I suggest, then, that we move as quickly as possible. Allow us time enough to make our way down the alley at back. Say five minutes. As soon as we hear you create a row at the front, we shall break in the back. With any luck, we shall have them at a stalemate between us."

"Five minutes, Your Grace," repeated Winslade, drawing forth his pocket watch and examining it in the pale gleam of the crescent moon overhead. "Have a care, Althea," he warned in a carrying whisper at their retreating backs. "None of your demmed female heroics."

Traherne, who could only echo that sentiment, was acutely aware of the slender form of his wife striding dauntlessly beside him. Ironically, he acknowledged to himself that he was in the full sway of the natural mechanism of a male's instinct to protect his mate. No doubt his determined duchess, on the other hand, was ruled by her overly developed feminine propensity to turn into a bloody damned tigress when one of her loved ones was threatened. He found himself hoping in this case the purely human capacity for rational action would prevail in the end. The last thing he could wish was to have Althea fling herself heedlessly into the midst of a fray in order to save her younger sister from desperate felons. With any luck and if they kept a cool head, they might be able to pull the thing off without resorting to actual violence.

Arriving at the carriage house and stable at the back of the house, Traherne and Althea paused long enough to ascertain that both were unoccupied. But then if Gloriana had indeed taken refuge in the rented house, she would surely have arrived in a hackney, just as she had always done when she had come to meet Althea and Effie there. With a sudden pang, Althea wondered where Toby was, and Mrs. Stoddart and Mirabel Jones and all the others. Fervently she hoped no harm had come to them, as she and Traherne crossed the open drive to the kitchen garden and beyond that, to the rear of the house.

Intent on making as little noise as possible on the gravel path, neither of them noticed the indistinct form of a man detach itself from the shadows and steal after them. Nor were they aware as, availing themselves of Althea's keys, they let themselves into the kitchen and made their way up the servants' stairs to the first floor, that that same shadowy figure entered the house after them.

Stealing into the dining room bathed in darkness, Althea could only be grateful for Traherne's reassuring presence at her back. Thus far they had seen nothing of the servants, let alone any supposed intruders. Save for the lamplit parlor at the far side of the dining room in which Traherne had earlier spotted the moving figure, the house, for all intents and purposes, seemed peculiarly deserted.

In spite of herself, Althea jumped at the sudden loud clatter at the front of the house. Winslade, she thought, clasping a hand to her thumping heart. Egad.

"Softly," murmured Traherne next to her ear. "Let us see if they send someone to answer it."

A second assault, louder and more insistent even than the first, must have left little doubt to those in the house that the caller, whoever it was, had no intention of going away.

Even as Traherne hastily pulled Althea into a murky corner, a low curse sounded from beyond the closed parlor door. "Kearns! Fetch the housekeeper to see who the bloody hell's at the door. Tell her to get rid of the blighter. As for you, lovely lady, it will be far better for you if you remain quiet while she goes about it. Indeed, I should not like to see anything happen to that pretty face of yours."

"I suggest you consider your own welfare while you still may," came the retort in cutting accents. "You may be sure my husband will take an exceedingly dim view of the manner in which you have chosen to detain me. I daresay you will find yourselves before long wishing you were at Jericho."

Even as Gloriana's captor gave vent to a cynical laugh, a fierce stab of joy shot through Althea. Gloriana! she thought, and from the sound of it, unharmed in body and most certainly in spirit. Still, Althea had known her sister too long not to recognize the brittle quality beneath the tone of hauteur. Gloriana was game as a pebble, but her nerves were stretched to the breaking point. And little wonder, if she had been in the clutches of heartless abductors for the better part of the night!

Traherne's warning hand on her arm brought Althea to the sudden realization that the parlor door was sliding open. Drawing deeper into the shadows, she beheld a burly form emerge, a flickering candle in hand, and turn to draw the door closed again.

Noiselessly, Traherne moved.

Straightening, the fellow froze, the touch of cold steel at his throat.

"Not a sound," whispered Traherne's voice in the silence. "I should not hesitate to cut your throat for you. Althea, the drapery cords. Quickly. Now, you, my ungentlemanly gentleman of Verona, downstairs to the kitchens."

Reaching for the drapery cords, Althea flung a startled glance over her shoulder. Good God, there was indeed an uncanny resemblance between the thickset fellow being conducted by swordpoint to the serving exit and the burly gentleman of Verona, who had come very near to inciting a full-fledged assault on Traherne only a couple of hours earlier. Althea, who placed little credence in coincidences of a significant magnitude, experienced a cold little chill at the realization that quite possibly Traherne had saved her from more than a mauling at Branscombe's Bacchanalia; that, indeed, Branscombe himself had averted more than a mere "regrettable incident."

Yanking the cords free, she hurried after Traherne.

"The devil, Lucius," she whispered moments later, as she applied herself to binding the gentleman's hands to the arms of a ladder-back armchair, "it *is* our friend from the ballroom. But how—"

"For now, wood sprite," Traherne interrupted, sheathing his sword in order to gag their glaring captive with the man's own linen neckcloth, "allow me to introduce to you Henry Kearns, who has the distinction of being one of the most sought after practitioners of the free trade in England. Be certain to bind his feet well. He has a talent for slipping out of the hangman's snare. But not this time. This time, Kearns, I am not laid low by a sniper's bullet."

Althea, visited with a flash of sudden enlightenment, gave the knot at the smuggler's ankles a savage jerk, which earned her a grunt of pain, accompanied by a murderous glare, from the notorious Henry Kearns. She had not the smallest doubt that this man had had a part in very nearly putting a period to Traherne's existence.

Straightening from the task of searching Kearns's pockets, Traherne dangled a ring of keys before Althea. "I suggest we repair at once to the cellars," he said, "where I believe we shall discover your housekeeper and the rest of the household held prisoners. Our friends in the parlor are expecting Mrs. Stoddart to open the door to their persistent caller. I should hate to disappoint them."

"That won't be necessary, Your Grace," issued a hoarse voice at Traherne's back. "I've already taken the liberty of letting Mrs. Stoddart and the others out."

Althea came sharply about, her face alight with wonder and surprise at sight of the ragged figure standing with his arm about the waist of a blushing Sally Higgens and the others of the household crowded behind them. "Dick Turpin!" she exclaimed. "By all that is marvelous. I could not be more pleased to see you are alive."

"No more than am I, miss," said Turpin, his homely face assuming a dusky color. "I've been hiding out in the streets, watching over Sally and the others, ever since Mr. Develin tried to cut my stick for me. Set his hounds on me, he did, as I was coming out of the Blue Boar. And after I paid him the blunt you gave me, too, Miss Althea."

"Her Grace, Dick," whispered Sally Higgens, giving his coat sleeve a tug. "She up and married the duke, just like you said she would."

"Begging your pardon, Your Grace," Turpin said, his pleasure writ plain on his face. "If you don't mind my saying so, I couldn't be happier for you both."

"You may say so. Indeed, having done so," interjected Traherne, "I suggest it is time we returned to the business at hand. Mrs. Stoddart, perhaps you would be so kind as to admit the gentleman at the front door. The rest of you, take yourselves out by the back way. Althea, come with me."

Without waiting to see in what manner he was obeyed and drawing the pistol from his belt, Traherne turned to exit the kitchens, Althea following close behind him.

Positioned once more at the parlor door, Traherne and Althea could plainly hear what sounded very like Winslade on the point of breaking down the oak barrier below.

"Hell and the devil confound it!" came from the parlor. "Where are Kearns and the woman? We shall have the neighbors down upon us."

"More important, what is keeping Develin? He bloody well should have been here by now."

"It would seem, gentlemen," said Traherne, sliding open the door, "that Develin has stood you up. Hold very still, Alastair. I should have very few compunctions about shooting you, especially after you were so kind as to direct me to Branscombe's gala. And who have we here?" he queried, his hooded glance taking in the set features and imposing build of the second gentleman. "It is the friar, is it not, who entertained unsavory designs on my wife, as it happens? You keep strange company, Alastair. First Kearns, and now, am I not mistaken, we have Sir Wilfred Pellum of the Port Authority."

"Now, see here, sir. There has been some sort of a misunderstanding. I—"

"Stow it, Pellum," said Alastair, coolly drawing forth

an exquisite enameled snuff box and flipping open the lid preparatory to taking a pinch of his favorite mixture. "I fear His Grace has us dead to rights."

"His Grace?" queried the woman, who sat stiffly on the faded brocade settee, her back held rigidly straight and her hands clasped tightly in her lap. "Are you—"

"Traherne. Yes, Gloriana," declared Althea, slipping past the duke to embrace her sister. "Dearest, are you unharmed?"

"Althea? Faith, is it really you? You cannot know how glad I am to see you. Effie! Is she—?"

It was at that point that a firm step in the hall outside the parlor announced the arrival of the importunate caller from below.

"Effie is fine, dearest," said Althea. "And here is Jack, come to fetch you home."

"Jack!" Gloriana's went suddenly white. "Then you know—"

"Yes, darling—everything, almost. And now we must get you out of here. Merrick might arrive at any moment."

Gloriana's face went even whiter than before. "Merrick? Good God, is he—"

The crash of the window, followed by the report of a shot, just as Winslade burst through the door, transformed the room into chaos. Flinging the contents of his snuff box into the duke's face, Alastair bowled into Winslade, sending the viscount careening backward into the carved mahogany vitrine cabinet, as Alastair bolted past him and out the door. Traherne dashed at his streaming eyes with the back of his hand and lunged after Alastair, followed by Winslade. Gloriana screamed at the deafening explosion of a second gun going off and collapsed in a swoon against the back of the settee, even as Althea, who had pulled up her skirts to snatch the gun from her garter at the first eruption of chaos, fired at the figure, glimpsed fleetingly in the dining room doorway.

* * *

Half-blinded, Traherne spared the carriage, driven at a splitting pace down the deserted street, a single glance before turning to clap a hand to Winslade's heaving shoulder.

"Never mind them for now. Quick! Althea and your wife!"

Traherne shoved past the viscount into the house and, taking the stairs two at a time, burst through the door into the parlor.

"Althea!"

"Gloriana!" exclaimed Winslade, arriving hard on Traherne's heels. Dropping on his knees before Gloriana, he began to chafe her wrists.

"Gloriana and I are fine, Lucius," said his duchess, straightening from examining the ominously still form sprawled in the chair facing the dining room. "The same, however, cannot be said, I'm afraid, for Sir Wilfred Pellum. The pistol ball took him square in the chest."

"Pistol ball. What the devil are you talking about?" demanded Winslade, glancing over his shoulder at Althea. "The shot came from outside. It could not possibly have struck the man in the chair."

"Obviously, that one was only a diversion to give Alastair his chance to escape," said Traherne. Never taking his eyes off Althea, he crossed the room. His hands coming to rest on her shoulders, he stood staring down at her.

"He was there before I knew it. He shot Sir Wilfred." Althea lifted her eyes to Traherne's. "It was Merrick. I am positive of that. I took a shot at him, but I must have missed. He turned and ran. It was all to no purpose, Lucius. Sir Wilfred is dead, and the others escaped. I daresay your Mr. Kearns has gotten away as well."

"Then you'd be wrong, Your Grace, on two counts," said Dick Turpin, shoving the bound figure of Henry Kearns into the room. "I owed it to you to hold him for you, Your

Grace, for placing your faith in me, when by all rights you should have turned me out. As for Develin, or Merrick, as you call him, he got away, but he was bleeding like a stuck pig. You winged him, ma'am, and that's no lie.''

"I should say you are wrong on *three* counts, Althea dearest,'' added a voice, which, though undeniably weak, was yet expressive of deep-felt emotion. "You and-and everyone saved me from Merrick.''

"Gloriana!'' exclaimed Winslade, carrying his wife's hand to his lips. "Thank God, you are awake.''

"Little do you care, Jack,'' said Gloriana, awarding her adoring husband a reproving pout. "You dashed out of here without saying a word to me, when I have been tormented with the thought that you could never forgive me for-for the lies. Effie is ours, and I never told you. I let Althea take all the blame, when it should have been my burden. Oh, Jack, I have been cowardly and-and weak. And now I do not know how I shall ever face Effie or Lord Guilmore and Baby Alice.''

"We shall face Effie together, my little peagoose,'' said Jack. "I am as much to blame as you for what happened. I should never have left you in Madras. I should have faced the colonel like a man and demanded your hand in marriage.''

"And then Merrick would have-have killed you,'' Gloriana did not hesitate to point out, "and, like Juliet, I should have wished to kill myself, though I cannot bear the thought of poison and I know I should faint at the merest sight of a knife, never mind a gun. I daresay I might have managed somehow to fling myself off the balcony, had I been able to bear the idea of having anyone see me in what I cannot but think would be a shockingly unsightly state. And as for drowning, you know I cannot tolerate even the notion of water with all sorts of dreadful things in it.'' She shuddered, no doubt visualizing clinging moss and debris, not to mention frogs and fish, snakes, and perhaps a crocodile or two.

"And, besides, there are still the dreadful letters. They will ruin you, my dearest Jack. They will tell everyone about Effie and that your wife gave secret information to the Pathan banditti, never mind that I told the colonel what Merrick wanted so that Papa made certain they never got anything he did not wish them to have. I daresay it was very useful for the colonel, as he was able to capture not a few of the bandits and to put them off on the wrong track when he had not enough men to protect a particularly vulnerable caravan. Not that any of that will possibly make a difference when Develin, who now Althea says is Merrick, puts the stories about. No one will believe it was all just a silly game. You should not have come after me, Jack. You should have let them carry me off. At least then I should be free of the hounding. Now it will never stop, and I cannot bear it, Jack. Not anymore. Really, I cannot."

"But then, my dearest Gloriana," said Althea, for whom a great deal had been made suddenly and abundantly clear, "you will not have to, not another day longer than it takes to draw them into a trap. Will she, Lucius?" she added, smiling up at her dearest lord duke.

Chapter Fourteen

Traherne felt a hot fist of anger, like bitter gall, in the pit of his stomach.

"You knew, Duval," he said. "All these months you knew."

"About Jacqueline Marot and Robert Alastair? *Oui, mon ami.* You said there was a woman who acted as a broker. They came to her, *non?*—the families with relatives seeking to escape France. To her, they brought money, jewels, whatever they had to offer of value—names, perhaps, of anyone who had ever said anything that might be construed as sedition against the revolutionary government. She would send word to her confederate in Paris. It was he who arranged everything. We had only to follow the clues to the names. In time, you would have found them yourself."

The devil, thought Traherne. There had been no more time. The names had eluded him. The woman and her lover, the illegitimate son of an English aristocrat and a French comtesse, the man who had denounced his own mother to the Directorate, had been as elusive as mist. Together, they had devised the scheme to smuggle French émigrés to England. Only, they had found it more lucrative to murder their clients for the possessions they carried with them. The addition of an informer with authority over the coast guard had reduced the risks of interception and capture. Traherne had known there was someone. He had never gotten so far as to name Sir Wilfred Pellum. Henry Kearns had been the key to it all. The smuggler, with his fleet of small boats, had known all the names. But then, Duval had known, too. All those months ago, as he, Traherne, had lain battling infection and the nightmares, Duval had followed the twisted trail of clues to Robert Alastair and Jacqueline Marot, and he had kept it from the one man who had at least earned the right to know.

"Marot, I have always suspected was not what she presented herself to be, but Alastair and Sir Wilfred Pellum hid themselves exceedingly well. And now Merrick. Where the deuce does he fit into the equation?"

"The answer is that he does not fit in. Your Mr. Merrick, or Develin, as he calls himself now, was never a part of the old scheme to murder and rob French émigrés. He came later, my friend. It is uncertain what his connection is to Marot and her lover Alastair."

"Or why, for that matter, he went to great pains to silence Sir Wilfred Pellum."

"In truth, that is most curious," Duval agreed with an eloquent shrug. "With the Reign of Terror at an end, it seems that the woman and Alastair have turned to blackmailing men of wealth who are foolish enough to fall victim to Marot's dubious charms. Viscount Winslade would not seem, on the surface, a likely candidate to interest them. His fortune is respectable, but he has never demonstrated any inclination to take up with a mistress." The handsome lips twisted in a smile of reminiscence. "On the contrary, he is rumored to be in love with his beautiful young wife."

"You may be certain that Marot holds little appeal for

him," agreed Traherne, who had been given to personally witness the extent of the viscount's devotion to his wife. "But then, it is not Winslade who is the object of blackmail. In this instance, it is Lady Winslade. Furthermore, you may be certain it is not Winslade's fortune they want, but something far more valuable. Winslade serves as liaison between the government and the Lords of Admiralty. Everyone knows the French Tyrant is amassing a flotilla of small crafts to transport an invasion force across the Channel. How valuable would copies of the orders to the blockade fleet be to Napolean?"

Duval's dark eyes shone, glittery, in the handsome face. "To know the exact number and class of vessels, their captains and the superiors who command them, the scope of their orders? I think these would be of the most use. Does the viscount have access to this information?"

In answer, Traherne gathered up his hat and gloves.

Duval frowned. "You are going after them, *vraiment?* You will need help."

"Not this time, Duval. This time I know who they are."

The former Comte d'Arbolet gave vent to a sigh. "What purpose would it have served to tell you? It was all over, thanks to you. If in the end we were able to put it all together, there was little we could do. To know who they were was one thing, but without proof?" Again Duval shrugged. "It almost killed you, my friend. And you had already done enough."

"It will not be enough until it is finished, Duval—one way or the other. And in future, old friend, I shall thank you not to presume to make my decisions for me."

Settling back against the velvet squabs of his carriage some moments later, Traherne deliberately unclenched the hard fist of his anger. The devil take Duval and the Ministry. Jacqueline Marot and Robert Alastair were traitors to the country that had taken them in and given them sanctuary. Worse, they had butchered innocent men, women, and children who had trusted them to bring them to safety. Proof? What proof was required to damn them? The victims of their treachery damned them.

He had come almost to believe that with Althea he would in time learn to forget, but how could anyone ever forget the thing of horror that had washed ashore off Beachy Head? The devil! What terrible quirk of fate had prompted Wendell Haverland to accept a position tutoring the son of a French diplomat on the eve of rebellion? Traherne did not doubt his former friend and mentor had perished trying to effect the escape of his young charge from the Reign of Terror that had made the boy an orphan. How ironic that the smugglers, flush with the stolen jewels of a comtesse, had not bothered to relieve the English tutor of an insignificant wooden quill stand, which, though crudely wrought, had yet borne the coat-of-arms of the Dukes of Traherne!

It was that relic of Haverland's years at Meresgate, carved by the hand of a twelve-year-old duke, that had brought Duval to Traherne, and Traherne to the house in Eastbourne in which had resided, preserved in spirits, Haverland's remains—what was left of them.

And now for the final irony, thought Traherne with scant humor. Having failed to bring Jacqueline Marot and Robert Alastair to account for the murders of Wendell Haverland, his young charge, the Comtesse d'Arbolet, and four-year-old Jeannine Duval, not to mention countless other unfortunates, he must stand by while the one woman in whom resided the sum total of his future happiness offered herself up as bait to his sworn enemies.

It was not a concept to give him any sort of comfort. Indeed, only the utter conviction that his dauntless wood sprite had devised the only feasible plan to draw the villains once more into the open prevented him from consigning her forthwith to the safety of the dungeons at Meresgate until the entire matter was finished.

By the time the business of Pellum's untimely demise had been reported to the proper authorities and Kearns had been safely locked away to await trial, there had been little hope of finding Alastair. His bachelor lodgings in St. James's Hotel showed signs of having been hastily vacated. Nor was there any indication that he had taken refuge with Jacqueline Marot. The French woman remained conspicuously in residence in her house on Portland Square, even going so far as to make her regular appearances in Hyde Park every afternoon at the hour of five, and frequenting the theatre and any number of private entertainments. As for Merrick, the former East India agent had proved as elusive as ever. Maintaining a constant surveillance on the Earl of Branscombe had thus far failed to yield anything of Merrick's secret lair.

There was little to be done, but wait in the hopes that someone would contact Lady Winslade with some sort of final demands. A week had passed, leaving but a sennight until the day Branscombe had claimed was the final deadline. Althea, anxious to have done with the entire affair for Effie's sake as well as her own, found the waiting more trying than she could ever have previously imagined. Indeed, she could not but consider it bizarre that, while her entire being seemed focused on the desperate plot of murder and blackmail into which she had been thrust, she should be suddenly swept up in the whirl of social events that signaled the opening of the Season.

It really was too absurd that, far from the snubs she had steeled herself to expect, she suddenly found herself being feted and fawned over as if she were not the same woman who only a little over five months previously had had to suffer the slights of shopkeepers who considered her beneath their contempt. But then, no doubt there was a world of difference between Miss Althea Wintergreen, the Nobody who had been branded a Fallen Woman, and Althea, Her Grace of Traherne, the duchess who was wed to one of the most powerful men in England. It seemed anything could be forgiven of one with the claim to a title second only to royalty, especially one blessed additionally with a large fortune and a vast influence.

That the Society into which she had been introduced under the auspices of Ophelia Keene might have found her delightful and charming, her manners unexceptional, and her bearing unpretentious never occurred to her. Indeed, she would have been exceedingly surprised to discover she had been accepted as much for her lively wit in conversation and her unaffected display of interest in those with whom she came in contact as for her unrivaled position as the wife of the Duke of Traherne.

She was judged an Original and an Incomparable, a Diamond of the First Water, the *ton*'s newest Reigning Beauty.

That her new consequence sat lightly on her—indeed, that she gave every appearance of being wholly unaware that the silver salver in the foyer overflowed with invitations or that she was sure to be immediately surrounded by a host of admirers wherever she went or that any number of ladies had adopted forest green apparel whether the color suited them or not—served only to reinforce the generally held opinion that the Duchess of Traherne was neither coming nor puffed up with her own consequence.

And the inevitable rumors going the rounds of every salon and assembly room that the new duchess was not all that she appeared to be—that, indeed, she possessed a checkered past that involved an illicit affair and the birth of a child out of wedlock—perversely added to her cachet rather than detracted from it. No one could say precisely how it was that the sordid details upon which the rumors were based should have come to take on the aura of a romance of the sort to move even the hardest of hearts to a tender sympathy. No doubt Ophelia Keene might have shed some light on the subject had she chosen to have done. Certainly, Lord Hilary had found not a little peculiar the fact that his dearest Ophelia had decided to pay a morning call on Wilhelmina, Lady Rutherford. His wife was privately fond of referring to the countess as "Willy-Nilly," due to her unfortunate propensity to gibble-gabble over every tidbit of gossip with the mindless relish of a pecking hen. Whatever the case, it was not long before the Duke and Duchess of Traherne began to figure largely in a misty tale of star-crossed lovers separated against their wills by tragic circumstances, which had involved the manipulations of a corrupt and evil villain. That Fate had intervened at last to bring them together again purely by happenstance, besides being faithful to the dictates of a true tale of Gothic adventure and romance, had served to endear the two principal players to their adoring public. The fact that His Grace was known to have instituted proceedings to legally adopt his wife's five-year-old daughter, who had already the distinction of being his legal ward, naturally would seem to support the widespread belief that it was a factual story. That made it all the more delectably marvelous.

Consequently, it was hardly surprising that Traherne, arriving home in the wake of his call on Jean Duval, should find his wife ensconced in the withdrawing room surrounded by gentlemen callers.

"I say, here is His Grace now," declared Sir Thomas Greene, a widower in his middle forties, who was a self-avowed fancier of scientific research into the phenomenon of electromagnetism. "The duchess was just in the midst of propounding her theories on harnessing the sun's rays for the heating of houses as well as for providing a usable energy source for the running of fully automatically operated machines. We rely on you, Your Grace, to help us persuade the duchess to submit her writings to *The Scientific Journal of Theoretical Research.*"

"Here, here, Traherne," seconded Lord Harry Wilcox,

who was hardly noted for his intellectual pursuits, but rather for those ventures of an amorous nature. "I daresay the Duchess of Traherne could do more to advance the cause of scientific research than a host of Oxford dons. You may be certain Harry Wilcox had never sat through a lecture on the phenomenon of polarization as applied to a voltaic cell before I had the pleasure of calling on your wife, nor am I likely to do so again, save under similar circumstances. I cannot think there has ever been a more charming proponent of the importance of practical scientific research than the lovely Duchess of Traherne."

"Pray do not listen to him, Lucius," said Althea, enchanting the entire room full of gentlemen with her laughter. "Lord Harry is far better informed on scientific principles than he would have you to believe. On the other hand, gentlemen," she added after a single penetrating glance at her husband, "I fear I must ask for leave to continue this discussion at some future date. Regrettably, His Grace and I have a prior engagement. I beg you will excuse us."

"I'm afraid, my dear," said Traherne a little time later, when the last of their guests had departed, "that I have no recollection of a prior engagement, a circumstance that can no doubt be attributed to my lamentable memory."

"Pooh, you know very well there is not the least thing wrong with your memory," Althea chided, shoving him down on the caffoy-covered easy chair near the fire and plopping herself down across his lap. "There is no prior engagement. I wanted you to myself."

"Why, I wonder, do I find that somehow fraught with dire possibilities?" queried Traherne, eyeing his duchess askance.

"I daresay, my dearest lord duke, it is because you are suffering the pangs of a guilty conscience," speculated Althea, running her fingertips through the hair over his temple. "You stole out of the house this morning without so much as saying good-bye, and you have returned in a veritable state of gloom. Pray do not deny it, Lucius. I could see it in your eyes the moment you walked in the room."

"No, did you? The very moment?" said Traherne, with the arch of an eyebrow. "But then, you have always had the faculty for seeing through my poor defenses. It is nothing about which you need concern yourself, Althea. Merely a disagreement with a former business associate."

"Is that what he is? Strange, but I had not the impression *Monsieur* Duval was in any way involved with business." Althea, sensing the barrier descend, steeled herself to continue. "I beg you will not be angry, Lucius; but I had to know, and Edward was so obliging as to step out for a moment. I stole a peek at your desk. You have spoken Duval's name in your sleep; and when I saw it, written in your calendar for this morning, I asked Edward about him. I really could not help myself. Naturally, Edward fobbed me off with some nonsense about old school acquaintances, which only served to convince me the gentleman is much more than that. He has something to do with what happened to you in France, that thing you said about a sniper's bullet. He is somehow mixed up in all of this mess with Jacqueline Marot and Alastair and Henry Kearns, I know it. If he is one of them, I should like to think you would tell me, Lucius."

"Then you will be happy to know that he is *not* one of them," said Traherne, resigning himself to the inevitable. Althea had made it plain that she would not stop until she had learned the whole of it. Surprisingly, he found an odd sort of relief at the thought of sharing it with her. "He is a French émigré whose wife and daughter were found washed ashore four years ago off Beachy Head, along with an Englishman named Wendell Haverland."

"Haverland." Althea's brow creased in a frown. The name struck a chord of memory. And then it came to her— the young duke on a walking tour in the company of his tutor, a tall man with a gentleness about him, which had struck her even then in the midst of her grief at the loss of her mama. Her eyes flew to Traherne's. "He was your tutor. He was with you that day you came to talk to the colonel about Briersley. I remember. It was the day we left."

"I wondered if you had. You could not have been more than eight or nine, and you had a great deal to occupy you at the time." Even then, Traherne reflected, she had had an arresting quality about her, as if, even in her insupportable loss, she had inner reserves of strength upon which to draw. She had looked straight at him, with the serious air of one who realizes her life has taken a turn from which there will be no going back again.

"You said you were glad I had purchased Briersly because you could not like the notion of leaving it without knowing there would be someone to realize and care that it had always been a happy house and would be so again one day. I believe you drew comfort from the notion that your mama would always be there, surrounded by the things she had known and loved, while she waited for the time when she would be rejoined by her loved ones."

Feeling her throat tighten, Althea laid her cheek against his shoulder. "I do remember. There was something in your face that told me I might trust you to understand." Suddenly, she lifted her head to look at him with startled comprehension. "That is why you never changed it. Lucius, you kept it as it was for her sake!"

"For yours, perhaps," corrected Traherne, lightly trailing a fingertip down the side of her face. "Or perhaps it merely suited my whim to leave it as it was. It hardly mattered, since I was seldom there. Now it is yours to do with as you will."

"Faith, I had not thought of that," Althea said, her brow wrinkled in a frown. "Somehow, the Old Mill House feels more like home now. But then, home will ever be where you are, Lucius. And-and Effie." She closed her eyes and shook her head. "But I am not ready yet to think about what is to be done about Effie." She opened her eyes to look at Traherne again. "Tell me about Wendell Haverland. It was because of what happened to him, was it not—the reason you went after those men and Jacqueline Marot? They killed your friend."

Traherne's brow darkened with the memories. "He was more to me than a friend—more to me than my own father. He did not deserve such an end, his hands and feet bound behind him, his throat slit like a butchered swine's. It was worse for the woman. Duval will carry that with him the rest of his days."

"You, however, pledged to find Haverland's murderers," Althea prompted gently. "It was all that was left to you to do. You could not bring Haverland back, but you could perhaps prevent others from a similar fate. My God, Lucius. You went to France under the cover of a disguise. With your command of French, you could easily pass yourself off as one of the scaff and raff."

"As a blind street minstrel, as it happens, and later a traveling physician, a beggar, an old crone, a crippled sailor. You would be surprised, my dove, at the scope of my repertoire."

"Personally, I have a certain fondness for you as a pirate," submitted Althea, smiling whimsically up at him. "What did you discover on these forays into enemy territory?"

"That there was a ring of treachery and deception spanning the shores on either side of the Channel, which preyed on the desperate." He told her all of it, things he had never told anyone before. The weeks and months of following a seemingly endless trail of clues, until at last he had uncovered all but the heart of it.

"I tracked down Kearns. Presenting myself as one with a considerable sum to venture in his smuggling enterprises, I persuaded him to take me in as a partner of sorts. In this manner, I learned the extent of the operation, the signals employed between boats and to communicate with the shore watch, the numerous landing places along the coast. It was enough to quash the network of smugglers, who preyed on the innocent, but not to expose the evil genius behind it. No doubt I owe it to Sir Wilfred Pellum that Kearns escaped the net. I have little doubt it was Kearns who fired the sniper's bullet that took me down on the doorstep of my own house.''

Listening to his dispassionate narrative of the risks he had taken, Althea felt a vise close on her vitals at the end of the final chapter. Faith, had it not been that a chance gust of wind had blown off his hat, her dearest Lucius would not have been there with her today! The first shot had missed by inches. The second had taken his leg out from under him as he dove for cover. And then had come the endless weeks and months of sickness and pain, with Carstairs and Greaves, not to mention the entire household staff at Meresgate, standing guard in fear that the notorious League of Gentlemen would return to finish the blood feud against the duke.

''I am glad to know about Carstairs and Greaves,'' said Althea, turning her face into the curve of Traherne's neck lest he see too much in her eyes. ''If I could not be there in your time of need, then at least I can comfort myself with the knowledge that you were well looked after.''

''I, on the other hand, can only be grateful I had not you as well as my aging butler and gentleman's gentleman to worry me,'' asserted the duke, who could little relish the image evoked of his indomitable duchess prepared to take on a band of murderous smugglers in his defense. ''There is still a great deal that is puzzling. Merrick was never a part of the smuggling and murder of French émigrés. Is there anything you can recall that might explain his involvement with Alastair and Marot? Can you think of a reason he would go to the risk of putting a period to Sir Wilfred?''

''I have been wondering about that. In the norm, I should have expected Merrick to take a shot at *me*. After all, he had gone to a deal of trouble to find me; and I did shoot him in the foot years ago, which did little to endear me to him. All I can think is that he was afraid Sir Wilfred could be made to tell us something that Merrick had little wish to have known.''

''That much, I believe we can assume without question, little peagoose,'' Traherne observed dryly.

''Devil,'' scolded Althea, wrinkling her nose at him. ''As I was saying before I was so rudely interrupted, it occurs to me, therefore, that perhaps it would help to know something of Sir Wilfred's past. Was he ever in Madras, for example? Perhaps he knew Merrick before he went to India. Perhaps equally relevant is what Merrick was about before he was sent to Madras.''

''As it happens, we have been unable to find anything about Evelyn Merrick before his employment with the Company,'' said Traherne, a curious glint in the look he bent upon Althea. ''It is as if, like Minerva, he sprang fully grown out of the forehead of Jupiter the day he was put on the rolls.''

''Is that not just a trifle curious?'' queried Althea, sitting up in sudden acute interest.

''I should say, if he sprang from the head of a mythological god, it would be curious in the extreme,'' contended Traherne. ''It would cause one to wonder about Merrick's references at the very least. I believe it is not the custom of the Company to hire agents to handle their affairs without at least one recommendation from a source of indisputable integrity—or a relative with influence in the Company.''

''You do not suppose he was engaged on the word of Jupiter, do you?'' queried Althea, who was obviously thinking along lines identical to Traherne's.

''We shall soon find out.'' Traherne, giving Althea a boost from his lap, rose to cross to the bellpull. ''As it happens, Edward has compiled a dossier on Mr. Merrick, which would hardly be complete without the Company's record of employment.''

* * *

"But I assure you it is all there in his dossier, Your Grace," said Phips some moments later. "The recommendation came from one high in the Port Authority. Sir—"

"Wilfred Pellum," said Althea in concert with Mr. Phips. "Lucius, Sir Wilfred knew Merrick before he went to India."

"Which is undoubtedly why Merrick cut his stick for him," Traherne observed thoughtfully. "I think it may be safe to assume that Merrick is nothing more than an assumed identity. In which case, instead of Evelyn Merrick, perhaps we should have been trying to find out what we could about *Monsieur* Develin."

"Develin?" echoed Phips, even to the French pronunciation that Traherne whimsically had given it. "Not Antoine Develin?"

"I am sure I could not say, Edward," admitted Traherne, eyeing his secretary with an air of expectation. "Who is Antoine Develin?"

"Faith, why did I not think of him before?" exclaimed Althea, in sudden animation. "Antoine Develin commanded the French fleet off the southern coast of India. It was generally held he was behind Hyder Ali's rampage across the fertile plains of Madras. When General Coote routed Hyder Ali, the English fleet drove Develin's ships back to France. Antoine Develin, however, would be a much older man than Merrick. In 1785, I was still a child living at Briersly."

"The cogent point, I believe, is not that Merrick could not be Develin, but that Develin does not rhyme with Evelyn," said Traherne with grim significance.

Althea felt a cold chill explore her spine. "Develin is not English. Good God, he is French!"

* * *

Still contemplating the ramifications of a French agent in a position of influence in Madras, Althea was singularly preoccupied as she sat beside Ophelia Keene in the carriage on the way to Lady Cranston's ball later that same evening. Indeed, a great deal that had puzzled her about Merrick would seem suddenly to make a deal of sense in light of this new revelation. How it was, for example, that an East India agent would go to the trouble of engaging in espionage against the governor of Madras, even enlisting the aid of the colonel's younger daughter to steal information from her father's desk. Really, when one thought about it, it would seem to make little sense unless the information was intended to be used to foment unrest among the various native princes for the sole purpose of disrupting British trade. How very clever of the colonel to turn it to his own advantage! No doubt had she herself not been utterly distracted by what gave every evidence of her sister's unruly plunge into pubescence, she would have realized that Merrick could not have been in the least amorously interested in a schoolroom miss—that, indeed, his sole purpose was to use Gloriana for nefarious purposes.

Really, she was out of all patience with Evelyn Merrick or Develin, or whatever the deuce his name was. Indeed, it had just occurred to her, not for the first time, that it was past time his propensity for meddling in their affairs was brought summarily to an end, when it was forcibly brought to her attention by her companion's sudden collapse into tears that Ophelia had apparently been speaking to her at great length without Althea's being in the least aware of it. Upon reflection, Althea did seem to recall mention of something concerning the sins of the parents being visited upon the child and the need to mend fences before much more grass was allowed to grow underfoot, though in lieu of a context upon which to judge, she could make very little sense of the utterances.

"Dearest Ophelia," she exclaimed, in acute mortification

at her gross dereliction of what was due her companion, "pray do not cry. Everything will be fine, I am certain."

"You cannot know how relieved I am to hear it, dearest," sniffed Ophelia, dabbing at her eyes with her lace handkerchief. "I have been so consumed with guilt these past several weeks, though I cannot see how I should have known the letters existed, when they have been packed away in a box in the attic all these years. It is all Hilary's fault for not taking the time to go through all of Crandal's things, though I daresay he had not the slightest wish to examine what he must have presumed to be billets-doux from that Woman. For if you must know Hilary never approved of his brother's infatuation for one who was little better than an adventuress, never mind that the affair endured for fourteen years. Faith, she was his mama's seamstress, whose sole claim to gentility was the work she contracted to do for her betters. I thought her a rather sad, quiet creature myself, not in the least what one might expect of a strumpet. And at least she was decent enough never to bring forth a parcel of byblows. Oh, dear, I do beg your pardon, Althea! I never meant—"

"Of course you did not, Ophelia," declared Althea, patting the other woman's hand. "I am not so removed from reality that I do not apprehend the complications of illegitimate offspring to a noble house. At least Effie is a girl and therefore hardly poses a liability to the succession. What happened to the duke's mistress—er, what did you say was her name?—in the wake of his passing?"

"I do not believe I mentioned her name, which is Milly Langston. After Crandal behaved in a wholly reprehensible manner in allowing himself to be struck down in a duel, she must surely have been cast from the house in Kensington, had not Hilary taken pity on her and intervened. Perhaps Crandal expressed somewhere a desire that she be given the deed to the house, for that is what Hilary did, though I daresay I could not say for sure any arrangement had been made for her. Nevertheless, I believe she lives there yet, quite retired in what Crandal was used to call his love nest.''

''But then, should not the letters go to her?'' asked Althea, recalled to the original topic of conversation.

''To *her?*'' exclaimed Ophelia, apparently considerably taken aback at such a notion. ''But what would *she* want with them? I daresay she would sooner toss them in the fire as to look at them, which I could very easily do myself if I were certain that is what should be done with them.''

''But I do not understand,'' said Althea, more than a little perplexed. ''Why would she burn them? Surely, after all these years, she is not still so deeply in mourning as not to wish to read letters that would bring back fond memories of a happier time.''

''Fond memories? I cannot think reading letters from the wife of the man to whom one was denied marriage would bring back memories of a fond nature. Indeed, I cannot imagine why Crandal even bothered to keep them, save perhaps to savor his mean-spirited revenge against a woman he wronged over the years and the son he delighted in belittling and humiliating.''

''The woman he wronged,'' Althea repeated, a glimmer of understanding beginning to break through the fog of misconception. ''Do you mean Olivia Traherne wrote the letters?''

''Of course she wrote them. I said so, did I not, not more than ten minutes ago. Three years' worth of letters. Not that Lucius was ever allowed to see them. Olivia must have known the duke would never permit them to be delivered to him. Still, I suppose she felt she had to try. Certainly, she was left little doubt that her pleas to see Lucius fell on deaf ears. The duke threatened to have her locked away in Bedlam and her precious Praetorius transported to the penal colonies if she ever so much as tried to talk to the boy. You may be sure he would have done it, too. And then the letters stopped. Heaven only knows why. But now I have had the misfortune to find them, and all because I would come up with the notion of displaying my mother's silver epergne, for which I have never entertained the smallest fondness, on the dining room table. I wish I had never set foot in that attic. Whatever am I to do with the letters, Althea? I am depending on you to tell me.''

Althea, who was still digesting the reality of the letters' existence and all that they might mean to Lucius and the dowager duchess, did not even hesitate to answer. ''Naturally, you are going to give them to me, Ophelia. And I shall see they go to Lucius, just as they had ought to have done twenty-six years ago.''

No more was said of the letters, as the carriage arrived just then before Lady Cranston's Town House. The long line of carriages waiting in the street, not to mention the stream of people entering at the front door, gave every evidence that the ball was to be a complete squeeze. Having relinquished her pelisse to a servant at the cloakroom, Althea, nodding and smiling, made her way with Ophelia down the receiving line. She paused at the head of the stairs to glance over the crowded ballroom below.

Traherne, naturally, would not make his appearance until after the second intermission. He had said something about meeting with Winslade. Nevertheless, in spite of the fact that she had been in circulation for only a sennight, Althea was pleased to recognize not a few of the faces below her. Sir Thomas Greene, having already espied her, was even then making toward her, while Lord Harry Wilcox, in conversation with a young blond beauty, did not hesitate to blow Althea a kiss in tribute to her stunning presence at the top of the stairs. Althea gracefully inclined her head in acknowledgment.

''Dear, I might have known it!'' exclaimed Ophelia in

anxious tones. "Just when I thought to have a pleasant evening. I should have remembered that she and Maria Cranston made their curtsies together. Indeed, they were bosom bows."

Glancing in the direction in which Ophelia was staring over the flutter of her ivory-handled fan, Althea was greeted with the sight of her mama-in-law elegant in a shift of white lawn, so light as to be nearly transparent and having Grecian patterns embroidered around the hem. Mr. Praetorius was equally striking in an *incroyable,* the narrow high-waisted tailcoat and high collar of purple velvet seemingly particularly designed to draw attention to his tall slender build, as were the yellow waistcoat, skintight breeches of paisley green, and slippers cut so low as to only just cover the toes and heels.

"Pray do not take it so much to heart, Ophelia," said Althea, allowing Sir Thomas Greene to lead her down the stairs. "They had to meet sometime. I should think tonight would be as good as any other."

"On the contrary," declared Ophelia, "there could never be a good time for it. I daresay Traherne will take one look and march immediately out of the ballroom, which will be exceedingly uncomfortable for everyone concerned. And what do you think you are doing, Althea? You cannot truly be intending to walk right up to her. I pray you will think carefully before openly acknowledging her. Dear, you know Lucius has expressly forbidden it."

"Pooh to Lucius," Althea said with a grimace. "Sir Thomas, have you had the honor of meeting my mother-in-law?"

"Indeed, Your Grace, I have not. I have heard she is a charming woman."

"You heard correctly, Sir Thomas. She is an exceedingly charming woman, and I shall take great pleasure in presenting you."

* * *

Traherne, ushered into Winslade's study, was immediately aware of a tension in the room, an impression that could only be abetted by the discovery that the viscount was not alone to greet his guest. Gloriana Winslade, a pale vision in rose sarcenet, stood with her back to the fire, her hands clasped at her waist before her.

"Traherne," said Winslade over the strong grip of hands. "Good of you to come. You remember my wife, of course."

"Lady Winslade."

"Gloriana, Your Grace, I beg you. We are family, after all. Please, be seated. Jack, perhaps our guest would like a glass of something. I myself should not be averse to a small libation of ratafia."

"Your Grace?" queried Winslade, indicating a grog tray, which had been replenished since the viscount's indulgence upon the event of his wife's decampment.

"A brandy would not be amiss. Thank you." He seated himself in the wing chair across from the settee upon which his hostess sank, taking care to arrange her skirts. Patently, the viscountess was nervous.

"It is strange that in view of all that we have already been made to experience in one another's company that we have never really even been introduced," observed Gloriana, who, Traherne could not but notice, bore a remarkable resemblance to her elder sister. Perhaps Althea was the slightest bit taller and demonstrated a greater willowiness of form than Gloriana. There was also a hint of petulance about Gloriana's lips that distinguished her from the indomitable Althea, but the two women were very alike in appearance. "I am keenly aware that I have been remiss in expressing how very happy I am for you both. I could not have been more pleased to learn that Althea had found someone to-to care for her as she deserves. I know it has not always been easy for her."

"I believe you may comfort yourself with the knowledge that Althea has not been unhappy these past years in the dale," observed Traherne in exceedingly dry tones. "On the contrary, I found her to be remarkably resistant to the idea of changing her single existence. Had it not been for the attempt to abduct Effie, I daresay I should, in fact, have been forced to marry your sister over the anvil."

It was made immediately apparent that Gloriana had been left in ignorance of the events to which he was referring. The viscountess, blanching, clapped a hand to her breast in every manifestation of horror. "Effie? Dear God, is she—?"

"Thanks to Althea's quick thinking, the child was made to suffer nothing more alarming than a brief flight alone on horseback, a circumstance which I am told she views in the light of the 'most wonderfulest of adventures.' I have no doubt Effie is slated to be a bruising rider."

"Yes, of course, she would be," said Gloriana, twisting her hands in her lap. "The Wintergreens have always been crazy to ride."

"Let us not forget the long line of equestrians in the Travers's line," Jack interjected, handing a glass to Traherne and another to his wife. "No doubt you will pardon my curiosity, Your Grace, but I have yet to even lay eyes on my daughter. Tell me, what is she like?"

Good God, thought Traherne. Effie was Effie. His very first impression of the little imp had been that she was the spitting image of the wood sprite with the red-gold hair. Over the months his opinion had not altered. What the devil did they want from him?

A heavy-ridded look of ennui descended over Traherne's handsome features. "You did not, I assume, ask me here tonight to discuss the child?" Setting the glass aside, he deliberately made to rise. "If you did, then I shall have to ask you to excuse me. As it is, I am promised to meet Althea at Lady Cranston's ball."

"No, please." Gloriana, leaning forward, implored him

with her eyes. "I beg your pardon for what must seem a gross imposition. We had no right to—" Giving a vague gesture of the hand, she did not finish, but instead drew herself up, her head lifted in proud supplication. "I beg you will stay, Your Grace. You are quite right. We did not ask you here to talk about Effie."

Althea, sitting in animated conversation with the Dowager Duchess of Traherne, was acutely aware that she was the cynosure of attention. Indeed, she did not doubt the entire room was waiting in eager anticipation for the arrival of the one remaining principal player in what had all the elements of a wholly scandalous row in the making. A small voice of conscience persisted in warning her that she was not playing fair with her dearest lord duke. An equally persistent voice, however, insisted that she really could not, in all conscience, have given Olivia Traherne the cut direct. To have done so would have been to go against her every sense of what was right and wrong. Not that she felt she was justified in having gone against her husband's express wishes. She knew she was on the horns of a dilemma.

"Where were you, Xavier," Olivia queried, her gaze knowing on her Apollo, "when Althea was performing her 'Dance of the Seven Veils'? You were not, by any chance, indulging your passion for sordid pleasures?"

"You wound me, Duchess," said Praetorius, clapping a hand over his heart. "You know very well my passion for sordid pleasures does not extend to prurient lusts, save behind the closed door of my lady's bedchamber."

"You are right, of course," smiled Olivia, her eyes twinkling with fond humor. "I ask your pardon, my prince of hearts. What, then, were you doing when Althea was fleeing the pack of wolves?"

"I, dear ladies, was beating a strategic retreat. Having espied a tall buccaneer eyeing our lissome Gypsy girl with the glowering aspect of a husband in the throes of a jealous rage, I judged our little duchess was in far better hands than mine. As it happens, I am being visited with a strikingly similar emotion at this precise moment. I believe I must ask you both to excuse me. I feel the urge for a glass of punch.''

Althea had hardly enough time to grasp the significance of Praetorius's queer behavior before, bowing graciously, the thespian was melting into the press of dancers. "Be not faint of heart, my dearest lady. The moment you have been awaiting is upon you.''

"Althea.'' The touch of Olivia's hand, tense, upon her arm left Althea little doubt what moment it was to which Praetorius was referring.

"Yes,'' she murmured, covering the other woman's hand with her own, "I see him.''

Faith, she thought. It would have been impossible *not* to see the tall figure—strikingly handsome in a double-breasted blue cutaway coat with gilt buttons, a waistcoat of pure marcella, and white kerseymere breeches—when the crowd on the dance floor appeared to split in the manner of the parting of the Red Sea to allow him to pass. A hard knot tightened in her belly, as it came to her fully what, precisely, she was risking.

She had willfully gone against his wishes, even to the extent of placing him in a wholly untenable position. She was forcing him to choose between his wife and his pride. If only there had been time to show him the letters, came the fleeting thought, the letters that must surely prove his mother had never ceased to love him. If only circumstance had not dictated that the choice should have to be made in full view of a ballroom filled with people. In just moments, Althea realized, her own brief dream of happiness might very well have come to an end.

Her dearest Lucius, however, must not be allowed to see that she was suffering from a sudden queasy sensation in the pit of her stomach or that she had forcefully to keep herself from fidgeting. For his sake, as well as for Olivia's, she must appear as if she were perfectly unaware that the ballroom had gone suddenly still or that every eye was turned on the Duke of Traherne as he came at last to a halt.

Only then, when she felt him standing over her, did Althea finally allow herself to look up.

She was not sure what she had expected—a chill stare, perhaps, meant to sear her soul with his contempt, or, more probably, banked fires of a slow smoldering rage. Certainly, it was not to discover the light piercing eyes fixed with a curious probing intensity on the face of the dowager duchess.

"Madame. You are much as I remember you."

"It is kind in you to say so, Your Grace," returned Olivia Traherne with the same solemnity of tone, belied by the hunger in her eyes. She smiled. "You, on the other hand, are a great deal taller than when last I saw you."

Althea's heart sank as she saw the cynical twist of Traherne's lips.

"Not the last time, surely, madame. You cannot have overlooked the occasion of my recent incivility to you. I beg your pardon, madame, for behavior that is unseemly in a gentleman."

Olivia Traherne's eyes held in searching wonder on the duke's before dropping at last to the lean strong hand held out to her. A murmur went around the ballroom, as, looking up again, she laid her palm in his and allowed him to lift her to her feet.

"You had reason to feel as you did. Lucius—?"

"We have a great deal to discuss, madame. However, this is neither the time nor the place. I regret that Althea and I must take our leave of you. We should be pleased, however, if you would join us for dinner one evening this week."

Olivia's face underwent a swift change of expression. "You are too kind, Your Grace," she said, carefully controlled once again.

Althea felt her heart ache for them both, even as she struggled against an insurmountable urge to shake Traherne for what could only be seen as a rebuff just when she had been trembling on the brink of rejoicing in what gave every appearance of a happy reconciliation.

Althea rose brusquely to her feet in the sudden taut silence. "Splendid," she said. "We shall expect you, then. Shall we say tomorrow evening?"

"Rather say Thursday." Traherne's gaze met hers and held.

"Yes, of course." Althea experienced an immediate sinking sensation in the pit of her stomach. The waiting, then, was over, she thought, hardly knowing what she felt. "Thursday would naturally be better."

"Thursday," echoed Olivia Traherne, gazing from one to the other.

Traherne's light piercing glance rested on the dowager duchess. "I regret we cannot stay—"

Smiling, Olivia shook her head. "Nonsense. I understand perfectly. You will be careful, will you not? Both of you?"

Traherne's hands came to rest lightly on her shoulders. "You may depend on it." Bending, he kissed her lightly on the cheek. "Thursday evening, then," he said. "Oh, and, Mother—you will naturally wish to bring your friend, Mr. Praetorius."

Chapter Fifteen

Traherne, ushering Althea out of the door to their waiting conveyance, was acutely aware that his irrepressible duchess was fairly bursting with barely suppressed excitement. And, indeed, hardly had they arrived at the carriage than Althea turned and flung her arms about his neck.

"Lucius," she exclaimed with a glowing face, "pray forgive me for ever doubting in you. What you did back there was—"

"Not a word, Althea, I warn you," Traherne sternly interrupted. "What I did was unavoidable. You made certain of that when you aligned yourself with my mother—against my express wishes, need I remind you?"

"No, Lucius," said his impossible wood nymph, gazing up at him out of eyes that fairly took his breath away. "No doubt I should apologize for that, but I did warn you I should very likely never make a conformable wife. And, truly, I could not help myself. You must see that I was on the horns of a dilemma."

"I see that you are exceedingly pleased with yourself,"

he said repressively. "Worse, you will very likely be moved in the very near future to say I have only done what you told me I should."

"No, how can you say so?" Althea said, moved to wrinkle her nose at him. "There is nothing so tiresome as an 'I told you so.' Besides, you have very obligingly said it for me."

"Little jade!" growled Traherne.

"My dearest lord duke," Althea sweetly retorted. Then, all at once, she sobered. "Lucius," she breathed, squeezing her arms tightly about his neck, *"I do love you so!"*

The next instant she had released him and, turning, climbed hastily into the carriage.

Traherne, left standing, silently cursed. His wood nymph had an uncanny knack for utterly disarming him in moments when he least might have wished to be distracted. He had entered the ballroom hardly expecting to find his duchess seated in the company of his estranged mother, though no doubt he should have done. After all, it was bound to happen sometime, just as it had on the memorable occasion of the exceedingly uncomfortable encounter at the theater. This time, however, he had not the option of playing the arrogant boor. To have done so would have been to sink his own duchess beneath reproach in the eyes of the world, a circumstance of which his meddling wood sprite must have been fully aware.

A wry smile twisted at his lips. The devil, she had outflanked and outmaneuvered him in a manner that must have been the envy of even an old soldier like the colonel. But then, his thoughts, unfortunately, had been otherwise occupied when he arrived at Lady Cranston's ball.

Brought back to the grim reality of what lay before him, Traherne stepped up into the waiting carriage.

"You might as well tell me straight out, Lucius," said Althea when they had gone for several minutes in silence. "Delaying the inevitable would seem to be to little purpose. What did Jack have to say to you?"

Traherne, who had been occupied with determining the best manner in which to inform Althea of the new turn of events, smiled sardonically to himself. Depend on the wood sprite to go straight to the heart of the matter. Furthermore, she was perfectly in the right of it: Nothing would be gained by putting off the inevitable.

"Late this afternoon," he said, taking the plunge, "a letter arrived for Winslade. Needless to say it was not of a felicitous nature. Besides the previous threats, it warned that his wife's recent experiences at the hands of abductors was only a presage to what would come if he failed to cooperate."

"But that is what we were hoping they would do, is it not?" queried Althea. "They did leave Gloriana instructions where to take the papers?" A frown knit her brow at Traherne's brooding hesitation. "Lucius, what is it that you are reluctant to tell me?"

"Only that as a demonstration of what might happen to anyone who thought to play them false, they directed Winslade to a house—" Traherne stopped, his eyes dark coals in the dim light cast by the carriage lantern. "Althea, there is no longer any need for you to play a part in the final scheme of things. Gloriana was not asked to deliver the papers."

"Then who?" demanded Althea, little liking the direction in which Traherne would seem to be heading. "Lucius? Who is to take them? Winslade?"

"No," said Traherne. "The letter named me."

"The devil it did." She had known before he said it. He meant to go through with the plan the two of them had devised. Only, *he* would be the one to walk into danger. Furthermore, he intended to go alone! Indeed, if she was not mistaken, they were even now on their way to Grosvenor Square and undoubtedly Winslade's Town House where Lucius planned to deposit her like so much excess baggage. It was all exceedingly plain to her.

"I will not have it, Traherne. This is none of Merrick's

doing. He would not have any reason to have done. This is Alastair's work. His and Jacqueline Marot's. It is a trap. You know it is. They intend to cut your stick for you, and I will not allow it, do you hear me! I will not let you go alone.''

"I shall not be alone. Winslade will accompany me.'' Traherne, grasping her wrists, held her. "At any rate, you have no say in it, Althea. This has nothing to do with you. This is about Bonaparte's plans to invade England.''

"Gammon!'' declared Althea, as the carriage came to a stop before Number 3 Grosvenor Square. "This is about Wendell Haverland, and pray do not try and deny it. I am going with you, Lucius. If you try to fob me off on my sister, I will only pry what I need to know out of her. You may be sure she will keep nothing from me, anymore than you can keep me from coming after you. I did not follow the colonel and the drum all those years to no avail, Lucius. You may be sure I know how to handle myself in perilous situations.''

Egad, thought Traherne, who hardly needed to be reminded that his maddening Althea had not been reared a hothouse flower or that she was perfectly capable of doing precisely as she had said she would. This time, however, he was damned if he would give in to her.

He had few doubts as to what might be waiting for him in the house to which the letter had directed him. It was no place for a woman, even if the woman happened to be the colonel's daughter who had experienced any number of perilous adventures growing up with her father's regiment.

"The matter is not open to discussion, Althea,'' he said, flinging open the carriage door. "You will obey me in this if I have to bind you, hand and foot. Is that understood?''

Althea, who had been reared most of her life among men, understood very well when one of them had clearly shut down all avenues of logic and rationality in order to put his masculine foot down. She saw immediately that she was given no choice but to employ feminine wiles against him. She reflected philosophically that it was really too bad of Traherne to make things far more difficult than they had to be.

"You may be sure that I understand perfectly, Lucius," she said, dismounting calmly from the carriage. "That does not mean I agree with you. Nor is there any need to keep the cattle standing on my account," she added, walking blithely past him toward the front door. "I am perfectly capable of seeing myself into my sister's house."

Traherne, who had hardly expected his redoubtable duchess to give in without so much as an argument, experienced, at Althea's orderly retreat, an immediate insidious birth of suspicion. The devil, he thought. The little rogue was up to something.

"Nevertheless," he said, striding to catch up with her, "you will allow me to see that you are safely inside."

"I'm sure you may do as you please, Lucius," Althea replied reasonably. "My only thought was for your prized pair of bays."

"Naturally it was," agreed the duke, reaching past her to give the knocker a resounding thump. "Indeed, I daresay it never occurred to you to hail a passing hack and follow me to my destination."

"I assure you the thought never entered my head, Lucius," declared Althea without the least hesitation. "But if it had, I should no doubt be grateful that several of the neighbors appear to be entertaining tonight. I daresay there are any number of hacks standing by just hoping to be hailed."

"They will not be hailed by you, however, will they, Althea?" asserted his grace in dire accents. "*You*, after all, will be spending the evening with your sister in a quiet coze, will you not?"

"Really, Lucius," declared Althea, awarding him a pitying glance, "you cannot actually expect me to exchange the latest *on dits* with Gloriana over tea while you are out somewhere doing your best to get yourself killed. You may be sure I shall be doing anything *but* having a quiet coze with my sister this night.''

"Nevertheless, you will remain here until I return for you," warned Traherne, who was perfectly aware he had just been given a royal roundaboutation. "I want your word on it, Althea.''

"Then no doubt you will have it," observed Althea, as the door was opened by the viscount's London butler. "You are, after all, too regrettably used to getting what you want, are you not? Please inform Lady Winslade her sister is here to see her," she announced then to the superior servant as she stepped into the foyer. Composedly tugging off her gloves, she turned to regard her husband with an inquisitively raised eyebrow. "Still here, Lucius?" she inquired with limpid eyes. "Was there not somewhere you intended to go?''

"To the devil, I doubt not," growled Traherne, ruefully aware that he found himself in an unenviable position—at a draw by perpetual check with his duchess. "Althea, I am not often reduced to asking anything of anyone. I am asking you, however, to honor my wishes in this matter. I doubt not that, while you are well able to take on any number of Pathan banditti, I am not equipped to risk my duchess's life on a questionable venture. I shall not be distracted from the business immediately at hand if I know you are with your sister.''

"And I shall not be *driven* to distraction, Lucius, if I am not made to wait in ignorance of what is happening to you. The truth is, I should have made an exceedingly poor soldier's wife, for I could never bear to remain at home as my mama did, wondering if I should ever see my husband again. Is it so very difficult for you to see me, not as a woman who must be protected, but as a seasoned campaigner who is well able to protect herself?''

Traherne was keenly aware of his wife, enticingly arrayed

in a white Mechlin lace evening gown cut low in the front and with a short train at the back. He found it utterly impossible to see her as anything but his wholly maddening, utterly adorable wood sprite, whom he would go to extreme lengths to spare the horror and disillusionment of what must surely be waiting at the designated house. He would, in fact, lie to her, if he were given no other choice in the matter.

"It is precisely because I believe you are well able to look after yourself that I wish you to remain with Gloriana," he said without the flicker of an eyelash. "I was reluctant to mention it before, but I am troubled with the feeling that this letter may be more than a ruse to draw me into a trap. It has occurred to me that it may be designed as well, to make certain Gloriana is left alone and helpless. If you think about it, it has a queer ring to it that they should demand *I* bring the papers. You yourself pointed out that Merrick would hardly have any reason to involve me. On the other hand, they must know Winslade would never stand to let me go without him, in which case, Gloriana—"

"Would have no one to protect her or the children!" Althea's face went pearly white at the mere possibilities. "Faith, why did I not see it before? I daresay that is precisely what they are planning. Indeed, it would seem to make perfect sense. Very possibly they suspect you will not bring the real papers, in which case, they will wish to have the added assurance of hostages. Jack would have no choice but to do as they demanded! Faith, it is precisely what I should do if I were in their place."

Far from experiencing any sort of satisfaction at having sold his logical-minded wife on a scenario he had merely invented to keep her out of trouble, Traherne found upon closer inspection that the made-up tale would seem all too fraught with dire plausibility.

Indeed, he was far from pleased with himself. Some twenty minutes later, after dropping Winslade off a short distance from the direction given in the letter, Traherne alit from the carriage in front of the house that only twelve nights before had been ablaze with lights and boisterous with the sounds of revelry. It was silent enough now, and bloody well dark with brooding.

Like a cursed tomb, reflected Traherne, which in all likelihood was what it was if there was in truth some grim memento within to demonstrate what happened to those foolish enough to cross the likes of the Gentlemen. Why the devil had they picked Branscombe's house? he wondered, unless it was the earl who, having declared freely to Merrick-Develin that he would not tolerate treason against King and country, had proved as good as his word. Traherne doubted not it would not have been either an easy or a quick death if that was the case.

It augured ill for someone that the door had been left ajar, like a baited trap for the hare. Where the bloody hell were the servants? Grimly, Traherne was reminded that the Gentlemen were notorious for never leaving witnesses to their black-hearted deeds.

Closing his fist on the handle of the pistol in his greatcoat pocket, Traherne shoved the door wide and stepped inside.

The foyer was subdued, the parquetry-tiled floor reflecting the light from a single candelabra set on the sideboard. Following the premonition that had come to him at his first perusal of the letter, Traherne took up the candelabra and made his way through the darkened house to the ballroom and the remembered exit to the private corridor. If Branscombe were to be found anywhere in the house, then surely it must be in the chamber that had obviously been his private sanctum.

The white paneled door edged in gilt opened noiselessly on oiled hinges, and Traherne stood, limned in the doorway, his gaze riveted on the scene made fantastic with its single black-garbed mourner, the plethora of burning candles casting weird shadows, and the body laid out in state in an otherwise empty room.

Slowly, his grip relaxed on the gun in his pocket. He withdrew his hand.

The sharp gasp at his back stabbed through his chest. He turned—and found Althea, staring past him, her eyes fixed and staring.

"Good God," she breathed. *"Merrick!"*

At her utterance, the black-garbed figure turned.

"Traherne," he said, taking in at a glance the grim-faced duke and the slender, breeches-clad figure at his side, diamond earrings dangling from dainty earlobes and a green satin reticule clutched incongruously in one hand. "And his beautiful duchess. This *is* a surprise. Splendid. You came. I was not certain you would. My missive so obviously reeked of a trap. And so it is meant to be—a trap to net a pair of murderous traitors and thieves. Pray do come in, and close the door, if you would be so kind. I believe there is yet time before the others arrive. Obviously, there are a myriad questions you would like to have answered."

"You may be sure of it," Traherne agreed, eyeing the other man from beneath hooded eyelids. "Although I believe much of it is now clear. Still, I should be interested to hear you tell it. You have, after all, gone to a deal of trouble, have you not, my lord Branscombe."

"It was a labor of love," replied Branscombe, turning back to finish the task of lighting the final candles set in the manner of a backdrop to the still form laid out on the magnificently carved, Italian late-Renaissance walnut cassapanca. "The final labor, as it were. My poor Evelyn. They treated you most unkindly, just as I warned that they would. A pity you would not listen. But then, if the French harlot had not slit your throat for you, I fear it should have been left to me to do, and that I could not have borne with any great fortitude. I do so detest violence in any form."

"Are you saying Jacqueline Marot did this to Merrick?"

asked Althea, chilled at the earl's passionless avowal. Even from where she stood beside Traherne, she could see all too plainly the slash across the throat, finely sutured and cleansed of blood; the ashen face, arranged to resemble an attitude of peaceful repose; the rouge on the cheeks and lips, a bizarre mockery of the horrid death it was meant to conceal.

"Actually, I fear you played some small part in it, Duchess," said Branscombe, dousing the candlelighter. "Not that I blame you. You were, after all, firing at a French agent who had planned and executed your sister's abduction. I understood perfectly why you should have done it. The pistol ball in Evelyn's shoulder, however, bled profusely. He was considerably weakened when I came home to find him collapsed into insensibility on my bed. Still, I daresay with my careful ministrations, he would most certainly have recovered. Unfortunately, I was at length forced to leave him. It was only for an hour, you understand, to restore my strength in quiet repose. When I returned upstairs, I found poor Evelyn beyond even God's help. From the window, I glimpsed the French harlot run from the front of the house to her waiting carriage." Carefully, the earl smoothed a strand of snow white hair from the dead man's cold brow. "I daresay Evelyn never knew what happened. I can comfort myself with the knowledge that she executed him as he lay, senseless, in a coma."

"Why?" asked Althea, swallowing against the sudden rise of bile to her throat. "Because he killed Sir Wilfred Pellum?"

"Undoubtedly," agreed Traherne. "And because he tried moments earlier to kill Alastair."

Althea's eyes flew to Traherne's. "The shot through the window. Faith, I should have known. Merrick was tying up loose ends. He had decided to rid himself of his partners, anyone who might have identified Merrick as Develin. He was preparing to leave England."

"Actually, we were going away together," supplied the

earl. "I have always wished to see Greece. Evelyn had taken the precaution of providing himself with a villa overlooking the Mediterranean. It was through my persuasion that he was severing his ties with the French harlot and her lover. That was before, of course, I learned he was trying to steal information that would aid in Bonaparte's planned invasion. Had he recovered sufficiently to carry through with his plans I should have been left little choice but to stop him myself. At least I was spared that, my dear," he remarked to the dead man. "Though you may be sure I should have chosen a more tasteful farewell—champagne, the attar of roses, a gentle playing of the harp, a sweet song to lure my dear to restful repose, a drop of poison in thine cup. I did try and warn you what the French harlot was."

Branscombe went suddenly still, his head cocked at an angle, listening. Then he turned, smiling, at the soft scratching at the door.

"It would seem our other guests have arrived. Come," he said. "The game begins."

Opening the door, Branscombe spoke softly to the servant in pale blue livery. Althea recognized in the slender youth the servant who had conducted them to the Countess Suite on the night of the revelry. "Leander," Branscombe had called him, though she doubted that was the boy's real name. His eyes shone, dark with fear, in a face as smooth and comely as a girl's.

Branscombe turned, then, to Traherne. "The French harlot and her lover are below in the ballroom waiting in anticipation of your arrival. Two of their hirelings are posted in positions to cut off your escape, both at the entrance. I suspect possibly a third outside on the terrace. I suggest, Your Grace, you dispatch the underlings before you attend to the main course. Leander will show you the way."

It came to Traherne, following in the wake of the servant

to wonder what part Branscombe had chosen for himself in his elaborate scheme of revenge and retribution. The earl had contrived everything thus far with the touch of a master. It was an aspect of their present situation which most rankled. Traherne disliked being made a pawn in a game not of his own making. But then, that was why he had taken his own precautions. If only he had not Althea's worrisome presence to complicate matters!

"Lucius," whispered that worthy, glancing up into the duke's stern features, "I mistrust the earl. Has it occurred to you that he has arranged for all of the principal players to be present in what promises to be a deadly finale?"

"If you mean Branscombe gives every appearance of a man tying up loose ends," Traherne whispered back, "then, *yes,* it had occurred to me. What the devil are you doing here, Althea?"

"When I realized the real reason you should have been the one to be asked to deliver the papers—because Merrick was already dead and the remaining participants thought to kill two birds with one stone, so to speak—I really could not stay away. Remember the twist the colonel employed against Merrick in Madras? What if Winslade's superiors are using it here? What if they *want* Bonaparte to get his hands on Jack's papers?"

"Then you may be sure they will succeed, wood sprite," replied Traherne, his eyes glittery in the faint flicker of the single candle carried by the servant. "What we must do is ensure that Winslade is not made to take the blame for it."

Althea had been worrying about that very possibility. Indeed, in her anxiety to reach Branscombe's Town House before it was too late to warn Traherne of her suspicions, Althea had been compelled to change into her borrowed clothes in the carriage. Now she could only breathe a sigh of relief that he should have so immediately apprehended the crux of the matter. But then, it was obvious he had already come to the same conclusions for himself. The devil, she thought with a grimace. Really it was too bad of him not to have trusted her with the truth from the very beginning.

It was only then that she came to the realization that Leander had stopped and was signaling them to come abreast of him.

Pointing to a closed door, the youth turned and fled without a backward glance, back the way he had come.

Traherne, uttering a curse beneath his breath, let him go. The boy seemed frightened of his own bloody shadow, and little wonder. The great house, hollow and empty and brooding in darkness, was enough to test the nerves of the hardiest of souls. Finding and clasping Althea's hand in his, Traherne groped in the dark for the door handle.

The spill of moonlight through bay windows revealed the long gallery and, at its center, the curved stairs descending in eerie splendor to the ballroom. It came to Traherne that Branscombe had chosen an odd setting for the evening's entertainment. Indeed, the posting of two guards at the top of the stairs would seem to make little sense in the context of what was supposed to be happening in the ballroom below. Presumably, Alastair and Jacqueline Marot were there waiting for the arrival of the Duke of Traherne with the intention of taking the documents that resided in his greatcoat pocket and then putting a period to his existence. Why, then, should they have men at the head of the stairs down which he would have to descend in order to make the rendezvous?

The answer was that Alastair and the French woman had no expectations of his arrival. The men were there to prevent any outside interference in what was obviously designed to be a meeting with the Earl of Branscombe. And then it came to him, the real purpose behind the earl's elaborate manipulations.

Motioning Althea to stay where she was, he glided forward.

* * *

Althea had also been questioning the rationale behind two men posted at the head of the stairs and had not been long in reaching conclusions similar to the duke's. She started after Traherne, only to stop at the glimpse of movement out of the corner of her eye.

It came to her all in an instant. Traherne, having reached the closest guard, was even then in the process of silencing the fellow with the hard clamp of an arm about the throat. But he had failed to take note that the second was coming around the curve in the gallery. Botheration, she thought. The only thing between Traherne and the approaching guard was herself!

Althea yanked at the strings of what she was fond of referring to as a lady's ridiculous ridicule. It was far too small to accommodate with any measure of convenience anything greater than a packet of Spanish papers, a comb, and a box of beauty patches, none of which, save for the comb, she was in the habit of using, let alone carrying about with her. She plunged her hand inside. It came to her with a terrible certainty, as she closed her fingers about the handle of her automatic mechanical igniter, that she was going to be too late. The figure of the guard appeared to loom over her. She dragged her hand free of the ridiculous ridicule of green satin fringed in lace. Turning her head away, she thrust her arm straight up in the air and pulled the trigger.

Blue flame shot from the barrel. Staggering back, the guard clasped at his eyes. The next instant, a hard fist cracked against the bewhiskered jaw, and the fellow crumpled into Traherne's waiting arms.

"Althea?" whispered Traherne, lifting his duchess to her feet. "The devil, are you all right?"

"I am fine, Lucius," Althea whispered back. "Never mind about me. I think it is time we discovered what the devil is afoot, and the sooner the better. I am heartily weary of the Earl of Branscombe and his thoroughly wretched sense of hospitality. Have you noticed that, other than Merrick on his grotesque bier, there would appear to be a peculiar lack of anything resembling furniture in this house?''

"You are right, of course, Your Grace," observed a deep-throated feminine voice from behind them—the French accent unmistakable. "It is most peculiar. But then, I daresay his lordship has no intention of returning here again. *Mais, non,* my lord duke," came in warning. "I should not try anything if I were you. Robert, you will relieve the duchess of her petite pistol. And bring the woman here to me."

Althea, in no mood to be manhandled, turned to face the raven-haired beauty, whose voluptuous form was draped in a black tunic dress open up the side to expose a leg to the thigh, and a red velvet cloak slung carelessly over one shoulder. In her hand was a gun, aimed at Traherne's midsection.

"Jacqueline Marot, is it not?" said Althea, suppressing a chill at the reminder that she was in the presence of a woman who had not hesitated to slit a man's throat while he lay in a coma. Her fingers tightened on the grip of her automatic mechanical igniter. Then, shrugging, she dropped it in the open palm of Alastair's hand.

The French woman, taking it from him, carelessly tossed it aside.

"So this is the scandalous duchess, who has had the temerity to foster another man's child on the oh-so-proud Duke of Traherne." Jacqueline Marot's dark eyes, framed in improbably long eyelashes, raked Althea's slender leather breeches–clad form from the incongruous dangle of diamonds at her earlobes to the diamond-buckled slippers with recessed French heels on her feet. "I was not aware you liked your women in leather and diamonds, my lord duke. It is *tres amusante,* I think."

"Jacqueline!" snapped Alastair. "Enough of talking. Let

us finish what we came here to do and get the bloody hell out of here. Or have you forgot we have a ship waiting?''

The French woman heaved an eloquent sigh. ''Robert is right. We are pressed for time. You will be so kind as to tell us where you have hidden the earl.''

''No doubt I regret that we cannot help you,'' said Traherne, weighing his chances of reaching Alastair before the man could get off a shot. ''It would appear Branscombe has stood us all up.''

''A shame, then, that you will both have to die to no purpose.'' Pressing her fulsome body up against the duke's, Jacqueline Marot ran the barrel of the gun deliberately down the side of his face to the front of his neck. ''Such a waste. Tell us where he is, and I will not make you watch while I slit the throat of your wife.''

''The way you slit Develin's when he failed to tell you where he hid the diamonds?'' Traherne's cold stare appeared to be too much even for the French woman.

She pulled away. ''Bah! He was out of his head, but he said enough for me to know he gave them to his precious Adonis. Branscombe is here. He would not leave without his passport to travel freely on the Continent. You have them, *oui?* The papers Develin was to sell to Bonaparte's agents? There can be no other reason you would come here. Robert, search him.''

''I found them!'' Alastair thrust his hand into the greatcoat's inside breast pocket and pulled out the folded packet. *''Do you hear, Branscombe?''* he shouted, holding the packet up high over his head. ''I have your bloody papers. Come out, you sniveling cur, and get them!''

It was all the diversion Traherne needed. Seizing the opportunity, he swept the pistol out of the French woman's hand. Marot uttered a scathing curse. Traherne slammed his shoulder into Alastair, carrying them both crashing into the banister. Even as Alastair struggled to bring his gun to bear,

Traherne's fingers clamped like a vise about the other man's wrist.

"Devil's son," gasped Alastair, his face contorted with hatred and rage. "I should have made sure of you when I had the chance."

Traherne's arm drew back. "The way you made sure of the English tutor you butchered." Traherne's fist slammed into Alastair's unprotected jaw. "I shall see you in hell for that."

The force of Traherne's blow sent Alastair plummeting backward over the balustrade. A scream shattered the silence, to be summarily cut off with the sodden thud of Alastair's landing.

His chest heaving from his recent exertions, Traherne straightened and turned—to be met with the less than gratifying sight of his duchess poised and ready to give an immediate demonstration of the finer art of the use of a fulcrum and lever. Thrusting her hip into Jacqueline Marot's middle, Althea sent the French woman flying head over heels over one shoulder.

"Egad," uttered Traherne, as the French beauty alit in a sprawl, to groan and then go suddenly still.

Dusting her hands off, Althea turned to regard Traherne with an unmistakable air of satisfaction.

"Now that that is taken care of, Lucius," she said, bending down to retrieve her automatic mechanical igniter, "do you think we might collect Branscombe and go home? I believe I have had enough danger and intrigue for one night."

"I'm afraid you are too late, Your Grace," declared Edward Phips. Looking rather dashing in a flowing caped greatcoat and curly brimmed beaver and not a little efficient with a pistol held in readiness in his hand, he made his appearance at the end of the gallery in the company of three modestly dressed gentlemen with a distinct businesslike air about them. "I saw his lordship depart in his carriage as, at our prearranged time, we made our way into the house. I regret that we were not quick enough to stop him.''

''I should not let it worry you,'' drawled Traherne, removing his greatcoat and slinging it around the shoulders of his scandalously clad duchess. ''I have the feeling Lord Branscombe is better left to his own devices. Oh, and, Edward, in addition to the lady, here, who has the dubious predilection for slitting people's throats for them, and our friend Alastair in repose on the ballroom floor below us, there are two ruffians lying about. I should be grateful if you would see that our Bow Street Runners gather them all up for us.''

''Bow Street Runners, Lucius?'' queried Althea, gazing inquisitively up at him.

''In light of certain recent developments, it did seem advisable to take some precautions, wood sprite.''

''I am sure you are in the right of it, Lucius,'' Althea did not hesitate to assure him. ''To which developments are you referring?''

''I say, Lucius,'' called Winslade, who had just entered the ballroom through the French doors, ''what shall I do with this?'' Reaching behind him, he dragged into view a disheveled figure, who, staggering drunkenly, gave every appearance of one who had sustained a rude awakening. ''I caught him lurking around outside with a pistol. It struck me he was up to no good.''

''I daresay you were not mistaken in your suspicions,'' observed Traherne, drawing Althea with him, as he descended the stairway. ''Allow me to present to you, *Monsieur* Jean Duval, the former Comte d'Arbolet, who is undoubtedly here to look out for the interests of the Ministry's latest investment.'' Traherne's eyes glittered coldly. ''You will be happy to know, *mon ami*, that Branscombe is successfully on his way. Alastair and Jacqueline Marot, on the other hand, are in the custody of Bow Street Runners. *They* will *not* escape. You will make sure of that. You will also see that Viscount Winslade is not made the scapegoat for the Ministry's little strategies." Traherne's steely voice took on a velvet-edged softness. "You almost had me killed, old friend, you and your superiors in the Ministry. Do not imagine for one moment I shall forget."

Duval gave his eloquent shrug. "It was most regrettable, but it is war, *mon ami.* I would use the devil himself to bring down the French Tyrant."

Traherne's face changed to a chiseled hardness. "Marot and Alastair murdered your wife and daughter. You have already bargained for your soul, Duval. I pray God you do not sell England to the devil."

Chapter Sixteen

Striding from the great empty house, Althea could not but reflect that she would be exceedingly pleased if she never again had to lay eyes on it or the Earl of Branscombe. But then, as she settled in the carriage between an ebullient Jack and her stern-faced husband, she was not sure if she had ever been given to see the Earl of Branscombe. Who was he, really? An image of the graceful Adonis in the midst of his beautiful things would seem hauntingly at odds with the black-garbed mourner lighting candles over Merrick's remains. And now, having spirited the packet of forged papers from Alastair's limp hand, he had vanished into the night—on a dangerous mission for King and country to give Bonaparte false information? Or to a villa in Greece overlooking the Mediterranean where a stolen fortune in diamonds would assure him a life of beauty and luxury? Or both, perhaps. Althea would not put anything past him.

She no longer cared what happened to the earl as they came at last to Grosvenor Square and Gloriana, eagerly awaiting them.

"If you had ever seen Althea help stand off a band of marauding bandits, you would have known there would be no keeping her from this tonight," declared Winslade to Traherne, as the two men waited in the study for Althea to change back into her dress. "The colonel was used to say she was worth any three raw recruits. She has never been one to lose her head in a crisis. Strange that she has no sense at all when it comes to one of her demmed machines. Did she ever tell you the story about her bloody trapeze-flying-kite? Devil of a thing. No more than ten or eleven when she came up with this kite bigger than she was. Built it herself out of wood and waxed linen. Climbed up onto the third-story balcony and jumped off. From all accounts the thing actually looked as if it were going to fly, till she hit a wall or some bloody demmed thing. The colonel made her swear to keep her feet on the ground after that, which was when she came up with her idea for a wind-sailing-buggy."

"The wind-buggy worked beautifully, Jack," declared a reproachful feminine voice from the doorway. "You know very well that it did. How was Althea to know that a sail-driven buggy would frighten all the dogs, horses, and persons, not to mention every sacred cow, in the street, causing a full-scale riot? Really, when you think about it, it was all exceedingly funny."

"On the contrary, it was not in the least amusing, when you consider the colonel confined me to a regimen of tatting and sewing for six whole months to make up for the trouble I had caused," Althea reminded Gloriana with a wry grimace. "You know how I detest needlework."

At this byplay, Traherne turned to be met with the sight of the two nearly identical sisters standing arm-in-arm inside the doorway, one charming in a mint green gown of flowing sarcenet, the other breathtakingly indecent in a black coat, leathern breeches, and knee-high riding boots.

"I say, Traherne," exclaimed Winslade, slapping a hand

to the duke's shoulder, "did two men ever have more beautiful wives?"

"No, never," murmured Traherne, his penetrating gaze, not on his wife's fetching, if wholly scandalous attire, but on her eyes, which did not reflect her smile.

"I believe His Grace has been rendered speechless," observed Gloriana. "And I daresay he has every reason to be. Althea's things were soiled on the floor of the carriage quite beyond wearing, I'm afraid. It was easier to lend her my riding boots than a dress and all the things that go with it, especially as she can think of nothing but home and her bed. You will see that you get plenty of rest before you set out to bring Effie home."

"Of course I shall." Althea frowned. "Are you sure you and Jack will not go with us? I told you it is only to Reading where she has been residing with Traherne's Cousin Eleanor, the Countess of Leister. I daresay she has been having a splendid time of it with her pony, Pegasus, and the earl's seven children. She was getting along swimmingly when we left her, though I shouldn't be surprised if she were not just a little homesick. She has Nessie with her, thank heavens, or I should not have been able to bear to leave her. It is the first time we have ever been apart, and I cannot but worry that she is eating properly and not making a nuisance of herself always asking questions. You know how inquisitive she is, Gloriana, and how I have taken pains to encourage that particular aspect of her character."

"Of course I do," Gloriana assured her. "Effie has always demonstrated a remarkable affinity for learning. In that, she undoubtedly has taken after you." Looking Althea straight in the eye, Gloriana pointedly added, "You need not worry about Effie, Althea. Not ever. We are all her family, but no child was ever more fortunate than Effie to have you for her mama."

Althea suffered a sudden pang in the vicinity of her heart. "Gloriana, I—"

''You don't have to say anything, Althea. Not now. You will see Effie, talk to her. Explain everything about Jack and me. Whatever is to come after is up to Effie. Jack and I are firmly agreed. Effie is as much yours as ours—more. You, after all, will always be her mama, and she has already come to love Lucius. I see no reason why we cannot all share her.'' Giving her sister's hand a squeeze, Gloriana nudged Althea firmly toward the door. ''Go home, dearest Althea. We shall talk it all out later.''

Seated in the carriage beside Traherne, Althea was acutely aware of a heaviness of spirit, which had little to do with the evening's harrowing events. Merrick was dead, the threat to Effie blessedly at an end. How strange that with Effie safe at last, she must surely lose her!

Faith, she did not know how she was to bear it. How did one surrender the child of one's heart? Where did one find the words? And when the thing was done and Effie's faith in her Althie was gone, how did one continue on?

She was no closer to any of the answers when they came at last to the Town House in the Campden Hill district and, climbing wearily from the carriage, she made her way into the house. Nor was she aware of Traherne's eyes on her as, wrapped in her own thoughts of Effie, she climbed the stairs.

Entering her room, she found Grayson, waiting to help her out of her things. She could only be grateful the abigail, no doubt sensing Althea was in no case to engage in chitchat, made no mention of her mistress's unseemly attire as she undressed her and slipped the nightdress of emerald silk over her head.

It did not occur to her until she stood, alone at last, staring into the ormolu looking glass, that Traherne had not come to her as he always did when she was just finishing up and Grayson, having laid the brush aside after brushing her hair, was wont to slip away. Really, it was too much, when now, more than at any time before, she needed him merely to come to her and hold her, if only to keep her thoughts at bay.

Hardly had that thought crossed her mind than the door opened behind her, and she was aware of a light thrilling step at her back.

"Lucius," she said, turning—and was met with the soft whirring of tail feathers and the plop-plop of webbed feet. A wholly unlovely "Honk-honk" assaulted the quiet, and Goosey Gander, its webbed feet moving with mechanical rigidity and its head swiveling from side to side as its beak snapped open and shut, waddled mindlessly into Althea's dressing table.

Effie, dressed in her night shift and held aloft in the cradle of Traherne's arm, squealed and clapped her hands together in patent delight.

"Goosey flew, Althie, for Lady Eleanor and the earl and everyone. Everyone wants one. Only Judith wants hers to be a duck, and Freddie will not settle for anything less than a frog. You'll do it, won't you, Althie? I promised you would."

"Of course I will, darling. Since you promised," agreed Althea, laughing and reaching to put her arms around Effie and Traherne. "Just as soon as I am at Meresgate. Darling, how I have missed you!"

"I missed you, too, Althie. I rode Pegasus every day, and now I am ever so much better at it. Now we can all go riding together, can't we, Lucius?"

Traherne's eyes met Althea's. "You may be sure of it, *enfant*. We are, after all, a family."

"A very large family, dearest," added Althea, clinging to Traherne's eyes for strength. "Tomorrow night you will meet Lucius's mama and her very dear friend Mr. Praetorius whom you will like very much because he is an actor of no little renown. And in a few weeks, we will be joined by your grandpapa, the colonel, who is coming home at last to

England to stay. And tomorrow, or rather today, right after breakfast, we shall go and see Gloriana and little Lord Guilmore and Baby Alice, who—you will be glad to know—are your brother and sister. And you will meet Jack, Viscount Winslade, who is very much looking forward to making your acquaintance because he is your—''

"Papa," said Effie, busy with pulling at the button on Traherne's waistcoat. "Gloriana told me all about her and Jack when they came to see me at Reading, and I liked him very much. He is ever so handsome and gay, don't you think?''

"Yes, darling. Jack is handsome and gay.''

"He makes me laugh. I shall like going to see them at Blydesdel on holidays. But I shall always live at Meresgate with you and Lucius, Althie. Gloriana promised I should until I am old enough to live wherever I choose. I shall, shan't I, Althie?''

"But of course you will, dearest," exclaimed Althea, who could not but marvel at Jack and Gloriana.

They had worked it all out together, the two of them, their only wish to make sure of Effie's happiness. Gloriana had said it that very night, only an hour or two ago. They were all Effie's family, and Effie was always assured of their love. But Althea would always be the mother of Effie's heart.

And Lucius, she thought, laughing and smiling through the mist of tears in her eyes as she watched the duke, who everyone knew was totally lacking in any of the softer human emotions, swing Effie, squealing with glee, up on his shoulders to march her off back to her bed, would be the rock on which they would build—she and Effie and the children that would come after.

No little time later, lying on her side facing Traherne in the bed, Althea listened as Lucius reminisced about his boyhood at Meresgate. He talked of his mother who had been young-seeming and sad until she laughed, and his father who—trapped in a marriage he had never wanted in order to beget a son whom he could never love—had seemed harsh and vindictive.

How strange to think that the late duke had lost his heart to his beloved Milly when he was little more than a youth and she a young apprentice to the seamstress employed by his mama. His pride would not countenance a marriage with one of her station, and yet his heart would not let him love another. Therein had been laid the seeds of future discord.

To Olivia Traherne, passionate of nature and yearning for love and adventure, life at Meresgate must have been like living entombed. And yet there had been Lucius. If he had not been a child of love, he had yet been a child, the child of her heart and her body. There had never been another. How sad that in fleeing the tomb, she had left her heart behind. It was little wonder that she had never married her dearest prince of hearts. No doubt she had seen it as the final severing of the only tie remaining to the son she had loved and abandoned. Milly Langston, living alone in her house in Kensington, had not even been left with that.

"In retrospect, Lucius," said Althea, running her fingers through the mat of hair on Traherne's chest, "I cannot but think your papa was to be in some measure pitied. I daresay there can be as little to envy in a marriageless love as in a loveless marriage if one is bound by the dictates of convention. And the duke, it would seem, was trapped in both at the same time."

"My father, the duke," replied Traherne repressively, "fashioned his own bed and was not averse to lying in it. I have every reason to believe he was perfectly content to live with his mistress while consigning his wife and the mother of his heir to oblivion. He had, after all, fulfilled his obligation to the succession. It was all that he ever required of the marriage."

''Which brings me to a topic that I have been meaning for some little time to bring up with you, Lucius,'' said Althea, apparently absorbed in studying the cleft in the duke's chin. ''I am well aware, my dearest lord duke, that I am hardly the wife you intended when it came to the business of setting up your nursery. And though it was never my intent to entrap a duke in marriage; that is, nevertheless, precisely what happened. In which case, it occurs to me to wonder how you will feel when I have fulfilled my obligation to you. And pray do not be afraid to open the budget. I am, after all, a freethinker and a woman who prides herself on her grasp of logic. I should like to think that ours is a marriage of rational minds. Though I should mind if you were to take a mistress, especially as I was perfectly content to accept that position for myself, I assure you I should understand and make the best of it. After all, I did give you my promise I should never leave you so long as you wanted me. But should you cease to want me—and, after all, the natural law of gravitational forces between two disparate bodies cannot be expected to be the only cement to bind a marriage together—I should like you to know that I could never leave, not so long as the children needed me.''

''The devil, Althea,'' exclaimed Traherne, who was experiencing no little difficulty in following the logical vein of his duchess's thinking, especially in the aftermath of their recent gorging at the feast of the senses. ''I haven't the least desire to take a mistress. And you may be damned certain that, if ever you did try to leave me, I should most assuredly come after you and drag you, kicking and screaming, back again, children or no children. I have not, after all, lost my heart to you and your overprecocious little Effie only to lose you out of some mistaken notion that you are not precisely the wife I should have chosen. I love you far too much ever to let you go. Indeed, I have loved you ever since you and your Automatic Mechanical Goose caused me to fall in the cursed lake, though I have had the devil's own time convincing you of it.''

It was on his lips to add that any further mention of mistresses and the entrapping of dukes would lead to exceedingly dire consequences, when the shimmer in his wood sprite's eyes, not to mention the dawning quiver of a smile on her lips, suddenly called his attention to the original topic with which she had begun the present line of conversation.

''Good God, Althea,'' he said, his gaze going with unconscious volition to the small mound of her belly then back again to her eyes the color of a verdant glen in early autumn. ''What, precisely, are you trying to say to me?''

''Only, my dearest lord duke,'' replied Althea, cradling his face between the palms of her hands, ''that, while being the mistress of the Duke of Traherne must surely have had its pleasant aspects, nothing could possibly compare with the exquisite joy of being your scandalous duchess.''

Epilogue

It was the end of September, and the beech and oak woods marching up from the shores of Ullswater had begun to show the first faint sheen of red and gold. Indeed, it was generally agreed there was a decided nip in the air, a sure sign that winter was fast approaching. In the green glen of Briersly, however, with the rowan trees heavy with red berries and the mingled scents of gorse, thyme, and sorrel sweet on the breeze, there was a decidedly festive air as was evidenced by the shrieks of childish laughter and the frequent arrivals of travel coaches, which disembarked gaily dressed passengers.

In Glenridding, Leach's Emporium and Thaddeus Elright's butcher shop were kept in a near frenzy supplying the orders that arrived daily from the big house. And Thomas Jessop was required to purchase a new cob in order to keep the deliveries of coal arriving on a regular basis—and all because the Duke and Duchess of Traherne had taken up residence in Briersly.

But then, it was not everyday that the dale was given the

opportunity to celebrate the arrival of a new scion of the house of Traherne. Mattie Treadwell was heard to remark to Miss Louisa Thedford that the young heir, save for gilt-green eyes the color of a verdant glen in early autumn, was the spitting image of his ducal father.

"Oh, indeed," replied the spinster, who had not been averse to making the most of her fleeting glimpse of the young Marquess of Traherne as the duchess had laid him in his automatic mechanical rocking cradle with the wind-up arm. "There's a fair family resemblance between the dowager duchess and her new grandson. But then, I doubt not that there might not be a dash of the colonel in him, too."

"Oh, you may be sure of it," agreed Mattie, who was later to liken the spinster's sagacious observations to the crowing of a puffed-up swell. But then, it seemed that there was not a soul in and about Glenridding who was not convinced that the Duke of Traherne had done the dales proud when he took to wed Miss Althea Wintergreen, who, after all, was and always had been one of their own.

And now what had Althea, Her Grace of Traherne, done, but determined to have an alfresco party with open invitations to the people of the dale in honor of an all-important occasion. Effie Marie Wintergreen Keene was to celebrate her sixth birthday with pony rides, clowns, hot-air balloons, and booths featuring every sort of delectable edible, not to mention the very first demonstration of the duchess's newly created automatic mechanical ice cream–making machine.

Mattie, viewing the gathering crowd, shook her head and smiled. Well, it was the way *she* wanted it, and now would come the reckoning.

About the Author

Sara Blayne lives with her family in New Mexico. She is the author of eight traditional Regency romances and two historical romances set in the Regency period. Sara is currently working on her next historical romance set in the Regency period—look for it in 2001. Sara loves to hear from readers and you may write to her c/o Zebra Books. Please include a self-addressed stamped envelope if you wish a reply.

Put a Little Romance in Your Life With

Jo Goodman